AF865752

SUBLIMATION

SUBLIMATION

ISABEL J. KIM

PICADOR

First published 2026 by Tor Publishing Group

First published in the UK 2026 by Picador
an imprint of Pan Macmillan
The Smithson, 6 Briset Street, London EC1M 5NR
EU representative: Macmillan Publishers Ireland Ltd, 1st Floor,
The Liffey Trust Centre, 117–126 Sheriff Street Upper,
Dublin 1 D01 YC43
Associated companies throughout the world

ISBN 978-1-0350-6552-3 HB
ISBN 978-1-0350-6553-0 TPB

Copyright © Isabel J. Kim 2026

The right of Isabel J. Kim to be identified as the
author of this work has been asserted in accordance with
the Copyright, Designs and Patents Act 1988.

All rights reserved. No part of this publication may be reproduced,
stored in a retrieval system, or transmitted, in any form, or by any means
(including, without limitation, electronic, mechanical, photocopying, recording
or otherwise) without the prior written permission of the publisher.

Pan Macmillan does not have any control over, or any responsibility for,
any author or third-party websites (including, without limitation, URLs,
emails and QR codes) referred to in or on this book.

1 3 5 7 9 8 6 4 2

A CIP catalogue record for this book is available from the British Library.

Printed and bound in the UK using 100% Renewable Electricity by CPI Group (UK) Ltd

FSC www.fsc.org
MIX
Paper | Supporting
responsible forestry
FSC® C116313

This book is sold subject to the condition that it shall not, by way of
trade or otherwise, be lent, hired out, or otherwise circulated without
the publisher's prior consent in any form of binding or cover other than
that in which it is published and without a similar condition including this
condition being imposed on the subsequent purchaser. The publisher does not
authorize the use or reproduction of any part of this book in any manner
for the purpose of training artificial intelligence technologies or systems.
The publisher expressly reserves this book from the Text and Data Mining
exception in accordance with Article 4(3) of the European Union
Digital Single Market Directive 2019/790.

Visit **www.picador.com** to read more about
all our books and to buy them.

To my mom and dad.

PART I

Back when tigers used to smoke tobacco, there was a fisherman who lived at the edge of the sea. It was widely known that the shore was a boundary like those between nations, and underneath the waves there was a kingdom of water spirits. Therefore, to dive to that kingdom was to risk the separation of the self from the self.

But one day, the fisherman met a water spirit, who beckoned him through the water.

—Korean version of a coastal folktale

SOYOUNG

"Do you think it's emotionally equivalent to murder?"

Yujin chokes on his latte. You take a smooth sip of your Americano. In retrospect, that was a morbid thing to say. It doesn't fit the setting. You're sitting in the basement of the Shinsegae Department Store, waiting for your instance in the cafe near the rotating displays that guard the entrance. The salespeople are loudly promoting dried persimmons in fancy gift boxes (Half off! Today only!). Commuters in nice clothing hurry past, using the food hall as a shortcut to the subway. Tourists examine the stalls and malinger.

The Shinsegae Department Store basement used to be your favorite place in all of Seoul. Your mom always took you through when you visited her at work, and you'd pick out something delicious (twigim, mandu, jun) to augment dinner at home. But these days, the physical reality of the basement always disappoints you. Everything is smaller, shabbier, too loud and not as wondrous. The jun don't taste the same. They got rid of the ice cream stall you liked. You wonder if your instance will feel the same way, or if the years between visits will preserve some sort of magic when she returns. You kind of hope it will feel perfect for her, because you'd like to experience that perfection again. If and when she agrees to reintegrate. Or else for you, the memory will stay bittersweet and choked forever, because Harabeoji is dead and you're never going to eat dinner with him again.

You feel regular about that. By regular, you mean very bad. Bad enough that you're blithely asking Yujin about whether reintegration would be murder. That's an awful thing to say to Yujin specifically, because Yujin talks about his other self like his instance will save him. But you can't help yourself.

You want to stop talking about death but it keeps seeping out through the seams. You're angry about that. Things shouldn't matter to you so much; Harabeoji's death shouldn't be affecting you so greatly. It was a foregone conclusion, and it's not like your mom or your fiancé or any of your friends or anyone *young* has died. This wasn't a surprise death. So you're in your twenties and your grandfather dies. So you knew it was coming. So you still feel like shit about the whole thing, and worse than shit, you feel guilty, because there's the relief mingled in with the sadness—the relief of foregone conclusions. He's dead and gone and you aren't waiting for the drop anymore. What a terrible grandchild you are! Except, no. You're allowed to feel however you want. Maybe you shouldn't even feel bad. You visited him every other week in the house you grew up in, choked with slowly advancing vines. And you're pretty sure he loved you the best, even if he called Minsoo his favorite, because Minsoo was the firstborn son. That love: another foregone conclusion.

"Murder?" Yujin says, and then in English, "*Murder?* Like, killing people?"

"Yeah, murder. Emotional murder."

You've been thinking a lot about reintegration and how it relates to death. Ever since you called your instance. But you're now feeling really awful for bringing this up to Yujin. You know instancing is a sore spot for him. And maybe you're also a coward, needing moral support for a meeting with your other self. You knew that without a friend's presence, you probably would've let the sick feeling in your stomach win, and you would have let your instance be someone else's problem. Not yours.

Except, no. You wouldn't have called your instance if you were a coward, even if you did call her at a terrible time—1 PM in Korea, which was 1 AM in New York.

She had picked up with a scratchy, sleep-sodden voice.

"Hello?" she said, in English.

"Is this Soyoung Kang?" your own voice said, in Korean.

"Yes." You were surprised that she had an American accent.

"Harabeoji's dead," you had said, and there was a thump as she dropped her phone. You told her the bare facts. You didn't know what else to tell her. You had almost wanted to laugh, during the conversation—her incredulity, contrasted against your own emotionless voice. How absurd. Harabeoji is dead, and he wants *you* here, even though you've never come back to visit. Even though you don't call him, anymore. Harabeoji's dead and he knew that I always wanted to know what you know, and I think telling you to return was his idea of a gift.

Your instance had been silent for a long moment. Then she had said she would come for the funeral.

You scratch the black cuff on your wrist. The raised letters MERGE-BREAK are cool and rubberized against your fingers. Yujin had bought it for you with his instance's employee discount. The matching cuff for your instance is in your purse.

"Sorry," you say to Yujin. "I don't mean that. I guess I'm just nervous about meeting her? I don't know. You should go, she texted me she was on the subway. I bet she'll be here any minute."

"You sure you don't want me to stick around?" Yujin says, leaning forward.

With his hair in his eyes, Yujin looks like your memory of him from high school, when you were just childhood friends who had fallen out of touch, when he was just another one of the boys in the uniform shirt and slacks and you were one of the girls with the regulation haircuts. You had only become close again after Yujin had instanced, after he had called you from the airport because you were the one person his age who had an instance. And now you vet his girlfriends and he shows you about how to download movies illegally and you have both forgiven each other for what you did when you were seventeen.

It hadn't been anything so bad—Yujin had asked you out and you had said no.

"I'm sure."

"Because I can stay, for moral support. I can make intimidating faces in the background. Or I can be super friendly so she-you likes you more. Whatever you need."

You shake your head. When you had instanced, you had gone home and then gone to school and you had marveled at the way that nothing in anyone's life had changed, how they didn't know that anything was wrong. This is how you feel now.

"It's family stuff," you say, handing Yujin your empty cup so he can toss it on his way out. "And I don't want to scare her."

You know that's a foregone conclusion. Of course you're going to scare her. She's you. And you're scared. You're sick to your stomach with want. You need her to love you so bad it hurts. Because then you get to be her. Then she gets to be you.

▮▮▮

An instance is a duplicate self cleaved mitosis-like from the original—though the duplicate and the original are both referred to as "instances" in modern American vocabulary. To become an instance is to "instantiate"; in the present tense, "instancing."

The oldest reference to instances is a line in Hammurabi's Code translated as *the foreign brother-self will receive no inheritance.*

Different cultures refer to instances with a Technicolor diversity: the sibling-self, the changeling, the one-who-does-not-return. The first requirement for instancing is a settled culture, and traditionally instances appear specifically in seafaring societies. In many civilizations the ocean formed an organic division between the familiar and the foreign.

The second requirement is intent. Sailors throughout history are recorded as having sailed from their home ports without instancing for decades, until one morning they board their ship and look back to see their instance standing at the docks. Something must have shifted in their heart, some secret admittance that their leave-taking is permanent, that their families have become foreign to them.

There is a folktale that is repeated in Japan, Korea, and coastal China, of a fisherman who is coaxed into following a water spirit into an undersea court, where he drinks and dances with the beautiful merfolk. But the night grows long, so the fisherman asks the water spirit to take him back to his home. The spirit warns him that time flows differently underwater, but the fisherman repeats that he wants to go home.

The spirit nods and sadly takes the fisherman back to the shore. When the fisherman's feet touch dry land, he ages thirty years instantly. When he walks into his house, he finds himself already inside, asleep with his wife.

A border is an artificial thing with practical consequences: the severing of the self from the self.

ROSE

You're trying to find your instance in the basement of the Shinsegae Department Store. You hadn't managed to sleep during the flight, which had been all roller-coaster turbulence and recycled air. But now, fresh out of the airport and cleared through customs, you're wired from sleep deprivation and strangely delighted by all the people running around and the coordinated chaos of the food hall, so foreign to you now. They don't make food halls like this in New York. The closest you go to regularly might be Eataly. And all your memories of Shinsegae are two feet lower, from the perspective of a child. You want to go look around. You want to buy an ice cream. You don't want to go looking for your instance.

Once you see your instance, all of this will become real again. The good feelings will start to sit wrong in your chest and you'll have to act like you've flown in for a funeral, because your grandfather is dead.

You *do* feel sad about it. Abstractly. It's the hollow grief of losing something you already assumed had dissipated into the past. Your instance had dredged up a whole dead history with her phone call in the middle of the night, waking you from a deep sleep.

"Hello?" you had said, accented with slumber.

"Is this Soyoung Kang?" your own voice said, accented with Korean.

"Yes." The only people who still call you Soyoung are family. Everyone else calls you Rose.

"Harabeoji's dead," your instance said. You had dropped the phone in shock.

You hadn't heard from Harabeoji in a decade. For a while there were phone calls on your birthday. He would say *happy birthday,* and you would say *thank you.* He would ask *how's school,* and you would say *it's okay.* Then you would ask *how is other Soyoung?* because you remembered the photograph of the little girl on the other side of the immigration checkpoint, wearing your clothes and your face and your memories.

Your instance.

Your-her grandfather would say *she's fine! She and her mother are doing fine.* Her mother. Your other mother. The instance of your own mother standing next to you and pretending not to listen to your conversation.

Okay, you would say. Harabeoji never told you anything interesting about the other Soyoung. You eventually stopped asking, because you had homework, field hockey practice, college applications.

This is what you remembered, when your instance told you that Harabeoji was dead. His silence about her. As if her existence was anathema to yours.

You picked your phone back up again and listened to your instance. She spoke to you in complete banmal, no formal suffixes for her other self. *Grandfather's dead. He wanted to see you before he died, but he died before we could ask you. Yes, we saw it coming.*

You don't have to come to the funeral, but he said he wanted you here.

Your instance said nothing about what she wanted, or why she was the one calling instead of an aunt or a cousin or your mother's instance. She said nothing about how she felt about Harabeoji's death, but you could guess her emotions based on the first ten years of being the same person. Maybe her sadness was like a foreign shore, which was how your sadness felt. You couldn't imagine how she felt about talking to you.

"Okay," you told your instance in the dark warmth of your bedroom. "I'll be there when I can."

You arranged plane tickets. You arranged time off from work. You arranged for your best friend to cat-sit. And now you're in Seoul, in a basement ripped from your memories, and you wish you were a tourist instead.

But, well. The phone calls. You owe your grandfather . . . something. Maybe not what you're giving him now. You should have owed him your presence when you were alive. But he had your instance, and your mother's instance. He had your aunts and your uncles and cousins and the ghost of your grandmother, and you and your mom had been the only two people in the family to ever conclusively instance.

You have always comforted yourself about the distance from your Korean family by considering yourself something of a vestigial limb.

▮▮▮

The distance between you and your instance is manufactured, not inherent. You know this. Your instance knows this. You both share in the creation of the space between the two of you, between yourself and your mother, between yourself and her-your Korean aunts and uncles, between her and her mother, between your mother and her mother. The only thing not your fault is the relationship between your mother and your-her grandfather.

Your instance and her mother get Korea, your-her aunts and uncles, your-her grandfather. They get the physical presence. They get Chuseok. They get your-her grandmother's grave. They get stationery stores and Emart and clean public transit, they get the ahjumma selling ginkgo nuts and roasted chestnuts at the foot of the hiking trails.

You and your mother get America.

You could call this a fair trade. You could call this the inherent outcome of your mother's feud with your grandfather, a wound not your own, which you never completely probed. You could have researched your instance—you know her name, her birthday, her school history until you left the country. You could have easily contacted her through your aunts. But you didn't.

It's not like you have anything against instances in the abstract. Your best friend from high school instanced nearly five years ago after transferring to the German branch of her company. She hadn't expected to instantiate, but Clarissa's heart apparently thought her future lay across the Atlantic.

You love both Clarissas. The last time the two of you spoke, German Clarissa told you she was planning on returning to America.

"It's been fun," she said to you. "But I'm ready to return. I think I want to reintegrate. Don't tell Clarissa, yet."

"She doesn't know?" you said, cradling the phone between your shoulder and ear as you rinsed dishes in your sink.

"No," German Clarissa said. "I haven't told her, it's not like we're psychic."

"You could extend your visa."

"I have to declare that I want citizenship with the embassy, then. And I've been thinking about it a lot. But. I don't know."

You had hmm-ed encouragingly. This hadn't been anything you had expected from Clarissa. You had assumed that she would naturalize because she had instanced. You had assumed she would seek citizenship overseas just from the blunt fact of her cleaving. But you supposed that she might have changed her mind, that the intervening years had made her feel differently. You guessed people could change.

"That's kind of a big thing. Reintegration. We don't know anyone who's reintegrated, right?"

"It's not a big thing in the States, yeah. People usually just . . . leave. And it's going to be a pain in the ass, dealing with the embassy. That's why I want to talk to her first."

"Sure. Hey, it'll be nice to see you again."

"What are you talking about?" Clarissa said. "You see me all the time. You guys get brunch like, every Sunday."

■ ■ ■

An instancing captures a static moment. A feeling in a specific time and place. The heart at the moment of stepping over a border. The mind when it knows it is leaving. A life is made of many static moments. What's felt when walking up to the tarmac is a different thing from what is felt sitting in a park two weeks later. What's felt when crossing a river with your belongings held above your head is a different thing from what is felt in the detention facility. What's felt when your mother tells you that you're leaving and puts you in your best coat is different from what you feel when you are twenty years older, sitting on the plane, returning. The only constant is that what people want will change, and the administrative state is there to log the outcomes.

Normally, American instances travel outbound on their original's passport and are required to log themselves at the nearest American embassy. America considers an instance as a whole and complete person, as mandated in the nation's founding documents. But if a person's instance wants to stay in the new country, that's a different question. The human heart wants what it wants. But a government is made of many human hearts.

■ ■ ■

You catch sight of your instance sitting alone at a table, typing on her phone. For a moment, it's like looking at a stranger, just the slick black hair and pale hands of any East Asian woman. Then she looks up and you know the shape of her naked surprise, the curve of her lip and the arch of her eyebrows. Here is your sister-self, your shadow-could-have-been, the woman you are in another country. Here she is, looking you over with your eyes in her face, though the lines in her face are not the lines in your face, yet you could have been her: Twenty years wind back to when one of you stepped onto the plane and the other stayed.

She smiles at you. She stands up and waves. You hurry over. You don't shake hands. You don't bow. She has a black band on her right wrist, like a broad watch strap with no watch.

"Did you get here okay?" your instance asks in Korean.

"Pretty well," you respond in kind. "Thanks for picking me up."

"Of course. We're family."

"Are we?" you ask, and she laughs, and you laugh. It feels something like release.

"Let me get you a coffee or something," you say. "What do you want?"

"You don't have to."

"No, I'm putting you through enough trouble," you say. Your instance's face twitches a bit at that, the same way you smile when something is *funny* but not *happy*. You can read her thoughts in that instant: *It'll make her feel better to buy me a coffee, I want a coffee and she wants to buy me a coffee, let's skip the posturing, I know that she knows that I know.*

"Black Americano, if you don't mind," she says. You nod to hide your surprise. You're a caramel macchiato–type girl. You've always taken your coffee sweetened, with cream.

■ ■ ■

Here is the second half of the sailor's folktale:

The sailor returns home and finds his instance asleep in bed with his wife. He looks down at their bodies. The slow rise and fall of his instance's chest. The way his instance's arm curls sweetly around his wife's waist. He forgets the endless beautiful night he spent in the underwater court and remembers only that thirty years of his life have been erased.

A great and terrible anger rises in him. How dare his other self be content. How dare his other self have three decades with his wife.

He picks up his instance's knife from where it hangs on the wall. He kneels above his other self.

He plunges the knife into his other self's breast.

His instance wakes in a great gasp. He claws at the air. He screams. His wife, waking, beats at the sailor's chest. *Husband!* she shouts. The sailor's instance grasps at his jacket, at his sleeves. The sailor holds the knife down.

His instance tears the wet fabric. He manages to grab the sailor's bare wrist.

And suddenly there is a single man lying there, bleeding from his breast wound, his own hand holding the knife in place. The sailor and his instance having merged, falling into a single self like a collapsing waveform.

In some versions of the story, the sailor survives his self-inflicted wounds. In others, he doesn't.

The message remains the same in either version of the story: Intention does not matter in homecoming. There is no requirement of desire to return for reintegration. What matters is the physical action, the touch of skin against skin.

SOYOUNG

You watch your instance leave all her luggage behind and go to the counter. You don't really want another coffee, but you do want the opportunity to observe. You drink in the sight of her. You had wanted to reach over and touch her hand, to examine the calluses and see whether there were similarities. Did she have the bump on her right middle finger? Did she pick at her cuticles? The thought of it gives you a shiver of illicit delight. There is an enormous taboo around instances touching without intent. If you had grabbed her hand right there and then, you would have merged back into a singular person. You haven't given her the MERGEBREAK paired to your own, yet.

You should have. But you hadn't known what to say to your instance. It's been two decades. You didn't know what to ask.

"So, I'm surprised you never even tried to stalk me on social media," you could have said. "I looked you up all the time, or at least I used to, until I started to feel a little bit creepy. Now I just look you up once a year. There's a girl named Rose Kang who goes to Oberlin, did you know that? And a doctor in San Francisco."

"So, how much of our childhood do you remember? I don't remember a ton of it, but sometimes I walk past our old elementary school in the spring and I remember being a kid and walking past the yellow flowers with Umma, and it's like I'm there again."

"So, how much Korean do you speak? Do you think in English? Do you think in pictures, or words? For me, it's all image and emotion."

"So, what's the States like?"

None of that would be endearing. Everything you wanted to know about her was too personal. You wanted to crack open her chest and dissect her heart. You wanted to ride her neurons. You wanted to fit inside her skin. Sometimes the size of your want scares you.

You could just ask: "Do you want to reintegrate?"

Except, no. That's too much. That's too fast. You know you have an ungirlish tendency to speak without thinking (see: asking Yujin about murder, asking your fiancé out first instead of waiting to be asked, and asking people how old they are, constantly). You've tried to learn restraint. Better instead to say nothing.

You watch your instance order. She's just close enough that you can hear her speak. Slightly accented, her voice a little lower than yours. How did that happen? You're similar, but not the same. The barista doesn't give her a second glance, doesn't gesture to the English language menu or anything. For a moment, it's like she lives here.

You want to look through her stuff. She brought a backpack and a small silver suitcase. No purse. Very practical. You want to carefully peel back the zipper and peer inside the black mouth of the backpack, you want to carefully slip your hand inside and feel the contours of the items inside. The smooth glassine of a pair of sunglasses. The rough leather of a bound journal. Crinkled gum wrappers with chewed gum inside.

Instead, you open your own bag and take the MERGEBREAK band out and place it on the table. The MERGEBREAK, placed in the middle of the table, neatly serves as both invitation and question, a reassurance that you both are aligned on not reintegrating. And then you can save the rest of the conversation until a more appropriate time. Better not to spring it on her sleep-deprived and plane-drunk. This is her first time back in Korea. You can't imagine returning to Korea. You've never really had to return anywhere. You feel a sudden stab of sympathy for her. You rest your chin on your hand and think about alternate universes while watching her shift from foot to foot, rolling her shoulders the same way you do when you're nervous.

Your phone buzzes. You scroll through your messages. Tae (the only person you have vibrations on for), asking how the meeting was going, asking if your day was going well. Minsoo asking if you were still doing dinner, and how did Rose look? Your mother, asking if Rose had gotten fat in America. The girls, talking about the trip you were going to take to Tokyo next summer, with copious use of stickers. Yujin, asking how coffee was going, followed by three memes and a couple of emojis.

You respond to Tae: *It's good we're getting coffee!! Still on for dinner with M, if Rose wants to.*

You respond to Minsoo: *Still on for dinner as long as Rose agrees.*

You respond to Yujin: *IDK how you talk to YJ all the time this is so weird!!*

You ignore the girls and your mother.

Then you snap a photo of Rose—it's a bad photo, blurry, her hand in motion as she reaches for the coffee, her head nothing more than a black smudge—and send it to everyone.

▪ ▪ ▪

When your instance returns with your coffees, she picks up the black MERGEBREAK like it's a life jacket and she's adrift in the Pacific Ocean. This makes you feel very bad. Almost angry.

"My life isn't so awful," you want to say. "My life is very good, actually. I'm usually very happy. This week is a terrible outlier. But you don't seem like you're usually very happy. Which is interesting, because you don't even seem like you regret leaving, or feel bad about Harabeoji dying."

And then you would continue and say: "Sorry, this is a really awful first introduction. Maybe we should set some ground rules about this. But Harabeoji told me that we should reintegrate. Right before he died. How do you feel about that? Do you want to? I want to know what he was thinking."

But saying that wouldn't be a very good way to make her like you. So you just watch her strap the cuff on, the perfect complement to your own, with the glossy MERGEBREAK over her wrist.

▪ ▪ ▪

You didn't mean it about the emotional murder. You try not to be morbid. But there was this game that you used to play with Minsoo, when you were kids and just learned about the Aztecs, which was called *human sacrifice*. You would pile up the couch cushions into an altar and one of you would lie down and try not to giggle and the other would say lots of stuff about the human sacrifice and say, "Stop laughing!" and then you'd use Minsoo's toy lightsaber to poke the sacrifice in the chest. And then the sacrifice would have to make lots of terrible noises. Obviously, your mothers would try and stop you from playing this every single time, so it became your favorite game for three months when you were seven.

When you tried to play it with Yujin, he agreed at first, because he wanted to use the lightsaber, but when you made him be the sacrifice he started wailing. It was, in retrospect, very funny. But at the time it was very serious and very annoying. You had yelled at him. You hadn't understood how he didn't get it: The getting-to-play-with-the-lightsaber was the exchange for the being dead part. To get to play with the lightsaber, with its beautiful fwoosh-fwoosh sound effects and pretty battery-powered glow, you had to lie around being bored and not laughing or whatever.

Reintegration conceptually feels the same as playing sacrifice. So that's why you're thinking about murder. It's an old memory from before you instanced. Your instance must also remember it, unless your childhood games have been subsumed under the rest of your lives, like a layer of sediment that has been buried under new loam.

ROSE

Your instance takes you to the parking garage where her small silver car is parked. She opens the trunk for you, but doesn't help with your suitcase. You struggle to lift it.

"Sorry," she says. "I know we're both wearing the MERGEBREAK. But—"

"Yeah, I get it," you tell her, and grunt as you push the suitcase in. The taboo between instances and physical contact runs deep. It leaves an icky feeling in your chest to think about touching her. A 5 percent failure rate. The suitcase isn't that heavy. You manage alone; you're used to that.

You get in the car and she turns on the engine.

"Where are we going?" you ask, pretending not to glance around the car. It reminds you of your mother's old car, not so much in appearance but in the smell of it.

Your instance drums her fingers on the steering wheel.

"The plan is for you to stay with me tonight, unless you want to stay with Keunimo, but I think she's busy with arranging everything, and Minsoo's got a futon but also like, the wife, the kid. And you missed the funeral home bits. But Harabeoji's being buried the day after tomorrow. So, we're just going home tonight, unless there's anything you want to do. Do you want to get dinner? I was going to take you to dinner. You can meet my fiancé. And Minsoo and his wife and kid will be there—our cousin, I mean. If you remember him."

You don't know if there's anything you want to do. You want to tell her you know who Minsoo is, and that you're sorry you missed the funeral home parts but this was the earliest flight you could get that didn't cost four thousand dollars. You want to tell her it freaks you out, how matter-of-fact she is. Shouldn't she be the sad one? Why is she talking about dinner? You don't know anyone who's died.

You want to go to the kalguksu place near Harabeoji's house where they would bring out huge pots of simmering clam broth and noodles. You want to go to a 7-Eleven and get a banana milk. You want to go back inside the

Shinsegae basement and buy yourself ice cream, fried mandu, the little glazed sweet potato things, and eat all of them at the food court in a feat of decadence your mother never would have allowed.

You wish you were home in your apartment in downtown Brooklyn, heating up a single serving of rice and leftovers, your cat purring by your side. You wish your grandfather wasn't dead and that you were not here in this country.

"I'm hungry," you say. "Let's get dinner."

■ ■ ■

Your grandfather isn't from Seoul. Your grandfather is from a town outside Pyongyang, which is the capital city of North Korea. You don't know the name of his hometown. You just know that he left, when he was young. Not that young. Maybe your age. You're more from Seoul than he is, though he lived there for longer than you've been alive.

You don't tell people that you're from Seoul, though you lived there for a third of your life. But the parts of your life that you feel matter, the parts of your life you feel that people can relate to, are the parts where you grew up in a suburb on the East Coast of the United States, the parts where you went to public school and played after-school sports and took the SATs and briefly joined a sorority. The parts of your life where you bought K-drama boy band merch from third-party resellers and went to karaoke in K-Town and only sang the American songs. You aren't your childhood.

■ ■ ■

Your instance drives you to a local Korean barbecue place (or, just a barbecue place, you suppose), where you meet up with your cousin who you haven't talked to in two decades, his kid (your niece, your instance's niece), and your instance's fiancé. You don't ask about the rest of your family. You'll see most of them at the funeral, you guess. You wonder if you should call the version of your mom in Korea and meet up beforehand. Or if you should call your mom back home, but you hadn't told her you were here. She's more estranged from your family than you were.

"Are we drinking?" Minsoo asks. He's sitting next to you, and had given you a big hug when he walked into the restaurant. He used to be your favorite cousin. He's not the kid you remember. He's an adult, with an adult's face. You don't know why this surprises you.

"Please, yes," you say, and Minsoo orders a few green bottles of soju for the table.

"Really?" your instance's fiancé—*Taehyung, but call me Tae, haha, yeah, like the band member*—says, with amusement in his voice. You've been trying not to think about how he's handsome. How he has nice hands.

"It's what Harabeoji would have wanted," Minsoo says. "Just a few toasts. We gotta honor his memory."

"You're just saying that, you drunk," your instance says with a smile on her face that mirrors your own.

Minsoo gasps in mock offense.

"What's a drunk?" the niece says, and everyone laughs. "It's not funny!"

"Just grown-up teasing," your instance says, giving the kid a kiss on the cheek that the kid squirms away from halfheartedly. You can't stop staring at the way the kid fits in your instance's lap like she belongs there. You wonder if she wants kids. You never wanted kids.

"Why'd Harabeoji want me to come, do you know?" you say, tamping down the discomfort bubbling in your chest. "We haven't talked in years."

"He talked about you a lot," Minsoo says. "Before he died. You and your mom."

"Family was important to him," Tae says. "I learned that when I asked him about marrying Soyoung. He was a big 'duty and loyalty' sort of guy."

"War generation," Minsoo says sagely. "I think not knowing about what happened in the north kind of haunted him."

"I think he always hoped you'd come back," your instance says. Your eyes snap up. You want her to explain, but she's looking away now, busy moving the kid to her own seat.

"What's living in the States like?" Tae asks.

"Well, everyone speaks English," you say, and everyone laughs. Then the food begins to arrive, and it's a scramble to clear the table so that the plates of banchan, meat, lettuce, rice in metal bowls, and kimchi can all fit around the grill. Conversation turns to cooking meat, pouring drinks.

"To the old man," Minsoo says, and you all clink shot glasses. This, at least, is easy. Like slotting into a life you had forgotten living.

▪▪▪

What's living in the States like?

America is Costco and Starbucks and freeways; America is H-Mart and boba and FOBs and bananas and first gen, second gen, third gen. America means KSA and APSA in college, and it means clicking the box that says "Asian/Pacific-Islander" on the job applications and the census, America means being asked *so, where are you from?* and nobody meaning New Jersey.

America means not knowing which of your friends are instances.

In 1776, the Constitution granted full rights to white, male, landowning instances—unheard of in Europe at the time—and not much to anyone else. Common knowledge states that instancing exploded globally from the Age of Discovery and onward, though, in truth, instancing records had historically been badly kept. But it's certain that colonization duplicated people across the globe. Immigration through Ellis and Angel Islands created vast swaths of instanced communities across the coasts. This is the legacy of the west: A mitosis-like duplication of the self across lands already populated.

Instancing is written into America's blood, into the story it tells itself: *Here is where instances immigrate.* Give us your tired, your poor, your hungry, give us your copies and let them be fruitful and multiply, let them homestead, let them become titans of industry, let them and their non-instanced children build cities and towns and railroads. Let them build chemical empires. Let them master their own fates.

The party line is: America assumes instances will stay forever.

Here is a free state for those who want to leave, America says, ignoring the fact that the land was already peopled, that the borders were brought to them unwillingly. Ignoring those brought by force in chains. Ignoring the deportations at the border and the raids in sanctuary cities. Ignoring the fact that *intention to leave* actually just means *acceptance of situations beyond your control.*

Living in the States means that you're blank-American. Korean-American. Mexican-American. African-American. Indian-American. Native American. America assumes instances leave their original country permanently and defines them by the self left behind.

And there is, perennially, the citizenship issue. The illegal immigrant issue. The border issue. The H-1B issue. The green card lottery issue. All facets of the same sort of problem. We want you here, but we want you on our terms.

▪ ▪ ▪

Halfway through dinner, Minsoo and you take a smoke break outside. He had offered. You don't smoke much anymore, but the atmosphere inside was getting to you. The way your instance and her fiancé held hands through most of dinner, the way she looked up at him through her eyelashes—you had grown out of that sort of behavior in college, although it could have just been that you didn't have anyone to do stupid couple things with.

You exhale clouds of smoke. Cold air, warm nicotine. It's nice. It was strange to watch Minsoo and your instance together. Good strange.

"So, what's she like? Soyoung, I mean," you ask Minsoo. You remember him being honest, as much as a kid is ever honest. "She seemed pretty high-strung during dinner."

Minsoo waves a hand in the air, trailing smoke. "Eh. She's having a rough time of it."

"Are she and her fiancé always like this?"

He laughs. "What, are you not like this with—are you seeing anyone?"

"No," you say. "And I don't act like—not even that, just, she's so cagey."

"You're not seeing her at her best," he says. "You know how it is, Harabeoji's last words to her were about wanting her to reintegrate. That was pretty shitty of the old man."

You stop, cigarette halfway to your lips. "What?"

Minsoo stops. "She didn't tell you?"

"No, all she told me was that Harabeoji wanted me to come to the funeral. Jesus Christ, did he really ask her that? *Dying wish,* ask her to reintegrate?"

You are abruptly reevaluating how much you knew about your-her grandfather. You know Harabeoji was born before the Korean War. You know your family is from the north. You know your grandmother died when you were very young. You know Harabeoji liked to watch baseball and that he kept sweet jelly cup snacks in his cupboard for you, even when your mom told him to stop buying them.

"Yep," Minsoo says, looking uncomfortable. "Look, you should talk to her about it, not me. I probably shouldn't have told you about it if she didn't tell you."

"No, you should have told me sooner! That's so fucked up. Who asks that sort of thing?"

"Well, Harabeoji did."

You know your grandfather was bitterly opposed to your mother moving to America. You know he and your mother had a blowup fight two nights before you moved, screaming at each other while one of your older cousins hustled you and Minsoo out of the living room. You know your grandfather drove you and your mother to the airport anyway, but didn't speak except to tell you to *be good for your mom, Soyoung-ah.*

You know your mom always handed you the phone, rather than talk to your grandfather.

Minsoo taps ash, stubs the cigarette against the ashtray. He offers you another cigarette and you shake your head. You're trying not to pick up old bad habits. One cigarette is stress. Two is a relapse. You had picked up smoking when you wanted to seem cool in college, and it had lasted all of two semesters before your mother had found out.

Minsoo doesn't take another cigarette for himself, either. He sways from side to side, as if he's contemplating walking back inside. You glance back. Through the clear glass windows of the restaurant, it's easy to spot Soyoung and her fiancé. Her head is tilted toward his. They look like they're laughing about something.

"How long are you staying?" Minsoo asks.

"Just a few days," you say, looking back out at the street. It's a warm night, and there're lots of pedestrians. Couples and groups of students, businessmen, moms and children. Minsoo taps his hand against his pocket like he wants another cigarette. He looks down at the floor.

"One second," he says. He hands you the box of cigarettes and heads around the building. You crane your neck to watch him, bemused. He disappears into the gravel parking lot. You give in, taking out a second cigarette, and you realize you don't have a lighter. You just stand there with a single unlit cigarette, thinking about that one John Green book that everyone was obsessed with when you were in college, and then Minsoo is striding back, holding a big manila envelope.

He thrusts it forward.

"Take it," he says. "Harabeoji left you some stuff. And he gave it to me to give to you. He said it's in the will, and for after—just, for after, but if you're not going to be around for when the lawyers sort all of that out, I guess I should give it to you now. I didn't want to mail it, you know?"

You unthinkingly stuff the cigarette box and unlit cigarette in your pocket and take the envelope. It's heavy. Half of you wants to open it right here and now. The other half of you wants to hand it back and demand that Minsoo give this to Soyoung. Let her deal with this. It's her family.

"Did he leave Soyoung anything?" you say. "What's the stuff?"

Minsoo shrugs.

"I don't know. I thought it'd be rude to look. Maybe it's just a letter for your mom or something. You know, for posterity."

"He told Soyoung to reintegrate," you say grimly.

"Well, yes," Minsoo says. "But, you know. Who knows what he was thinking. He was really old, Rose, and—"

Then Minsoo's kid, whose name you've already forgotten, runs out the door and into his legs, and you laugh, more out of shock than amusement, and Minsoo doesn't finish his sentence.

▪ ▪ ▪

The Korean Armistice Agreement was signed in 1953, creating the demilitarized zone that splits the peninsula into North and South. The Republic of Korea has the fourteenth largest nominal GDP in the world, globally consumed entertainment exports, and a remarkably high percentage of plastic surgery among its populace. The Democratic People's Republic of Korea has nuclear weapons, a fascist dictatorship built around a cult of personality, and a thriving black market for international media. The two countries never formally ended the war. Both countries post blank-faced soldiers with mirrored sunglasses on their side of the DMZ.

Crossing a border creates an instance. Creating a border manifests the capability for instances.

For a short time during the Korean War, it was possible to cross the DMZ with the right papers. The DMZ wasn't quite a border yet, not coalesced in the hearts and minds of the people as a "border." So much had happened to Korea in the past decades. Japanese occupation, name changes, comfort women, the phasing out of the Korean language. The theft of thousands of cultural artifacts. Global war, local war, foreign powers playing toy soldiers with foreigners, ideologies grappling in Korea before moving to Vietnam.

Soyoung's grandfather crossed a border-becoming-a-border. He didn't look back at who he might be leaving behind.

SOYOUNG

You're busy keeping Jangmi from getting ssamjang on her shirt so you don't realize your instance has gone outside with your cousin until they're already gone and Jangmi's hands have been wiped with a wet towel. It's just you, Tae, the elementary schooler, and half a grill of assorted meats now. Jangmi squirms away from you, and you let her get back to mixing all the sauces together in a little dish. Kids are crazy. You look across the restaurant, across the tables to the shadow of Minsoo and Rose against the frosted glass. It's impossible to tell anything from their silhouettes.

"She's not what you expected," Tae says. You look away from your cousin and your instance.

"No." You wrinkle your nose. "I don't know what I was expecting. But she's—I don't know! I guess I expected her to be less Korean? But other than the accent she's . . . Maybe she's funnier? Do you think she's funnier?"

"I can't legally answer that," Tae says.

"She tells *jokes*. I wish I was good at telling jokes."

If Rose agrees to be you, then maybe you'll be good at telling jokes. Reintegration is a plot point in at least seven of the webnovels that you keep up with. The main character's instance has some incredible power, or some plot-relevant weird skill (deep-sea fishing, in the last one you read), and so the main character has to somehow find his instance, convince him to return, and then reintegrate. Then there's usually a huge flashback sequence, a training montage, and then they're one person for a while before they separate again, because the instance had some sort of meaningful reason to want to leave afterward, now having both sets of memories, and a whole lot of character development. It's one of your favorite tropes.

"Tell me a joke right now," Tae says.

You stuff some rice in your mouth to keep from answering. Tae just keeps watching you with a patient, amused smile. You chew even slower. He grins.

You have to keep yourself from smiling with a mouth full of half-chewed rice.

You swallow.

"No."

"I'll tell you a joke!" Jangmi says.

"Jangmi-ya, go get your daddy," you say, pushing her gently off your lap. She goes readily.

You and Tae watch her run across the restaurant, out the door, adding her own little shadow to the two standing there.

"So," Tae says.

You pour him a shot, because he's taking the subway, and you don't pour yourself one, because you're going to be driving.

"I think I like her," you say.

Tae takes the shot.

"I know you're not okay, but are you okay?" he asks.

You haven't told Tae about your grandfather's last request. This is another thing you feel bad about. A good fiancée would have told him about major life decisions like: My grandfather told me as his dying wish that he wanted me to reintegrate, which makes me wonder whether he told my mom the same thing, but I haven't asked my mom, because asking my mom would be a cruel thing to do right now, and I don't have time to have a breakdown in front of my mother and we've already cried all over each other. Right now, I'm trying to figure out whether my American instance would want to know what I know. Would want to feel what I feel. So I need to feel like a person who is worth inhabiting.

You would like to pour yourself a shot. You don't. You pour Tae another instead. He frowns at you. You shrug.

Normally you're a good fiancée. Normally, you tell Tae all the things he needs to know and he tells you the things you need to know, sleepily under the covers late at night, over coffee and toast, in the soft odd hours when you're both supposed to be doing other things but are choosing to spend time together instead. You've talked about your future together. You're getting married next year. You both want kids. You're grateful for him. Based on what your girlfriends have said, sometimes it feels like you've found the one good man in all of Korea. He knows how you feel about Rose. He doesn't know what you're hoping for.

Outside the restaurant, you can see Jangmi's small shadow, next to your instance's shadow, identical to your own.

"I'm okay," you say. "I'll be okay."

■ ■ ■

What can you offer your instance? You have the following: a fiancé whom you've been with since college. You have a rented apartment that is anemically furnished. You have your mother, who is equivalent to her mother, except for all the ways they are different. You have friends and KakaoTalk group chats and a favorite cafe you like to read in. You have a stable career working as a business analyst at a chaebol group. You have a family. You have two decades of memories with your cousins and your grandfather and your aunts and uncles and you dream in Korean and speak in Korean but you don't know how much that matters to her, anymore.

You can offer her information. Emotional richness. Grief.

Maybe you don't say the last bit.

■ ■ ■

When Rose walks back inside, she's holding a large yellow envelope.

"What's that?" you ask.

Rose looks at Minsoo. He shrugs. You frown at him. He shrugs again.

"I don't know. I haven't looked inside yet," Rose says.

ROSE

You want to open the envelope in the car, but the light's fading. You let the papers rest in your lap as you look out the windows. Seoul at night is lit in cooler tones than New York. More fluorescents, more LED billboards, and brightly lit 7-Elevens next to corner stores with their closed metal shutters. Soyoung veers you off the side roads and onto a larger throughway.

You don't know where exactly she's taking you. You know in the abstract: her apartment. Where she lives alone, without her fiancé, because it would probably be a whole thing if she lived with him before marriage. But you don't know where it is, what neighborhood. You wouldn't recognize any of them anyway. You're very tired. You've eaten too much grilled meat and you've slept too little. Without the dazzle of the restaurant, your eyelids are drifting closed. It's not a bad feeling. When you're this tired, all your emotions feel very far away. So what if you're in Korea for the first time in twenty years? So what if you had to meet your relatives? So what if you were given a mysterious package you don't want to deal with? So what if you had expected an uncomplicated visit, that you would do your filial duty and get out without any emotions? It's hard to be nervous now. You let gravity win, and close your eyes. Just one moment.

You wake up in a parking garage, with something prodding against your shoulder. You jolt awake, jerking the seat belt forward.

"Sorry!"

Soyoung's fingers on your shoulder. She's shaken you awake. Two layers of fabric separate your skin from hers, along with the MERGEBREAK.

"Sorry," she says again. "You weren't waking up."

"It's fine," you say, in English, because you dream in English and it's the first language your brain jumps to. Even though it's not fine. She touched you. A 5 percent failure rate. No skin against skin, but what if there had been a hole in your jacket, perfectly layered against a hole in your T-shirt, and what if the skin of her palm had touched the skin of your shoulder, and then you wouldn't be you anymore, and she wouldn't be her?

But nothing happened. So it's fine.

"I made sure I wasn't touching you," Soyoung says, like she can read your mind. She's keeping her hands carefully far away from you now.

"I appreciate that," you say. This time in Korean.

You take refuge in action, unbuckling your seat belt. This is when you realize the envelope is missing, no longer sitting in your lap. You swivel your head around wildly. It's a big document. It should be immediately visible. Did Soyoung steal it?

"Did you take my envelope?" you demand.

She looks at you flatly.

"It fell on the floor," she says, gesturing at your feet.

You look down. The envelope is wedged there.

"Sorry," you say, using the word for "sorry" that denotes higher formality. You're ashamed of yourself. You've been very suspicious of Soyoung for no reason. It was one thing to think of Soyoung in the abstract, and another to be faced with the physical reality of her. She hasn't breathed a word of your grandfather's request. She might not even know. She hasn't tried anything, with you. She's been a good host. Better than you would have been. You're the asshole.

Soyoung unbuckles her own seat belt in lieu of saying anything. She opens the car door. She pauses before she gets out.

"If you want, I can drive you to Umma's place. Or to Minsoo's apartment. Or one of the aunts. You don't have to stay with me if it's too weird."

"No," you say. "No, it's fine. I really appreciate it. I'm just tired."

"Okay."

You don't think she believes you. But there's no way to tell. You both get out of the car. She pops the trunk and gets your suitcase out. The odd thing is how normal it feels with her, when you don't think about it too hard. You work in synchronization, like the movements you're doing are choreographed. Yes, this is the order of operations you would take. Yes, this is the route you'd wind across the basement garage to the elevator, which has a mirrored door on which you can see your reflected faces.

Soyoung in her neat work clothing, more formal than you ever wear to work. She doesn't look like a T-shirt girl. She's wearing a full face of makeup, and her lipstick isn't even smudged, although you saw the way she shoved lettuce-wrapped beef into her mouth.

Meanwhile, you look like you spent sixteen hours on a plane, and are carrying a large manila envelope like it's a shield. This is the face of the American dream.

"I'm sorry I accused you of stealing my envelope," you announce.

"It's okay," she says. It's clearly not okay.

"Minsoo gave it to me, and told me that Harabeoji left me some stuff inside, and that this was all listed in the will. But Minsoo didn't tell me what it was. Do you want to look at it together?"

"Sure," she says.

The elevator comes. You ascend.

▪ ▪ ▪

Instances having to work together is a staple of modern media, although the trope only became codified outside of folktale and myth after the advent of the rail system in the western world. In the older stories, the return is a magical thing. The son returns to his mother's house and finds himself chopping wood, and he is cast out as an interloper. The runaway bride returns to her father's kingdom and begs her instance to reintegrate with her. The fisherman rises from the sea and finds his other self contentedly asleep.

But in modern stories, the instance doesn't reintegrate immediately, nor are they immediately cast out. The story luxuriates in the encounter. The tension is in whether there will be a reintegration. It's a plot point, a way to refresh a character that is growing stale. A way to reset relationships. In soaps and telenovelas, instancing and reintegration are used like a death, a coma, a long-lost twin. This is not how it feels to have an instance. An instance is you in all respects but one. An instance is you, until you make enough choices that you are no longer them. An instance is what would have happened, if you had gone, or if you had stayed. It does not feel like having a twin. And in reality, instances don't tend toward conflict—they know too much about each other, and it's too easy for them to anticipate each other's actions. What they want is often too similar to be separated.

▪ ▪ ▪

You arrive at Soyoung's apartment and some part of you is surprised that it looks nothing like yours. It's white where your walls are blue, the lights occasionally give off a weird fluorescent flickering, and all the cabinets are too shiny. Soyoung has set up an air bed in the corner. It's not bad. It's just not where you live.

You go to the couch and open the envelope without any ceremony before shaking the contents onto the coffee table. Papers slide out. Folded letters, heavy cardstock, notebooks. A very official-looking piece of cream-colored paper, sealed with a red stamp. Soyoung sits across from you, leaning over the document. She unfolds it.

"It's a deed to the house," she says.

You pause from where you're picking up one of the cards.

"Shut up," you say.

She passes it to you wordlessly. It's all in Korean. You think it's talking about property, and it lists an address. Your grandfather's house. The house you grew up in.

"It's his house," Soyoung says, like you wouldn't remember his house. "He gave you his house."

"But I don't want his house," you say. You're not sure how to feel about this. Your grandfather is a man mostly faded from your memory. You remember him in the way he sat in his armchair and crossed his arms, you remember him in the house like they are one and the same. Your childhood memories are in that house. You grew up there. You don't think about that house a lot, not every week, not every month. Only when you see forsythia. You don't need to own property in Korea. You *really* don't need to own an antiquated house that hasn't been updated since you were a kid.

"I don't live here!"

You toss the deed on the table. You can't read Korean legalese. You can speak Korean conversationally. You couldn't read a dense novel, or have a business discussion. You can talk about family things. Friend things. Restaurants and where the bathroom is and where you're going, you can talk about your feelings, a little, but you wouldn't know how to write any of it down properly. This says something about a transfer. Legal ownership. You don't know how this works or what the document is supposed to have—you really wouldn't know in English, either. She picks it up.

"What does it say?" you ask your instance. Her knuckles are white.

If this were a movie, this would be the moment she told you about your grandfather's last request. To reintegrate. She'd tell you like it was a relief to have the secret out, and she'd say that she thought it was a fucked-up request from a fucked-up old man, and you'd say, "Yeah! This whole thing is super weird," and you'd tell her that you still don't know why you agreed to come.

And you would tell her that you had been hoping for some sort of closure, maybe. And she would nod, because she understands closure. And seeing you would be closure for her, final proof of what-could-have-been, and then she'd translate the deed and the will and understand what's going on, and you could bond over that, and you would say that you're sorry for never getting in contact, it's just that you thought that she wouldn't want to talk to you, because if you were the one left behind you would have been mad about the whole situation, and you had never really wanted to think about how there was a whole other life being lived by someone who is *you*.

But this isn't what happens. Soyoung stands up. She walks away.

"Soyoung," you call. It's odd to be calling another person Soyoung. To you, you're Soyoung. Soyoung for your mother and your late grandfather and the one white ex-boyfriend who insisted on using your *real* name and for no one else.

Soyoung turns. She tilts her head.

"Are you okay?"

She smiles.

"Honestly? I'm really pissed off, and I don't want to say something I'll regret. So I'm going to go to bed. Good night."

You're too tired to chase her. Fine. Let it lie. There's all of tomorrow, and you're angry too. Not at her, but maybe at yourself.

SOYOUNG

When you wake up, Rose is gone. Her suitcase is open and her pajamas are neatly folded on top. She's left a note: *I went for a walk. Here's my number, in case. I have international roaming so OK to call.*

You don't see the envelope. She must have taken it with her. You're still angry in the clear light of morning. Not at her, but at your grandfather. He gave her the house. The house you grew up in. What do you get? You get the mandate to reintegrate with her. And the documents stipulate that the house belongs to your instance, or your future reintegration. Not *you*. You wonder if your grandfather's playing some sort of complicated game from beyond the grave, or if these are a bunch of loose, unconnected threads that you're creating a nonsensical map out of. What does he want from you? What does he actually want you to do?

In the warm wet embrace of washing your hair, you're awake enough to run through a laundry list of questions. Why was your instance so mad about the house? If she was so mad about getting the house, why did she come back to Korea? Why are you mad that you didn't get the house? You hadn't expected the house to begin with, you didn't know anything about your grandfather's finances and you had thought that if anyone was going to get anything, it would be your mother. You don't even want the house, you just want her not to have been given the house. Your mind conjures plots, schemes, tangled webs. But you already know the family secrets, and most of them are about dead people.

You step out of the shower and towel-dry your hair. You think about how most of these questions aren't really relevant. You wipe condensation from the mirror and brush your teeth. You think about how mostly, people don't know why they do things or why they want them.

You apply your moisturizer and makeup, blow-dry your hair. If your instance asked you bluntly why you want to reintegrate, you wouldn't have an answer that would make sense to her. You step into your underwear and day clothes. You think about how your instance is you, and you imagine how you might feel, alone, among strangers-who-aren't-strangers, but your imagination fails you so you give up. You pick up your phone and text people back—the girls (*yes, I'm free next week to go for drinks!*), Minsoo (*I'm not babysitting for you, today. Get Mina to do it*), and Tae (*that shirt looks good on you!! Looks like a cute girl with an amazing sense of style picked it out* 😘). You make a call.

"I think I need your advice," you tell Yujin. "Can we meet up? I'll buy you a coffee or something."

ROSE

You're up before the sun rises. For a moment, you think you're at home, underneath your duvet, and that your cat is going to come running in begging for his breakfast. But then you blink, and the ceiling isn't your ceiling. The sagging air mattress underneath you isn't your bed. You're halfway across the world. Your body believes it's supposed to be seven at night and that it's time for dinner, not breakfast.

You rub your eyes. You pick up your phone and check the time. Six in the morning. The apartment is quiet. Soyoung probably isn't awake yet.

You're a heavy sleeper. You make an educated guess that your other self will be as well, and quietly slide the bedroom door open. The soft slump of your other self's sleeping body is a dim outline. You go back to your suitcase and pull out a pair of socks. You pad into the bedroom silently and stand over the bed, breathing shallowly.

So this is what you look like when you're unconscious. Her hair is splayed across the pillow, her mouth open. She's curled up in a fetal position, with one arm tossed across blankets. It's not particularly attractive, and you feel a sudden self-consciousness. You step back, and slowly turn your head to take in the whole room. It's too dark to make out the particulars, like the color of the curtains or the text on the spines of her books. But you see framed photos of her and people you don't know. Photos of her and the Korean version of your mother. Photos of her and her fiancé. A lot of them look like they were taken in photo booths, the kind you loved as a kid.

Apart from that, her room is neat. No haphazard clothes pile on a chair. No cat toys that have been batted into weird places. No cat. You should check on how Dr. Crouton is doing at Clarissa's.

You could imagine living in this room, but you don't much like it. You wonder why Soyoung lives alone. If you were engaged, you would be living with your fiancé. But maybe it's a cultural thing. Some of your more Korean friends, the Korean Christian ones who go to church every Sunday, have talked about the same thing: No moving in together before marriage.

You suppose you could ask. But you don't need to know that much about her life.

Soyoung shifts in her sleep. You make a hasty, silent retreat, carefully closing the door behind you. You step into the kitchen and exhale quietly.

You decide to open all her cabinets. Plates, bowls, cups, all very *Korean* in a way that is less cultural and more in the way that you remember using a similar style of bowl as a kid. Maybe these are actually Mom's bowls. You look through her pantry cabinet and her fridge, and you're amused to see that it's very similar to your own: more snacks and condiments than actual food, half-eaten takeout containers. See, you think. We have the same bad habits. The glee at the moment of connection shocks you: You had thought you didn't want to be her.

▪ ▪ ▪

What does the fisherman think when he goes into the water? When he slides into the cool ocean, when he steps into the wet sand, when the buoyancy lessens his weight and he goes, hand in hand, with the water-nymph-siren-mermaid into the undersea court? Does he think about his wife? Does he think only about the lights underneath the water? Does he think, who will take care of my boat, who will take care of my house, my ailing parents, my wife, my unborn sons and daughters? When does he know he will not return?

▪ ▪ ▪

You take a very quiet shower using unfamiliar products that smell like mint and citrus. You dress yourself. You stare at the envelope sitting innocently on the kitchen table. You haven't flipped through the documents inside, yet. Your instance's anger unnerved you. You knew you had a temper; you've never seen it on display. You're learning too much.

Suddenly you really just want to be out of this apartment. Soyoung's possessions are a reflection of her, and she's a reflection of you, and you're struck by the sudden complete understanding that the longer you spend in this space, the more you'll know about yourself, and you didn't come back to this country for self-discovery. You always hated that trope. An instance returns to the place of their birth, and has some sort of important cultural experience, meets the people that they grew up with, and in doing so, learns something about themselves before leaving again. It's always bittersweet, sentimental. You don't want bittersweet or sentimental. You have a life already. You want the closure of a chapter of your life that you had already considered dead and buried. You were never really one for thinking about your childhood. You had overestimated your tolerance for nostalgia.

Fine, then. You'll take a day to work through your emotions and then there will be the funeral, and then you can go home. You'll take a few more days off work and claim bereavement, and spend them playing video games and watching reality TV and hanging out with your cat and going out with your friends. But first you need to figure out what you're going to do with the envelope. And for that, you need to understand what's in it.

But right now, you want to leave the apartment, so you do.

▪▪▪

Of course you loved your grandfather's house. Of course you loved the way the windows glowed when it was dark and sunset shined laterally through the blinds. Of course you loved how it felt to sit in your bed at night surrounded by plushies that you or one of your cousins had won from a claw machine. Of course you loved the dent in the wall where you accidentally slammed your soccer cleat because you had been so excited at winning the tournament at school. You had been happy there. But you don't want it anymore. You loved it like something you had already lost, like something you were always meant to lose.

▪▪▪

Soyoung's apartment leads to a pedestrian pathway bordering a small road. You pass storefronts selling fish cake and twigim and tteokbokki, 7-Elevens with cardboard K-pop stars advertising soft drinks and soju. You pass five thousand coffee shops, none yet open. There weren't this many coffee shops when you were a kid. You've passed two different Starbucks and a Coffee Bean in the last fifteen minutes.

You walk through the neighborhood and cross into another. You walk across broad roads and up staircases and down hills and you stop in at a

FamilyMart to buy a packaged coffee that you pour into a cup of prepackaged ice. You drink as you walk. Around you, the vague character of the neighborhoods change, though the stores keep repeating—another Olive Young, another Caffe Bene. You eventually walk around a large local shopping center, and pause at the corner. Something about it is strange. By now Seoul's waking up, and there are people here—a couple of old men and women setting up to sell vegetables, a few shopkeepers still pulling up metal doors that cover their shops, a few kids buying some little snack before school.

You frown. You sit on the edge of a windowsill. From this angle, the world is familiar. Then it hits you. You've been here before. You've been here dozens of times. This is the little grocery market near your grandfather's house, which your mom had always claimed was a little overpriced. You had bought candy here as a kid. There had been an arcade machine that was always broken, outside. You and Yujin and Minsoo had played at the playground nearby. Your grandfather's house, the one that he's trying to give to you from beyond the grave, is a five-minute walk away.

You think about turning and leaving. Going back to Soyoung's apartment. Going anywhere else. But it's so close. It's like an invitation. It's like how once you had heard that your grandfather had wanted you back in Korea, there was no other option for you but to return. The door is open, so, you have to walk through.

You'll just take a quick look. And then you'll leave.

▪ ▪ ▪

It's not curiosity that creates instances. Not the desire to know the world outside your own boundaries. Marco Polo famously didn't instance. You can travel the whole world and still return home and stay singular. It's not a bad thing, to instance. But it means that you were of two minds. It shows a desire beyond wonder. It suggests a desire for escape, an understanding that either the world outside is so beautiful it must be permanently inhabited or the world inside is so terrible that it should be escaped. Instances often are annoyed when asked how they knew they were leaving. It's like falling in love, the cliché goes. You just know.

▪ ▪ ▪

You had expected your grandfather's house to have changed after nearly two decades. It hasn't. It's a redbrick house with a wrought-iron gate, covered in vines. Yellow forsythia and blooming purple azaleas line the fences. You feel a punch of emotion in your throat. You didn't ever think you would be back here. You feel as though if you opened the gate and stepped through the front door, you could call for your grandfather and he would look up from where he was watching the television, and say, *ah, Soyoung, back from school?*

You stand in the street, staring at the house. You guess you were hoping for some sort of closure. But this isn't a movie and you hadn't felt bad about leaving, anyway. It had just been a fact of life. You had moved to America because your mom said that you were moving. It was just something that happened to you. Though you had missed the house. It had taken a long time for your mom's new place to feel like home.

The door opens. A face identical to your mom's pokes out.

"Soyoung, what are you doing, standing there in the street?"

"Umma—" you say, forgetting for a moment. No—that's not your mom, that's Soyoung's mom.

"Soyoung-ah—"

"It's Rose," you say. "From New York."

"Oh, Rose," she says. She says your name accented. The *s* turning to a *j*. The emotion in her face has turned from light curiosity to something deeper. She's staring at you. She looks exactly like your mother. "Do you want to come in? I'm just here doing some cleaning. I started boxing things up."

You are gripped by a sudden visceral desire not to go in. You don't want to go into your childhood home and drink coffee as if you're a stranger. You don't want to remember this place like it's somewhere you don't belong. You like the warm memories of your childhood. You don't want to overwrite them.

"Not really," you say. You wouldn't say that to your mom in the States. It would hurt her feelings. You shouldn't be saying it to any version of your mom. But you really don't want to go inside.

"That's fine," Soyoung's mom says. It's so mild. Your mom is never so mild. She walks out the door and closes it behind her. "Do you have time to talk now?"

"A little," you say.

She comes over to the gate. She looks older. You can't tell if there's any differences from your mom. They look the same to you. She smiles at you. You have the feeling that she wants something from you and you have no idea what.

"So. How have you been? What do you do?"

You blink.

"I'm good. Um. I've been good, mostly. I'm a software engineer. Why are you asking me about this?"

"I'm asking you now because I don't know when I get to ask again," she says. "Your mother and I—anyway. Are you happy? Do you like living in America?"

Do you like living in America? It's not so much that you like it as it's where you live. You live there because you live there. You live in New York because you went to school in the tristate area and you grew up in New Jersey. You live there because it was somewhere to live and you had no compelling reason to go anywhere else.

Were you happy? You weren't unhappy. You considered happiness to be a fleeting state, but there wasn't anything you were discontent with. Someday, you might want something more out of life but you liked your current life and the holding pattern it was in. Anyway, you couldn't give your mother's instance a different answer than what you would have given your own mother.

"I'm good," you say. "I'm happy."

"Good. That's good."

She just looks at you. You just look at her. You think about asking her about the deed to the house, about what your grandfather—her father, had asked of you. Of what he had asked your instance. You want to ask her whether he asked anything similar of your mom and her.

"Do you still live here?" you say.

"No. I moved out, after Soyoung was going to college. When we didn't need the space so much. I share an apartment with one of your aunts. We took turns coming back and taking care of your grandfather, at the end."

The use of the words "your grandfather" seem like a deliberate stab.

"Did you ever want to move out of the house, when we were living here?"

"Of course I wanted to leave, Rose," Soyoung's mother says. "I left for America, with you."

She looks so matter-of-fact about it. Like it didn't hurt her, to be the instance who stayed. You can't ask about the deed to the house. Your phone buzzes, and you pick it up and pretend that it's time sensitive.

"Sorry, I have to go," you lie.

"Wait—" Soyoung's mom says. You pause. You turn back. You think she's going to call out your obvious ruse. You think she's going to open the gate and step out and hug you. You would accept it. She's your mother. She's a version of your mother.

"See you tomorrow," she says. "Be safe getting around."

SOYOUNG

You're waiting for Yujin in the cross-section of the underground mall. This is because he's got a date later with some girl he met last week—not important enough yet, in the grand scheme of things, to be given a name—and there's four subway lines out of the underground.

You've bought Yujin a cheese-cream-foam-strawberry-ice-latte since it sounded disgusting. It was a thing with the two of you, as kids. Making potions. You grew out of it and then grew back into it. Now you get each other terrible coffee drinks when the baristas don't look too harried. You also bought him a red bean bun. You're not completely heartless.

It's early enough that you didn't feel bad ordering an awful drink. You like Seoul best when it's quiet. Sometimes you think about moving out of the city core, but that feels like a later decision, after you're married. When you want to raise a family. You're supposed to babysit Jangmi the day after tomorrow. The awful drink slowly coagulates.

Yujin comes bounding over, sliding into the seat across from you with more enthusiasm than you think 10:30 AM on a Saturday deserves. He's wearing date clothes (button-down shirt, real pants), and he's styled his hair. The thing about funerals is that other people still go on dates.

"You look cute," you say. "Do I get to meet her, yet?"

"Nope. Not until after a few more dates. I like Youngmi, though. I think this could be something. Damn, is this *congealing*?"

He picks up the cheese-cream-foam-strawberry-ice-latte and takes a long sip before making a face.

"Oh, this is even worse than it looks."

You smile a bit, then slide him the red bean bun. He takes it and bites down with too much enthusiasm. Red bean paste smears on the corner of his lips. He wipes it.

Through a mouthful of pastry, he asks, "So, wha's up?"

"How do you talk to your instance?"

He swallows his food. "Mostly over Wi-Fi."

"Not logistically, I mean like . . . how do you try and convince YJ to do anything? What's it like talking with him? Do you guys ever fight?"

"Things with Rose are going well?"

"Oh, shut up. I'm serious. Do you have a good sense of what he's feeling, most of the time?"

"You've gotta give me more context, Soyoung. Did you guys get into an argument or something?"

"No," you say. "Some funeral-related family stuff has come up and I don't know how to talk with her about it. I kind of thought it would be easy. But it's really hard talking with her. Is that normal?"

Yujin is the only person you know who regularly talks with his instance. He frowns. Runs a hand through his hair, messing up the styling.

"When I talk with YJ, it's like . . . I know what he's thinking, most of the time, so he's actually not really helpful if I need an outside perspective. But when we talk, it's like . . . do you have conversations in your head? Do you think in language?"

"Sometimes?"

"It's like that. Like when I ask myself in my head, 'Do I want to buy the new Pokémon game,' and then tell myself, 'No, we're too old for that,' and then I say to myself, 'Well, come on, you know you want it, and besides, you don't really give a shit about being too old for anything, you're just worried about how it looks, so buy it online and play it at home. Get over yourself.' It's like that, but I say the words out loud. A stream-of-consciousness dialogue."

This is so foreign from your experience of talking with Rose as to have come from another planet. The expression on your face must make this obvious. He frowns.

"Do you want to listen in on a call with him?"

"Now? Here?"

"Sure. I was going to call him anyway."

Yujin pulls a set of earbuds out of his pocket and hands one to you. He pops the second in his ear. He fiddles with his phone for a second, and while the KakaoTalk jingle plays, he says, "Just be quiet."

You say quietly, "Are you sure this is okay?"

He shrugs. "I don't have to tell him everything immediately. We'll know about it eventually."

You want to say something about that. How your listening in feels like a lie of omission. It seems at odds with the way Yujin spoke about his relationship with his instance. But then the call connects. And YJ's voice, fairly clear, sounding tired, with identical cadence and tone to Yujin's: "No, I haven't had time to call Dad yet. I got his message. I'll call him in the morning."

Yujin laughs. "Yeah, okay. But he's bugging me about bugging you, so just get it over with."

To your surprise, Yujin speaks in English, despite the fact that YJ was speaking Korean.

"Yeah, yeah. I'll call him. Are you out?"

"Getting coffee with a friend, yeah. Sorry, did I wake you up?"

"Kind of. Petra's asleep."

"Tell her I say hi. Just kidding. Don't."

"I will," YJ says.

"You're not getting back together with her, right?"

"No. She's just—she's moving out, end of the month probably. It's just—"

"Sure. I only asked 'cause I'm seeing this girl, and I think it could be—"

"That's fine."

Silence, for a moment. Soyoung holds her breath, afraid that the whisper across her airway will make it obvious there's a second person on the line. Yujin takes a long slurp of the bad drink.

"So I'm buying a new pho—"

"No you're not," YJ cuts in. "You got a new phone last year."

"But I want the new model."

"You're never going to use the camera."

"Don't tell me what I won't do."

"Do you use the camera now? I don't use the camera."

"Maybe you don't use the camera because it's not good enough."

"They're pretty much the same camera!"

"Three lenses, YJ," Yujin says. "Get over yourself, you know you want it too."

"Look, all I—"

YJ's sentence is broken with a yawn. You're surprised by how fast the conversation went—less than thirty seconds of rapid-fire back and forth, the sentences more like half-formed thoughts than anything fully coherent.

"I'm going to go back to sleep," YJ says. "Send me the specs for the phone. I'll call Dad. 'Night."

"Bye," Yujin says, and hangs up the phone. He takes out his earbud. You take yours out as well and hand it back to him. You're unnerved. That wasn't what you were expecting from the conversation. YJ had used complete ban-mal, perfectly informal, and neither of them had been *nice*.

"Who's Petra?"

"His ex-girlfriend."

"She's sleeping with him, still?"

"They're sharing an apartment until she moves out. Sleeping in the same bed. It's psychotic. I've been trying to tell him."

"She knows about you?"

"More or less."

You almost want to ask him about how much they share with each other about their dating life. You're pretty sure Rose is single.

"Did that help, at all?" Yujin asks.

"Not really," you say. "Sorry, I'd lie to you, but we're friends."

He snorts.

"YJ and I are basically the same person, developmentally. And we're planning on reintegrating before we're thirty, so it's not like your scenario. I don't think it's weird that you're having a hard time talking with Rose. Have you asked her about reintegrating, yet?"

"No. That's the problem. I don't know how to bring it up. And—get this, my grandfather, god knows what he was thinking, left her *the family home*."

"Like, property?"

"Yes, like property. Like my grandfather's house. *House*-house."

"Wait—your house?"

"Yeah," you say. You had always thought of it as your grandfather's house. It had belonged to him for so much longer than you had lived there. It had felt like a fact of the universe, that he had lived there. That was a lie, though. He had grown up outside Pyongyang, when that was something still possible.

"And she got all weird about it. So I got all weird about it. And now I can't bring up the reintegration thing without it seeming . . . all predatory. I was a jackass to her last night, too."

"When's she leaving?"

"I don't know. Soon after the burial. I don't know why she came, anyway. You get why I want to talk with her without things being weird, right?

But whenever we're in the same room it's like . . . I'm thinking about all the things I would say, if I were her. And then I don't say anything."

"There's your problem. Have you tried saying something?"

You kick him in the shin. He kicks you back.

"You haven't talked with her since you were a kid, right?"

"We've never talked before."

"*Never*-never? Really?"

"Why's that so weird! It's not like we had our own phones. And if she wanted to talk to me when we were kids, she could have always asked for Harabeoji to hand me the phone."

"Maybe she didn't know you were there."

"Well she could have asked!"

He drinks more of the horrible drink. He drums his fingers against the table.

"Sorry, Soyoung. I don't know if I have any good advice for you. You're not the easiest person to get to know. I think either she or you probably needs to man the fuck up and talk about your feelings."

"Ow. I thought we were friends."

"We are. That's why I can say those things."

He smiles at you, the bastard. You kick him in the shin again. You're always strangely pleased by how childish the two of you act around each other. It's a different sort of friendship than your girlfriends, or your cousins. It's friendship, like, when you look at him, mostly what you see is the seven-year-old missing a tooth, daring you to pick up the worm in his palm. Sometimes you think that's what keeps the two of you friends, more than the instancing-related reconnection. That you're friends because both of you like peeking back into the portal to your childhood.

"Come hang out with me and her, before your date," you demand. "Please."

"Sure," he says, easily. Ah. Things in your life can still be easy.

ROSE

You get out of the subway and don't know where you are. The stairs have spit you out between a busy road and a warren of storefronts that have colorful displays of immensely touristy-looking hanboks, pretty hair pins, and cheap jewelry, the roads thronged with strangers, girls with dyed hair, and boys with artfully tousled perms, wearing twenty different kinds of streetwear. If you were sixteen you would have been delighted. You would walk right into the streets and start buying cat-shaped earrings and twinkly headbands and chunky knockoff heels.

Your instance is somewhere in the middle of all of this, hanging out with a friend. She hadn't apologized for last night.

You plunge into the crowd, your phone clutched in your hand like a shield. It feels a little wrong to be walking here. Everyone is a little too alive. It's too much fun. It's a street made for a vacation, not your grim familial duty. In this crowd, death is an abstract concept. Responsibility was left by the subway station. Yet your instance came here the day before your grandfather's funeral, to meet a friend. You wonder how she feels.

You navigate past stalls selling honeycomb soft serve and stores that only sell rhinestone hair clips and finally you find a staircase with an arrow that points up. You walk up the stairs and a sliding paper door automatically opens to a dimly lit bar. It's all dark wood and paper lanterns, with slick lacquer-like floors. It's practically empty—too early. The sound of the street below is muffled, like the dull roar of an audience somewhere far away.

It's exactly like something you'd find in New York. Except that when the man at the far end of the bar waves at you, there's your other self, sitting next to him, getting elbowed in the arm, turning and smiling. You're very pretty when you smile. Soyoung gestures for you to come over. You walk over. You don't sit down.

"Hey."

"Hi," she says. "I thought it might be nice to do something not-family, since tomorrow is going to be the whole family again."

"This feels vaguely sacrilegious," you say. Soyoung looks fresh, smiley, no hard edges. You can't tell what she's thinking. "Nothing to do funeral-wise today?"

She shrugs, nods. "Umma and the aunts are doing most of the prep. I offered to help, and they said it would be good if I helped with post-funeral stuff."

You take a deep breath.

"I don't want the house. I'll figure out a way to give it to you, or your mom, or whoever. Okay?"

You don't mention that you had gone to see the house earlier. You don't mention running into her mother earlier. You don't mention the reintegration request. She doesn't know that you know. She hasn't brought it up yet, and you're hoping that it can lie like a corpse, dead and buried under more pressing material concerns. If you turn this into a conversation about property it doesn't have to turn into a conversation about feelings.

She blinks.

"Okay. That makes sense. Thanks. I don't care about who owns the house. You just surprised me last night."

"Okay," you say, unmoored. You hadn't expected such a complete acquiescence. Wasn't she going to bring up the reintegration thing?

"Okay," she repeats, and smiles a little.

"No, please," the guy says. "This is like a K-drama. Have you seen *Image,* yet? This is just like that."

Soyoung elbows him and then gestures at an empty seat. You notice that she's wearing the MERGEBREAK camouflaged under a stack of bracelets and her filmy black sleeve. Yours is just plainly tied on your wrist. You sit down.

"So. Something fun," you say. "Who is this?"

"You don't recognize me?" The man clutches at his heart theatrically. "Ah, here, maybe if I fix this."

He smooths his hair down ineffectually. He sticks his tongue out. You frown. Something in his face is very familiar, but you can't place it. He looks like someone you might know, but what you've come to realize is that once you get old enough, everyone in the world looks like someone you've met before. He's an attractive stranger with a fancy haircut, who your instance is friends with. He looks like the sort of guy you'd write off as an asshole in a bar where all the drinks cost twenty dollars. You shake your head.

"Stop playing around," your instance says. "That's Yujin."

The axis tilts. Your brain rearranges his features, imagines them two decades younger and half-formed. Yujin was a neighborhood kid, one of your classmates. Yujin was a kid you were friends with when you were like, five. He once made you pick up a worm with your bare hands.

"Holy shit, you grew up hot," you say before your brain can catch up with you.

Yujin cracks up.

"I like her better than you," he says to your instance. She elbows him a second time.

"We reconnected after college. He called me crying because he had instanced."

A flash of something dark across his face, like a brief sun-shower. Your instance doesn't notice, looking toward you.

"Hey," Yujin says mildly. "We don't have to go down my personal history."

"I don't know, I'm kind of sick of dealing with my own," you say. "Might be a nice change of pace."

A smile that doesn't reach Yujin's eyes. "My instance is in New York. You should look him up."

∎ ∎ ∎

You're offered the choice between staying at the bar and ordering something, or doing some exploring. Soyoung says that these streets are a good place to buy souvenirs. She says that she really liked coming here as a teenager. The red pill or the blue pill. Do you want to talk, or do you want to act?

You pick the blue pill. You thread back down the narrow staircase and into the press of people, following Soyoung and Yujin. You stay in a loose triad through the crowd. Strains of random pop music from stores, snatches of other people's conversation. You could get swept up in it. You feel like you're reliving an adolescence that doesn't belong to you.

You peruse through racks of sunglasses. You buy a touristy magnet for a work friend, a new hair clip for yourself. Something in you relaxes to see your instance in a context that isn't funeral-adjacent. Like she's just a person and not some sort of malevolent specter. Strangers give you the occasional double-take, but there's not any judgment. Unless they look carefully at your wrists, you could just be identical twins. Everything has felt so heavy, the last thirty-or-so hours. Like every conversation you have, every interaction you've had, has some psychic weight. Like you've been standing in front of the Egyptian god of the dead and he's weighing your heart against a feather. Weighing your life against hers. The metaphor is a little inexact. Maybe you just feel better now that you've cleared things up about the house. But the question of the reintegration knocks about in your mind like a stone in your boot. It's on the tip of your tongue.

"Are you going to buy that?"

You turn to see Yujin standing next to you. He gestures at the bracelet you're holding.

"Not sure."

"Mm. The ahjumma is starting to look annoyed, that's all."

"Ah," you say, and put the bracelet down and put your hands in your pockets. You glance at your instance, who's trying on hair bands. You walk out of the store and lean against the decorative railing. You read somewhere in an internet forum that *leaning against things* is a particularly American affectation that has to be trained out of spies and undercover operatives. Yujin follows you. You're a little annoyed.

"What actually happened, when you instanced?" you say.

"That's kind of personal."

"Isn't Soyoung basically your best friend? You guys seem pretty close."

"You're not Soyoung."

You smile. You're *not* Soyoung.

"Is she cheating on her fiancé with you, or do you have a crush on her or something?"

Yujin turns his head to you with an expression of perfect confusion.

"Fuck, what the hell? She said you two were having communication issues, you clearly got a different memo, why would you ask me that?"

You shrug. "Have you ever been on one of those dates, where ten minutes in, you know it's going nowhere, so you both end up going way too deep and personal because you know it's never going to matter?"

Yujin grimaces. "Yeah, I have, but still. Damn."

He's quiet for a moment. You think about going back inside and buying the bracelet.

"We're friends. We're not anything but friends. I'm friends with Tae, too.

We play on a recreational soccer team together. I asked Soyoung out in high school, once," Yujin says. "She turned me down. Which was fair, we were both shitty teenagers. After that, we didn't really talk much until halfway through college. I was doing a study-abroad program at NYU and I came home for break, and . . . Well, YJ's in New York. And I'm here."

You sneak a glance at his face. Not much visible expression. That's one of the stereotypes that Asians get in America: emotionless. Inscrutable. The stigma had surprised you. You always felt like you exposed too much.

"Did Soyoung bring you as some sort of 'Oh, if Rose meets someone who has a sad instancing story, she'll feel sympathy for me' sort of thing?"

Yujin shakes his head, laughs a little. Just a brief bark of sound.

"Soyoung brought me for moral support. You scare the shit out of her."

"Me?"

"She doesn't know how to talk to you. She really wants you to like her. I think she's always been a little hurt that you never tried to get in contact. We talk about it, sometimes."

"Do you have support group meetings while you talk about your instances?" you say, lacing your tone with as much irony as you can, trying to drag the conversation back to safer ground. He's easier to talk to than Soyoung. This is dangerous.

"No, mostly we just get coffee."

You laugh. He laughs. It's almost comfortable.

"I don't know why I came," you admit. "I really don't want to go to the funeral tomorrow."

"I'm sorry for your loss," Yujin says. He almost sounds like he means it.

You shrug. He's a stranger. It doesn't mean anything coming from him. He should save it for your instance.

▪ ▪ ▪

NPR ran a few episodes about instancing when Rose was in high school. The first episode was on instancing research: covering the instanCenter at Stanford, the instancing start-ups that had popped up trying to overthrow Mergebreak, and the earlier, barbaric Victorian and WW2 experiments. In calm, methodical tones, the narrator explained that new research from the instanCenter has found that 30 percent of instances were surprised by the cleave. That they hadn't consciously expected that they would duplicate. This was up from 15 percent, a century ago—although of course with the allowances that the older studies are less accurate, and survey a smaller demographic pool. The narrator postulated that this was related to the increase in human migration in the twentieth and twenty-first centuries, and the increase of infrastructure surrounding air travel.

▪▪▪

Yujin leaves before you do. Something about how he has a date. He gives So-young a hug, and you get a nod and a wave. You're left standing with your instance.

One of us only tells the truth, the other one only tells lies, you think, the memory of watching *Labyrinth* floating through your head. Your instance rearranges her purchases. She seems happy. You think about how the day after Clarissa checked into inpatient treatment for her eating disorder, you went to the mall and bought three makeup palettes you never ended up using. You think about how after you had a blowup fight with your mom, the fight that led to you couch-surfing for a month over the summer in sophomore year, you had wasted forty dollars on movie tickets.

"So I know that Harabeoji asked you to reintegrate," you say. "All cards on the table."

A long pause. Your instance runs a hand through her hair.

"Oh. Minsoo told you, I'm guessing?"

"Yeah. At dinner. He told me to talk to you about it. But I thought you would bring it up if you wanted to talk."

"When have we ever brought anything up?" she says. You laugh. She laughs. Neither of these are very happy laughs.

"I wanted to wait until after the funeral," she says.

"You should have just said it when we met. I would have appreciated it."

"I didn't know how to say it. Why are you bringing it up now?"

"I don't know," you say. "It's pretty fucked up, right?"

"So fucked up!" she exclaims. That sentence contains the most beautiful expletive you've heard. You and her, in alignment. Yes, that was a horrible thing to do! No, neither of us are happy about it.

"Like, what was he thinking? Between that and the house . . . He's crazy."

"Don't say that," she says suddenly. "You don't get to say that."

"Oh, I didn't mean—"

"I know," she says. She says it curtly, two syllables in the lowest register. Plain banmal. Tomorrow, you're going to bury your grandfather, and every time you talk to your instance, you say the wrong thing.

"I just mean," you say, and then sigh. "I'm sorry you're having a tough time. I'm sorry that Harabeoji asked you to reintegrate. I can't really imagine what you're going through."

"You're kind of blunt," she says. "Have you changed that much?"

Time, space, the American public school system. You don't know if change is something that happens to you all at once, or if you could chart your life in millimeters and that maybe years ago you could have understood each other.

"I didn't know you had a life like this," you say. "I didn't know you had a life at all. I didn't think about you, or your relationships. I didn't know that Harabeoji could be someone to ask so much of you. I don't think you should do anything you don't want to do. I don't want to do anything you don't want to do. I'm sorry this has been so messed up. I'm sorry that we're getting jerked around by our dead grandfather. Okay?"

"Yeah, okay," she says. And she wipes her eye with the back of her sleeve, and the movement tugs her bracelet stack, revealing the barest edge of her MERGEBREAK wristlet.

SOYOUNG

You take care to walk around the apartment quietly. The sliver of moonlight through your blinds paints everything silver. Rose is a soft slump in the indent of the air bed. Her short black hair is a small halo around her pale face. She has one palm splayed upward. She's still wearing her MERGEBREAK to sleep. This is a little hurtful. You're not the sort of person to do anything while the other party is unconscious. Of course you're thinking about it, though. But you're mostly thinking about her confession earlier. How she spit out the words: *So I know that Harabeoji asked you to reintegrate.* She said it like she had to stutter it out, or like she was biting off some sort of poisonous snake. And you didn't know what to say to her, how to get the answers you wanted.

You carefully bend down next to her backpack. You unzip it slowly, millimeter by millimeter so that the click of the zip against the teeth doesn't sound. You pull out the envelope. The slide of paper against cloth is so loud, in the dark. The crinkle of the package opening. The rasp of the contents being poured out onto the floor. You sit cross-legged in your pajamas and start reading, squinting in the dim moonlight. You want the deed to the house to contain some special, secret knowledge. You want to unravel its contents.

But Rose shifts in her sleep. So you put all the papers back in the envelope, and you put the envelope in the bag, and you push the bag gently back into the shape that you found it in, and mostly you just wish your grandfather was alive again so he could explain things in his creaky, assured, old-man voice, and that he could tell you that it would all make sense someday, and that you'll figure out what to do next.

▮ ▮ ▮

Most people report having the "instancing nightmare" at least once as children. It is roughly as common as the dream about all of your teeth falling out, or the dream when you're naked in class and get called on. The instancing nightmare is usually some variant of the child crossing a boundary (usually the threshold to the child's home or a garage, or an airport or rail station, if the child has traveled extensively) and then instancing. Dreamers have almost unilaterally described their experience as being from the point of view of the instance left behind.

ROSE

Your instance drives you to the gravesite. It's rush hour in Seoul, and you both sit uncomfortably in your black clothing. Your instance's fiancé will be coming later in the day, but you almost wish he was here now. You try not to watch your instance, but her visage is reflected in the passenger window. She's unavoidable.

Seoul crawls past in fits and bursts, block after block. You have never more desperately wanted to initiate a conversation. A dialogue. An interrogation. You want to ask about Harabeoji's last request to her, how she feels, what she wants to do. You want to ask her your questions without fear of the answers, except you know that the moment you ask is the moment she will refuse to speak. Because *you* would refuse to speak. It would scare you, to talk. It scares you now.

You know that she knows that you're scared. So, you can't ask.

You watch the scenery instead. High-rise apartment buildings, signs for after-school tutoring facilities, bus stops, and subway stations. Dozens of coffee shops. You don't remember this many coffee shops. You hadn't expected Seoul to change so much—the Seoul in your memories was a static snow globe.

Your family has lived in Seoul for two and a half generations. Your grandfather relocated here after the war, and your mother and her sisters were born here, and you were born here, and you could have lived your whole life in this city. Your grandmother and now your grandfather have died here.

"It was old age, right?" you ask. "Not a heart attack or cancer or anything."

"He was eighty-seven," your instance says. "Isn't everything old age at that point?"

"Sure." It always surprises you when your instance says things you wouldn't. It surprises you more when she says things you would.

"We kind of saw it coming," she says, looking straight at the road. "I mean. Eighty-seven, right?"

"Right," you say, daring a glance at her. She looks perfectly calm. She glances at you before looking back at the road.

"I'm sorry I was so rude to you, the other night. I didn't apologize. I'm sorry I'm kind of having a weird week. I thought you had enough to be dealing with, without my problems."

"No, it's okay," you lie. "It's really all okay."

"I hope it's been okay, other than . . . the funeral stuff. I wanted you to have a nice time, if you could. I promise my life usually isn't like this. But I wanted to ask—why did you come back?"

"I hadn't had any reason to, before," you admit. "I wanted an excuse. I guess this was an excuse."

"You were never curious before?"

"I was busy," you say. "And plane tickets are expensive, and before that, my mom would have had a lot of opinions about my leaving. But I *was* curious. Harabeoji never told me anything about you."

"He used to call you when I was around," Soyoung says.

"I didn't know that. He never said anything about you, no matter how much I asked."

"Well, here's how you should picture it," she says, rolling to a stop at a red light. "He's on the phone, sitting on the sofa, half-watching me and half-watching baseball. And I'm sitting at the kitchen table doing some homework I didn't finish at hagwon. And he's talking to you, and you're talking to him, and I'm doing my best to be really quiet with my pencil so I can hear what you're saying."

You can picture the house with the clarity of a reconstructed childhood memory. The smooth glass tabletop. The creased leather couch. The way it smelled a little like smoke, even though Harabeoji only ever smoked outside. You can imagine Harabeoji holding the old landline against his ear. You can imagine yourself sitting at the kitchen table doing homework. Listening.

"I don't know what to do with that," you say after a long pause.

"Well. I didn't, either."

You drive in silence for a while.

"Sorry. I didn't mean to say all of that," she says. She smiles a little, and it's the same smile that you do when you're feeling a little awkward, a little sad, when you're not exactly sure which public sentiment is the correct one to be displaying.

■ ■ ■

In many ways, it's easy for the man in the folktale. He never had to speak with his other self. And besides, what's three days compared to thirty years? One beautiful, strange night in a foreign country subsumed under thirty years of eating dinner with his wife, raising his children, taking his boat across the glittering shore and casting his nets. Time polished the memory of the undersea court to a pearl, something carefully tucked away under the rough cloth of his weekday worries.

Or he dies, bleeding out through the self-inflicted wound.

SOYOUNG

You used to dream of being the one to leave. Not like, metaphorical "god-I-wish-I-had-left" dreams, but literal dreams. Dreams where you stepped through the immigration checkpoint and walked through the airport, dreams where you landed in fictional American airports that were cobbled together, kaleidoscopic dreamscapes stitched from magazine articles and your memories of Narita and Hong Kong and Incheon. You'd wake up from these dreams sweating, and would walk around your grandfather's house, inspecting every corner to make sure this was the true reality and that you were still in Seoul.

The truth of it was that you had felt some secret relief, leaving the airport and getting back in the car with Harabeoji and your aunts and your mother, even though you threw the mother of all tantrums. Even with the disappointment of not getting to go on an adventure, part of you was relieved you'd be going back to the rest of your life, to elementary school and the playground, to after-school ice cream bars and hagwon and flute lessons. The things you loved would continue to be the things you loved. You would continue to be the thing that was loved.

Your true and bloody desire for your instance's life was a thing that grew like moss on a still rock, or a fungus threading its way through rotten wood. It grew from the tinny conversations you overheard as a child. Nine at night while you worked on homework and she chattered about her day. She always sounded happy. Distracted. When you were older, you peered at her Facebook photos and imagined yourself in her place. You saw her name in the graduation announcements posted online, briefly in the newspaper once for a community service award. It was mostly curiosity, a little bit of longing. Easily quashed.

Once, in middle school, you asked Harabeoji about why he called her. You remember watching him hang up the old phone with the bouncy cord and the clear plastic numbers. You remember watching him turn to you and smile wryly, his cheek creasing up with wrinkles.

"Don't be jealous, Soyoung-ah," he said.

"You always call her," you had whined. "How come I can't talk to her?"

He would make a thoughtful noise, shuffling over to the fridge and opening it, pulling out the big plastic jug of cold barley tea. You always considered that very much an old man drink because of him. He poured you a glass, and then himself.

"If she wants to talk to you, she'll ask."

"But I want to talk to her, and I'm asking."

He slid the glass over to you. You picked it up begrudgingly and drank the cool, slightly bitter tea.

"It's harder, when you're the one to leave. Let it rest until she's ready, Soyoung."

"Fine," you said. And then you never talked about it with him again.

You remember this conversation like an old video cassette played too many times on a VCR. But now you're wondering if you're remembering it the other way around. Maybe your memory is fallible, and you were the one who declined to talk with her, because *you* thought Rose should get a choice. Because your grandfather respecting Rose's autonomy seems strange, since his last request was for her to reintegrate with you. But he was probably an instance himself, so maybe her autonomy did matter to him, just until it didn't. Or maybe it was a long game of emotional manipulation, which you could almost respect. Or maybe he loved you more than he loved her. You can't ask him. He's dead.

Isn't that what it comes back to? He's dead, and you can't ask. All you have now is your instance, here in the car with you. Her face your face. Her grief not your grief.

You want to go home.

You glance at Rose. She's still staring out the window. You look back at the road.

She gets the emotional distance. She gets the different language. She gets to look at the funeral through foreign eyes and foreign perceptions, and you don't want to be her but you want to understand how she sees. You want to be able to see through eyes that are not your own. And in your heart of hearts, you admit that you would like to be someone not yourself.

ROSE

A traditional Korean funeral is held over three days, ending with the burial. Most people are cremated now. Korea is a small country and has only so many mountains. But your grandfather was semi-traditional, and his burial plot has been purchased for decades. Your grandmother is buried here as well.

The gravesite is familiar. A hill on the outskirts of Seoul, a clearing in the middle of the forest underneath the blue sky. This is why you're wearing black hiking boots instead of heels. All around you, family and friends and strangers in black, their wet eyes, your aunts and cousins exclaiming over you. *You must be so tired from the travel! It's so good to see you again! How's your mother?* You nod at your other mother. You speak Korean and stumble over your syllables.

The burial happens. The coffin. Shovels. Dirt and sod.

Your grandfather's grave is a large mound of earth encased in a stone foundation with a shiny black granite marker. Your chest hurts to look at it, the sort of bone-deep dull sadness when a part of you that you thought was already dead dies.

Your instance walks over. You glance up as she approaches. She had been standing near her fiancé, while you stood near Minsoo and his daughter and your other cousins.

"It's weird being here when it's not Chuseok," she says. Her eyes are red-rimmed.

"Oh *you* think it's weird to be here?" you respond, and she laughs and you laugh and the laughter feels like a thin soap bubble film stretched across your conversation.

"Don't laugh," Minsoo says, without any heat. "The aunts will get mad."

"Sorry. It's just that, you know. This still doesn't feel real."

Minsoo peers at you. "Are you okay?"

Two days ago, you were home in downtown Brooklyn. Your biggest emotional hurdles were making sure you did the laundry before you ran out of socks or updating your dating app profile or deciding whether to get dim sum or American brunch with Clarissa over the weekend. You hadn't thought about your instance, your family in Korea, or your grandfather, in months, and even when you thought of them it was in passing, as if they were a dream you only vacantly remembered, something tamped down and deliberately buried.

A beat of silence that stretches too long. Your instance laughs. You don't laugh.

"Shit, of course she's not okay!" your instance says. "She just learned Harabeoji died two days ago, and now she had to fly all the way here for the fucking funeral, what were you expecting?"

"Uh—" Minsoo says. Your instance's voice had spiraled into a shout. Everyone's staring.

"Are *you* okay?" you cut in, staring at your instance. Her face has gone all blotchy under her makeup.

"I'm—I'm going to get some air," she says, and you almost reach for her when she turns on her heel, but Minsoo catches your hand instead.

"Let's give her a moment to cool off," he says, but you chase after your other self anyway.

▮▮▮

A plethora of related terminology borrows the language of instancing. For instance, software development. When Soyoung "Rose" Kang, in her real-true-American-job, downloads a copy of her company's repository from the cloud, that's called instancing, the same way the three steps across the immigration gate was instancing. A perfect copy is duplicated in a new location.

When Soyoung "Rose" Kang is done making her changes to the file, she will de-instance it, merging the file with the original on the server. The changes slot into the original, and the new copy becomes the official version on the server. The original copy without the changes is overwritten by the instance. Integration of the other into the self.

SOYOUNG

You are standing against the car, peeling your MERGEBREAK off your wrist, and the way you feel is not something you can articulate. It is not something you want to understand.

ROSE

You catch up to your other self. She's come back to where the car is parked, and she's leaning against the side, pretending not to wipe her eyes.

She looks askance at you. "What do you want." A statement. Her voice your voice. Her hurt unlike your hurt. You feel like a stranger all of a sudden, so far removed from the way she sounds, unable to understand the way she feels.

"*Are* you okay?" you say. Plain banmal.

"The messed-up thing is that it would have been so easy if Harabeoji hadn't asked," she says.

"What?"

"If he hadn't asked me, and made it a whole family thing, and given you the house, then I could have just asked, and it wouldn't have been a whole string of family stuff. It wouldn't have had to mean anything," she says, a flood of words more intense and tangled than you've heard from her before. "But he had to go and die, and he had to leave me here with all this shit! And the only reason you're here is because he's dead. And I'm—I'm really mad, okay?"

She wipes her eyes again. She looks at you. Your eyes are perfectly level.

"I lied. I always wanted to reintegrate."

And now you finally recognize the expression in her face. Embarrassment. Shame. Hunger.

"Do you want to be me?" she says.

▮▮▮

The fisherman looking down at his other self, clothes and cold air the only thing between them.

▮▮▮

Your surprise, naked on your face. Her hunger tucked away again behind her blank mask.

"Ah. I guess you didn't expect me to ask," she says.

"Why didn't you forcibly reintegrate me, then?" you ask. She had the opportunities. When you bought her coffee. When you were in the shower, and the MERGEBREAK was sitting on the bathroom counter. Reintegration is about physical contact, not about mutual desire.

"You said it. *I don't want to do anything you don't want to do,*" she says, echoing your American accent, your inflected Korean. It sounds strange through her mouth. That must be how it sounds through your mouth. She smiles at you, a sarcastic twist of the lip. "Could I live with myself, if I did that?"

Maybe you should be glad there's no instance of you that is cruel.

▪▪▪

Instances cannot read each other's minds.

▪▪▪

"But I want to," she says again. "I've always wanted to know what it was like, to live somewhere else. To have been the one to leave. I wondered about you. When I had to take the CSAT. When I would fight with Mom. When Tae proposed. Did you ever wonder about me?"

You did. You thought about your other self when you picked your college major. When you fought with your mother. When it was Chuseok and you were alone in your dorm room, eating tteok that your mother mailed you.

"I did," you say.

A part of you wants to know how she loves her fiancé. How she loves her family. How she talks with her-your cousins and how she goes to work in her silver car and how she orders at restaurants in Korean and how she speaks in Korean and dreams in Korean and how she misses Harabeoji as more than a crumpled memory.

"I guess it's selfish, to want to know two lives," she says. "But I can't help what I want."

▪▪▪

Soyoung's grandfather always regretted not looking back across the border.

▪▪▪

"I know it's a lot to ask," your instance says. "And it was shitty of Harabeoji to ask me, and it would be shitty of me to force you. And it was shitty of him to tell me to reintegrate, and it was shitty of him to give you the house and no instructions, but I think it was shitty of Mom to leave Korea without explaining anything, and it was shitty of you to never get in contact. And I'm telling you that I'm happy here, and I love my fiancé, and I love my family, and I don't know who you love, but you could love who I love. I could love who you love. If that changes your decision at all. It doesn't have to be permanent. But I would like to be you."

Your heart thumping in your chest. Your dry mouth. Your instance standing a scant three feet away, smiling at you. She holds out her hand. Her wrist is empty underneath the slice of her black sleeve.

She's taken her MERGEBREAK off. But she's not reaching forward. She's not a bad person. You know this, because you aren't a bad person. This is only an invitation.

"So, let me know what you want," she says.

▪▪▪

The three keystrokes it takes to push a de-instancing request to the server.

▪▪▪

You want to take your other self's hand and fold her into your existence. You want to hide in your apartment with the soft warm weight of your cat in your arms. You want to call Clarissa in Germany and commiserate. You want to smoke outside barbecue restaurants with Minsoo. You want to go back to your grandfather's grave and apologize for taking so long to visit.

You want to kiss your instance's fiancé and have him be your own. You want to have grown up in Korea. You want to have grown up in America.

You want there to be only one of you. You want your other self to be happy. You want to fulfill your grandfather's last request. You want to be happy. You want to go home.

■ ■ ■

There is a multibillion-dollar industry built around human longing.

■ ■ ■

"It's not that easy," you say. Your instance's face crystallizing in her smile. You can't look at this, because even if it's not your feelings, you understand the way that disappointment feels in her heart.

"You'll remember, if we reintegrate. It's not that I become you. Or that you become me. You'll remember, and I'll remember, but it's not going to make us happier. It won't make Harabeoji and Umma make up retroactively, and it won't stop me from having left, and maybe it's selfish, but I have a life. I have a job, and I have a cat, and I have friends, and they could be ours, but then they wouldn't be mine. And it won't make Harabeoji happy, because he's dead, and what he wants can't be more important than what I want, and I'm sorry about that but it's true. And I wish there was a way for me to have everything—for *you* to have everything—but there isn't. I can't live my life and live yours at the same time. Fulfilling his wishes doesn't bring him back."

You are suddenly achingly homesick. Home like your grandfather's house, twenty years ago. Home like falling asleep in the back seat of your mom's car. Home like waking up in your childhood bedroom. You won't ever get any of that back, and losing that wasn't your choice, but you can choose how to live with the loss of all the people you used to be.

"If we reintegrate, America becomes a memory for you. For me. Just like Korea is a memory for me. You'll remember, because I'll remember, and you'll regret, because I've regretted. I know you will. I know about regret. I miss Korea, sometimes. I'd miss my life more."

You don't know how to explain the way you feel about the States to your instance, who has never had to leave home. How she-you will long for worlds that no longer exist, for countries that only exist in your memories, how you've had years to come to terms with the tension that sits in your belly when you think about the homes you've left behind, how you have changed enough to miss America, now, and you can bear the loss of one homeland but not two. How to explain she would become a foreigner.

"I don't want that for you," you say instead. "Or for me."

Your other self's smile melts into something less cracked. You smile back in relief.

"If it's only *regret*," Soyoung says, and reaches for your hand and this is the first time you've seen her bare wrist, white and smooth like your own, and—

■ ■ ■

The knife in the heart, held in the fisherman's hand.

PART II

Tell me, O Muse, of a complicated man,
Whose instance wandered widely
After sacking that famous town of Troy.
Where he went, while his other remained,
How he suffered while his other withered,
And how he worked to save his life and bring his men back home.

—Homer, *The Odyssey*

SOYOUNG-ROSE

In her dreams, Soyoung sits next to herself and they don't touch. In her dreams, Soyoung is Rose is Soyoung is nine years old and has never seen herself doubled. In her dreams, Rose is wearing Soyoung's clothing and walking through an apartment she's never lived in. In her dreams, Soyoung sits in her grandfather's house and does her homework with Minsoo and Yujin and she is nine years old forever.

In her dreams, Soyoung tears the band on her other self's arm and beats her black and blue and bloody.

When she wakes up, Soyoung goes to the bathroom. She splashes water on her face.

She tells herself: "People reintegrate every day. You shouldn't be having so many goddamn problems with this."

She tells herself: "You have everything both of you ever wanted. And you've seen both worlds now. It's not like one of them is better. Who cares why Soyoung chose this?"

She tells herself: "You need to man up and call the American embassy. And change your registration with the Korean government. And quit Rose's job. Just get it over with."

Sometimes the pep talk is enough, and she slips back over to the bed and slides between the sheets. If Tae's sleeping over, he'll mumble something as she moves his arm gently. Will hold her close when she slides in with him. When he's asleep, he forgets that they're fighting. When he's asleep, he forgets that she's half-stranger. And in the warm black of her bedroom, it's easy for her to forget to be a foreigner.

Other nights, the dream ends closer to morning, or leaves her hands shaking. So she pads into the living room. It'll be quiet. Only the slow roll of cars. Birds chirping. She'll turn on the television, with the audio low. She turns the channel to SBS, which airs an English practice program at four in the morning. It's soothing. Information that she already knows, that scratches the itch of the not-knowing. The presenter will pronounce American words and write them on the digital blackboard, and slowly the living room will brighten as the sun rises, and eventually she will fall back asleep, on the couch, and then when she wakes up, the TV is in Korean again, and it's like the educational program was a dream.

Sometimes Soyoung speaks the words along with the presenter in her perfect American accent. But only in a whisper. Soyoung's fiancé sleeps lightly.

■ ■ ■

An American passport holder is allowed to visit the Republic of Korea for tourism for up to ninety days, after obtaining a K-ETA from the Korean government. The K-ETA is an online application that takes fifteen minutes to complete, and is almost never rejected. The registrant must indicate their ethnicity, and if they are ethnically Korean, they must declare whether they are an instance of an existing Korean citizen, or if they are foreign-born. There is a third box that can be checked which states "other." This is the box that reintegrated individuals must check, and then they have to explain their circumstances in the text field in under five hundred characters.

If the individual reintegrates while in the Republic of Korea, they are required to declare their new status through an online portal hosted by the Korean government and must choose a citizenship status within the next thirty days, the decision of which will be evaluated by a panel of cross-government officials. This is for those designated with "F" under "Sex." Those with a designation "M," under thirty years of age, fill out a near-identical form, except with the inclusion of a section describing military service. Korean male instances are required to complete military service by thirty, or else show naturalization in another country. This is five years earlier than non-instanced citizens, and has been criticized as discriminatory.

■ ■ ■

The English word "nostalgia" derives from the Ancient Greek "nostos," which refers to a genre of epic literature involving safe homecoming by sea. "Nostos" is contrasted against "kleos," the glory earned through great deeds. The two are not necessarily mutually exclusive—Odysseus's nostos is his kleos. His return to his wife, meeting his son, and the acceptance of his instance are simultaneously his triumph against Poseidon, his wife's suitors, and his own self-doubt.

In the narrative, Odysseus dislikes the man his instance became after he left for Troy—weak willed and unable to stand up to his wife's suitors. Only by leaving, by fighting for ten years at Troy and spending another decade attempting to return to Ithaca, does Odysseus become a man he recognizes as himself. Yet it is the embrace of his own faults that allows him to finally return home, completely and wholly.

Odysseus's story is an outlier—no other epic focuses so heavily on the relationship between instances, or creates the sort of conflict that Odysseus has between himselves.

YJ

"Do you want a distraction?" your other self says in English.

"Not really," you say in Korean, popping the call to speakerphone so you can have your hands free to finish buttoning your shirt up. You have to concentrate. You're going full corpo-formal today, you're thinking about suit jackets. You thought perhaps a vest, but that's a little too IB for you. You don't want to look like one of the IB guys, you want to look competent and cool, NYC meets SF, but you're not a technical lead, so no T-shirts. But a suit jacket could look like you're trying too hard. You wish you were a code monkey. Then you could wear T-shirts every day of your life.

Thinking about your wardrobe is better than thinking about the meeting you're dressing for. Thinking about your wardrobe is better than thinking about updating your résumé, reaching out to recruiters, saying goodbye to your H-1B1 status, starting all over from scratch.

"Hey, should I wear a suit jacket?"

"No, we look like an asshole when we wear a suit jacket. Calm down. You're overthinking this."

"I'm not overthinking this. You're not the one getting fired today."

"You're not getting fired today."

"I'm getting fired today. You ever get told we have a baby face?"

"No, but you work with—hey, what was the word for 'baek-in' again? Is there a specific term for them?"

You and your instance like to use your phone calls for language practice. You speak Korean regularly. He doesn't use English except to watch American shows without subtitles.

"No, just say 'white people,'" you say, in English. "Okay, so I'm going to wear the blazer."

"Your funeral," he says. "Look, you'll be fine. You need a distraction. I'll give you a distraction. Guess who I've been hanging out with?"

"Jesus, I don't know. Do we have to do this now?"

Your instance makes an error noise with his mouth. You finish buttoning your shirt. You pull your nice blazer out of your closet, ignoring all the clothes on your floor. Someday you'll be good about this sort of thing. But Petra moved out a week ago and the mess feels protective. When you clean everything up, you have sort of a suspicion that your loft is going to look too empty.

Besides, aren't you allowed to have a bender after a breakup? Aren't you allowed to lose your mind when you're about to be fired? Not that you have time to lose your mind, because you're in the middle of losing everything else in your life.

"Soyoung, you know, from high school."

"Yeah, and? Don't you guys hang out all the time?" you say. You don't really think about Soyoung. She lives in the part of your brain that the rest of your childhood lives in. Soyoung is hagwon and ice cream bars and pretending really hard you don't have a crush. Soyoung is the remembrance of getting rejected the first time you tried to ask a girl out. You don't miss her, the same way you don't miss the acne and the sweat and the cramming for exams. Someday, after you and your instance reintegrate, maybe she'll mean something to you again.

"I hung out with *American* Soyoung," your instance says.

"Huh," you say again. "So . . . Soyoung's instance? Visiting Korea? Wait, is that who you needed the MERGEBREAK for?"

He hadn't really explained why he needed your employee discount, but you had presumed it had been some sort of favor for a friend, an expat returning back for a couple months. You trust yourself. You and he share email addresses, a Netflix subscription, and most of your social media passwords, because you had still been a single person when you made them.

"Yeah," he says. Looks like you were right; he was trying to impress a girl. If you weren't so stressed, you'd be annoyed. You and he have an agreement. Only one of you can be pursuing a long-term relationship at a time.

"How'd she look?"

Your last memories of Soyoung are from high school graduation. You had hugged each other, and she had said *good luck in college,* and then she went to KU and you went to SNU and then you did that semester abroad at NYU which led to your instancing at Incheon Airport at the end of winter break, after which your instance transferred to KAIST, out in the boonies, while you scraped your life together in NYC.

So you kind of lost touch with Soyoung. You had other things on your mind.

Thinking about Soyoung makes you think about Petra, and you really don't want to think about Petra right now, even less than you want to think about your imminent career nosedive. You look at the time on your phone.

"—hung out, but it was weird. And the first time, I just watched them meet from across the room, which, hey, do you think that was creepy?"

"Yeah, that's creepy. Look, I have to go. Can't be late to my guillotine. Spend the time thinking about how not to creep on girls you're friends with."

"Fuck you, talk tonight! You're not getting fired. Tell me how it—"

"Fine, yeah. Bye, man."

You end the call before he can say goodbye. You don't feel bad about it. He'll call back tonight and pick up your conversation right where it left off.

You contemplate making your bed before you leave, but you don't and just shove your shoes on and head out the door, shaking off the dread of the little blue blocks that had been added to the calendar: MEETING WITH D. THORSSON.

And then after that: MEETING WITH HR.

▮▮▮

You haven't been back to Korea since the day you instanced. You could go back—for Christmas, or for Chuseok or the New Year or something, some manufactured excuse. It would be good. It would be good to see your parents again. To see your friends. To see Yujin in the flesh, which you've never done before. It would be good to be back in Korea, where you speak natively and without any self-conscious hint of an accent. Where you would just be *Yujin, who's working in America,* which would give you some exotic clout.

To go back would mean that your mom would start guilt-tripping you about staying, would ask you about girlfriends and why you aren't married yet. To go back would mean your dad would ask about you getting a job at a Korean company. And going back would mean accepting the possibility of military service. You're still a Korean citizen. Your thirtieth birthday is coming up. Yujin's up for his service soon. You've heard of people getting detained at the airport—you don't know if the stories are true, but you have friends who won't go back to Korea because they don't want to accidentally end up wasting two or three years of their life. You don't think it's going to happen to you. But you worry.

So, best not to risk it. Best to tell yourself that all the good memories can stay with Yujin, until you can become him.

∎∎∎

For a brief, delicious moment as you exit into the world outside your rathole, you feel like a person with a capital *P*. You're divorced from your messy floor, divorced from the looming workplace failures, divorced from the divorce. Not a divorce. The breakup. The clean, bloodless, amicable breakup.

"I don't want to do long distance," Petra had said.

It was bullshit, and you knew it was bullshit. You could have done long distance: Planes existed, and you *liked* California, you would have dutifully flown across the country twice a month, and she knew it, and you knew she knew it. So the problem wasn't the long distance. You didn't want to ask what the truth was. It was all an excuse. You really hated the idea of Petra staying with you out of pity, or because it was easy. You wanted her to stay with you out of—you don't know. Love? Even thinking "love" makes you squirm. But you had thought you maybe could have loved her.

So you had said, "Okay, yeah, that makes sense. Sure. Cross-country move. Doesn't make sense. I get it."

And Petra had smiled at you and said, "Thanks for understanding, Jay."

Petra always called you Jay. She was the only one. You were YJ to pretty much everybody else. You liked "YJ" better than hearing "Yujin" with the American accent, and Yujin was your instance now. Yujin lived in your parents' apartment in Seoul. Yujin hung out with your high school buddies and dated pretty Korean girls with glossy mouths and perfect hair. But you were Jay to Petra, because you had been trying something new that month (you had also been trying: dirty martinis, going to the movies regularly, keeping a daily planner).

You had liked being Petra's Jay, even if it had culminated in Petra sitting next to you on the couch not looking at you. Across your clean living room *The Good Place* played silently on the television, and Eleanor exclaimed to Michael in closed captioning all caps: THIS IS THE BAD PLACE!

You didn't look at Petra.

"We had fun, right?" you had asked.

"It was fun," she said.

On the screen, Michael smiled.

That night, you had both gone to sleep in the same bed (you had thought about taking the couch, but your couch had a weird bump in the middle, and anyway, Petra was breaking up with you, you weren't breaking up with her), and in the morning you both went to work, and you kept not talking about the looming specter of your breakup at all until Petra offhandedly mentioned that you could keep the furniture, because it was too expensive to hire cross-country movers, but it might be nice if you could compensate her for it, because, well, the couch had been rather expensive.

And you said *yeah,* and tried to fold up the part of you that had wondered when everything had gone wrong.

"Work," Yujin had said. "You work way too much. Petra's checked out because you're never around."

Sour anger in the back of your throat. Did Yujin think you liked being a workaholic? Did Yujin assume that the year before college entrance exams was the true shape of your soul? You worked for him. You were working so that you wouldn't just be entered into the green card lottery, but guaranteed dual citizenship. So that you alone wouldn't just get American citizenship, but your recombined instance could get dual American-Korean citizenship. So that you could have his memories and his life. So he could have yours.

"What do you think is paying for the couch! Christ," you had said to Yujin, laying your head against the cool glass of your apartment window. By then, the living room had begun its transformation into the rathole. You much preferred to look out onto the street.

"Okay, if you're going to be like that, I'm hanging up," Yujin said, and hung up before you could say anything else. Like all the pain in the ass H-1B1, green card stuff, was nothing to him.

Then it had just been you, the window, the rest of Manhattan. Just the faint sound of sirens. Of someone's fading laughter outside. Music from somewhere. A television laugh track from your neighbor's living room.

You had wondered whether there was some other version of the world where you and Petra had stayed together. You had tried to squash that thought. But so little time had passed since you had driven her to the airport and hugged her goodbye. You knew you would get over it. You had watched

Yujin get over a breakup two years ago, so you knew the stages of your sadness. He had gone cold, and then sad, and then he found equilibrium. At the time you had felt a little superior to him, and a little relieved, since that meant that you were allowed to get serious with Petra.

The subway station smells like the inside of your apartment looks. You walk past a Hispanic woman in a full pastel Lolita outfit, a black man in a jumpsuit. A couple of Asian women in pretty matching suit sets. And white people, so many white people. The thing you miss most about Seoul was the way you could dissolve into the population. The anonymity. Ethnically homogenous populations have a dissipative effect that you don't get in America. But the New York subway system during rush hour is its own dissolution.

▪▪▪

There's a horror story that they tell the new hires in the glitzy sweatshop client-services industries—Biglaw, IB, consulting, Big 4 accounting. It's one of those stupid urban legends touted out every year like a particularly pathetic scarecrow.

It will be inevitably told during busy season, during the night before a closing, during the three hours before the slide deck is due and everyone's on their seventh straight day of sleep deprivation, when it's all bad temper papered over with polite emails, eye drops blooming over burst blood vessels. There'll be one tiny pool of fluorescents still lit and a single team huddled over their laptops and one of the associates will turn to one of the first-years and say: "Did anyone ever tell you about Doug?"

"Who's Doug?" the first-year will say.

"Doug's a VP," the associate will say. "You know, Doug that sends the four AM emails. Doug's always working."

"Yeah, I know Doug."

"No, you don't get it. Doug's *always* working."

The first-year will squint. "Is this the setup to a joke?"

"Nah. Doug's always online 'cause he can't leave the building. Ten years ago, Doug was really grinding at it, twenty-four seven real sigma male shit, coming in early, leaving late, and then one night, he swiped his ID card and stepped through the gate and . . ."

The associate will make a gesture like he's slicing something invisible in half.

"Doug instances. And the version of himself that got out the gate fucking books it. Because he hates his job. And the version of Doug that was inside the building tries to run after his instance but he can't leave. And his outside instance never comes back after him. Just keeps collecting the paycheck. Never shows up again. And Doug on the inside, well, he can't leave. He could kill himself, but he can't get out."

The first-year will scowl. "You're fucking with me. That's not how instancing works."

The associate will shrug.

"Just be careful swiping out tonight."

■ ■ ■

You've folded yourself back up by the time you're walking out of the BDFM station next to Bryant Park. You've accepted failure into your heart. You even looked at the meeting invite on your calendar to make sure you remembered which conference room you'd be meeting Drew in.

Drew Thorsson, despite being the COO of Mergebreak, and one of the investors for Condensco, and now the combined C-something for the merged entity, doesn't have a permanent office in New York. He doesn't have one in San Francisco, or Hong Kong, or London. He calls reception whenever he's in town and gets a temp desk. You've seen Drew sitting at intern desks, at VP desks, at the big conference tables with a laptop and a secondary screen, drinking iced matcha and always wearing a hoodie that has the MB over the heart. He seems nice. You've never *talked* to him, though, other than pleasantries during meetings. Megan's your usual buffer between you and the C-suite. Megan usually called him *eccentric*. Italics included.

You can deal with eccentric. Mergebreak is filled with Apple and Google refugees, Nike guys, post–Big Pharma PhDs, psychologists who realized that corporate was more lucrative than trying to get insurance to pay out. You've heard that Condensco was more of an after-school robotics club, mostly startup grindset freaks, but so far you haven't made any judgment.

You swipe your card to get into the building. You don't look at anyone in the elevator. You don't want to make small talk. You stare at the door instead. You're thinking about metrics. You're thinking about Project Parachute, which had been successful, and Project Ring, which hadn't. Parachute had been a location-tracking app that Mergebreak now sold as a companion to the MERGEBREAK. Ring had been the failed acquisition of a small start-up that was working on a way to make the MERGEBREAK smaller, less a cuff, more of a chunky designer ring. You're thinking about your lack of an MBA—was that an issue? Did Drew care? Drew had dropped out of college.

All you know is that these meetings are apparently about your performance.

You're not nearly important enough for Drew to fire you, Yujin had texted you when he first found out. You sometimes hated the way Yujin could read your mind.

You stand outside the conference room. Drew hasn't noticed you yet. You tell yourself you'll get another job, if you get fired. You're an intelligence worker. You're white collar. You're not the disposable sort of immigrant. This is a lie you like to tell yourself. Everyone's disposable. You saw the layoffs, a few years ago. One of your friends was literally deported, since he couldn't find a new job in time. You never want to be in his position.

You open the conference room door. Drew looks up from his laptop. He smiles. He has a very American smile. Broad, showing all his teeth.

"YJ! Just the man I wanted to see! Come in, come in. Sit down. Unless, of course, you'd prefer to stand. Actually—let's go for a walk. How do you feel about a walk?"

"Sure," you say, helpless against his scattershot speech. "Nice to see you, Drew."

"Excellent. Leave your phone."

He abandons his laptop, his second screen, and his papers, and weaves around you to open the conference room door. You exit. You let him take you down the glassy hallways and up the office stairs to the floor above.

"Megan says great things about you," Drew says.

"Oh?" you say.

You're only good at targeted conversations. You're best when you're selling something, when you know what someone wants. But you don't know what Drew wants from you. He's wearing a hoodie that has Mergebreak's mascot instances shaking hands. He's wearing sneakers with no socks.

"Yeah—great work with the Ring girls. Heard you were the one who almost convinced them to sell. How'd you do it?"

"But I didn't," you say.

"Still," he says.

Drew's playing with his food. You clear your throat.

"Well, I knew for sure they were going to refuse—Hannah's independently wealthy—so I figured might as well find out why they didn't like us. I mean, I get it. Mergebreak's the conglomerate monster in this space. Not that I mean—"

But Drew just laughs. "Go on," he says.

You flush. You're saying all the wrong things in the wrong order. You should have said something about the statistics. The math. The roadmap. The way that you led a team to coordinate with outside counsel, the finance guys, how you're good at leadership and a team player and how you can quantify success, that you like the work you do here, that—

"I don't mean it like that. But I understood how they might see us, and I didn't want to leave on bad terms. So, I asked if Ayumi and Hannah had time for a postmortem, and we got coffee."

You bite your sentence off. It's not a very good story. It had been an awkward meeting in a too-fancy coffee shop, which trailed into an awkward silence upon which you cast the weak conversational lifeboat of: *Why an instancing start-up?*

Hannah had punctured your lifeboat by telling you, with a vicious smile, about her grandparents, and the Holocaust. How they got out right before it was impossible to get out, and how there was a second version of her grandparents, who had survived the camps, who had come and found them again when Hannah's grandparents were visiting family. And how her grandfather, the instance, had pushed his other self off a roof rather than live with the knowledge in his own brain.

You hadn't known what to say to that, so you had just told her the truth about your family. That an instance of your grandfather defected to the communist North, and then your grandfather in the South was disappeared by the Korean government. Everyone in Korea has a sob story like this. Hannah hadn't laughed.

"Is that why you're in the industry?" Ayumi had said. "You didn't strike me as sentimental."

"No," you said, because to hell with postmortems. To hell with people who use their family trauma as their conversational nuclear weapon.

"I got into the game because my instance in Korea wants us to get dual citizenship before we reintegrate, so that he can avoid the military draft. So, you know. I'm just a garden-variety international bourgeois."

"Oh," Hannah had said, and something in her had relaxed a little. But she then leaned forward and asked, "So why Ring?"

You thought you had them, then; the three of you had talked for two hours, circling an agreement that never came.

They killed the deal the next morning.

▪ ▪ ▪

The instancing industry comprises 2 percent of the American technology sector, though that number rises to 5 percent if the entire instancing economy is considered—services, vacations, immigration and travel, counseling. America is currently the largest instancing market in the world, though statistics show that the Chinese market has overtaken the American market. Talking heads quibble that the numbers released by the CCP are obviously doctored.

The origins of the modern instancing industry have roots in the Second World War, though the American sector specifically exploded during the 1950s with the increasing interest in chemical solutions to neuropsychological symptoms. Not to mention the increasing concern of Soviet agents infiltrating American society during the Cold War. Intention was mutable, intention was amorphous, intention was chemical, just like depression, anxiety, seizures, suicidal behavior, long-term pain management, and being a frigid mother.

The largest player in the space is Mergebreak, whose titular product, the MERGEBREAK, is said to prevent reintegration. Independent sponsored studies have shown that the MERGEBREAK has a 95 percent protection rate when both parties apply the prophylactic. The MERGEBREAK is most often worn by avid travelers, or wealthy deportees, who aren't interested in reintegration. It is cheaper than an iPhone, but not much cheaper.

A number of other start-ups have attempted to enter the instantiation space, but in recent years the technology has stagnated. Mergebreak's stock has also declined slightly in recent years.

▪ ▪ ▪

Drew leads you down a second corridor, this one lined with a beautiful cascade of glass windows. He stops in front of the outdoor garden. You squint in the sunlight. The windows face east, and the sun is a bright white speck in the sky.

"And after you got coffee?" Drew says. He sounds fascinated. Like he really does want to know, like the mechanics of a failed solution are of great interest to him. But you don't want to tell him about Hannah's family, your family, your instance's desires.

"We just talked, about why we were all working in tech, and what made them look to the instancing industry in particular. It didn't work, though. You know that."

"You're good with people," Drew says, like a pronouncement. Why is he saying this about you? He opens the door. You follow him out onto the terrace.

The Midtown wind tunnel is in full effect. Your eyes immediately water. You walk over to the edge. Below there are all the little people who look like ants, the teensy yellow cabs, the big square of Bryant Park. This would be a great place if you wanted to push someone off the building and have it look like an accident. Hannah's grandfather would have had a perfect alibi. Oh yes, Officer, the railing was just so low, and the wind just so harsh.

"Great view, right?" Drew says. "We should advertise this terrace more. Anyway. I didn't want to have this conversation in the fishbowl. Too many ears."

You turn to him. You want to throw yourself off the building.

"Am I being fired?"

He looks blankly surprised. Then he laughs. "YJ, man. So negative! No—I'm trying to promote you."

He holds up his phone. Presses down the power button, deliberately showing you as he swipes the device to dead.

"What do you know about Project Mitosis?"

SOYOUNG-ROSE

"This isn't working," Soyoung says. She's sitting in the front seat of the car. Next to her, Soyoung's fiancé is driving. Behind them, Jangmi is fast asleep in her car seat. They're on their way back from Lotte World. When Soyoung was a kid, when she was singular, she went to Lotte World with her cousins and her mother and her grandfather. And when she was older, instanced, she had taken her cousins' kids to Lotte World, to Everland, to Caribbean Bay.

Rose hadn't been to a kids' amusement park in years. The last time she visited was when she was fourteen and went to Great Wolf Lodge on a school trip. She remembers the terrible pink swimsuit she wore and how self-conscious she was about it, the chlorine smell of the water, losing her glasses in the wave pool. The memory mingles with the last time she took Minsoo's daughter and her friends to Caribbean Bay. The chlorine, the screaming children.

The doubled memory is nauseating, all dissonant imagery and emotions. Soyoung tries to breathe through it, just like the online therapy exercises suggested. The cognitive dissonance is supposed to get better with time. Soyoung and Rose both thought therapy was full of shit. They haven't gone yet. Not they. She.

Her fiancé stares fixedly at the road. There's no point. They're wedged in traffic. Soyoung studies Taehyung's profile.

"Baby, what are you thinking?" Soyoung says. Or not exactly. She says "oppa," not "baby," because Soyoung and Taehyung had been the sort of gross couple where Soyoung called Taehyung "oppa." Sometimes serious, mostly half-joking—cosplaying a sort of couple that they once had been. Rose would have gagged. But from the inside Soyoung understood the shape of it. They had met in college. They had grown up together and around each other. They had been puppy love left to simmer too long. Past Soyoung is sort of horrified that she now has to ask Taehyung anything about his thoughts. But the part of her that is Rose is horrified that she has a fiancé. The part of her that is the whole, now, the part that is all of her recombined self, the chrysalis of sludge that the caterpillar has spun itself into, mostly feels nothing. None of the underpinning warmth of good feeling that had lit her neurons up previously, when she saw Taehyung, none of the bodily warmth, the desire to curl up next to him.

Do you understand now, Soyoung thinks savagely at herself. *It's losing, not gaining.* But just like every time before, her nonexistent instance, the tulpa of her other self (which other self?) doesn't say anything back.

Taehyung's jaw twists. Clenches.

"You can't just make these decisions without me," he says.

"I'm not deciding anything," Soyoung says. "I'm stating a fact. This isn't working."

"What isn't working? What are you referring to?"

This was the problem between Taehyung and Soyoung, which Rose knew not at all and then all at once. They had a shared vocabulary of ambiguity that only made sense because they both shared the same referent of the specific. They spoke in generalities. But Rose had knocked their private language out of alignment.

It doesn't help that they're whispering. There's the kid in the back of the car, asleep. Not their kid. But the horrified part of Rose, the eager part of Soyoung, both of them know now that taking care of Jangmi had always been practice for her future.

"This," Soyoung said, gesturing between her and Taehyung. Between her and the rest of Seoul outside the car window. The black, useless MERGEBREAK she still wears on her wrist is stark against the pale skin.

"Soyoung," Taehyung says, and maybe Soyoung in the singular, Soyoung before her recombination, would have perfectly understood the emotion reflected in his speech. But Soyoung who had stood on a mountain and grabbed her other self, the Soyoung who was the other self being grabbed, reads anger and not sadness.

Or maybe Taehyung's anger was his sadness. Maybe these were the same emotion viewed through a different lens. Or maybe Soyoung was interpreting Taehyung as a reflection of her own frustration at herself. She almost wishes that there was something *actually* wrong: that Tae had a mistress, that the instance of Rose had a boyfriend, that one of them had said something despicable to the other. Anything but the simmer. They're supposed to be getting married. She thinks they might be breaking up.

The light turns green. Taehyung inches the silver Hyundai forward. Soyoung thinks about getting out of the car and marching through the lanes. She imagines walking down into the subway station and making the trip on the airport line all the way back to Incheon. She imagines smiling through immigration and showing Soyoung's American passport, landing in JFK and calling an Uber back home to her apartment. Her plants are all probably dead. Clarissa still has Dr. Crouton.

It's a nice dream. It would last until someone realized that Kang Soyoung, Korean citizen, had disappeared, and her recombined self had illegally flown back to America without declaring her reintegration and sorting out her citizenship. That's the sort of thing that gets you placed on No-Fly lists.

"Soyoung," Taehyung says again, almost a sigh. "I don't know what to do. To help."

The niece makes a soft sound in the back of the car. Soyoung glances in the rearview mirror.

"Oh, Jangmi-ya, are you up?" she says.

Jangmi nods sleepily and smiles. At least one of them had a nice day.

"Are we there yet?"

"Not yet, Jangmi-ya," Taehyung says.

The car stops and starts as it winds through the city. They're on the road next to the river, which glitters in the late afternoon sunlight. They have to drop Jangmi off at her parents' place. They have dinner plans with Taehyung's coworkers.

"You should go back, if you're unhappy."

Taehyung keeps his eyes on the road. He merges onto the exit. The river slips away.

This life in Seoul is everything the previous version of Soyoung wanted. This is everything Rose hadn't longed for. An imminent marriage. A singular future. It was everything Soyoung had assumed she would always have. In America, Rose has a job and a cat and a constellation of acquaintances and she never calls her mother.

The funny thing is, despite her perfect life, Soyoung had still kind of hated being herself. Rose hadn't realized that until she was Soyoung, and then she knew it all at once.

"I'm not unhappy," Soyoung lies. "I'll tell you if I'm unhappy."

In the world where Soyoung gets out of the car and walks to the nearest subway station to Incheon Airport and calls the embassy from the airport lounge, in the world where a sympathetic government official buys her case for sole American citizenship, in the world where she flies back to JFK, nothing changes. She misses Korea the moment she touches ground. And then there's Soyoung's mother, Taehyung and the broken engagement, her job, her family, and in this world her Korean life becomes a memory, and all of it just seems so present, so real and current, that losing it seems—she knows what it feels like to lose it, once.

"Okay," Taehyung says, and she doesn't know what that means, either. She can't stand to be in the car any longer.

"We're like ten minutes from the train station, right? Drop me and Jangmi off there. I'll take her home and meet you at the restaurant. We're probably going to be late if we take the car all the way to Minsoo's and back."

"Are you sure?"

"Yes," she says, and glances back at her niece. "Jangmi-ya, do you want to take the subway with Gomo?"

Jangmi makes a cheerful noise of assent. She's the sort of little kid that likes crowds and bright noises and adventures. She's mildly baffling to Soyoung.

They drive to the train station without any further conversation. Taehyung drops them off next to the nearest subway stop. Soyoung helps Jangmi out and straightens the kid's coat and kisses Taehyung on the corner of his mouth out of habit and then she's slamming the door and disappearing down the subway steps, Jangmi's tiny little hand warm in her own.

The billboards flash with advertisements for probiotic yogurt hawked by Korean singers, for American superheroes and CGI lasers, for kids' cartoons bouncing jauntily across the big-screen displays. Newscasters talk about the storm hitting Jeju this week, about monsoon season.

"Will you buy me a grape drink?" Jangmi asks, like they didn't just spend the entire morning and most of the afternoon at an amusement park.

"Sure," Soyoung says, because she's the fun aunt and not a mother.

They get the grape drink from a vending machine. Soyoung gets a bottle of barley tea. And then they get on the subway.

On the subway there's an advertisement for MERGEBREAK slotted in between the yogurt and the kids' shows. A cartoon man shaking his own hand and smiling.

Soyoung looks down at her hands. The interesting thing is that Soyoung's middle finger callus still exists. But so does the scar on Rose's left palm from when she cut herself while slicing an apple. Soyoung had read about a case where a person merged with their instance, who was an amputee, and the amputated limb had stayed missing. And other reintegrations, where blindness was miraculously healed, or appendixes grew back. Soyoung and Rose aren't such special cases, though. Soyoung and Rose were ordinary. There's no world where they don't have to choose between Korea and America. Oh sure, vacations exist. Visiting exists. But she'll have to decide: Where's home? What language does she speak in, dream in? She doesn't really get to choose.

Soyoung cracks open her barley tea. She'll call the embassy tomorrow. No, tomorrow is the weekend. On Monday. She'll call Monday.

God. She misses her cat.

■ ■ ■

It's not so much that Soyoung's and Rose's perspectives are separate or like there's a clean divide between the two of them. She had tried to explain that to Taehyung, to Minsoo, to her Korean mother, but none of them understood.

There is no split point of view, no dual vision, just that on the inside it feels almost like there is a lens that dials in. It's subtle, sometimes. A shade toward one life or another.

The uncanny thing is when her thoughts feel normal. Regular. It feels like her decisions are organic and clean, the perfect route from thought to action, that this is who she is and these are the choices she's making. And then hours later, when she looks back at her thoughts, they've become alien. This is the part that scares her.

That, and the way that she no longer knows what she wants. Soyoung and Rose had both known. They had known so hard they have, functionally, died for it, but that's an uncharitable thought, toward people who no longer exist. There is no point hating the past self. Selves.

■ ■ ■

Jangmi demands that Soyoung let her press the buttons on the elevator, and they end up stopping at the second, the ninth, and the fifteenth floors of Minsoo's building before getting to his apartment. Then, Jangmi insists on ringing the doorbell, even though Soyoung knows the door code. A dog barks. The door opens.

"Daddy!" Jangmi cheers, running forward.

"Jangmi!" Minsoo cheers, picking her up and twirling her around.

"Hey," Soyoung says. "Did you get the rental truck booked?"

"Yeah. Thanks for taking her out, she would have hated coming."

"Oh, I'm always happy to take her," Soyoung says. "We had fun. Didn't we have fun?"

"Mm!"

Jangmi smiles and nods emphatically. Minsoo gives his kid a kiss on the cheek. Soyoung's own smile crystallizes on her face. The thing that always gets to Soyoung is the intense fucking normality. The way she unconsciously takes her place in all the existing dynamics of her instance's self. She's dropped Jangmi off a hundred times. This is the first time Rose is experiencing it. It feels like everyone acts like she's Soyoung from before, that the continuity of her existence is unbroken, that Rose is a novelty, that the entirety of Rose's life is her perfect American accent and nothing else.

The square of tile outside of Minsoo's apartment suddenly feels like the same sort of trap that Taehyung's car feels like, that her own bedroom feels like, the same sort of trap that dinner with Taehyung's coworkers (who have met his fiancé, who like his fiancé, who are invited to their wedding) will be, and it makes Soyoung want to scream, that the grooves of Soyoung's mannerisms are so etched into her gestalt self that the only thing left of Rose is her dissatisfaction.

"So I'm going to go," Soyoung says.

"Oh, okay," Minsoo says, sounding surprised. "Not coming in?"

"We've got a dinner thing."

He nods. "Have fun. See you Sunday?"

And she nods, and without thinking Soyoung leans in to give him and Jangmi a hug, and Minsoo returns it like this is every week of their life, and Jangmi puts her stupid little arms around Soyoung's neck and then Soyoung says "Bye sweetheart," and she untangles the kid's arms from her hair and walks down the hall.

▮▮▮

In the most commonly translated version of *The Odyssey*, Telemachus leaves Ithaca un-instanced, singular, in direct contrast to the way Odysseus instanced upon his leave-taking. In a few versions resting upon the alternate translation of a few key phrases (hotly debated in academic circles, and nowhere else), Telemachus leaves an instance behind. His leave-taking and his search for his father is then transposed into an escape: He wants to leave his useless father's house filled with suitors, he wants to leave his mother's side, he is both escaping responsibility and the emotional turmoil of his adolescence. It is an abdication.

■ ■ ■

Seoul is a city of slopes, studded with apartment towers like so many dominos lined up against the sky. From the descending elevator the stark slices of skyscrapers circle little playgrounds and neighborhood groceries and corner stores and tutoring centers. The ones in Minsoo's neighborhood are nicer than the ones near Soyoung's apartment, nicer than the ones in Rose's memories.

Soyoung's childhood memories are locationally bound. Sitting on the back porch of Harabeoji's house. The elementary school she attended until she was nine and a half. The purple azaleas that ringed the apartment sandbox where she collected BB gun pellets. She remembers sifting the plastic bubbles from the pale sand. She remembers the delight when they'd find a colored bubble—pink, or lime green, or electric blue. She couldn't have been older than Jangmi is.

It's nice to remember something that doesn't make her nauseous. Seventeen is double vision—seventeen might be split between hagwon and field hockey practice but seven is the clean remembrance of her pre-existing, singular timeline.

Soyoung takes a deep breath when she gets outside. The streetlamps are on now, even though it's still bright out. And it's quiet. On the weekdays it must be busier with parents and children and teenagers going to school and office workers going to their cubicles and all the stupid people going about their stupid days. In New York, it's morning. Sunday there, still, so the likelihood that Clarissa is awake is low, and it's afternoon in Germany, so Clarissa's instance is probably out. Rose's American mom must definitely still be asleep. Soyoung could call her mom here, though. But that's not who she wants to talk to.

She needs to call Yujin back. He had texted her after the funeral. She hasn't responded. She doesn't want to talk to him. She does want to talk to him. She wants to shake him by the shoulders and say, "Listen, Yujin, reintegration is a horrible idea and I hate it. Just do your stupid military service and get on with your life. I know you want to go back to the States because you feel cheated of a life you didn't get to live, but this really sucks."

She'll call him in a couple of days, maybe.

Soyoung scratches her useless MERGEBREAK. She walks back to the subway. If she goes back up the elevator, Minsoo would let her in without any comment. Or she could go meet her fiancé at the restaurant and it'd all be copacetic.

Soyoung walks down the subway entrance stairs. She waits at the platform and boards the subway that takes her to the transfer station. As she gets closer, the subway car fills up. The subways in Korea are neat and silent. Contrasted against New York, they're not as bad as she used to think they were. She watches the advertisements. Soy milk. MERGEBREAK. A new type of air-conditioning unit. She examines faces. The older you get, the more everyone looks like someone you already know. She swears she sees her aunt, Minsoo, the Korean version of her boss, Clarissa, an ahjusshi who looks just like a younger version of her grandfather.

Soyoung remembers her grandfather's slow deterioration. She remembers taking walks around the neighborhood with him as a teenager. She had always been particularly annoyed about it, she remembers, because that was time she could have spent on her computer, texting her friends, getting homework done so she wouldn't have to touch it later. The part of her that is Rose examines the memory like it is a particularly rare gemstone. Her memories of her grandfather are all out of date. He's perpetually younger, in Rose's memory. When he called her phone she had always pictured him frozen in the appearance of the day she last saw him.

There's a small, slow wave of numb nothing in her heart where the grief is supposed to live. She bites her cheek. The car swells. They get to the transfer station. Soyoung drifts, out and through the corridors, past the women selling cheap dresses, the knockoff shoes. Past the stores that sell fresh fruit juice and the waffle-and-fresh-cream vendors. There are signs for four different trains.

If Soyoung were to take a left here, she could get on the train to Incheon. One hour and eight minutes on the Seoul metro. She could buy a ticket to Newark Airport, or JFK, or LaGuardia. Fourteen hours and twenty minutes. She could cross the border again and hold her breath, and pray that she stays singular. And then she'd have to lie to the embassy, lie to immigration, pretend that the Soyoung in Korea died or something.

But there's a chance that she looks back and there the new instance of Soyoung-Rose would be, twenty-nine years old and unable to leave. A second instantiation, this time the instancing would be with the full continuity of consciousness. She would still be Soyoung. She would still be Rose. Every commingled part of her would continue to exist. Her memory would continue in duplicate. There's no guarantee she would be the division of her consciousness that gets to leave.

Soyoung takes a right, instead, to the train line that will take her to Taehyung's work dinner. She doesn't have either Rose's or Soyoung's passport on her, anyway.

∎∎∎

In the versions of the story where Telemachus doesn't instance, the singularity of his person is contrasted against Odysseus's doubled self. Implicit in this translation is the idea that Telemachus is a superior version of his father because of the way he is able to hold the single goal and single home in his head. Odysseus, filled with ambiguity, leaves his weakness in his palace to go fight a war.

YJ

Call me when you wake up, you text your other self, poking at your phone with numb fingers. You had been shivering by the time you re-entered the building, after you had walked back down with Drew to the conference room. Drew immediately began packing up his laptop, his extra screen, his wireless mouse.

"I've got to catch a flight. You'll get an email packet," Drew said. "And Stacey will get you all signed up. If you've got any other questions, give me a call. I'll be back in the States in a few months. But nothing for you to do now, really. You got any questions?"

You had a lot of questions.

"Where are you going?"

"London office, and then Paris, and then Berlin."

"That's a lot of travel."

He shrugged, slid his MacBook into a protective sleeve. "I don't like to stay in one place too long, you know? Too much baggage. The longer you stay in one place, the more likely you are to create an instance when you leave it. They've done studies on it."

You didn't ask him if he has an instance, or multiple instances, whether there were versions of him all around the globe that he didn't acknowledge. Drew took his phone out of his pocket and powered it back on. While the screen blinked to life, he flashed an absent smile at you.

"But seriously. You'll be great," he said. "I have absolute faith in your abilities."

And then he left. And you picked up your phone and typed the message to your other self in the two minutes between Drew leaving and Stacey knocking on the door.

"Facilities will be boxing up your old office, moving you up a floor. We can just get your paperwork signed, unless you've got another meeting now? Congrats on the promotion, YJ."

You wanted to tell her that you need a minute. You needed to press your forehead against the cool glass of the window of your office (now your *old* office) and think about the situation.

The situation is: You've been promoted, and Megan's quit, so you're the new Megan. Megan had *been* Mitosis, and now it would be your job to oversee Mitosis. Mitosis was *the* Condensco-Mergebreak project, and apparently the sole reason for the merger.

"We need a new face for the project," Drew had said. "Just someone to carry this over the finish line. I'd take it over, but I hate press. And Megan recommended you."

"Why not Megan?"

"Megan wasn't interested."

And you didn't ask: What did *not interested* mean? Was Megan leaving voluntarily? Why did Megan recommend you? You had heard of Mitosis, only in the sense that it was something that Megan complained about once in a while, and had meetings on her calendar labeled PROJECT MITOSIS SPONSOR DISCUSSIONS. Had Megan already left? Was it appropriate to go ask if she was still in the building? What were the optics of pushing out a woman and replacing her with an Asian man? *What was the purpose of this?*

"You can say no," Drew had said. "But let me know now. No harm, no foul."

Well, no. You couldn't say no. That was obvious.

"I'd love to be a part of this," you had said. And Drew had looked supremely pleased, and you had smiled and tried to make it look natural.

Then he dropped the bombshell: "Mitosis is our new reintegration-reversal product. It rewinds time."

Drew must be insane. Drew had watched too much *Doctor Who*. Drew had taken the Marvel Cinematic Universe too seriously. Drew's smile didn't fade.

"Are we talking *time travel*?"

Drew laughed.

"No, no. Got you good, though. That's just the marketing. Reintegration-reversal. It separates the memories and segregates the reintegrated individual," he had said. "Only works for the first six months after reintegration, though—though they're working on it. You came out of R&D, right?"

"No, business development."

"My bad, right. Well, either way, we'll roll out your new appointment with the press release—so sorry about how fast this is moving. We can't afford to delay the soft launch any longer, we're pretty sure someone talked to a *TechCrunch* reporter, or someone at the *Verge*. But after this weekend, everything will be out in the open. No more top-secret. For now, go introduce yourself to the guys who work on twenty-six. Don't worry about the tech, yet, all that's been done for months. Just concentrate on the optics."

He smiled at you, and he managed to make it seem sheepish. "Look, honestly, it's a paper promotion, things are really moving too fast to bring another person in, and it was kind of—between you and me—*fucked* of Megan to leave now. But hey, I don't mind you getting the glory instead of her."

"Why me?"

Drew had looked surprised you would ask. "Because she recommended you."

And then Drew had gone into detail about the project, the point people, the actual process you'd be going through (mostly overseeing R&D, and integrating the Condensco team, and there would be a significant media-outreach component, you weren't the boots on the ground, you were doing *strategy*), how you would be Drew's direct report now. You didn't ask any questions until the end.

"This is the first new product in a decade, isn't it?"

"Look at you, little company scholar," Drew said. "Yeah. We're patching up our five percent."

And you didn't say: The promotion would look really good on your application. This was the opposite of losing your H-1B1 status. This was the sort of role change that might allow you to apply for citizenship under the extraordinary ability visa clauses. An EB-1-1, with the addenda about your instance having abilities that would augment yours, giving your dual-citizenship addendum at the IIS the weight that an ordinary person might not be given.

■ ■ ■

Dual citizenship is a status where a person holds a passport to two countries, and every potential instance of that person is considered the same legal person. In effect, it means that an individual can reintegrate and be a citizen of two countries simultaneously, which is a status unavailable to most individuals. In the United States, a dual citizenship petition can be strengthened by having a particularly specific job, being a prominent individual within your field, or your instance having a particular skill set that would be of benefit to the United States. Dual citizenship requests are considered on a case-by-case basis and are considered addenda to the holistic citizenship application.

Between South Korea and America, an American acceptance of a dual citizenship petition automatically translates to a Korean one. It allows the individual to reside permanently in South Korea. It gives the individual all the benefits of American citizenship. It removes the Korean military service requirement. This is an extraordinarily lenient rule set, dating back to the historical backing of South Korea and the American military presence that continues in Korea to this day.

■ ■ ■

"YJ?" Stacey says, snapping you out of your thoughts. You blink. You try to dial your smile and body language up to "confident."

"Right, sorry. Facilities can box my stuff up. Can you get me a keycard to twenty-six?"

"Of course."

She leads you out of the fishbowl and back to the reception desk, then farther behind to a different, private area. She hands you a stack of paperwork.

"The only difference between this and your previous agreement is that this one comes with a heftier NDA, and a higher salary. But of course, read before you sign."

She rummages in a drawer. You feel that if this is such a confidential project, the cards shouldn't be kept so easily accessed. But then you watch her press the keycard to a machine and tap some buttons on the attached terminal, and then you feel a little stupid for assuming Mergebreak wouldn't have good operational security. You turn to the paperwork while the machine hums.

You don't know what you're looking for, other than them not screwing you over too badly. You don't mean that with any malice. Mergebreak's using you for whatever it can bleed you for, but you're using them as well—first for the H-1B1, and then for sponsoring your green card, for the chance at being labeled *important*. Workers in the instancing industry have a 34 percent better success rate at petitioning IIS for dual citizenship, across all visa pathways.

It's all for Yujin. Except, no, that's unfair. If you reintegrate, Yujin gets your life. And you get the memories of your family, your friends in Korea, all that warm familiarity back. You're both using each other. And you'll both get both places, if you're dual citizens. Free travel between borders. Live wherever you want. All your memories, all Yujin's memories. No military service, either.

▪ ▪ ▪

In a best-case scenario: You instance at the airport, and you fill out the rest of the paperwork that confirms that you were ready to instance, and confirm that your new instance is being sponsored by your university, your school, your family. In the best-case scenario, you had previously applied for instancing approval, rather than having to do it postmortem. Your heart and your paperwork are aligned. You know what you want and you get it.

In a worst-case scenario, you instance when you are ripped away from your family and your community and your life and you are trafficked across state borders when you catch a glimpse of the sign that demarcates where your country ends. Or somewhere in between, you instance because you realize that the only real choice you have in life is to leave your beloved, broken shithole, and cross the border into a different broken shithole, one with more access to capital, an overripe melon that you will be able to gnaw the rind from before sending back the scrapings. Lands of opportunity, which don't want you and would never approve you if you went clean and legal. But, too bad. You know this is the only opportunity you have, to leave.

In those circumstances, you send money home to your instance, and you live with their resentment, or their relief.

▪ ▪ ▪

It's hard not to feel trapped by Yujin sometimes. Without Yujin, Petra wouldn't have broken up with you because of your bad work-life balance. You would have applied for regular American citizenship without Yujin—the standards for that were far lower. You wouldn't be standing here reading this contract had Yujin not existed. You wonder if you should talk to Yujin before signing it. Except that would take too much time. And Yujin isn't you—sharing it would count as sharing sensitive employee data. No, you have to make the decision now. Sometimes it's exhausting trying to think of a future for two versions of yourself.

"Here's the card," Stacey says. "All look okay? You can take the paperwork up with you, if you want."

"No, I'm good," you say, and sign on the dotted line. You take the card from her hand. It's faintly warm from the machine.

You hand her your signed paperwork. She smiles at you.

"Congratulations, YJ. Again."

"Thanks," you say, and make your escape. You go to the elevator. You hesitate. A part of you wants to swipe your card and go down to twenty-six. A much larger part of you wants to get out of here for a minute. Get to somewhere you can breathe. You acquiesce to your nerves and push the down button.

Your phone starts ringing. You check the caller ID. It's your instance. It's one in the morning in Seoul. You glance up. You can't tell if there are any cameras or microphones embedded in the elevator. Legally, Yujin isn't you. Yet.

You cancel the call. You get in the elevator. You'll talk to Yujin later.

▮▮▮

The Odyssey is mostly concerned with Odysseus's seafaring instance. The one who is brave. The one who wants to return home. Scholars have written long papers regarding his instancing—if Odysseus left Ithaca with the intention of always returning, then he shouldn't have any instance. Something changes in him, during the war, to make him desire a homecoming. Something changes in him, to have his desires send him back across the sea.

SOYOUNG-ROSE

Soyoung slides into the passenger seat of the rental truck. Minsoo's sitting in the driver's seat, wearing cloth-and-red-rubber gloves and a ratty T-shirt.

"You look like a construction ahjusshi," she says.

"You look like a cleaning ahjumma," he says. "Ready?"

"I guess," Soyoung says, and then her cousin reverses the rental truck and they get on the road to their late grandfather's house.

Professional movers are coming next week. But Soyoung owns the house now, and her mom says that she's done her part already, cleaning up, and the aunts have all agreed that the moving part is the responsibility of someone young and strong, and also, they're bitterly jealous of her getting the house. And so Soyoung's guilt-tripped Minsoo into helping her tag and sort all the furniture, and into helping her cart away all the small precious things the aunts have asked for. They had discussed this before the funeral. Rose is a passenger in these plans, but Soyoung thinks that the Rose-version of herself still would have agreed to help, since her memories are filled with moving vans—two houses with her American mom, college, graduate school, three moves around the NYC greater metropolitan area.

"I almost went to the airport yesterday," Soyoung says as Minsoo backs out of the parking space.

Soyoung remembers watching her instance walk across the immigration checkpoint, the feeling of being stuck to the cold tile, of wanting to take another step forward and being unable to do so, watching her other self run blithely away, with a single wide-eyed glance back. The memory is in double vision. She doesn't begrudge her other self her adventure. But the envy. God, the envy. Soyoung cried in the car in her mom's lap while Harabeoji and her mom had a long, adult conversation, and Minsoo tried to distract her with his toys. She remembers this because she threw his Squirtle figurine out the window of the moving car on the freeway, and then everyone in the car had more pressing problems to contend with.

She examines the memory with the clinical detachment, the deep surprise of an adult learning the contours of a child's sadness. Every hurt is the worst hurt when you haven't been hurt before. For Soyoung, her childhood tantrum had been sanded down into a background anecdote. *And I was the remaining instance, and I was so mad about it!* For Rose, the childhood tantrum is a little sunburst of profane emotion, belonging to a child she doesn't feel any connection to.

This is the worst part of it: Every bit of the past feels fake from the dissonance, the sheer divorce of her past selves from her present decisions coloring even the combined memories. Her prior emotions are dead things in her chest. Like the stickers she saved as a kid, pretty little scraps of paper that meant something a long time ago, but have no meaning now.

▪ ▪ ▪

Odysseus instances a single time, between *The Iliad* and *The Odyssey.* Throughout *The Odyssey,* he is always leaving. He leaves Polyphemus's island uneaten. He leaves Circe's island cleanly. He leaves Tiresias's island unscathed. He leaves Calypso's island unharmed. He never instances again. His goal, over years, never faltering. He stays singular. He knows what he wants, showing the same clarity of vision as his son.

Papers have been written about the fact that Odysseus does not instance leaving Troy, though he instanced when leaving Ithaca. He should have instanced: He was at war in Troy for ten years, he instanced to reach it.

▪ ▪ ▪

Minsoo pulls the rental truck into the street. "Well, your mom would be pissed you didn't tell her. Have you made up your mind to stay, then?"

"Do you think I'd instance again, if I tried to leave?"

Minsoo makes a noise like he's not sure. She guesses it's not a fair question to ask him. They're close. Or one version of her was close with him. And he named his daughter after her foreign self—Jangmi is the Korean word for "rose." Which is a thing that Soyoung and Minsoo never talked about. And Rose hadn't brought it up when she came back for the funeral. It had seemed inappropriate. And it felt like to ask *now* would be to open up a whole can of other familial issues.

Rose had done her undergrad thesis on optimizing search engines. This later led to a boring job helping build software that sorts through aggregate data. But the interesting thing, to her, had always been that more information was not necessarily better. More information often meant more junk—more noise, less signal. With twice the data, it became orders of magnitude more difficult to answer any question.

"Never mind," she says. And she turns on the radio in the rental truck, and they drive the rest of the way not talking, listening to old, swoopy Korean music from the predawn of the K-pop era.

Minsoo parks in front of the house. It was weird that their grandfather had a *house*. There isn't much single-use housing in Seoul. He had never sold it to a developer. It was postwar property. He used to talk about how most of his friends had sold their land.

Soyoung and Minsoo carry flat cardboard boxes and rolls of tape into the entryway. Minsoo fumbles with the keys. He opens the door. Soyoung tries not to think about how she was here before, as Rose, standing at the entrance and unable to go inside. And then they go in.

The interior of the house is like a time capsule that smells like barley tea and dust. It doesn't smell like death at all. It smells like Harabeoji stepped out for an hour while the ahjumma who used to come by every week has come by and cleaned everything. The glass tops on the kitchen table and the low living room table are spotless. The blankets that usually live crumpled across the couch have been folded. Nobody has taken any of the pictures down yet. There're filmy black-and-white photos of her grandfather and grandmother, family members Soyoung never knew well, and formal wedding pictures. Soyoung's mom and late father. Minsoo's parents. All the other aunts and uncles. People smiling in hanboks and in western suits and frothy white dresses. Scrawled crayon drawings labeled neatly in the corners in pencil: *Soyoung, age 3; Minsoo, age 6; Jiya, age 8,* and so on and so forth, a parade of kiddie ephemera from children who had been subsumed into adulthood. God. The whole concept makes Soyoung so fucking sad, all of a sudden.

Part of her wants to walk right back out the door. Leave the house forever in a time capsule from her childhood, and pretend that the next time she comes back it will look the same for the rest of her life, that she can preserve the lost little-kid version of herself if she just never comes in here again.

"Soyoung, can you help me tape these boxes?"

"Yeah," she says, and looks away from the picture wall. "What are we going to do with the photos?"

"I don't know," Minsoo admits. "I didn't want to ask who wanted which ones."

"Right." Soyoung remembers making the scribbly bunny that's taped up next to a scrunchy-looking photo of her and Minsoo, age seven. She can't imagine anyone wanting it.

"I guess we'll just box them up and let everyone figure it out later."

"Mm."

Soyoung folds cardboard. Minsoo starts taking down photos and delicately removing Scotch tape from the walls. Ghostly rectangular patches emerge where the photographs have been removed. The photographs go into the boxes, followed by the blankets, and the smaller tchotchkes that litter the living area. Soyoung picks up a clunky little statue of the Empire State Building that Rose had sent when she had just moved to the States. She had forgotten about it. She remembers sending it. She picks it up and puts it into a box. She wipes her eyes, but they're not moist enough to make that satisfying, and anyway, she feels like the worst sort of cliché for being moved by this.

"This sucks," she says.

"Yeah," Minsoo says.

"I have to stay, don't I?"

"I mean. I'd be happy if you stayed. Though you should do what you want."

"What sort of psychopath reintegrates against their instance's desires?" she says, and sighs. "Don't answer that. How come our moms can't do the packing? We're his *grandkids.*"

"'Cause they'd start crying about it," Minsoo says, and takes a cuckoo clock off the wall.

"I'm going to stay," Soyoung says. "I hated that clock."

"Yeah, we all know you hated that clock."

Soyoung wraps the hateful clock in a towel and puts it in a cardboard box. She feels lighter now that she's made her decision. None of the back-and-forth of yesterday. This time her decision feels real. Her mom in the States will be disappointed. But Taehyung will be happy to have been chosen, and her mom here will be pleased. And maybe she'll feel good in her heart, eventually. Maybe she can fit herself back into the contours of Soyoung's life and snip out all the excess, and maybe eventually all the meaning will come back, form before function, water filling the shape that has been presented to it.

And it'll be easier. Reintegrated instances are generally subsumed into their state of original origin, not their naturalized countries. She's ethnically Korean. She won't have to climb through bureaucratic hoops, she won't have to justify her citizenship, she won't get kicked down to a visa. She won't have to break up her impending marriage, she won't have to make her family unhappy, and it might not be the decision that makes her happy, or what she wants, but how can anyone ever know what will make them happy? You can't always know what you want. All you can do sometimes is pick a direction and run. She'll be satisfied in her concrete choices. Soyoung was unhappy to begin with, anyway. And Rose was an emotionless freak. There is no perfect world. There is no return to the imperfect world as it was before.

"Remind me to call the embassy on Monday," Soyoung says.

"Sure."

They work together for the next few hours. They construct an absurd number of cardboard boxes. They get all the photographs off the wall. They go through Harabeoji's kitchen drawers. They clean up the spare rooms, which had been emptied years ago. One of these used to be Soyoung's bedroom, and she tries not to feel strange about how it's being used for storage. She leans on Rose's memory—tries to remember her teenage bedroom as the room in Fort Lee that she had decorated with boy band posters, not the room here, which had been decorated with different boy band posters. It fails. She feels strange. She pushes through it.

They tentatively open the door to Harabeoji's bedroom, which neither of them had ever been in before. There's pills on the nightstand, and the room smells a little like old man, but not in a bad way. Just in a lived-in way. There's a faded, framed photograph of all the kids, sitting on a windowsill. Minsoo and Soyoung box up the pills, the photograph, some of the other things that look valuable or important. They empty drawers. They open cupboards. They examine photo albums and creased, expensive hanboks. They put everything in cardboard.

The sun is high in the sky by the time they've gotten to a good stopping point. She stretches. Her forearms are sore.

"Let's get delivery jjajangmeon," Minsoo suggests. "I feel like we earned it."

Soyoung nods, and Minsoo walks over to the fridge where the magnet with the delivery number is written. They could use an app. But this is the place they've been ordering from for a decade. Soyoung lies on the couch.

"Get tangsooyook, too!"

"Okay!"

She feels around for the remote to Harabeoji's ancient television. She clicks it on. SBS. The daily international news is playing. She closes her eyes. Like this, with the TV playing in the background while she lies on the couch, it could be ten years ago for Soyoung, twenty years ago for Soyoung-and-Rose. Maybe when she opens her eyes again she'll be a kid and everything in the intervening time will have been a strange dream. When she opens her eyes, it'll be her mom waking her up to go upstairs and sleep in her bed. She needs to figure out what to do with the house.

The television announcer speaks in bitten-off formal syllables. Behind her, Minsoo's stumbling through ordering, changing his mind three times mid-order. She grins a little, because it's funny. When Minsoo's an old man, he's still going to be the same kid who cried after she threw his toy out the window.

The language coming from the television swaps to English. Soyoung opens her eyes and turns her head. It's a prerecorded press conference in some anonymous conference room, with cameras popping every few seconds, making it hard to get a good look at the people inside. There's a smiling white guy and a big screen next to him.

"We are so delighted to be here with you today—"

The audio from the recording quiets. Subtitles roll. The Korean newscaster speaks over it.

"In business news, Mergebreak announced the development of their first new product since their inception—"

Soyoung sits up. On the screen, a man in a black jacket (who has now been identified as DREW THORRSON) gestures at the screen, which begins to play. The newscast cuts to a clean version of the smaller screen, and the prerecorded animated trailer begins to play.

A little purple stick figure waves and walks through a gate, splitting into red and blue versions of the purple original. They both wave at each other, and run off the screen in opposite directions. The word MITOSIS scrolls across in a slick, futuristic font.

As it plays, the newscaster continues speaking. In a precise, neutral tone, he explains that the new service will allow for reintegrated instances to reverse the process of reintegration, separating themselves back into the component parts with separate memories. He announces that the new service is being announced in the wake of Mergebreak's merger with Condensco. He announces that this is a revolutionary product which can unwind a reintegration within six months of the event.

The animation spirals into charts and figures. Into global instancing statistics, into the average amount of travel done by the average first-world individual, into the wry admittance that Mergebreak has never been able to solve the 5 percent failure rate. But they're in the last stages of being able to reverse it. Expect public availability next year, likely partnered with local governments and travel authorities. The rising hope in Soyoung's chest immediately crushed. A year. She can't wait a year.

Cut back to Drew, in the conference room. He's still smiling. The screen behind him is still playing something after the animation.

". . . We're very excited about the product, and our new leadership team in New York. Please reach out to our leadership team with any questions."

And on the screen behind him, between all the other smiling faces, is Yujin. Not Yujin like Rose remembers him (at the playground, sitting in front of her in class), or Yujin like Soyoung knows (with his floppy hair, leaning over his coffee), but a grown-up-adult Yujin. American Yujin in a nice suit, smiling with the fakest smile she's ever seen.

Soyoung feels the same hunger she felt when staring at Rose, ten feet from their grandfather's grave.

▮▮▮

Odysseus, staring down the barrel of his past life, across the wine-dark sea. Nothing stops him, no gods, no monsters, no lovers, no ghosts of dead heroes or relatives, no enchanted feasts, no sirens, no sorceresses, no wayward crew. He is going to get his life back. He is going to go back home.

▮▮▮

"Soyoung," Minsoo calls. "Can you help me clear the kitchen table?"

"Sure," Soyoung says. She turns away from the television. She still hasn't called the embassy. She still has an American passport. One month since her reintegration. Five months until her reintegration is permanent, according to the newscast. The technology to separate her exists. The American instance of Yujin is the face of the project. He has access to it. And she has Yujin's number, and Yujin is best-fucking-friends with his American instance.

She's ready to eat.

PART III

Arirang, arirang, arariyo . . .
[You are][Your instance is]* going over Arirang hill.

—*"Arirang," standard translation*

*Subject is not specified in Korean.

SOYOUNG-ROSE

Soyoung wakes when the captain speaks: *Please put on your seat belts and bring your chairs into the upright position to prepare for landing.*

She rubs her eyes. In the dream she had been sitting somewhere very clear and beautiful and it's gone now, washing away the memory of her plans. She looks around the cabin: the half-sleeping strangers in the half-light. Businessmen closing laptops. Businesswomen putting tablets away. Mothers and fathers cleaning up their children. Other young women dabbing at their faces with oil-absorbent papers, leaning into the lurch of the plane's stuttering descent.

When she lands, Soyoung has a thousand tasks to complete. Calling both versions of her mother and letting them both know she's alright. Scheduling lunch with her American mom, as a pretense to give her the envelope from her grandfather and letting the house become someone else's problem. Calling Soyoung's fiancé and telling him that she landed safely. Finishing the emails to Rose's work letting them know she's back from Korea. Finding Clarissa, who's picking her up from the airport.

But first, Soyoung has to get through security.

The plane tilts downward, landing turbulence shuddering through the seat. Soyoung grips the armrest on reflex, then consciously relaxes. It's strange. Rose had no fear of flying. Rose flew without care, only complained about turbulence in how it kept her from sleeping. But flying had made past-Soyoung want to scream. Every little bump of the plane hit some animal hindbrain part of her, some little terrified piece that has dwindled into nothing ever since reintegration. Soyoung, as she is now, had gotten on the plane and marveled at how it felt like nothing. How something that had filled her with terror no longer existed. Where in the body did fear live?

The swooping sensation of a turn. The plane continues to lower. Out of the window, the landscape looks like a miniature toy set, and it sets something like relief in her chest, to see the little ticky-tacky boxes making up the New York metropolitan area.

Rose had always been glad to come home, but Soyoung's delight at the scene feels almost like greed. The landscape grows. Here, the individual cars. Here, the looping highways, the little pockets of green space, the buildings, all the buildings. When flying into Incheon, mostly what you see is sparkling water.

Soyoung looks away. She goes through her purse reflexively. Phone, wallet, keys. American passport, boarding pass. Soyoung's Korean passport is safely tucked away in her carry-on, sandwiched in a paperback that she jammed in between her socks and underwear. Bringing the passport felt like too much of a risk, but a crucial one. Without her Korean passport, Soyoung couldn't return to Korea after being separated from her other self.

Soyoung wasn't committing any sort of obvious crime. Just one that ICE could deport her for, were it discovered. But it wouldn't be discovered, and she wouldn't be in New York long enough for it to become a problem. She had Rose's whole life here that she could slip into. Nobody will ask, she tells herself. Nobody will know. Rose and Soyoung were, individually and collectively, a five-foot-two East Asian woman wearing a cardigan, neither strikingly pretty nor shockingly ugly. In high school, teachers had regularly called Rose by her friends' names, even though they looked nothing alike, just by virtue of their ethnicity. In high school, Soyoung had sat in the back of the class and hadn't spoken much.

The plane lands in a single, bone-jolting bounce. Soyoung half expects to see a newly instantiated version of herself falling onto the floor on the first thump. But no second body appears. It was unlikely to begin with—instances usually appear at immigration checkpoints. That was part of the *point* of an immigration checkpoint at an airport or railway, it was a controlled space for an instancing. It was a type of social technology. A solidified border, so that instances didn't appear spontaneously in the air or so they didn't pop into existence upon reaching the second landmass.

There are ghoulish rumors about that, which circulated the same way that people like talking about airplane crashes. That bodies just appeared in the air and fell after takeoff. There had been an Australian kid who had stowed away in the hollow parts of the landing gear of a plane, about a decade ago. When the plane took off, he dropped from the sky. For a while there had been rumors that he was an instance, but it turned out he was just someone who died.

No such drama for Soyoung. The seat belt sign turns off. She gets up and gets her bag from the overhead compartment. She stands in line to leave the plane. And nothing happens when she crosses the threshold through the tunnel to the airport gate, nothing happens when she exits the tunnel, and nothing happens when she scans through the immigration checkpoint and goes to collect her single suitcase.

■ ■ ■

The cultural programming around the naming of instances differs societally. In many patronymic societies, the leaving instance takes a surname derived from their progenitor and is either given a new name by their progenitor, or chooses a new name for themself (the best examples arriving from Russia and the Balkan states). In societies with larger numbers of instances, there often arises the pattern that the leaving instance is the one to carry the name, and the remaining instance must pick a sort of shadow-name, like they're some sort of ghost (common in East Asia in certain centuries). The ancient Romans used the same custom for their twins as for their instances, "Name" and "Anti-Name," which seems grimmer when you don't know that girls were named for their father and given numbers (Prima, Secunda).

But in most modern societies, instances carry identical names. This is the American tradition, which spread like the other American diseases (capitalism, Starbucks, McDonald's). Soyoung Kang in Korea is the same as Soyoung Kang in America, the same name on two passports, barring any visit to the courthouse and any legal name change.

"Rose" is a nickname. A handle for the western mouth to bite. Rose had thought of herself as Rose, most of the time. Except sometimes in her head, she still sometimes called herself Soyoung. It was still her name.

■ ■ ■

Soyoung emerges from the airport and both of her past selves are thrilled. Finally home, finally an adventure. It's the joy of homecoming twined with the joy of novelty and her skin feels awful and she wants a shower, but in that moment, she's never been happier. This is the first time that her reintegration feels like a gift. The sky is clear. The sun is bright. Everything is going to be just fine. She's going to fix everything.

She scans the pickup area and catches sight of Clarissa waving out the driver's window.

Clarissa hollers, "Hi! Get in! Before we get ticketed!"

Soyoung laughs, pulls her bag up to the curb and shoves it in the back seat, slams the door closed and gets in. In her head: memories of Clarissa drinking awful plastic-handle vodka, of getting really awful cheap pizza together, of crying over breakups, of saying goodbye to Clarissa at the airport, and driving the remaining instance of Clarissa back home while they silently listened to My Chemical Romance. Soyoung turns the memories over in her mind with wonder.

"Seat belt," Clarissa says. Soyoung obeys.

"Hi," she says. "Thanks for picking me up. And for watching Dr. Crouton."

It's the first time she's seriously spoken English in a month. She stretches her mouth around the syllables and tries to fill them organically. Rose doesn't have an accent. Rose spent years grinding away the edges of her English so that nobody would ask her where she was from. Rose had been a pretty optimistic teenager, all things considered. People still ask where she *really* comes from.

"Yeah, no problem, I love your cat son. I'm not giving him back."

"Please, my boy," Soyoung says, as Clarissa turns onto the main road.

"*My* boy now," Clarissa says, and she laughs, and Soyoung laughs, and it's nice, it's easy, it's something so divorced from Rose's family and its history.

"So, he's still at your apartment? I am noticing a distinct lack of meowing in this car."

Clarissa nods, her short blond hair bobbing.

"Yup, we'll grab him from my place and then head to yours. I thought he probably wouldn't like the carrier for so long, and JFK, you know, the delays. You hungry?"

"Caffeine?"

"Starbucks?"

"Okay, *suburbia*."

"It's the fastest!" Clarissa protests. "They have a drive-through! I thought you were in a hurry to see your boy."

"I'm kidding, I'm kidding."

They drive for a while. They go past the little homes that look nothing like the tourist's version of New York, the gas stations, the mysterious warehouses, the large ethnic food depots, the billboards that advertise pharmaceuticals and personal injury lawyers, and then Clarissa swerves them across two lanes and into the Starbucks drive-through.

Clarissa drums her hands against the steering wheel, glances at Soyoung over her shades.

"What do you want?"

Soyoung is hit by a staccato series of sense memories so strong that they almost make her gag. Rose at fifteen, Rose at seventeen, Rose at twenty-two in the car with Clarissa getting coffee. They spent so much time getting coffee. Something about the cadence with which Clarissa had asked, contrasted against the slant of the light, hits Soyoung's neurons.

"Grande Americano, black, and, um, one of those egg and cheese breakfast sandwich things?"

"Black coffee?"

Then Soyoung remembers: Rose liked her coffee with cream, with more sugar than necessary. Rose was caramel macchiatos and java chip Frappuccinos. Rose knew the names of the Starbucks breakfast sandwiches, had Star Rewards. Soyoung was the one who drank her coffee bitter unless it was for Instagram.

"Yeah," Soyoung says. "They've got crazy amounts of Starbucks in Seoul now, did you know? I was so surprised. They sell these insane drinks that have like, pudding in them, sometimes. Frappuccinos on steroids. There weren't really any coffee shops when I was a kid. Or maybe I just didn't pay attention since I didn't drink coffee."

"Jesus, pudding?"

"You slurp it with the straw."

Clarissa edges the car forward. Rolls down the window and rattles off their orders to the Starbucks employee. Soyoung passes her Rose's credit card. Clarissa pushes it back and rolls the window back up.

"How was Korea?"

"It was good," Soyoung says. Clarissa gives her a weird look.

"Cool."

Soyoung bites her lip. Was "good" the right thing to call the trip? Is this what was expected of her? Would Rose have been honest here? Soyoung tries to remember. Her pasts blur together. She doesn't quite remember what Rose-Before would have said. Only the clarity of her previous emotions and the outcomes.

She remembers calling Clarissa and asking if Clarissa could come pick up her cat, and explaining that Rose had to go to Korea for a funeral. She doesn't remember whether she explained about her grandfather, whether she explained anything about why she was going, whether she showed any emotion through her speech or body language. She had felt very clear, in that moment. Like every action that followed was a natural outgrowth of the prior experience, water down a slope.

"So, um. Funeral went okay?" Clarissa asks.

"It was fine," Soyoung says. "Kind of weird being back. But everyone was nice. It was kind of nice, I guess. To see my family again."

These are the wrong words. She knows it the moment she says them. They're too light. Rose had mourned her grandfather with the grief you would give to the death of a distant star. Soyoung had felt it like a wave that had scoured a piece of glass to a soft and edgeless finish. The flinch before the hit, so that the hit was almost a kindness. It was less that he was dead and more that a part of her childhood had died. That was too much to explain. It would have been too much to explain even if Clarissa had known Soyoung and not Rose. But she only knew Rose, and Rose's sadness should have been a bloodless, clean thing. Intellectualized. Rose would have talked about how the trip had been a nostalgia bomb, how her other self had been weird, how the funeral was nothing like she had ever gone to, not in a bad way, just in a weird way, just in a way that divorced her from her past.

"It's cool if you don't want to talk about it," Clarissa says awkwardly, rolling down the window so that the other Starbucks employee can hand them drinks and a limp sandwich bag that she passes to Soyoung.

Soyoung unwraps the sandwich. Takes a bite. Shoves down the nausea at that familiar-foreign taste. She almost wants to tell Clarissa the whole truth. Here's what happened to me in Korea. Here's who I am now. I am a different person than when my past-self got on that plane. Clarissa, your instance is three years out of sync. Get her back while you still can. No, never let her touch you. Clarissa, can't you recognize that I'm no longer the girl who handed you a cat carrier, back then?

Soyoung takes a second bite of the sandwich. Crumbling egg, congealing cheese. It needs hot sauce. She remembers being the person who got overly expensive Starbucks-ciabatta-bacon-egg-cheese before class (not the person who got gilgeori toast for breakfast before class, even though the sandwiches were cooked in bad oil), remembers being the person who grew into the opinion that these were a pale imitation of a bodega baconeggand-cheese. She remembers being someone who says baconeggandcheese all as one word.

"No, it's fine," Soyoung says. "I guess it was just an overall weird experience? Like I didn't really know my grandfather that much, and so it really wasn't that it was like . . . sad, as it turned out there was a bunch of business shit to sort of out with his estate, and his house, and all that family junk. And I was staying with my instance, which was stressful. I mean, not because of the reintegration potential—she had a MERGEBREAK, I had a MERGEBREAK—but because, well, it's not like a twin, you know? I mean, you know."

"I get you."

"Yeah, you know."

As if repetition is truth. They merge back into traffic. The sun is blinding. Time feels like wobbly eggs. Soyoung feels like she's made of wobbly eggs. Sleep deprivation is one of those forms of torture that they use on political prisoners; the sense of self starts to unravel. In Korea, it's two in the morning.

"What's your instance like?" Clarissa asks.

"A lot like me," Soyoung says.

"Okay, I mean, paint me a word picture," Clarissa says. "Come on, you talk with my instance all the time."

Soyoung closes her eyes. Imagines herself. Her other self, in the present tense.

"Soyoung looks like me. Pretty much the same hair, just a little longer than mine. Dresses better than I do—I think that's just cultural differences, though. Everyone in Seoul dresses so nice. Well, everyone our age. She wears makeup. I think her skin is a little worse? Not a lot worse, but I kind of thought it would be better."

Soyoung had spent a long morning, a few days after the reintegration, examining every square inch of her skin.

"And personality . . . I don't know, it's hard to tell. Like, what am I even like?"

"Did you guys get along?"

Soyoung waves her hand ambiguously. "Do you like your instance?"

"Yeah, actually. Clare-Squared is great. She sends all my breakup texts for me."

That startles Soyoung into laughter. Breakup texts. They're on good enough terms for breakup texts. Soyoung can't imagine. Soyoung needs to text Taehyung and let him know that she landed safely. She still hasn't. She forgot.

"I'm really happy for you," she says. "It really wasn't like that for me."

"Me," meaning Soyoung. "Me," meaning Rose.

"Well, I'm sorry it was weird," Clarissa says. "Less sorry about that than the funeral, but still sorry. Does it help if I say that I'm glad you're back? I missed you."

"Yeah, I missed you too," Soyoung says. In many ways, this is the first time she is speaking with Clarissa. There is no word in the English language for nostalgia for a relationship you never had.

▪ ▪ ▪

A popular folk song in both North and South Korea is "Arirang." It's an old folk song, a resistance song during the Japanese occupation, a song that is taught to schoolchildren on both sides of the border and to expatriates whose kids grow up nine thousand miles away. "Arirang" isn't a word that means anything, though the term likely refers back to the Auraji, which is a body of water connecting Pyeongchang and Samcheok with the Han River, and the associated legend. It is the sort of song that sounds like a lament, and doesn't explain anything about the underlying story.

YJ

You miss Yujin's call while you're doing an interview. A reporter from the *Times* who wanted to talk about Mitosis and was following you around all afternoon to add "color," which marketing thought was a good idea. The phone rings while you're talking with him, and you glance at your screen and shove it back in your pocket.

"Sorry about that," you tell the reporter.

"No, by all means, if it's important," he says. You've forgotten his name and you feel really bad about it. You think it began with a *W*.

"It's really not—just family."

"Sure," the reporter says. "Hey, speaking of your family—if you don't mind being on the record for this."

"Depends on the question."

Your phone buzzes again. You glance at it. Yujin, texting you: *Call me back when you get a chance?*

"Did your relationship with your family, and the fact that you're an instance, affect the way that you're steering this project?"

"Only in that it gives me a lot of empathy for our customers," you say easily. "Hey, I thought this wasn't a personal profile."

"I'm asking everyone I talk to about this," he says.

"I miss my family," you say. "But if I didn't want to be here, I wouldn't be here. You know? And if I were to go back, and if I were to reintegrate accidentally with my instance, then I'd be really glad to know that Mitosis exists."

▪▪▪

You never expected the separation, so you never had the chance to say goodbye. Or not even goodbye, explicitly, but *goodbye*. You never had the chance to say thank you to your parents, or to bow at your grandparents' gravesite, or to pack up your good summer clothes, because it was winter when you flew. You guess this is a silly thing to feel strange about, in the grand scheme of things. People have real problems. People cross borders with only the clothes on their backs. People pay mules to be transported across country lines. People instance in ICE facilities. But you feel the strangeness anyway. You would have liked to have gone to your favorite bookstore while knowing it was the last time. You would have liked to have said goodbye to your parents. You know it would have been a futile gesture, because Yujin would soon exist and they would get to keep a version of their son.

■ ■ ■

You escape the reporter by going to the bathroom. You sigh—quietly, because you don't know if there's anyone in the stalls. You check your phone again. No other calls. You lean against the sink. You call your instance back. He picks up. You can hear the vague sound of music behind him.

"Is this a good time? I have a minute."

"Yeah. It's fine." His voice isn't exactly muffled, but there's a background ambience like he's in a crowded area. Your own voice echoes off the bathroom tile.

"Are you out?"

"Yeah," he says. "I had a favor to ask. Well, not for me. Not an us favor."

"Sure," you say. You lean against a sink. The back of your shirt gets a little wet.

"So, Soyoung wanted to talk to you about something. I don't really want to get into it now—"

There's a large burst of yelling from his side, as if to punctuate his point. You wince at the noise.

"Maybe now's not the best time to talk," he concedes. "But it's kind of serious. So if you've got time this weekend—"

"Sure yeah, I can talk with her. She's back in the States? American Soyoung?"

"It's kind of more complicated than that. But—you're at work, right?"

"Yeah. I'm calling you from the bathroom."

"You're in the bathroom."

"Nobody's in here."

"Sure," he says, and his statement speaks volumes. He's judging you. He's imagining you in the bathroom with your phone jammed against your ear by your shoulder, the same way you're imagining him stepping out of some nightclub, his phone held languidly in his hand.

"Shut up, man. I've been followed around by this reporter all day. I needed a break."

"A reporter?"

"For the Mitosis stuff."

"So you're hiding in the bathroom."

"Hey, don't be—"

"I didn't say anything. Okay. I'm going back inside. Get out of the bathroom."

"Yeah, bye," you say, and then you're hanging up, and you're laughing, because you're in an office bathroom and you've been followed around by a reporter all day and you're supposed to be someone important and sometimes you have to wonder, when exactly your life went weird.

SOYOUNG-ROSE

She goes over the plan in her head for the seventh time while brushing her hair, picking out her clothes. It's not a good plan. She's just going to ask. She's going to say hi to Yujin's instance and talk a little bit about things that are inconsequential, maybe talk about Yujin a bit, and then she's just going to ask, blunt like a hammer to a head. *Will you let me into the clinical trials for Mitosis?*

She had discussed the ask with Yujin. It had been the first thing she did, after seeing YJ on television, walking out into the garden of her grandfather's empty house and punching his name into her phone and calling him on speaker.

"Your instance was on TV," she had said.

"What?"

"Turn on a replay of this morning's SBS," she had said. "Or google your name or something." She had heard some noise, as if he was getting up and getting to a device.

"Huh," Yujin had said.

"Could you get me a meeting with him?" she had said, no preamble. "If I was in the States?"

"Why?"

"Mitosis."

A long silence. The wind rustling through the leaves and late-summer grass. Soyoung wondered who would live here, next. Whether it would still be a family home. Whether it would get razed to make way for a larger building.

"Yeah, I can ask. He'll do it."

"Are you sure?"

"Yeah. He trusts me and I trust you. He'll do it."

She hadn't understood the conviction. She couldn't imagine being so sure of her instance's actions, even though she now had the mélange in her head. But she trusted Yujin. And he trusted his instance.

Now her grandfather's garden feels like a dream as she stands in the wet tile of Rose's bathroom, blow-drying her hair. Now it feels less like Yujin's instance will say yes. He's a stranger, after all. He has no reason to help her other than his connection to his instance. It's a big favor that she's asking.

Soyoung tousles her hair. She makes a face at herself in the mirror. Soyoung and Rose weren't so interchangeable, though it's difficult to remember the shape of their bodies from inside. Both Soyoung and Rose had viewed their own flesh with a sort of brusque self-consciousness. Sometimes they thought they were beautiful. Sometimes they thought they were a monster. They had both considered plastic surgery when they were younger.

Soyoung rubs her eyes, remembers the action will make them bloodshot, and pushes her hair out of her face instead. She sort of wants to talk to Taehyung about all of this, because Soyoung had been accustomed to talking her plans through with him. She kind of wants to call her mom—which version of her mom? She's not sure. She wishes she could have told Clarissa about what's going on. She just—she hates feeling bad at things. Rose and Soyoung, both of them, they weren't good at people in either version of her lives. She had fallen into all of her friendships, her relationships. She was always better at telling people "no" than asking for help. How to convince someone to help her? She had failed so hard with her instance. Her instance had failed so badly with her.

She guesses she'll just go in and ask.

▮▮▮

The legend associated with "Arirang" starts like many other stories. A man and a woman, meeting on the banks of a river.

YJ

You walk into the bar, which has a soft velvety interior done in dark blue paint and dark wood, with a constellation of little glass lights hanging from the ceiling. It feels nostalgic. You and Petra had spent a lot of time inhabiting the "fancy cocktail place" stage of dating. You walk over to the podium where a hostess is standing decoratively.

"Hi. I think my friend is inside, actually? Do you mind if I just—"

"Go ahead," the hostess says, waving you in. You walk past finance bros in their vests, women in fashionable clothing who work in marketing, and a group of tech guys in T-shirts crowding the space all the way to the back.

You don't know if you're going to recognize Soyoung. But then she turns her head, and you catch the side of her profile, the straight line of her nose, the curve of her lip and that's Soyoung, from high school.

Soyoung catches sight of you. She waves.

She grew up hot. That is, embarrassingly, terribly, the first thing you think. Your ancient crush on her means that you notice all the ways she's changed: Her hair's longer, she's filled out in her hips, she's got sort of a sharper cast to her face, like the last bit of her kiddie softness on her cheeks has been filed away, but the lips and her eyes have stayed the same. You have the urge to stand up straighter. To impress her. Oh, who are you kidding. When she looks at you, she must see the stupid teenage boy you always were with her.

But wait—no. This isn't Korean Soyoung. The last time American Soyoung saw you, you were just kids. She has no memories of you as an awkward teenager. You can pretend that none of that ever happened.

"Soyoung? Hi, wow. It's been a while."

"Hi, YJ. It's really nice to see you again."

She holds out her hand for you to shake. You shake it. Her hand is warm. You really hope your palms aren't sweating. She's smiling at you, not like it's an obligation, but like she's actually pleased, a smile that twists her whole face in a beautiful crease.

"So, what's up? Yujin said you wanted to meet up with me? Did you guys reconnect in Korea?"

"I had a really normal experience with him and my instance, yeah," and she sounds exactly like you remember from high school, and it surprises you, that she would sound the same in two languages, in two lives.

You take a seat at the bar.

"Well, it's nice to see you, even if it's been a while."

It's the truth. You'd rather be here with an old friend, than sitting across a bar from a stranger. Though, you have to keep remembering: American Soyoung is a stranger. It's hard to keep that in your mind, when you're remembering her Korean self so vividly, along with all the things that come with her Korean self. The badly air-conditioned rooms in your high school. Going to the 7-Eleven and buying shrimp chips. It's as if her presence is a totem pulling the memories out of your head.

Normally Korea feels like another universe. A parallel dimension. The country of your childhood and adolescence. Adulthood, for you, is synonymous with New York City. It's synonymous with English. You don't know the words for "leveraged buyout" or "taxable income" or the "blood-brain barrier" in Korean. Most of the time, you aren't homesick. But now, looking at Soyoung, you suddenly miss being sixteen.

"What are you drinking? Anything good here?"

"Old-fashioned," she says, holding up her glass filled with amber liquid. You must look vaguely puzzled, because she folds her arms.

"I like smoke," she says. "I was one of those kids who wanted to like black coffee, too. Don't be so sexist."

"Hey. I just remember the last time I saw you drink it was green-grape soju."

She laughs.

"When we skipped hagwon! And went to noraebang, and got Minsoo to buy us drinks, since he worked at the convenience store, and then—"

Soyoung hesitates. She's also remembered the end of that night. Your pathetic confession. You really hate thinking about this, and most of the time you don't—it lives in the part of your brain that contains your CSAT grades and the three weeks you seriously thought about walking halfway across the Han River bridge and climbing over the railing, except then some kid at school did that first, and after that, it would have seemed derivative.

Soyoung belongs to the period of time when you had felt like you could still be anything. One night you had all gone to karaoke, above the fried chicken place, and it always smelled a little like sweet spicy sauce and oil, but the place was cheap, and they didn't make any fuss about the clearly underage patrons ordering alcohol, and they had a decent music selection, including a bunch of American music that Soyoung liked.

Soyoung had been wild about foreign music, then. You could take or leave music, but you had listened to some of it because she had liked it, and you had liked the way she stuck her pink tongue out while she was concentrating. Liking her had also made you feel pretty gross. Soyoung was Soyoung. She was "digging around in the dirt when you were six" Soyoung. She was "we didn't talk for four years in middle school and the beginning of high school" Soyoung. What did you like about her? You liked her sense of direction. You liked the way she looked. You liked how she knew who she was.

It hadn't been a planned confession. It had happened after you had stumbled out, filled with the good feeling of alcohol and camaraderie and you had mistaken all of this for closeness.

You had tugged Soyoung back behind the others.

"Kang Soyoung," you had said. "I really like you. Will you go out with me?"

She had looked at you. And she had laughed.

But that was the other Soyoung, Korean Soyoung. This Soyoung hasn't seen you since you were ten. You remember there had been a classroom party for her on a Friday. And then her instance had been back, next week. So this is who that ten-year-old grew up to be. You can't blame her for anything.

In the present, Soyoung's smile twists, a little embarrassed.

"I'm sorry," she says. "I didn't mean to laugh at you, when I said no. I don't think I ever apologized. I was just really surprised. I mean, I wasn't interested, but I was just surprised. It probably came across kind of mean."

"It's fine," you say. You find yourself surprised to mean it. Nostalgia aside, the boy you were back then and the man you are now are so divorced as to be different people. His hurts are no longer your hurts.

Wait. How does Soyoung remember rejecting you?

The memory should be inhabited by Korean Soyoung. Not the version of her that went to America.

You frown.

"Did your instance tell you about this?"

Either she's heard about this from her Korean version or from Yujin, which, you could see him thinking that was funny, or she *is* her Korean version, which, why would she be in New York? And what had Yujin said? *It's kind of more complicated than that?* But what would that mean?

Soyoung's smile goes plastic.

"Did Yujin not tell you?"

"Just that you needed a favor."

She stares at you. Her eyes like dark pools of water, a liquid sort of emptiness. It's racist to say that Asians are inscrutable. You took one Asian American studies course, in college, and you didn't really relate to any of it. The only point being: You've always found Korean women really hard to read.

"Can you get me into a trial for Mitosis? One that ends with separating the reintegrated instances," she says, the words a blur of too-fast English.

"What?"

"The clinical trials that your company is doing," she repeats again. "The ones you've talked about happening, on TV. Can you get me into the right side of the control group? The side of the control group that isn't the control group, I mean. The non-control group. The side that gets their memories and selves split apart."

She's still talking too fast, all her words are just strings of syllables in your brain before the meaning coalesces. And you still don't understand, even after the words make sense.

"What?"

"Can. You. Put. Me. In. The. Mitosis. Trials?" she repeats, slower. "In the non-control group. Please."

She says "please" in Korean. There's no word for "please" in Korean, but she uses the closest analogue. The word you use during desperation.

"Why?"

"Yujin," she says, slowly, like she thinks you're stupid. "Why do you think?"

You squint. You imagine being Kang Soyoung. You imagine going to your childhood friend you haven't seen in years and asking for something insane. You imagine stepping into the laboratory on the twenty-sixth floor not as an observer, but as a participant.

"This isn't American Soyoung or Korean Soyoung I'm talking to, is it? It's both. You've reintegrated."

Soyoung-Rose nods. Single dip of her head. A wave of dark hair.

▮▮▮

Most governments force instanced returnees to reintegrate if they don't obtain citizenship in the country that they migrate to, barring exceptional circumstance. It's framed as administrative necessity. Most governments will refuse to grant instances citizenship if there are no grounds under ethnicity, heritage, blunt biology. The law doesn't care about the heart.

In the United States of America, instancing-related issues are handled by the USCIS underneath the DHS after 9/11, prior to that having been folded into INS, in a department called IIS—Instancing Immigration Services. Historically, instancing policy was set by states, and it was only in the 1900s that SCOTUS ruled that federal jurisdiction over instancing was appropriate. In the current day, IIS is a well-established agency, working with other departments in DHS to control the border. Nearly all forms of migration and human movement, legal and illegal—immigration, refugee, and asylum claims—are touched by the IIS.

▮▮▮

You stare at Soyoung-Rose. Her present could be your future. Reintegration. You and Yujin. You-as-Yujin. The version of your self that is amalgamate, the one who remembers the last decade in Korea, who remembers your family.

There's a tightness to the way Soyoung-Rose holds her mouth. The points of her nails dig into her flesh where she's holding her elbow. These are the sorts of things you wouldn't have noticed until things started going south with Petra, but now you know a lot about the way women express *tension* without saying anything. You really fucking hated that with Petra, the way she wouldn't just *say* things, the way that it was all—just silences. Body language. Why can't people just say what they feel? But you didn't want to ask, you didn't know how to ask, you hadn't—you don't have the vocabulary for that, emotionally, and this isn't Petra, you tell yourself. This is not about

Petra, this is not about you. You are being an asshole. A childhood friend is coming to you for help and you are being an asshole.

You should say, "What happened?"

You should say, "Why do you want to separate?"

You should say, "Seriously, you didn't know Yujin didn't tell me anything? This wasn't planned? You're not playing a weird elaborate social experiment on me? Is there a camera?"

Instead, you say: "How did it feel?"

The words come out all wrong, you wanted to hit casual but your voice hits *fervent,* like you *want* to know, the same tone you hit when you asked her out, all those years ago.

And Soyoung-Rose laughs at you, again.

"How did it feel!" she repeats.

■ ■ ■

The story associated with "Arirang" begins with a man and a woman who fall in love picking camellia blossoms near the banks of the Auraji, before parting. A storm causes the waters of the Auraji to rise, separating the two lovers. This happens in every version of this story.

■ ■ ■

"I shouldn't have—"

Soyoung-Rose waves her hand, shakes her head, her hair undulating in a neat wave.

"It's fine, it's just, Yujin asked me the same thing immediately, when I told him."

"You don't have to tell me if you don't want to."

"I don't mind," she says. "I told Yujin, anyway. He'll probably tell you."

She looks down at her drink.

"They put something weird in this. Rosemary, I think?"

"Seriously, don't tell me. It's fine."

She shakes her head again.

"No, I just—figure out what you're ordering, okay? Give me a minute."

"Sure."

The bartender enters the periphery of your vision.

"Can I just get a whiskey-soda? Uh. Suntory?"

He nods. You nod back. It still feels like winning a game whenever you interact successfully with a service professional. You always feel like you're doing it wrong. It's the little things. You think, sometimes, that this is because you're kind of a foreigner. The things you learned as a kid were all—not incorrect. But a half step removed. Sometimes you're afraid that this isn't a cultural conditioning thing, it's just that you're not very good at people. But you are. Good at people.

▮▮▮

Reintegration is required on reentry into certain states, after the expiration of the citizen's visa in another country. It is mandated in Russia and China for political reasons on re-entry from the United States, and from most South American countries, as well as Mexico. A political science doctoral candidate at Yale published a thesis that drew the connection between overpopulation and required reintegration. He published a follow-up charting how in countries where reintegration was more heavily mandated, but the political apparatus didn't have the bandwidth to police reintegration, citizens were more likely to lie and stay separate, or to lie about having an instance for access to social services.

▮▮▮

Soyoung-Rose puts her glass down and leans toward you. You pretend not to notice her cleavage.

"Do you remember playing human sacrifice?" she says.

"Vaguely," you say. You haven't thought about that in years. It was Soyoung and her cousin's game. You only remember that it involved stabbing each other with Soyoung's cousin's lightsaber, and you hadn't liked it that much, because it mostly involved Soyoung demanding that you lie down and let her stab you with the lightsaber.

"Sure. Okay. Different metaphor, then. Have you ever gotten pushed into a swimming pool?"

"Once or twice."

"It's like that moment, falling in. First, gravity. Everything goes weightless for a second. Like when you're falling, and you're scared, but you don't have time to be scared, because now you're in the water, like, the cold plunge of it, right? The way it slams all your breath out of you, and for a moment, you're just . . . You're nothing. You don't remember where you are or what's happening other than the cold and the pressure and then you're trying not to breathe, and then you're surfacing out of the water, gasping, wet, all your shit's drenched, if you're wearing clothes."

Soyoung-Rose takes a breath. She smiles, briefly. It transforms her face. Suddenly she's the girl you remember, and then it's gone.

"After you're reintegrated, it's like, you're in the ocean. Not a pool, anymore. You're in too deep, and the waves are coming, and you can't catch your breath, because it's like, the waves are rolling through you, like, you know what I mean? How it feels. It's like that, but in your head. Over and over and over. All the rest of your fucking life. So. Yeah. Or, I don't know. Everyone's different. Maybe it'll be good for you. Since you want it. Unlike us."

She's fully leaned over on the bar. You're no longer trying to ignore her cleavage. You couldn't pay attention to her cleavage if you tried. She's tilted her face in a way where her eyes are large, luminous, upsettingly so, the black circle of her iris cut by her eyelid in a way where it's hard to tell whether she's staring at you or past you, and it scares you, the way her face has gone completely blank. *Us*. The plural.

■ ■ ■

You hadn't anticipated the separation.

In your memory, there was no moment when you looked back at Yujin across the immigration desk, or across the border after getting your luggage and locked eyes. In the television shows, there's always that moment, paired with a swell of music and the high-pitched metallic tone that is supposed to denote something brainbending is happening. Sometimes then you get the silhouette shots of the instance walking away. The other instance standing there, the actor with a curated blank expression on their face.

No. You remember walking through the terminal, and then there's just a long blank space in your mind that ended with your waking up on the plane. You hadn't even realized anything had happened, you hadn't thought anything was *wrong* until you touched down at JFK and turned your phone from airplane mode and swapped out the SIM cards and you had voicemails from your mother's phone, your father's phone, from your mother (shouting, hysterical), from your father (stern, exasperated, paternal), and from your other self, on your mother's phone.

Your instance had sounded superficially calm. It was unsettling how you were instantly able to tell he was freaking out. That shouldn't have been apparent from his tone, the timbre of his speech and the steadiness of his language. But he was you. You knew how you felt when you sounded like that.

So you called yourself back. Or rather, you called your mother's phone, and your mom picked up, and she was hysterical at you, and you asked her to please put your instance on the phone. You remember that your voice was still very calm.

She put him—you, at the time, you had thought of him only as *you*, as there was only seventeen hours' difference between you and your other self, and his thoughts were your thoughts, and it was so strange that you suddenly, intrinsically understood why some cultures thought that instances were of the devil and should be killed on sight—back on the phone.

"I didn't think—"

"—not consciously—"

"We're back home now, did you—"

"On the airplane, I didn't realize what had happened."

"I keep telling Mom that but she keeps yelling about it. I'm putting her back on, you deal with—"

"I have to get my luggage—"

"Did you know you wanted to leave? Did you plan this?" your mother's voice cut in. You supposed she had taken the phone from your instance.

"No," you said. It wasn't a lie.

Instancing was want turned so deep that it manifested in reality. Instancing was pure white-hot desire. Did you consciously know you were leaving forever? No. You didn't know what part of your self wanted to leave. Except—the way it had felt like freedom, this past semester, to be so far from home.

It wasn't even about New York. It could have been anywhere. You could have been in the middle of Kansas, London, Sydney, Beijing, Hong Kong, it was about how you had learned you wanted more. You had lived in the same city all your life. And then suddenly, you didn't. You hadn't known that you liked feeling like an alien, that you enjoyed the unmooring from your family, your friends. You liked that you could be someone else, you could absorb new ideas and new languages, you could think about the world outside the box of your life.

A surprise instancing wasn't uncommon. This was a situation that they warned international students about, that schools factored into their study-abroad programs. It was one of the hazards of foreign travel, and one of the reasons that it was so difficult to get a student visa, why there was an extensive interview process before an international student was accepted, even for just a summer program between sister schools. There was also a specialized sort of insurance and waiver that you had to sign, in order to not hold the school liable in the future.

"We'll pay for your flight back," your mother had said. "Come home."

And. Well. God, for a moment it was tempting. For a moment you imagined getting back on the plane, not even going through customs. You imagined smashing back against your other self and regaining the memories of the two days you spent apart. Canceling the rest of your study-abroad program, apologizing to the directors and your professors, who you were sure would be understanding. This happened a few times a year, you had heard. The division between the head and the heart. The dreams and the reality, meeting the cold truth of debt, plans, life.

But there is no world where you said yes. The version of yourself that could have said yes was not the version that instanced.

You couldn't go home again; you didn't want to.

"No, Mom," you had said. And you had collected your luggage. You had gone to your dorm room. You had filled out the student visa paperwork, noting that you were an instance and your continued presence in the country had been approved. You had gone to potluck friendsgivings. You had applied for jobs and taken driving lessons in Queens. You got your first job, and then your second. You became an adult in America.

In your head, you still think of yourself as "Yujin." You were Yujin (Yujin-ah, Lee Yujin) for twenty years of your life. And you have, in your head, always used the plural "we" to refer to yourself. Even before instancing. You don't know why. Just an artifact of your self-perception.

So, maybe your instancing was fate. Or just something strange in your brain chemistry.

■ ■ ■

Soyoung looks away. She grimaces.

"Sorry. That was an insane thing to say. I shouldn't have said that. You wanted like, a technical description, right?"

"No, it was fine," you lie.

"No, it wasn't. I meant to be—I wanted you to help me, I shouldn't be saying ominous shit."

"I want to help you," you say. And then you hesitate.

Wanting something doesn't mean you can actually acquire it. You feel bad for her position. You don't want her to be unhappy. You want to help her. Yet—you don't know that you *can* help her. There are two reasons: the first, that you don't know the extent of the clinical trials that are still in place. The product is near market. It works. All the testing for human viability is complete. The second is that you don't think that allowing Soyoung-Rose into a clinical trial is technically within the bounds of your job. Technically, allowing a friend into a closed clinical trial, if one were to exist, would be corruption. Would be the sort of thing that a reporter—like the guy whose name began with *W*—would be excited to report on. Would be the sort of thing that would get you unceremoniously fired. And you need your job for your visa. For any pathway to citizenship, dual or not.

It's very frustrating. You never really *feel* like you have any power, despite your new big desk and your signature on all the documents. You've inherited the project, but you're not the decision-maker: Everything was in place before you were dropped in. What Drew told you was true: You were here because he didn't like doing interviews. You were trying to get a handle on what was going on, but it mostly meant being copied on email chains fifty messages deep and poking around the public access areas. You haven't been discouraged from looking at the files on twenty-six but you haven't had time to look around.

You're taking too long to answer.

"So you can't help me," Soyoung says.

SOYOUNG-ROSE

"I can't," YJ says. "No, I mean that I can't give you an answer now."

She stares at him. He looks serious. She can tell when Yujin is telling the truth, usually. She thinks YJ is telling the truth. But he and Yujin are, as she needs to keep telling herself, not the same person. Only derived from the same past.

"*Why?*"

No, the wrong word again. Just accept what you're given, Soyoung! Don't ask, because you don't actually want to know, because everything in life that other people want to give you is so uncertain, and you don't want to give them a chance to conclusively say no. She remembers, vividly and suddenly, sitting at the kitchen table in her grandfather's house. Harabeoji on the phone. At the same time, she remembers holding her mom's landline up to her ear, too big for her face. The memories cascade together. Sudden nausea. The desire to hurl.

"It's complicated," YJ says. "I need to see if there's any study still running that I can get you into, first. I want to help, but—"

"No, it's fine," Soyoung says. She tries to keep her voice normal. Shoves down the echo-memory of Harabeoji talking to her and not talking to her simultaneously. Shoves down her desire to ask why YJ can't just tell her yes. "I get it."

"I'm sorry," YJ says. He swirls his water. "I'll let you know."

She wants to ask, *when?* But that feels—she's already pushed him too far tonight. The nausea passes. She swallows. Bites her lip. She imagines how she would work on convincing Yujin. Well—she wouldn't have to convince Yujin—they're friends. He already cares about her. He wouldn't need a reason, their ledger is already full of back-and-forth. What's one more entry?

It's so very weird to be having such a stunted conversation with any version of Yujin. This feels like when Soyoung and Rose met each other. The cautious, neutral statements.

"I really do want to help you," YJ says.

Soyoung frowns. Leans forward.

"Is there anything I can do for you? To change your mind?"

"I don't need anything," YJ says. "Unless you can get me a green card."

"Rose—American Soyoung—is single and an American citizen. If you separate me, I'll marry you," she says. His eyes widen.

Soyoung waves her hand. "Sorry! Bad joke. Bad timing for a bad joke. I don't know why I said that."

She's embarrassed. That came out of nowhere.

"God," YJ says. He rubs his eyes. "It wouldn't help me, anyway."

"Because you want dual citizenship," Soyoung says. "And you won't qualify for that on a spousal visa."

YJ looks up.

"Yujin told you about that?"

Soyoung nods. Yujin had told Soyoung about his and his instance's plans a long time ago. When the instancing had been fresh in Yujin's brain.

"I haven't told anyone about it," YJ says. "Here, I mean."

Soyoung doesn't know much about YJ, other than by proxy. She knows the parts of him that are analogous to the parts of Yujin. He laughs the same. He has the same face, the same mannerisms. He seems a little more subdued than her Yujin, but that might just be that he's wary.

Soyoung feels seized by sudden impulse. Confession booth impulse, stranger on a first date impulse, the sort of thing where it is easy to speak to a wall, rather than to tell your mother about all the things you did in college. The past between Rose and YJ is so unmoored as to be nonexistent, they're constructions of a different country than their shared childhood.

"I can tell you about me and Yujin," Soyoung says. "Everything about what he told me, about you, if that's something you want to know. And I can tell you about how it's been, being reintegrated."

YJ drums his fingers on the table. Soyoung can't read the expression on his face.

"That really won't change my mind, Soyoung."

"No—I don't mean it as a bribe or anything. I just think—he misses you. I figured you missed him."

"He can't miss me, I'm him," Yujin says.

He glances at his phone, before looking at her clear in the eyes.

"But. I would—I would like that. I didn't eat dinner. Do you want to go get French fries or something?"

"Yes," Soyoung says.

▪ ▪ ▪

The first delineation in versions of the legend associated with "Arirang" stems from how the lover acts in the face of the heaving river. Does he decide to cross, or does he decide to stay? Do the lovers sing to one another from across the banks of the Auraji, or does the woman sing a lament after her lover's drowning?

The second delineation is whether the man instances, when he decides to cross the water.

▪ ▪ ▪

They get a second round of drinks before getting fries from the Belgian place with a thousand different sauces. YJ brings over two cones of fries and two little sauce cones. He sits across from her. Steeples his hands. Moves them back. Makes a sort of an aborted, slow-motion clapping gesture that smashes his hands together, before gesturing at her. His hair is plastered to his forehead with sweat.

"So, what's he told you?"

"That you want to reintegrate. That you're eventually applying for citizenship and you've got an H-1B1, but you've put off really pushing forward the process for green card stuff until you're in a good place to get dual citizenship. Is that right?"

"Yes," YJ says. "Why'd he tell you everything?"

"We're friends. He—he didn't tell you about this? He came to me after you instanced. Since I was the only person he knew who had an instance."

YJ frowns at her. Underneath the lights, he looks older. Soyoung supposes they are, that there's a long divide between the kids they used to be and the grown-ups they are now.

"What's the difference between going through all this trouble with Mitosis and just instancing for a second time? Did you instance a second time?

I'd assume you'd instance if you hit any sort of border. I'm kind of surprised you're in New York at all."

She eats a French fry.

"It's not clean," she says. "I want the sort of clean, perfect separation like we can pretend that these last months never happened, with all my memories sectioned off into the right person who needs them. I didn't know how important memory was, to how you moved through the world, how you felt about the people around you. How you move forward in life. Rose and Soyoung . . . they weren't aligned, and it is very hard to be a singular person when you—well. Have you ever gotten everything you wanted and then realized it wasn't what you wanted at all?"

"No," he says.

"Yeah, well. It's like that. If I instance again, without Mitosis . . . I think I change. I don't think I go back to either Soyoung's or Rose's life, like I am now. And they had been—not happy. But they hadn't wanted to change how they felt about the world. They wanted things to stay the same. But it happened. And I want it to not have happened."

She puts her head on the table. She looks out at YJ through half-lidded eyes. He's a blurry shadow against the fluorescent light. He could be anyone, like this.

"So it's bad, and I shouldn't reintegrate," YJ says, and he says it like a joke, in the same cadence that his instance would, if he were afraid.

"No," she says. "It just—it depends on what you want. What do you want, out of reintegration?"

"I want—" he says, before looking down. "I guess I want to preserve as many options as possible. I want to have as much freedom as possible."

"But why do you want this, specifically?"

He frowns. He gestures with a French fry.

"So. It's like—I want to remember being home. Living at home. And Yujin wants to remember ten years of being here. And Yujin wants to skip military service, if he can. And I can't go back without potentially getting flagged for my own military service. Or becoming him and having to do his—ours? And—this way we get everything. All of it."

Soyoung nods. "Yujin wants your life. He wants your life like Soyoung wanted Rose's life."

"Yeah. And I want his. So."

"What do you want about it?"

"It's—I don't know. Seoul's home. And—you know, just, I guess I miss it. I think the worst future I can imagine is that I'm like . . . you know those old guys who instanced when they were young, because it was just way harder to go between countries, who instance a second time when they're older when they go back to Korea? Yeah. That. I'm trying to avoid that. You know?"

"Yeah," Soyoung says again. She looks at the storefront. There's a couple of college students buying French fries. They look young and giggly and as if nothing bad has ever happened to them. Soyoung had more fun in college than Rose did, she remembers. She looks back at YJ.

"The other thing that happened, is my grandfather left me his house, in Korea. He gave me an ultimatum about it. The house was sort of a bribe. He wanted my instances to reintegrate."

"Huh," YJ says.

Soyoung wanted to reintegrate, too, she doesn't say.

"I reintegrated a month ago, give or take. A little more. And I saw you on TV, when they introduced Mitosis. I can't wait for the official release. The timeline doesn't work out. Six months, right?"

"I get it," YJ says.

He drums his fingers against the table.

"I should probably say no," YJ admits. "But I want to say yes. So, I'm saying maybe. I'm saying I'll look into this for you. Is . . . that okay?"

It felt like a smaller favor, when she wasn't sitting in front of him, asking. When he wasn't flesh and blood and he was just the concept of Yujin's instance, rather than the reality of him.

"Yeah, of course. It's fine," she says.

It's not a lie. But she would have preferred that he had just said yes.

YJ

Morning. Probably morning. Sliver of sunlight across your face, your alarm ringing. You scrape yourself up from your couch. You fell asleep there again, you hadn't taken off your work clothes, it tastes like something slithered into your mouth and died. Your back hurts. You stayed out too late.

You had called Petra four times between French fries, more drinks, and going home. You had thought to yourself—three hours between New York and San Francisco, she's probably still awake. You had found yourself telling Soyoung-Rose about the breakup, in between drinks at a worse bar and walking with her to the ACE. You had offered to take the subway with her. She had said no. You had thought about offering to let Soyoung crash at your place, and then remembered your mess, and then reconsidered. It wasn't that you minded her seeing. It was that she would probably tell Yujin about it.

You lift your head and feel immediate regret. You grope around for your phone, squint at the screen and your low battery. Petra didn't call back. If Petra had called you back you would have killed yourself maybe.

Did you get home okay? you text Soyoung. No immediate response. You check the rest of your personal messages. Nothing. Okay. Good.

You think about last night. You had talked more than you had meant to, the same way you've had deep conversations at three in the morning in a stranger's dorm room. It was all stuff you hadn't talked about with anyone else but Soyoung had already known. When you described your relationship with Yujin, she nodded like it was something she had heard before. It had felt simultaneously like she was someone you could talk to because she was so divorced from your life here, and like she had already known you and how you felt about everything. Like slipping into a bath and having it be the perfect temperature. And you had also been happy to listen to her talk. You had forgotten how intense she was, when she spoke. How she was magnetic.

But in the cold light of morning, in the loneliness of your apartment, your brain throws logic at you. Let's say there *was* a clinical trial that Soyoung-Rose could be folded into, that wasn't dangerous, that would give her the clean and perfect unraveling that she craved. And if there was a trial like that, then including Soyoung-Rose in it would be, if not an abuse of your power, a misapplication of it. It doesn't look good. It would be hard to keep secret. The reason for her inclusion would need to be kept out of all the official documentation—it needs to look like an evenhanded decision, nothing with your fingerprints.

And objectively, whatever Soyoung-Rose has gone through is something that doesn't have any connection to your life, she's not your sister or your mother or one of your cousins, she's not Petra or one of your ex-girlfriends, she's not a coworker, and she's not a girl you're trying to score with, she's not anyone who you are obliged to.

But it would be easy to help her. As long as she didn't talk about it. As long as your instance didn't talk about it.

You check the time on your phone. It's past noon, barely. No wonder the sun is at such a high slant. It's been a while since you've seen your place in broad daylight. You stand up. You survey your kingdom. Laundry. Laundry basket. Socks on the floor. Crumpled blazer. Empty bags of chips. Empty energy drink bottles. Bag of recycling you keep meaning to take out and not taking out. Dishes in your sink, dishes piled up next to your sink. Cups. Bowls you started using after you ran out of cups.

You put on a good show everywhere else but in the heart of your heart you sort of feel that this apartment is representative of the state of your soul. You need to clean this thing up. You want to be able to bring people back here. You need to be able to walk through your apartment without stepping on a bag of chips that is nine-tenths empty and one-tenth crumbs. You don't understand why the things that are hard are easy for you and the things that are supposed to be easy are very difficult. If you were a different sort of person, you could live a different sort of life. But you're not. You're just you.

It's midnight in Korea. Yujin will still be awake.

You call him. The phone rings, then he picks up. This time, the background noise is quiet. You can hear him typing. He must be at home. Probably playing a game.

"What's up," Yujin says. He sounds distracted.

"I talked with Soyoung," you say.

The typing stops. "Yeah?"

"Yeah. You should have told me what she was going to ask. It blindsided me."

"Sorry," he says. He uses the casual "miyan" instead of the formal "jesong." "I thought it would be better coming from her than from me."

"It's fine," you say. It's not fine. "But seriously, did you even think about it before sending her to me? I can't just say yes, Yujin."

"Why not? You're in charge of the project, just add her name to a study, get her in there to use the Mitosis machine, pull her two selves out, American Soyoung stays there, Korean Soyoung heads back to Korea."

Every once in a while, you become acutely aware that even though Yujin and you have two decades of the same memories, he doesn't have your context.

"It's not that simple," you say. "I can't just say yes. I don't even know if we're still running any trials. The product's almost to market. And adding her, if I can, to a study, means that *I'm* doing it, means that if anything goes wrong, *I'm* on the hook, means that *you're* on the hook, means that I get fired, lose the H-1B1, and then if I don't get another job, I'm going back to Korea and you're—I'm—doing military service, reintegrating, and okay, I guess we pivot back to doing something in Korea, or maybe we try to do foreign grad school but then, what was the *fucking* point of my last ten years?"

"Are you done?"

You sigh. You're sweating a little, at the temples. "Yeah. I'm done."

"I told you to start the appli—"

"It wouldn't have been as stro—"

"Okay, but you procrasti—"

"I'm doing my best, okay," you snap. "Maybe I was wrong. But we talked about it. This is the best chance we have for the application going through with everything we talked about."

"Fine," he says. "Sure. Yeah. No. I know."

"Why does it matter to you that I help Soyoung?"

He's silent for a moment.

"It matters because she's my closest friend," he says. "Because it'll give her back her life. Lives. And it's an easy thing to give her. I think you're overstating the danger."

"I don't know Soyoung. Do you trust her? To be able to keep things secret, to not talk about what's going on. Like—how can I know I can trust her?"

"I trust her, and you trust me," Yujin says.

He doesn't ask it like a question. He says it like a fact.

"Soyoung's not the sort of person who would try and ruin your life. Besides, we have—what's the word for when you have the ability to stop someone? Because you know something about them? So they can't tell on you?"

"Blackmail."

"Yeah, blackmail. You can blackmail her. Ah, this sounds bad, but she's not supposed to be in the States. She didn't register with—you know. They don't know she reintegrated."

"She's here illegally," you say.

"Yeah," Yujin says. "Maybe don't say that out loud."

■ ■ ■

Citizenship is a piece of paper. It is a few lines of code, a single variable hosted on a computer somewhere. Without citizenship, without borders, some experts have argued, instances would not exist. Other experts argue that borders are the natural shape of the world. The line between the sea and the sand. The curving bend of a river between two cliffs. The imperceptible line dividing the ground from the sky. These natural-border arguments are sometimes a dog-whistle for more specific prejudices, followed by the argument that people weren't meant to leave their original homes. But more often, it's part of an argument for an environmental studies department to get more funding. Artificial or not, the knowledge of existing borders delineates the world. They are a social technology that creates emotional reality, that creates a physical reality.

■ ■ ■

You had just assumed that everything was aboveboard, last night, that everything was clean-legal, Soyoung's paperwork neat-and-tidy. This feels like—border crossing, illegal immigration, coyotes, crossing the Darién Gap, this feels like the world that other people live in that you read about on the front page of Reddit, in interviews in the *New York Times,* articles shared by your more conscientious friends. It alludes to a part of reality that you don't think about that much, despite your immigration status. That's a world completely divorced from yours.

Yujin breaks your concentration.

"Hey, you still there?"

"Yeah."

"I'll talk to her, if you think it's best to say no," he says, conciliatory. "Save you an awkward conversation. I should have told you first. It just felt—"

"Yeah," you say. "I get it."

If one of your friends was in the country illegally, you wouldn't have wanted to talk about it over the phone, either.

"Yeah," he says. "Listen, it's late. I'm going hang up, okay?"

"Sure. 'Night."

He hangs up. You wipe imaginary dirt from your hands. You decide: First you are going to clean up your apartment. Then you'll clean up the rest of your life. You'll figure out how to handle Soyoung. You'll take a look at the trials for her. And then you'll use your best judgment and decide what to do.

This would be a much easier decision if you didn't actually want to help her, but you do.

▪▪▪

During the first six months after you instanced, you and your other self got really into *League of Legends*. It was sort of embarrassing. It was all late nights and early mornings, ruined sleep schedules, you and your other self playing a game that you thought you were too old for.

It's not a good game. Or it is, it's very compelling, but it's not a *good* game. It takes too much time. It's addictive. You knew that playing together was a bad habit, it was narcissistic, it was navel-gazey and both of you had other things to be doing. The thing was, playing a real-time video game with someone with exactly the same brain you possessed was incredible. You didn't have to speak to talk about strategy. There was perfect alignment in what you were thinking. You started winning and made a little bit of money. You started thinking about esports.

You had long conversations while you played. You talked about why there weren't more people who tried to optimize for efficiency with their instances, about how your various classes were going, about the bureaucracy each of you was trying to navigate. You talked about whether you would keep sharing a personal email account, whether it was better for Mom and Dad to be talking to both or one of you. You talked about your future.

And you imagined a world where you had absolute freedom to go wherever you want and still got to keep everything from your past. And you liked that idea, as much as both of you liked skipping the military service, as much as you were grateful that you were the one who left. If you could have everything, you wanted everything. If you could build yourself a future that you wanted to live in, you were happy to do so. So much of your adolescence had been subsumed in the mechanisms of *success*. You could keep going, for another decade. You had your whole life ahead of you.

You had asked yourself: "Do you want to reintegrate, someday?"

And you (the other you) had said, "Yes."

It was nice, in a way. Two in the morning. Computer screen glowing. Imagining a future for yourself. One where the whole world was open to you, and there were no borders. Or, well, two countries, at least. But that was better than one. You don't know why you wanted these things. You just did.

YUJIN

"Have you heard from Soyoung?"

Tae punctuates his question with a kick. The soccer ball goes flying, hits the target set up across the gym wall. It's pouring outside. Sheets of rain thrum against the glass window. The streets are flooded, wind and rain going nearly horizontal. You hate monsoon season. The planned team practice had been canceled, so you had ended up at the indoor gym with Tae and a couple of the other guys.

"What?" you say. You toss another ball in Tae's direction.

"Have you heard from Soyoung," Tae says, bumping the ball a couple of times in the air with his knee before sending it slamming to the net.

You speak before you can think. "Man, she's your fiancé. Has she not called you?"

This was rude. This implied that Soyoung and Tae had problems, which you knew that they did, because Soyoung had implied as much, because Soyoung was gone and not here. Tae was holding onto the fact that she hadn't instanced a second time, when leaving last week. That he saw her singular self as proof of her eventual return to him. You and Tae weren't the sort of friends that talked about feelings. And you had always felt that he didn't dislike you, but you knew that he didn't like the concept of you, as much as he thought you, as a person, were fine. You were Tae's fiancé's friend. His fiancé's male friend. When things were good for them—which was most of the time—until now, it didn't matter.

You would never bring this up with him. It would hurt his pride. If you brought it up, then he might ask why you were thinking these things. He might accuse you of sleeping with her. There would be no good way for you to explain that you wouldn't do that. You didn't mind jerking around people you didn't care about, but like you told your instance, Soyoung is—you like Soyoung. You like Soyoung a lot, actually. Too much to sleep with her. If you slept with her—wow. That's ruined forever. You don't have a lot of friends who are girls.

Soyoung's the only person you really feel like you can talk to, other than your other self. She's—the thing about Soyoung is that she's been really kind to you, as an adult. There's a part of you that's forever going to be the kid who got turned down by her, but you always go back to thinking about the night after you instanced, when she let you fall asleep in her dorm room and helped you avoid your family while you figured out how you wanted to handle things. Soyoung *got* you. You got her. You wanted her to be happy.

And yeah, okay. If Soyoung had been single when you reconnected, you might have asked her out again. But by then she had apparently found the only nice man in all of Seoul, so you gave that up easily as a loss. You didn't want to try *twice,* anyway. That was too much for your pride. You didn't have so many friends that you could lose one. And it kind of helped that your best friend was a girl. It made other girls trust you faster.

"She texted me when she landed," Tae says. "But I was wondering if she had talked to you, because of her plans. Your instance."

"Nope, she hasn't called me," you say. You don't want to tell Tae about your conversation with your instance. That's not his business.

You take a shot yourself. Feint to the left, then kick. Clean corner shot.

"Nice," Tae says.

You never really understood what Soyoung saw in Tae. You didn't really know what women wanted, actually, other than by trial and error. Women wanted a nice guy, except when they wanted a bad boy, except when they wanted you to read their minds.

"Why Tae?" you had once asked Soyoung. This had been soon after you had reconnected. Tae had seemed just—bland. Just some guy.

She had frowned a little, scrunched up her nose.

"It just feels comfortable with him," she had said.

"I don't get it."

"You'll get it when you meet the right girl," she had said, drawing the last two words out all dramatic. You had rolled your eyes at her and thrown a napkin at her, and she had shrieked, and you had laughed.

You pick up the ball, bounce it a couple of times, off your knee, off your elbow. Horsing around. Not getting anywhere. You glance at Tae.

"Why didn't you go with her?"

"She didn't want me to," Tae says. You toss him the ball. He catches it. Tosses it a couple of times in his hand. "She said it might look suspicious."

He puts the ball on the floor. Kicks it, catches it with his foot on the rebound.

"Do you think it'll work? Mitosis?"

"Yeah," you say. As long as your other self helps. You had been so sure, until you had talked with him.

Tae scratches his head.

"It had seemed all on track. Before—I just—" he says, and then sighs. Raises the ball in his hands, slams it into the net like he's trying to destroy the wall behind it. "If she says anything to you, could you tell me?"

"Sure," you say. The storm surges. Your voice is drowned by the rain.

SOYOUNG-ROSE

Soyoung wishes that the public transit in New York didn't smell the way it did. Other than that, the subway is fine. A couple of confused-looking tourists. A few artsy-looking kids laughing about something, and then two guys in sweatshirts who look like they're headed grimly, sleepily toward their jobs.

The subway runs down parallel tracks in Soyoung's head. Her Korean self is fascinated by how each stranger is a different sort of stranger—the way they dress, the slant of their features. There's a different quality of light in these subways. The thought collapses into the feedback loop of schizophrenic memory–not memory, because Rose hadn't thought about the NYC subway in years, but the *Korean* subway had been a totally foreign experience for Rose, so the memory divots itself, crumples inward, foreign delight at *clean subways,* the doors that slide open separating the platform from the train car, the clear white fluorescents, the burst of sky and sunlight when the orange line came out of the tunnel and over the Han River, and this is so *strange,* no it's utterly *familiar,* no, it's not anything that ever—

The train car rattles, and Soyoung unconsciously counterbalances against the force, doubled muscle memory because at the end of the day, standing on a train is standing on a train, the gravitational pull of the earth is 9.8 m/s^2 no matter where you are on the planet. Synchronization. She takes a deep breath of bad-smelling air.

Think about the near-past. Think about the past so close to the present as to become the future. The last seventy-six hours from touching down in the plane. Getting picked up, getting to Rose's apartment, small talk with Clarissa, Dr. Crouton purring and winding around her ankles, unpacking, texting her mother in Korea, texting her mother in America, texting Taehyung, texting the girls and pretending that she's just on an offsite, taking an anti-emetic, checking her work emails, collapsing on the couch, falling asleep dreamless, waking in the middle of the night and not knowing where she was, wishing that she had someone to *talk to* about all of this, falling asleep again, waking up and showering the night sweat off, logging into work remotely, dressing all nice and then—drinks with YJ, French fries, being given a non-answer about whether he would help her or not.

And now: waking up, dressing, the A train, which will connect to the laminate-and-tile hellscape of Port Authority, where she'll board the bus to Fort Lee, where she and her mom will have lunch.

Soyoung pats her tote bag. She can feel the envelope against the fabric. She was worried she would forget. She's recently been very paranoid about forgetting things.

At the top of the A train, the advertisement reads GOING TO THE AIRPORT? AREN'T YOU FORGETTING SOMETHING? And behind the text, there's a pretty white woman with a MERGEBREAK that looks more like a fancy knotted scarf around her wrist, and behind her, a handsome Black man with a MERGEBREAK that looks like a futuristic watchband. Premium options, *expensive* options. Soyoung looks back down and across the subway car.

If YJ doesn't agree to help her, then she guesses she'll go back to Korea. Or would she instance when she hit the immigration terminal at the airport, going back? She hadn't thought about what would happen if YJ didn't help her. She made the same mistake that Soyoung made with Rose—assuming that knowing a version of someone means that she knows every version of them. That Yujin's help would translate into YJ's. Why would he help her? There's no red string of fate between him and her. He cares about Yujin. He doesn't care about her.

She hugs her tote bag to her chest.

▮▮▮

The MERGEBREAK's basic model comes in six different colors, though black is the most common. Victorians used to wear black for mourning. Rose learned that in school: all-black clothing, and then gradually the black was lifted away, inch by inch, seam by seam, until it was just the barest trim. In Korea, in China, in Japan, they wear white. White chrysanthemums on graves. There had been heaps of them in floral arrangements at her grandfather's funeral. They had been kind of beautiful. Like the white spaces on the wall, in her grandfather's house. Her house, now, unless things change.

▮▮▮

Soyoung had been careful to dress like Rose. Rose had been East Coast practical, more Asian American than American: no flourishes, dark colors, muted-to-no makeup. Soyoung had dressed in beiges and the occasional pastel, with a full face of CC cream, eyeliner, blush, eye shadow, lip gloss.

Today she's wearing black pants and a dark blue button-down, a staple of Rose's wardrobe. She doesn't stand out among the other people on the bus. Two-thirds of the people taking it are Korean. Rose's mom had moved closer to the part of the suburb that was very Korean, after Rose had moved out.

Soyoung wonders how many people on this bus are instances. This isn't a new thought; she had been curious about it, as a kid, in the way kids are. There had been a kid from Japan, when she was in elementary school, who everyone called an instance, though he claimed otherwise. When Rose had moved to the United States, it had surprised her, how many of her classmates mentioned that they were instances, or their parents were instances, or one of their aunts or uncles was an instance.

She tugs the cord and gets out at the bus stop. The town looks like Seoul from fifteen years ago, a little—something in the design of the buildings and the signage. It's a transposition of the world that no longer exists. Like Soyoung has time traveled and returned to the Seoul from when she was a teenager. And then she blinks and the world around her returns to being the backdrop of Rose's adolescence, the town is just the town, it's just where she grew up, and it's not Korea. Pay no attention to how half the signs are in hangul, because a quarter are in Spanish, and everything has English subtitling underneath. Nostalgia, no, not nostalgia, just the faint feeling that something is missing from the way she is supposed to feel about this place, as if she is unmoored from the current presence of it.

Soyoung begins walking to the restaurant, the same one that Rose always meets her mother at. If Fort Lee feels like a time capsule to an antiquated Korea, then this restaurant feels like a time capsule to the years before they started putting gochujang in aioli. She goes inside, nods at the server, looks around the room to spot her mom, and there her mother is, sitting at the same spot she always takes.

"Hi, Umma," Soyoung says, and her mom gets up to give her a hug. This is pretty much as maternal as her mom gets. That, and cutting fruit for Rose and bringing it to her when she was studying.

"Hi, Soyoung-ah, it's so good to see you," her mom says, or the approximation of that phrase in Korean.

"Hi," Soyoung says again, and squeezes her mom, and her mom squeezes back, and for a moment everything in Soyoung's brain is suffused with the illusion that everything's going to be okay.

"Soyoung," Rose's mom says, and draws back. Rose's mom puts her hand on Soyoung's face. Tilts it to the left and the right before Soyoung can react, and besides, this is Rose's mother. This is her mom. She looks the same as Rose remembers and different from Soyoung's mom in ways that are hard to articulate, only that it's obvious that this is a different woman from the one who Rose met with, who Soyoung was raised by. The wrinkles on her face are different. Which version of them was happier? Rose's mom has more laugh lines. Both versions of her mom smell the same.

"So, you reintegrated?"

Soyoung whips her head back and out of her mom's grasp.

"How the f—"

Pure Rose, down to the excised expletive. How did she know! Is this what motherhood is? Can she tell from Soyoung's face? Something about her expression? Something she wore? Something ineffable from Soyoung's demeanor, how did Rose, purely herself, carry her weight, how did she move, what were the *differences*?

"Soyoung, I'm your mother," her mom says. "And your aunt told me what happened."

Soyoung sits down. Her face feels very tense.

"You still talk with people in Korea?"

"Sometimes," her mom says, and then nothing else. She sits down.

Soyoung looks down at the paper placemat. Advertisements for Kumon, a dentist. She moves her chopsticks around. Takes a sip of water. Looks back up.

"You wouldn't have been able to tell, otherwise?" she demands. "Just from looking at me?"

"Look, they have a lunch special now."

"Mom," Soyoung says.

Her mom makes a gesture as if she's brushing something away from her.

"I don't know, Soyoung. I think I would have been able to tell. I'm your mom. But I knew already, so."

"Mom," Soyoung says again.

She's thinking about how her mom in Korea had mistaken Rose for her. How she had looked at Rose, until she realized who she was talking to.

She looks at the menu. It's the same menu that this place has had for decades. They haven't changed anything except for the prices, which have been crossed out and handwritten.

"I'm getting the soondubu," Soyoung says. Rose always got the soondubu. Soyoung hadn't had a standard Korean restaurant order. Her mom is still looking at her. Soyoung doesn't like it. Her mom frowns.

"Are you doing okay, Soyoung-ah?"

The packet in Soyoung's bag feels like a physical manifestation of a lump in her throat. Like if she unwraps the package the entirety of Harabeoji's house will unfold in the space around them and they will be sitting there again and she will be ten years old and her mother and grandfather will be shouting at each other across the kitchen table.

"Why did we move to the States?"

Rose's mom looks surprised.

"You know, because of my work. You know."

Oh sure, work. The new job that her mom had gotten, a month before their move. They had talked about it, in the sense that her mom had talked about it at Rose, because her mother had always prided herself on being blunt with the facts. *Soyoung, your father left us. Soyoung, I got a new job in the States. Soyoung, we're moving to New Jersey, yes, this is where it is on a map.* But there were never any explanations. The world was described matter-of-factly and the rest of it was left to imagination.

"No, I mean, why'd you get the new job? Why'd you want to come to the States? Why were you and Harabeoji fighting so much about it, the entire time? Like—Mom, come on. What were you thinking?"

Neither Soyoung nor Rose had ever asked that question before, to either version of their mothers. Soyoung had never thought about it much. But Rose had. Rose had sat in sixth grade English class and only been able to read two-thirds of the words on the worksheet. Rose had been asked where she was from and told them New Jersey and it had never been the answer that anyone wanted. Rose had needed to make new friends, had needed to learn the social dynamics of American middle school and there had been a lot of weird, lonely moments, when she had felt like a little alien, or that she was surrounded by aliens.

Soyoung gestures at herself, as if to encompass her entire existence.

"That was, like, you get that was my entire life, right, Mom?"

"Soyoung," her mom says.

"*Umma.* Harabeoji gave me his house," she says, taking the envelope out of her bag.

Her mom looks small and old and alarmed and Soyoung doesn't care.

"He gave me his *house. Me.* Rose, or her reintegration. Not Soyoung alone, not your other self."

She shakes the envelope and spreads the deed to the house on top of the Kumon advertisements. She pushes it toward her mother like it's a dead piece of meat. Rose's mom picks it up.

"Soyoung, what do you want me to do?"

"Why would he do that?" Soyoung asks. "Give me the house, I mean. The way he did."

"You would know better than I do, Soyoung. I haven't talked to him since we moved."

"You're literally his daughter, Mom. You're deflecting. That's deflecting. Is he, like—what was the point of this? He didn't leave it to Soyoung. He left it to Rose, and he told Soyoung to reintegrate. What—why—"

She doesn't know the question she wants to ask other than in the vague thrust of the emotion, and she's surprised to care at all about this.

"Soyoung, he's dead. I haven't talked to him since I left. I can't know what he meant by giving you this."

Rose's mother looks so bleakly sad that Soyoung wishes she hadn't gone down this line of questioning, except for the parts of her that want to twist the knife, to ask every cruel question, to uncover every stone, to find the cracks in her mom's façade that will lead to answers if bashed open with a linguistic knife. She is thinking about standing in the forest next to her grandparents' graves, she is thinking about Rose's face in her perfect blank surprise, Soyoung's face and her set mouth, how it felt to be behind these faces, how it was like she wanted to hammer a response out of her other self, how she wanted honesty, how she didn't want to turn into her mother.

"Why didn't you go to the funeral?" Soyoung says, and her mother's expression is so blank and surprised that the emotion underpinning it can only be anger, but then the waitress steps up to their table and asks, in perfect, accentless Korean, what they would like to order.

■ ■ ■

A popular horror-gore story told by labor and delivery nurses is that of the fetus that instances when it drops out of the mother's womb, leaving a copy stillborn inside. There is no record of this ever happening, but that doesn't stop trainee nurses from discussing the possibility. They discuss other horror stories too: twins who turn out to be instances, babies and toddlers who instance when getting on a plane. International adoption agencies prefer to adopt out babies under the age of two, to conclusively prevent an instantiation event. When the children are older, adoption staff are instructed to lie to the toddlers, and promise that the children are going to return. That they are just going on a little trip. That this leave-taking is not permanent. This usually works because children don't know anything about borders, permanence, or death.

■ ■ ■

"Can I get the soondubu?" Soyoung says to the waitress.

"And the galbitang," Rose's mom adds as the waitress scribbles down their orders and leaves. Rose's mom folds her hands over each other.

"Rose, why did you go to the funeral? You never cared."

"I did care," Soyoung says, speaking before she can think, while in the back of her head she's doubled, the version of herself watching the conversation happen—this is not how Rose would respond, Rose would have said this viciously, Rose would have felt like this was an attack and would have attacked wildly, ineffectively, but the version of Soyoung that exists now, integrated, plural-turned-singular, has every impulse and no filter. Right now, it feels like a superpower. The version of her mother here is only a version of her mother. When it doesn't matter, you can ask.

"Look, answer my question. Why'd we move here? Why were you guys fighting? Why'd he want me to reintegrate?"

"Why didn't you ask your other mother about any of this? Ask her!" Rose's mom says, her face contorting. Some sort of pain, Soyoung thinks, as if from very far away. Rose's mom keeps speaking.

"We could have gone back. I could have taken you back, at any point. I could have apologized to my father and you could have gone back to school in Korea and we could have been back, like it never happened at all, other than the memories. Okay? Is that what you want to hear, Soyoung? Is that what you want me to say? I'm sorry, Soyoung. All Umma's fault, okay?"

Soyoung stands. She puts her hands on the table.

"Yeah, it is! Yeah, this one's on you! This one's *actually* you, Mom!"

"Why didn't you just go back, then! You're an adult, Kang Soyoung! You could *leave*! Anytime before now! So go!"

"I won't," Soyoung says, almost shouts, too loud for the restaurant, and she's still standing, because it feels like it'll make her point stronger, and really, she's just angry. She's just suddenly so angry. "I'm not leaving. I didn't want to leave the first time, and you can't make me now!"

"You didn't instance this time, coming back to the States," Rose's mom says, and all the wind is knocked out of Soyoung's sails.

She sits back down.

∎∎∎

When Rose had been a kid and they had moved to the States, it had just been Rose and her mom and the apartment. The apartment had been fine. It had been different than Harabeoji's house in Korea, but not worse. There were no heated floors. The kitchen had a gas stove instead of an induction burner.

Rose had just finished elementary school, or at least, she had gotten through the first half of her last year. The semesters in America finished at the beginning of summer, while the semesters in Korea finished at the beginning of winter. She was leaving half-done. But it was better to start at the beginning of sixth grade, it was what the adults had decided. So that was when they had moved. It had all been okay. She doesn't remember how her mother took it.

∎∎∎

"Soyoung," her mother says. "You didn't instance when you left Korea, this time."

"No," Soyoung says.

"So you're not staying," her mom says. "You don't want to stay."

Not a question, a statement. If Soyoung hasn't instanced when returning to America, then that means that she has no intention of being American. It means that this version of her is a temporary visitor in this country.

"Mom," Soyoung says, a little helplessly. The same pathetic way Rose always talked to her mom, and the same pathetic way that Soyoung always talked to her mom.

"I'm sorry I raised my voice," Rose's mom says.

Soyoung wants to tell her mom everything about her plan. That she wants to disentangle herself, that Rose would stay. She wants to tell her mother that she is very fortunate, despite everything, because she has the opportunity to reverse her reintegration, as long as a version of her childhood friend agrees to let her use the Mitosis machine. She wants to tell her mom about how she's worried that YJ won't help her. She wants to talk to a version of her mother who would be receptive to Soyoung's concerns. She wants to reassure her mother, which is an odd feeling.

"Mom, it's fine," she says. "I'm going to fix everything."

"Soyoung," her mom says. "There's nothing to fix. You just have to live with your choices."

"No, you don't," Soyoung says, because talking with her mother makes her feel about eleven years old, all the time. "Let's just eat. I'm sorry."

■ ■ ■

Intention is cheap. Intention has people making proposals they don't mean, intention has kids declaring majors to make their parents happy, intention has people gambling their entire fortunes on individual stocks and losing every single cent they own. Intention has fathers going out for milk and then never returning. Intention has people leaving and returning and leaving and returning and intention has women turning into people who they do not understand.

■ ■ ■

The food comes out. They eat. They talk about easy things. They talk about her mother's friends and the new television drama that they had both been watching. They don't talk about the future. Soyoung's soondubu tastes different than she remembers from Rose's recollection but she doesn't say anything about it.

They finish eating. Soyoung tries to pay but Rose's mom doesn't let her get the bill. Soyoung hugs Rose's mom goodbye.

She walks back to the bus stop. She checks the messages on Rose's phone. Social media app notifications, work emails, an old message from YJ.

You get home ok?

Yeah, Soyoung texts back.

Little dots. Pause. More little dots.

Okay, good

No yes or no. She runs her hand through her hair. At least she's used to waiting.

YJ

You pretend you're not watching the hallway from your glass-walled office. You pretend to be looking at important documents on your computer that have important words on them that you need to examine in great detail, but really, you're watching your coworkers' icons turn yellow in the NY-OFFICE Slack channel, and then occasionally glancing up to see them physically walk past.

A couple of them wave at you. You wave back. Stacey pokes her head in.

"Still working?"

"Still working," you lie.

"You're going to end up like Doug if you keep staying this late," she says, which makes you smile.

"I already instanced once, and I take my laptop home to work."

"Just watch out," she says and walks away.

More of your colleagues walk past. It's late now, dark outside, though the world is still half lit by the little boxes of light from the office building across the street. You putz with your mouse.

Your plan is to go down to twenty-six with your redacted Excel sheet of clinical trials and dates and pick through the paper records and the files that are kept in isolation, since you've exhausted the limits of what's been shared with you on the public network and what you've learned from talking to the people who you're nominally managing. You say "nominally," because you didn't really need to do much managing. You had run interviews with all your new direct reports. Half of them were existing colleagues. The other half were being integrated in from Condensco, and all of them were already diligently working on various silos of the Mitosis project. Their research spanned handfuls of disciplines: biology, technology, physics, philosophy. There's one guy whose degree was in *comparative mythology,* of all things.

As you should have expected, the Mitosis project didn't just revolve around the single reintegration-reversal product. There were other technologies being tested under the project's umbrella, even though they were seemingly unrelated to the core Mitosis product. There were studies on miniaturization technologies, tests on novel polymers. Studies into the wavelengths of the harmonic resonances and how they affected the body. Yet, every person talked about their part of the project in a one-track silo. There was no cross-pollination between them.

This was a little odd—Mergebreak was an established tech company. Condensco had been a relatively mature start-up. You had floated around this space for long enough to know that the culture here was inherently collaborative. Once you were on the same team within the same superstructure, you'd end up discussing the project—at happy hours, during coffee breaks, while you were going for a quick walk around the office to clear your head. At the levels people were at here, there was no turning off their brains. But there was no reference to each other's projects. No word on how their silos were related. Your best guess was that this was related to the fact that the project was still tightly under wraps while Mergebreak tried to preserve their advantage in the market.

That wouldn't have surprised you—Mergebreak had one of the largest private repositories of instancing research, second to the instanCenter at Stanford. But the MERGEBREAK, and the principles behind the MERGEBREAK and the causal principles behind reintegration and instantiation were common knowledge by now. Instancing was about desire—psychology. Reintegration is about physical reality—physics. With reintegration, the current research indicates that on the operative level the truth of physical reality overwrites the subjective experiences of the instanced individuals. The metaphor that is used in all the textbooks is that each instance is a waveform that collapses into each other through a pure failure mode in a particular harmonic resonance frequency.

The MERGEBREAK worked by disrupting the resonance through a series of proprietary technologies that reverberate through a mirrored novel polymer that the cuff is made out of, which is powered by microcharges harnessed from the user's latent bioelectricity. Paired MERGEBREAK bands effectively prevented the two instances, on a material level, from recognizing each other as the same object in space.

It's the killer app. Variants of MERGEBREAK have included discreet jewelry, scarves, a couple of exploratory attempts at belts. Research had shown that MERGEBREAKs were partially effective through their psychological effect, which compounded the resonance disruption: a more visible MERGEBREAK had a lower failure rate. Belts were too inconspicuous, unless they were ugly (according to focus groups). There were ancillary technologies, as well: trackers that both instances could wear to see each other's GPS location (banned in several countries), discreet buttons that would tell someone whether their instance was in range. But Mergebreak never managed to make anything that prevented instancing in the first place, or something that could definitively tell if a person would instance, prior to the event itself. *That* would have been useful, just speaking from experience. And sure, Mitosis was a revolutionary new product. But it also had a smaller market than MERGEBREAK did. The marketing revolved around the *LAST 5 PERCENT.*

It was unclear how the company was going to make a profit on this. They might sell access to Mitosis like insurance. Or it would be marketed as a psychological security thing to help sell more MERGEBREAKs. Except that MERGEBREAKs sold regardless, because anyone who needed a MERGEBREAK would buy a MERGEBREAK. So who was Mitosis for? Were the edge-case scenarios worth the development budget? Your mind wandered to the babies who were born with esoteric genetic defects that needed gene therapy, which no drug company was interested in developing a treatment for because it would be prohibitively expensive and there was no market other than a few sick kids. Mitosis was like that. Who needed to be unwound? Soyoung Kang. Just a few regretful adults. It was a niche product. It didn't make sense to develop, other than as foundational research that might eventually lead to something more interesting.

But that was all upstream musing from your actual search. There wasn't much on the public network, just a lot of redirects to things like "see file-number-whatever in restricted network," or "trial complete." And most of the clinical trials had been finished, since the product had been announced as human-safe. But there were still some research studies that seemed like they were recruiting test subjects, and maybe one of them would do the job. Hypothetically. If you still wanted to help Soyoung.

So you were going down, after hours, to twenty-six, just to to look around a little. You thought that going late might prevent any discussion of what you were checking on. Not that it was suspicious. Going down there was within the purview of your job. You were just self-conscious.

Finally, the corridor empties. You get up. You flash your keycard at the elevator before proceeding down the dark hallway. The overhead lights flicker on as you activate the motion sensors. You don't shiver—you've been at the office late enough times that you've gotten over your fear response at the emptiness. You don't think about Doug—you hated that urban legend. There are no cameras on twenty-six. The research inside is so proprietary that cameras were deemed a security risk. Only about ten employees have access, and most of them are Condensco hires.

You punch in the door code to the laboratory and go in. Manila envelopes in boxes, machines in bubble wrap. Unplugged monitors, machinery that was still branded with Condensco. Sharpie-markered masking tape. Soldering irons. Boxes of MERGEBREAKS in various colors and in various states of construction.

In the middle of the lab, there's a set of steel-looking bars that are set at parallels in the floor. The test version of the Mitosis machine, reminiscent of a guillotine. The clean steel lines of the gate hid an insanely complicated piece of technology. In front of you now, the machine looks like an inert piece of metal. Surprisingly delicate, with seams where it could be taken apart.

You had watched video interviews taken after the Mitosis machine was tested, where each instance was asked questions about their life. Each instance of the subject had seemed scattered. Like a lobotomy, you had thought. Even separate from the logistical issues that helping Soyoung might cause for you, you didn't want her to end up in a trial that had her looking at that.

You poke around at the main computer terminal, attached to a black-box server severed from the rest of the network. You click through file trees. You skim documents. There are nine-hundred-page-long technical specifics and research papers and Excel files. You cross-reference against your notes on the existing trials. You keep glancing at your watch, watching the minutes tick by. It's getting late. Your eyes hurt.

But you find your target: documentation on a research study that included a final separation of the subject. It would start within two weeks. There's an Excel file of subject names, contact information. You scan the list. Soyoung wouldn't be out of place here.

Now it's just a question of whether you should add her. You rub your eyes, you look away from the terminal. You don't want to think about this while sitting here.

You get up. You turn the computer off. When you get back to your floor to pick up your bag, you glance at the security camera in the corner of the hallway. You don't think this was particularly suspicious, but you don't know. Maybe you shouldn't have done this. But you felt like—well. You checked for her. It still doesn't mean that you'll say yes.

YUJIN

Your doorbell rings, but you're not paying any attention. You aren't expecting any visitors—your friends and coworkers don't usually visit you at home, you meet them outside, in cafes and bars and places where your mother isn't around. You hear her get the door.

"Ah, wrong apart—" you hear your mom say in her accented English. You swivel in your chair. You open your door and peek out into the hallway. The front door is open, and you can see the faintest silhouette of a woman's body. You can't tell anything about them—probably a delivery person, or a lost foreigner.

Then the stranger speaks, in clear American English.

"I'm sorry, does Yujin Lee live here?"

You get up, walk out of your bedroom.

"Hi," you say, in English. "Who am I speaking with?"

"Yujin-ah, who is this?" your mom says, in Korean, ceding the door to you.

"I think this is one of YJ's friends," you say in Korean, even though you have no idea if this is true. Your primary thought right now is that you want to get this woman away from your mother, before she starts asking questions. If this is YJ's mess that you're cleaning up, you don't need your mom getting in your business.

The woman looks at you at first as if your face is familiar, and then her expression shifts to something more guarded. She smiles like she's trying to be reassuring but landing on concerned.

She's an ordinary-looking woman, you think, other than the fact that she's a foreigner, and you can't place a name to the face. She's definitely not Korean. She's wearing professional clothing. She doesn't look like she's slept.

She does a shallow, unpracticed bow, like she's heard this is the thing to do but hasn't internalized the motion in her body. You dip your head.

"Hi, Yujin? You don't know me, but your instance does. I'm Megan. I worked with your instance. It's very nice to meet you."

"Hi," you say, again. "Can I help you?"

"I don't mean to intrude. Is there somewhere we can talk?"

You don't want to do this in the living room, where your mom will be eavesdropping from the kitchen, where she'll bring tea and ask questions. You don't want to take her back to your room—who is this woman? What will she learn about you, if you bring her back to your bedroom? Would it be bad for you to be in public with her? Why didn't YJ tell you that she would be visiting? Does he not know?

"We'll go talk in the hallway," you say, and lead her outside.

∎ ∎ ∎

Some international students at wealthy international schools are deliberately coached to adopt a specific sort of feeling toward the country where they attend school. They're pushed toward emotional statelessness, a feeling that they don't belong in anything so gauche as a country, or a deliberate emotional closeness, a patriotism, because their families believe that an instance would be professionally or politically useful. The kids aren't told anything, of course, although they might suspect. The knowledge would alter the shape of the feeling in their heart. It might tilt the scales in one direction or another.

∎ ∎ ∎

Megan looks around the corridor like she's never seen an apartment complex before. You guess they don't have these sorts of buildings in the United States, or at least you hadn't seen them in New York. YJ has told you about traveling out to the suburbs and it being like the countryside, except without the rolling mountains and rice paddies.

"So, who are you?" you say without any softening. You don't know how to be polite in this situation, much less in a language you don't speak regularly. She knows more about you than you know about her.

"I used to be YJ's boss," Megan says. "He has his parents' address listed as his personal contact."

You look at her, as if looking at her would change her face, drag it into familiarity. It doesn't.

"What are you doing here?"

"I'm here because I wanted to talk to you. You're close with your instance, right? You'll pass on a message? Can you get him some stuff from me?"

"Why didn't you just talk with him?"

She makes a face. She crosses her arms.

"Because I have fundamental disagreements with how Drew is handling this, and I think YJ should know what's going on. I think Drew's treating your instance like you're stupid, and I think he thought I was too hard to control so he's overcorrecting in the other direction. I expected Drew to kind of minionize your instance, but I hadn't expected him to put you on PR duty without the whole picture. That's fucked of him. And I expected your instance to come talk to me. I referred you because it would be *good* for you, not because you'd be easier to push around. And I kind of feel responsible for putting you in the situation. Sorry. I don't mean you. I mean him. But you get me?"

Your words fail you. It's been a while since you've spoken English with anyone who isn't your other self, and you're feeling a sort of awkwardness. You understand the words in order, but the details escape you. You get the general gist of what she's saying but she's rambling and using casual turns of phrase too quickly. What does "minionize" mean? You wish you were fluent.

"Say that again, please?"

Her face falls. She uncrosses her arms, rubs her eyes with her hand.

"I don't know why I didn't think about the language barrier," she says.

"I speak English," you say. "Most people here speak a little English at least. You're just talking with a lot of—"

What's the English word for "figures of speech"? You don't know. She looks confused. You're trying not to let the frustration show on your face.

"Should I just call YJ for you?"

"No," she says, sharply. "I don't want anyone to pull any phone records, if it comes to that."

"Is it something serious?"

Megan scratches her arm, and then abruptly moves to swing her backpack down. She looks away from you, and opens the bag. She plunges her hand inside.

"It's a little serious," she says. "But it's nothing that bad. I'm sorry. I'm making this all sound worse than it is."

You feel as if you have been thrust into some sort of bad spy novel. You think you've seen this exact same storyline in the web serial you're reading, where the spy shadows the main character's instance and intercepts them in a grimy alleyway, kicking off the plot where the bad guys start chasing the instance. You are the instance, in this scenario. You wonder if you should have just had the conversation somewhere that wasn't outside. Your mind conjures visions of a sniper rifle, buildings away, centering the red dot on your forehead.

"Doesn't it look bad that you're talking to me now?"

"I don't think anyone's really paying attention. And this is a layover, anyway. I'm going to Japan next. Vacation. Funemployment before I start work, you know?"

You nod, though you're not completely sure what she means by "funemployment."

She pulls something out of the backpack and holds it out to you. It's a small pink USB drive. It looks like the sort of thing a high school girl would use to hold her homework.

"Um. Can you please give him this, somehow? Mail it to him? It's encrypted as well. The password to access it is 876212."

You don't know if you want to say yes. Is this your problem? This has to be your problem. You are YJ. He is you. You wish she had gotten to you when Soyoung was still here. Then you could have handed Soyoung the USB drive. It could have been so much easier. You're not sure how you're going to get this over to YJ now.

"Sure," you say. You take the USB drive from Megan. You put it in your pocket.

YJ

You're playing *Minesweeper* when your phone rings. You startle. You misclick and all the bombs go off. You pick up the phone, and Drew's voice comes tinnily across the speaker.

"Hey, you busy?"

He sounds fresh, like he just woke up.

"No—hey, where are you calling from?"

It's 7:14 PM on the East Coast. The last you heard, Drew had been somewhere in Europe or Asia. You wonder how screwed up his sleep schedule is.

"Rome. But—insomnia, you know. You still at the office? I thought I'd have to call your cell."

"Got a date later," you lie. It's not a date. It's meeting Soyoung, but it's just easier to say that it's a date. This is why you're still at the office—you figured you'd meet her somewhere public to talk about things. To let her down easy. You didn't want to pawn this off on Yujin; you felt that this deserved an actual conversation.

"Fun, who's the girl?"

"Just someone I went to school with. Moved to the States, we reconnected a while ago."

"Cool. Very cool," Drew says.

"Yeah," you say.

If you hadn't been caught off guard, you'd be better at the small talk. You don't have a lot to say to Drew that isn't either platitudes or the sort of question that's too deep to plunge into in the middle of the office.

"So, nothing crazy. Just noticed that you'd tapped into twenty-six."

"Yeah?" you say slowly. "Are you checking my—are you checking my keycard logs?"

"What, no! That'd be crazy. Like *1984* or something. No, I just get a log of everyone who's tapping into twenty-six. Just saw you punch into the lab for the first time."

Your shoulders are suddenly very tense. You realize you're clenching your teeth tight enough to hurt your jaw.

"And?"

"I'd appreciate if you didn't do that again for a bit," he says. "Sorry. But the technical stuff shouldn't affect your day-to-day, anyway."

You take a deep breath. Your jaw hurts.

"Drew. You put me in charge of the project. Yes, I'm just following the plan that was previously given to me, and realistically, I understand this, I get what my role is here, but in *practice,* this all feels a little like I'm being shafted. Like—"

"No, man, I get it! Look, we gotta get some red tape sorted. I don't want to go into it over the phone, but there's a couple of issues because you're not a citizen, and because you're an instance. Nothing insane, just—it'll take a minute. So if you don't mind staying out of the sensitive stuff for a bit, like, the lab stuff, it'd be good."

"Drew—"

"Just a couple months, nothing that affects things for you, honestly."

"You couldn't have mentioned this when you promoted m—"

"Honest to god, I thought it was red tape that we'd cut through faster," Drew says.

"What sort of red tape is this?" you say.

He's silent for a moment. You frown.

"Do we have a government contract for Mitosis? Is that why?"

It was the first thing that jumped to mind. Why would something be barred from your view, too sensitive for you, if it wasn't something government? If it was just private industry, then there would be no reason to bar you, unless Drew was trying to mess with you for some reason. And if he was trying to mess with you—well, you couldn't do anything about it. He's your boss.

"Jesus, I love and hate it when the people I'm working with are smart. Look, if this was something government, I wouldn't be telling you about it over the phone. You're here on an H-1B1, yeah?"

You nearly bite through your cheek. You try to take the most surreptitious deep breath possible.

"I don't think this is an appropriate topic of conversation."

"No, hey, no. Another thing I was going to bring up, since we're talking. Look, we can get the lawyers to fast-track your citizenship stuff. Whatever arrangement you want. I know that it usually takes a hot minute."

He says it so easily. Like he's not dangling the carrot in front of you: a bribe to get you to shut up. Like it's a simple thing to give, and a normal thing to offer.

■ ■ ■

For a long time, you had been bitterly, embarrassingly desirous, throat-clenchingly greedy, almost lustful, over Yujin's memories. It had been the worst, the first six months. Whenever Yujin talked about your Korean friends, or what he was doing with your parents, or—sometimes the craving would hit at the strangest, most offhand moments. When he said something about getting Baskin-Robbins. When he mentioned going to noraebang. When he said your mom was thinking about getting a new couch. It was never anything that had made sense. But god, you had wanted his memories. You still want them, sometimes. But you don't miss it. You've learned to hold your desires in and sharpen them to a narrow point.

■ ■ ■

"I'd appreciate it," you say, heart in your mouth, trying to keep your voice level. "I've been angling for dual citizenship, if possible."

"Sure," he says. "Alright. I gotta get some sleep. Appreciate if you could keep my request in mind. Good luck on your date."

"Thanks," you say, and hope that it doesn't sound too hollow.

He hangs up.

You rub the space between your eyes. What was that interaction? Why did he offer you citizenship, unprompted? It was only tangentially related. You don't like that he can play with your emotions like this, that your future is something that is so easy for him to give that he can dangle it casually in this conversation, that he thinks you can be bribed. You're angry that you *can* be bribed. You're angry, for the same reason you have been angry your entire adult life. But you need this. You need this more than you need answers. Every job you've had has just been a means to an end.

You look at the glass walls and the faint sight of Manhattan beyond. Your reflection stares back. You imagine Yujin, sitting there. You imagine Yujin no longer existing. You rub your eyes again. You text Megan. Politely. Just a *hey, wanted to talk to you about the promotion, if you're free? Sorry to keep following up.*

You wish you could still have rolled up to Megan's office and said, *Megan, do you want to go get a coffee*? And she would have said, *outside or inside*? And you would have said, *outside*. And then you could have gone across the street and asked all your questions, in a non-work location, where your fucking *keylogs* weren't being tracked.

You think for a moment. Then, before you can overthink it further, you scroll to your messages with Soyoung, and ask her to meet you at your apartment instead. She texts you back quickly: *No problem.*

You text her your address and shove your phone into your pocket. You stand up. You're going home to clean your place up. You have a not-date.

▪▪▪

Instancing has historically affected populations bimodally, at least in settled societies that are not organized around migration. The lowest rungs of society in settled populations are the most likely to be transient against their will—either herded by the higher rungs or fleeing an adverse condition or sold into slavery or slavery-equivalents. The highest rungs of society, in contrast, are mobile, as they control the resources necessary for travel. In the past, kings and queens marry their offspring off for alliances. In the present, the global elite send their children to international schools in Switzerland.

In short, if you're worried about instancing, you have been born either very lucky or very very unlucky.

SOYOUNG-ROSE

Soyoung brings dinner with her. It had seemed like a better idea when she had placed the order, less of a good idea when she had to carry a paper bag full of steaming packages four blocks to YJ's apartment building. It's nicer than the apartment that Yujin lives in with his parents.

The doorman gives Soyoung a side-eye. She raises the bag a bit. "Delivery for apartment 14F."

"Sure, go ahead," the doorman says.

YJ must have told them to let food deliveries up. Rose had lived in buildings where she'd told them that—YJ must order out a lot. Rose had ordered out a lot. Thinking about how they're similar is better than thinking about what YJ is going to tell her. She's trying not to read the tea leaves, but it's hard not to speculate. Does moving their conversation to his apartment indicate that he's more or less likely to help her?

"Thanks," Soyoung says, and goes over to the elevator bank.

▪▪▪

There are approximately thirty-six thousand variations of "Arirang," which have in turn been derived from sixty versions of the song. The refrain stays the same between versions—the plaintive, *Arirang, Arirang* verse being included in every rendition.

▪▪▪

Soyoung knocks on YJ's door. It opens just a crack, and YJ's face peeks out.

"Hey," he says.

Soyoung can't help but feel the ball of nervous tension in her stomach when she looks at him. So much hinges on his approval. He looks tired, serious, stoic. She can't read disapproval or approval in his face, she can't tell whether he's going to lean one way or another. She thinks she should be able to: His other self is her friend. She holds out the takeout.

"Hi. I know it's not a social call, but I brought din—"

"Let's go to the roof," he blurts out. "My place is a mess. You shouldn't see that."

And the image of him as collected, as someone in charge of her future, collapses. He's just a man now. She can talk to him. He's someone she can understand. Someone whose mind can be changed.

"Sure," she says.

▪ ▪ ▪

The plethora of "Arirang" compositions raises the question: How much can a single song change, before turning into something different? What single thread needs to be kept identical for versions of a song to remain interchangeable, for a person to hear one version and remember the other?

YJ

You take the bag from Soyoung because it feels like the polite thing to do before walking with her over to the stairwell. You're nervous.

"Is this a bribe?"

"Only if a bribe would work," she says, which startles you into laughter.

"I'm not going to say no to free food," you say.

It's only two floors up to the roof from your apartment, and the elevator doesn't go all the way. You start climbing the stairs. You pause to see if she's following. She is. She looks at you with clear eyes. She doesn't look nervous at all—if it was you in her position, you would have been so very nervous.

"Is this from Sun Palace?"

"Yeah. If I'm being real—I brought food because I wanted an excuse to go there."

"Did you get the dan dan noodles?"

You unlock the door to the roof and walk out. Dim late-summer sunset. Other rooftops, windows into other apartments. There are tables and chairs and though it might be a nice place to hang out, you mostly only came up here to smoke weed. Sometimes you came up with Petra, to drink a glass of wine. Get some fresh air and talk a little after spending a few hours tapping on your computers.

It's a nice view. Not like the view from the Mergebreak offices, but pretty good.

"Of course," Soyoung says, walking past you and putting the bag on the table. She has nice hands. You've been trying really hard to not notice how nice she looks in general, but she has nice hands and it's just a thought you have that doesn't need to mean anything.

"I should come up here more. But I always forget. I always want to do things, and then—where's the time? I always feel like I'm wasting New York."

"Ha—that's sort of what Soyoung thought about Seoul, too."

You lean against the table. You open the plastic takeout containers. You realize that you're stalling for time with Soyoung. The food smells wonderful. You realize you're also starving.

"You really shouldn't have."

"I have two full-time jobs, I can afford to buy you dinner," she says.

You frown.

"How's that working out?"

You hadn't thought about the logistics of her situation before. If she hasn't told anyone what has happened, then she's responsible for two lives—two jobs, presumably, two sets of friends, family, two different schedules and worlds and time zones.

"It's going okay," she says. "I couldn't keep this up for longer than a few months, but it's doable for now. I think it's going to start being obvious what's happening after that, but—you can get a lot done by just telling people you're sad, or traveling, or by posting photographs online of you doing things. Mostly people are busy with their own lives."

She picks up a fork, rips the plastic. Takes the noodles. If you didn't know she was reintegrated, there would be no way to tell. She furrows her brow.

You make a sort of apologetic gesture. You hadn't meant to be caught staring. You feel like you're stalling for time, because you are, but you also feel—depending on how the next conversation goes, you might not have the chance to talk with her again. She might no longer want to talk with you. The thought of that makes you kind of sad. You want to keep talking with her.

"If you don't mind me asking, how does it . . . How do I word this? How does it . . . What is the feeling of remembering like?"

▪ ▪ ▪

You had taken a class on diaspora, in college. You had thought that as an instance, as a first-generation maybe immigrant, you could get an easy A. You could write some bullshit about how you felt alienation from the culture around you in ways that were indescribable.

Did you feel alienation from the culture around you? You remembered being a kid, and being picked last in soccer games. You remembered getting yelled at by your mom and your dad silently looking on. You remembered standing in the middle of a crowded bus in Seoul and getting a breakup text.

You didn't know that the feeling of landing in JFK was qualitatively different from that.

You had written a lot of nothing, for that class. But the interviews stayed with you. You remember watching the old interviews of instances while sitting in a very uncomfortable plastic desk chair and then going back to your dorm room and comparing their reactions against the way you felt.

▪▪▪

Soyoung frowns. She puts the noodles down. Drums her fingers against the table. Her gaze pinned to the skyline. Her profile is almost flat, just the sharp and elegant plane of her cheek.

"It's like it happened twice, and they're both real."

She shakes her head.

"No, that's not helpful for you. It's more like you have twice the amount of data in your brain, but you don't really get the context. Or when you do get the context, it's the wrong context. Like, hm. Okay. Soyoung had never been to New York, right?"

"Sure."

"She'd never been to the States at all. But she had wanted—well, she wanted a lot of things, but one of those things was to have everything that Rose had. All of her life. So she's bringing this crazy perspective of, almost a sort of *wonder,* to the way she sees New York. And it's so fucking infuriating as a filter on the way I see the world, because I can't deal with wonder. I've lived here for *years.*"

"So it makes it obvious you're not from—"

"Not even that, it's just—there's a mental gap. Like a glitch between what I know and what I also know. It's—you'll get it, when you reintegrate."

"Sure," you say, again.

"What's that tone?"

"Nothing."

A jolt of surprise somewhere in your neurons that she was able to read the apprehension in your voice so easily.

"Your birthday's soon, right?" she says. "Yujin was worried about—"

"Military service. I know."

The sword of Damocles that hangs over your other self's head. You know.

Three years of your life. His life. You know. *You know.* You have been thinking about this all day. It had been the malicious undercurrent to the conversation with Drew. You have been thinking about this for the last ten years of your life.

Soyoung smiles faintly, apologetically.

"I'm sorry, I shouldn't needle. We already talked about this, anyway. The gap—" she says, gesturing back at her head. "We can just talk business. I shouldn't pry."

"No, it's fine."

"YJ," she says. "Wait—YJ or Yujin, actually?"

"Either is OK," you say. "Maybe YJ. Since. Well, everyone calls me that. Is it Soyoung, for you?"

You laugh. She smiles. She holds the takeout container out to you with her pretty manicured fingers. There's a chip in her index nail. You don't want to compare her to Petra, but there's something about the eerie domesticity of it, the way Soyoung feels comfortable enough to hand you an open takeout container and the fork she already ate from.

"Soyoung is OK. Rose called herself Soyoung sometimes. But tell me what you've got. Can you help me?"

Your laughter stops. You take a deep breath. You take the food from her; you eat from her fork.

▮▮▮

In every version of the story, though, the man at the edge of the water looks across the bay. His lover at the other side, and the whole of the storm between them. He knows that this is dangerous. He knows that eventually, the water will recede. He knows that there are more important things than hypothetical love, that this might not be the most important relationship in his life, that there's a lot of other things he needs to be doing rather than pining after some inconvenient girl. But. The girl.

SOYOUNG-ROSE

YJ takes a bite of the noodles, leaving a red oil slick over his bottom lip. He sets the carton down. He runs a hand through his hair.

"So. The majority of the clinical trials have already concluded. But we're still running a few more research studies, because there are avenues of research that have opened up since we're looking into processes similar to Mitosis. Make sense?"

Soyoung nods.

"The problem is that most of these aren't really testing *Mitosis* anymore, and you need Mitosis."

"Is this the part of the conversation where you turn me down?"

She says it lightly. In reality, her heart is in her throat. She's thinking about plane tickets. She's thinking about landing at Incheon Airport, with all her hopes conclusively dashed, everything over and done with.

"This is the part of the conversation where I admit that I was going to turn you down," YJ says. "I wanted to help but it wasn't—it would have caused problems."

Soyoung doesn't say anything. She picks up the carton of dumplings and stabs one with a chopstick. YJ keeps speaking.

"But I wanted to tell you honestly. So, I went looking on the restricted floor to at least confirm things, before I told you no. The one I'm supposed to have access to, because it's *my* project."

Soyoung eats the dumpling. YJ twirls noodles with his chopsticks and doesn't pick them up.

"Then earlier today, my boss called, and told me not to look around, not until I got some sort of clearance. And he basically bribed me with fast-tracking my green card. Said he could expedite it. Said, *whatever I want.*"

He puts the carton down.

"So, I'm saying yes to you, instead. There's a research study that makes sense to slot you in. And, if you see anything weird, during the research study trials, or get a chance to look through any of the files, I would very much appreciate if you could let me know what you see in there."

"You mean spy on your company for you," Soyoung says. The joy of him saying yes tempered by apprehension at his request.

"I wouldn't put it that way," YJ says. "It's not conditional. I want to be clear about that."

"But you want me to help you."

YJ nods. He keeps twirling his noodles.

"They've offered to help me and Yujin. I want to just make sure—it's probably all just fine! But. I don't know why Drew's offering, and I can't push back. I—Yujin, we've cut it really close, timeline wise. Like—you know."

He finishes spinning the noodles, puts them in his mouth, and chews.

The realization hits her not so much like a lightning strike but as if a set of lenses have been placed over her eyes, bringing her vision into focus. Like looking at Yujin in the bar in Korea and realizing that he wasn't a handsome stranger, he was her friend, the arrangement of his features collapsing into something familiar. The way he's avoiding the question, how he talks in vague abstractions, the contrast between how he and Yujin talk about reintegration.

"You've been putting this all off on purpose. You don't actually want to reintegrate with Yujin," Soyoung says with wonder. "You've been lying to him."

Surprise blooms across YJ's face, an inkblot spreading across the page. For a second he looks lost. He looks like the night where Soyoung laughed at him and turned him down. Soyoung suddenly feels like an asshole.

"I'm sorry—"

"I'm not doing it on purpose," YJ says. "Why would you say that to me?"

"But you've been putting it off," Soyoung says, tilting her head. "You want—"

"Don't tell me what I want! You don't know me. You don't know *him*."

She realizes that she's leaned forward, her face close to his. Soyoung is in YJ's space now. Too close for strangers. Hot enough to feel the warmth of his skin against hers. He's got a look on his face that she can't read. Is he going to push her back? Is he going to throw his drink at her?

"I know you, Lee Yujin. Do you think I don't? Do you think you're so divorced from your other self that you can be unseen? I've known you for twenty-nine years, Lee Yujin, and, if you're jerking yourself arou—"

YJ surges up from where he's sitting and—

▪ ▪ ▪

The Auraji had risen to levels never seen before. Water is one of the strongest boundaries in human history. One version on the shore. The other dreaming of crossing the water.

YJ

—you kiss her.

▪ ▪ ▪

Maybe the girl on the bank of the river just gets him! Maybe he's sick of his other responsibilities! Maybe he sees the other side of the shore and thinks to himself, *God, I wish I were anywhere but here,* and maybe it's easier to embody that feeling in a person, to project it onto her, than it is to feel it abstractly, to admit to his inner self that he wants to leave.

▪ ▪ ▪

The press of Soyoung's lips against yours. Why did you do that. What are you doing here. This is stupid. This is an idiot move. You don't know why you did this. She has very soft lips. You are angry at her. How dare she know the you that you no longer are, the you that you wish you were. How dare she read your mind. You had once dreamed of this in the stupid teenage way that you had also dreamed of what sex would feel like and also, more damnably, the imagined fantasy of where the line of her body against yours would meet, the warmth of it. Why did you do this? She feels nothing like Petra. Yes, you wanted this. You wanted this from the first moment you saw her again. You are trying so hard all the time to be normal about things. You don't understand why your other self wouldn't want Soyoung. What the difference is between you and him. You want her to stop fucking with your head. You feel lower than a worm for that thought; she is a real person with hopes and dreams but you are also a person with hopes and dreams and you are not your other self and you are tired of being conflated. Why is she being so familiar? She doesn't know you.

Are you angry? You feel something. Probably anger. Or desire. What should you be feeling? You shouldn't be feeling anything about her. You should be trying to dig yourself out of your hole. You don't have time for anything like this. You should be thinking about your future. You are so tired of feeling trapped. You are so tired of never doing what you want to do. You are just really tired.

SOYOUNG-ROSE

Soyoung grabs YJ's arm instinctively, her fingers gripping the fabric of his sleeve. YJ's mouth is warm, tastes vaguely like Sichuan peppercorn and flesh, just in the way where he's a human being, physical and real and made of meat and bone. This is reality. They exist in the world as real entities. She is real. She shouldn't be kissing him back. Soyoung has a fiancé, and she loved him. This is unfair. This is cruel. This is analogous to cheating. This is the other version of her best friend. This is a stranger that she needs a favor from. This is a stranger who is asking her to commit corporate espionage.

Her teeth on his lip. He tastes like skin.

∎∎∎

You meet a guy on the shoreline and you meet again, again, again. He's divorced from your life, he doesn't have any context for you. But he's familiar. He does the same thing you do, he understands the rhythm of the water, the tides, and you don't know if his family is wealthy, and he doesn't know if you're married, but none of that matters on the shore. How do you fall in love? Is it fast, or is it slow? Is it that you know the moment you lay eyes on someone? Is it built on shared familiarity? Is it that you can look across a room at someone and feel instant chemistry? Is it that the man on the shoreline is someone you remember playing with as a kid, in the sand next to the river?

∎∎∎

Soyoung-Rose is not just some conglomerate ghost of past women's wants, she is her own person and she is capable of her own desire outside of her dead selves. She is not Soyoung. She is not Rose. This is not a decision they would make in any world. There is no world where this happens if they were separated. She is a temporary entity that exists from the combination of two separate lives that should not have been reintegrated. She is a ghost and she is not a woman and ghosts are not able to commit sin.

So. She kisses him, open-mouthed.

YJ

You break away.

"You're right. I don't want to reintegrate," you say. The confession falls from your mouth.

Soyoung stares at you. You stare at her. You look away.

"And I shouldn't have done that. I'm really sorry."

At first it had just been the sheer animal enjoyment of her lips against your lips, the ego-pleasure of the fact that she had kissed you back. Your knees are still touching. You want to pull back. That would be showing weakness. You stay very still.

"Why did you reciprocate?"

"I wanted to," Soyoung says, and then laughs, a sharp clear sound. "Fuck. I shouldn't have done that. Why did *you* do that? You started it! You asshole."

You are a bad person. You are lower than a worm.

"I'm sorry. I really shouldn't have done that."

"You said you didn't want to reintegrate."

You blink. Why is this what she's focusing on?

"I didn't mean that."

The lie is easy and automatic. She gives you a look that you can read as perfectly as if she is your instance and you are hers: She doesn't believe you.

"Okay. I meant that sometimes it's like I'm not really sure what I want out of life, and it seems that Yujin does. Or that he's just waiting to take over my life. I guess I don't really like that feeling. It's easier just not to think about it."

You look away.

"I don't mean to jerk Yujin around. I wasn't consciously taking too long, I just—I wanted to get us in the best position. But I grew up. I started wanting different things. It's too late to change my mind now."

You look back at her.

"I'm sorry. I didn't mean to cause a situation that's pressuring you into anything. Like, I said I'd help, and I mean it. I'm not—it's not—"

She makes a sharp gesture with her hand.

"I reciprocated."

She speaks so smoothly. You almost wish you were Soyoung for a moment, with clear-cut problems and goals, not your own messy heart. You rub your eyes.

"I don't know what I'm doing. My girlfriend broke up with me last month and I don't think I was ever in love with her but I want her back."

Soyoung's looking away from you, out at the skyline. You wonder what she's thinking.

"I don't know why I keep wanting to tell you things. I'm sorry."

She looks back at you. She's frowning a little.

"I think you're kind of doing the thing that guys do, when they want to tell their feelings to a woman to get them to interpret their emotions for them, because they seem like a safe person. And I think the way that you're acting is really, like, this is rebound energy for you."

"No, I—"

"I don't mind," she says, like it's a surprise for her as well. "I think I kissed you because I wanted to do it, because neither Soyoung nor Rose would have done it, if that makes you feel better. You're a rebound for my entire life. You're revenge for the fact that I exist. So this was fine. But it can't be anything more than—this. Just this, right now."

She pauses.

"I don't know if Yujin told you, but Soyoung's engaged."

She smiles.

"So, you know. I'm not good people, either."

Engaged? Yujin never told you, you don't think, or he had told you in the sort of vague passing that slid in through one ear and out the other. It hadn't been relevant to your life until now.

"I never understood why he didn't ask you out."

■ ■ ■

There are three versions of the story behind "Arirang." In the first version of the story, the man falls into the river and drowns. In the second version, he never tries to cross at all, and instead the lovers sing from across the river in the way that only people in mythology do. In the third version, he steps off the banks of the river and leaves his other self behind.

■■■

When Yujin had started talking about Soyoung, you had thought this was an unspoken girlfriend situation that he didn't want to disclose to you. You had assumed he just felt strange about it, because you would have felt strange about it, at the time, with the divide between your selves so new. Yujin had just said that he and Soyoung had reconnected in college. That he could have friends without your input. He said it so reasonably, so matter-of-factly, that you hadn't asked any further. But you knew yourself, so you had been a little surprised that he had never tried anything. Soyoung being in a preexisting relationship would explain that.

Soyoung drums her fingers on the table. She makes a sort of thoughtful noise.

"I think Yujin likes girls . . . a bit girlier? And Soyoung's been with Tae during the entire time they reconnected."

She gives you a look like she's seeing you here, in your entirety. It feels like she's looking at you and not seeing Yujin.

"YJ. I'll make you a trade. I'll try and look around for you, on floor twenty-six, and I'll hold off on telling Yujin that you don't want to reintegrate until you feel comfortable with it. And you let me into the research study that makes sense. And we can be friends."

You are so tired of letting the sensible, good part of you dictate your choices. You are tired of being lonely. You are tired of being alone. You look away. You close your eyes.

■■■

In the versions of the story where the man risks the deluge, when his desire for connection overwhelms his common sense, the story branches again. Sometimes the man who crosses dies, and the only living instance of him is the one separated by the Auraji. Other times he lives, and there are two versions of him on the bank. In some versions, he is drowned by his lover.

■■■

"But you will tell him."

"Only if you don't," she says. "But it won't end well, if you don't."

"I'm not like you."

"Well, not yet," Soyoung says.

You're quiet for a moment.

"I know that we have some complicated history, and I guess I don't have all of it yet, because it doesn't belong to me until Yujin and I reintegrate, and I don't want to seem like I'm pressuring you into anything. I accept your terms—except for the last one. The—I don't want to be friends with you by agreement. I don't want you to take pity on me. I don't want you to kiss me because you think you have to. So, this is unrelated to the rest of it. All the business stuff. I'll add you to the research study, and in return I'd appreciate if you kept things quiet with Yujin, and if you could let me know if you see anything interesting in there. But I would like to be friends, without strings. I'd like to have—it doesn't have to be permanent. It doesn't have to mean anything. I'd like to see you—like, socially."

You pause.

"Please don't laugh at me, again."

You try to say that like a joke, but you don't think you succeed.

The space behind your eyes is warm black. When you were a kid, you used to press your eyelids to create glowing halos and sparks. You don't do that anymore.

"I'm not laughing at you," she says.

■ ■ ■

It's not that all Korean folktales end depressing. It's not a requirement. But Korea is also the country that developed the culture-bound word "han": resentment, grief, sorrow, a sort of longing and anger against the rest of the world.

All the old stories are bittersweet. The sun and moon separated from each other, the rooster stuck in the well wailing at the moon, the man killing his other self after returning from the undersea palace. The man on the other side of the bay, weighing his life and his love. Like it's unrealistic to have something and not lose something in return. Like it's unrealistic to have love without loss. The old stories understood that.

PART IV

Then the LORD God said, "See, the man has become like one of us, knowing delineation; and now he might reach out his hand and take also from the tree of life, and live forever."

Genesis 3:22

SOYOUNG-ROSE

The Mergebreak offices are in a great glass monolith in Midtown Manhattan, a slick tarnished silver building with multiple levels of security. The first hurdle is at the entrance, where Soyoung hands Rose's driver's license to an unsmiling, besuited receptionist before the receptionist checks on a printed list and calls over the phone. Soyoung stands there, shifting from foot to foot, watching as the elevators come and go as shoals of employees walk out and in. Then she's waved through the gate.

"Floor thirty," the receptionist says.

Soyoung nods, punches in the number, and gets in an elevator.

∎ ∎ ∎

In the most common translations of the Book of Genesis, the story of Adam and Eve was laid out as such: After God created the earth, every animal and plant lived in peace. The world was an endless paradise, with no edges and no boundaries, and Adam and Eve were masters and kings and first among the animals, and they had no fear, pain, hunger, they wandered the earth delighted, blind, childlike, they crossed the border between the sea and the land without fear of what they might be looking forward toward or leaving behind. All the world was a home and all the world was a garden named Eden.

∎ ∎ ∎

Soyoung gets out of the elevator and walks into a reception area that's all marble and light wood. A white man in a yellow sweater walks over to her.

"Hey, Rose?"

"That's me," Soyoung says. "Nice to meet you."

"Nice to meet you! I'm Gerry—I'm part of one of the research teams for Mitosis. Follow me."

Gerry leads her to the last elevator in the bank. He swipes a keycard next to the elevator and punches in floor number twenty-six.

"I'll come and grab you, every time, for the study. If you come back."

"If?"

"Well, we have one last intake check and the initial test run," he says and then the elevator comes and they get in and go down.

On floor twenty-six, they go through a receptionist's room with blue sofas and a generic millennial-corporate affect. Nobody is manning the desk. Gerry leads her to the back wall, and punches in a code on the keypad next to the door, which is labeled AUTHORIZED PERSONNEL ONLY. Soyoung watches the whole maneuver out of the corner of her eye. She tries not to pay any overt attention. This isn't yet the part of the facility that YJ wanted her to observe.

Soyoung wonders where YJ is. He won't be here, she knows.

He had been very apologetic about it, when he was explaining the specifics of what she had signed up for.

"The research study is a final calibration test of the Mitosis machine. It's to document what happens to the brain at various levels of frequency lesser than the level used for the full separation. The last session in the sequence involves a full separation. It starts in a week. It runs for about a month and a half. Would that work?"

Soyoung bit her lip. A month and a half. She had sort of thought that by entering the study, under ideal conditions she could be separated sooner. That the research study would mean that she would be neatly cleaved in an instant, rather than subjected to the linear march of time. A month and a half. At least it was comfortably ahead of the six-month mark.

"Yes," she'd said.

"Okay," YJ had replied. "Okay, we're doing this."

He seemed to be trying to convince himself.

"Someone from work will send you the info for it, then. And let's talk, after the first session. I can't go in with you, but I'll meet you af—"

"You don't have to," Soyoung had said.

"No, I will," YJ had assured her. "I mean, I want to."

"Okay," Soyoung had said, surprised, a little pleased.

And just as he had promised, she had gotten an email from an "@merge break.com" email address, which had given her all the details for the study. And now she's here.

The keypad chirps and Gerry opens the door to the final testing chamber. He holds the door behind her.

The laboratory is plain, white walls and white linoleum flooring, surrounded at all ends by some sort of machinery. There are workbenches and a computing terminal that looks a little more robust than Rose would expect to see in a corporate building. The place looks more similar to a university mechanical engineering lab than anything else. In the middle of the room, there are two steel bars in the floor, set at an interval that almost creates a doorway. The Mitosis gate. It's less intimidating than Soyoung had been led to believe. In the video that YJ had shown her, there had been a mind-bending light effect that buzzed between the gate, which the person would walk through and be separated. On camera, the field that it projected between the steel bars was a glowing white spliced through with jittery black, almost like a luminous, glitchy barcode scanner. In the footage, the machine looked unreal. It looked like old-school special effects. Here, there was no visible effect on the surrounding world. But it hadn't yet been turned on.

Gerry walks over to the computer terminal and rummages around in a cupboard before pulling out a video camera and pressing a few buttons before sitting down. He gestures at the second chair.

"Intake," he says.

Soyoung sits down at the desk. She tucks her hair behind her ear. She's thinking about the Korean passport hidden in her sock drawer.

"I didn't know there would be video recording. I thought all the data was being anonymized?"

"It's just this and the exit interview," Gerry says. "The rest of it is just readings."

She bites her lip.

"This won't be shared with anyone, right?"

He shakes his head.

"All the video content is stored in a secure server disconnected from the larger network and only accessible through physical upload and download. All the written documentation is stored in the archive here, and not uploaded anywhere. Unless we get sued, nobody but the research team is looking at it."

"How likely is that? The suing, I mean."

"I mean, likely never? But hey, by the time it gets to that, we'll all have bigger problems. If everything got out, haha, wow. Wow."

Soyoung looks away and up to the dead black camera eye, past to the rest of the room and the Mitosis machine sitting inert in the center. She wonders if the device had been designed to evoke the metal detectors and full body scanners that were placed in every airport, ship port, and some train stations. It probably wasn't purposeful—there were only so many ways to create a machine shaped like a gate.

Gerry coughs. She looks back at him.

"If you're uncomfortable—hey, I don't know your situation but we've worked with a lot of undocumented im—"

The way it felt, sitting across from her mother in the restaurant. Not being able to look at Taehyung in the car as they spoke. Walking through her grandfather's bedroom and feeling like it was a place devoid of any color. The reintegration, how it felt to swallow all of her other self's memories. Sitting next to YJ and making choices with her mouth that neither of her past selves would have understood. She wants all of this to be a bad dream.

"No, it's fine. You can record me."

▪▪▪

On the screen, an Asian woman blinks and then smiles at the camera. She's wearing a dark shirt and minimal makeup. Behind her, there are two steel bars bolted into the floor.

"My name is Soyoung Rose Kang. I reintegrated recently after instancing when I was eleven, moving from Korea to the United States. I reintegrated accidentally when one of my instances forgot to wear her MERGEBREAK, and my instances physically touched."

She smiles a little wider. She looks away from the camera.

"I'm excited for the opportunity to be separated. I plan on going back to my lives as soon as I am separate."

She doesn't look uncomfortable.

▪▪▪

Gerry looks up from the terminal.

"Okay. Machine's on, sensors calibrated. Ready?"

"Yes."

She glances at the two metal bars behind her. There was no effect other than that the indicator light at the bottom of both bars began to flash red. The visual strangenesses that were captured on camera were invisible to the naked eye.

"Don't walk through until I give you the signal. You might experience some dizziness or disorientation afterward, but it should pass quickly. If you need to sit down, let me know. There's a few readings we need to take."

"Like giving blood."

Gerry laughs. "Yeah! Mental blood. Take off your MERGEBREAK, also?"

Soyoung pulls back the black cuff on her wrist. The rubberized fabric sticks to her wrist before peeling back. It doesn't exactly hurt.

"I don't know why I'm still wearing it," she says, inanely. "I've always wondered. How do they work, anyway?"

Gerry nods, the same way you'd nod when an idiot student asked a surprisingly good question. She appreciates that he doesn't call out how she's stalling for time.

"The cuff disrupts a charge between the two individuals, preventing the morphic fields from recognizing each as the same material—it's waveform collapse prevention. You might want to talk to one of the other technicians, though. I'm originally from the Condensco team, never actually worked on it."

He turns back to the computer, clicks a few more buttons. She should be paying closer attention, but she's starting to get nervous, a jittery sort of energy keeping her looking away from the gate. She'll look around more carefully in future sessions, she tells herself.

"Okay, you're all set. Please go stand by the Mitosis gate."

"Which side?"

"It doesn't matter. It just matters that you're in the field."

Soyoung walks over to the side farthest away from the console.

"Okay. I'm turning it on."

Soyoung feels a sharp sudden sensation that can only be described as the feeling of when there is a stranger with you in a dark room but you cannot see them. It is not a sound or a scent. It raises the hairs on her neck. She breathes in sharply, involuntarily.

"Yeah," Gerry says, softly. "It hits everyone like this the first time."

There's no physical effect. There's only the sense that there is something very wrong with the world behind the Mitosis gate, something immutably strange, a different, foreign plane of existence that exists on the other side. It repulses her. It feels like if she walks through the gate, she will end up in—

Her grandfather's house. Her childhood bedroom in Korea—in America. The corner of the library that felt like home, in high school. Her mother's arms when she was five years old. Drinking hot chocolate while watching the snow. A deeply seductive feeling of content, of returning, knifing its way through the strangeness.

"That's how it works, isn't it," she says, keeping care to keep her voice steady. "By creating a psychological effect?"

"It's more complicated than that," he says. "But that's materially part of it. Please walk through."

She does not want to walk through this gate. This feeling originates from her hindbrain. There is nothing logical about it. There is something very wrong with the machine, something that should not exist, something wrong and bad and in complete opposition to the world on the other side. This is a truth that she knows in the deepest recesses of her brain: There is no good future on the other side of the gate.

"Is it supposed to feel this way?"

Soyoung can't keep her voice from wavering.

Gerry looks up from the console. He pulls a piece of paper out of the drawer and unfolds a list. He reads it. Quickly.

"We understand that you may be experiencing a sensation that is foreign to you, which you were not expecting. You may be feeling displacement. Alienation. Longing. Please walk through the gate anyway."

Soyoung takes a deep breath. She is thinking about how Soyoung felt in the moment before she reached for Rose's hand. Gerry continues to read.

"We understand that there may be a feeling of tension in the base of your skull. This is normal. We assure you that the gate is safe. Please walk through."

She's thinking about the split second during which Rose was able to perceive the way Soyoung moved toward her with such smooth and organic motion. She summons the feeling right after their combination. The vertigo. The sharp betrayal like a knife in her stomach. The anger.

She walks forward, and—

I am nineteen years old and I am going for a run on the riverbank, and the sky is hazily smeared with the dead yellow pollution-and-dust that streams over from China in the spring.

My secret is that I think it's beautiful, sometimes, the way it paints the sky in antique colors, but it is objectively bad and my mother tells me to wear a mask on the days that the dust load is particularly high. But I'm not wearing a mask.

I'm going for a run, and right now I feel like the early morning belongs to me, and I am the only person in existence.

And suddenly the sky feels like a great bowl, and I feel a fleeting sense of vertigo. I laugh. The whole world is something I can understand.

This is the one tru-

I am nineteen years old and I am sitting in a dorm room crying. I am crying because I am lonely. I don't know why I'm lonely. I broke up with my boyfriend two weeks ago. I didn't cry then.

I am away from home for the third time in my life. The first time was when we moved to America. The second time was when I went to summer camp. The third time is now.

I know I need to fold this feeling away. I do not want to be the sort of girl who cries. That's not a sort of girl I can be, and survive here. Here being the world. Here being college. Here being the entirety of my life. I don't know why I feel this way. But I feel it. Perfectly. Sincerely.

The dorm room feels too small around me and I feel like I am trapped.

This is the one tru-

—So-Ro-Soyoung collapses through the other side of the Mitosis gate and falls to her knees. Her hands spasm. Her face involuntarily twitches, she nearly blacks out. It feels like she is melting. It feels like she is—I am—you are—I—is, she is, she is, she is going to hurl.

"Trash ca—" Soyoung gasps. A small recycling bin is thrust into her hands. She throws up messily in it. Sour bile. Her breakfast.

"Are you okay? Do you want a seltzer? Or water?"

So-Rose-Young feels like there are strings inside of her unraveling. Like the component memories that make her conglomerate self are pulling apart. It's not a bad feeling as much as it is a strange one, like a foot has fallen asleep but the foot is her memories, and there's a sense of pervasive lightness. Like there's nothing in her head.

"I'm fine," Soyoung says. "I'm—"

She heaves into the bucket again. Nothing comes up.

"Here," Gerry says. He holds out a paper cup of water. Soyoung takes it.

▪ ▪ ▪

Instancing is not a physical phenomenon. It is not a cleft of meat and bone, there is no physical severance. It is the cleave of one future from another. It is psychological change as denoted through physical reality; it is metaphor made flesh. The physical effects are downstream from the higher-order changes taking place.

▪ ▪ ▪

So-Ro-Soyoung drinks the water. She goes down the elevator. She exits the building like she is a foreign object being expelled from a cellular body. She takes slow, deep breaths. She walks down the street. The sky's dark now, and everything *feels* like it's lit up differently, like the world she has walked down into is a different world than she had walked up into, or that she is subtly a different person, as if the perspective of her vision is coming from a few inches to the right of her eyes.

She catches sight of YJ, waiting, haloed underneath a McDonald's sign. For a moment, she's thrown by how this is familiar, how this maps so neatly to her memories of Yujin waiting for her in the streets of Seoul, how he would look up at her from his phone and smile in the same way. She walks up to him.

"How did it go?"

She thinks about the way it felt to be unraveled by the Mitosis gate. The psychological assault, the unraveling. The way she wishes she was somewhere else now. How she feels ephemeral now, temporary, ungrounded. How—she is going to exist for such a short amount of time. She's going to become different people. It feels like something she knows in her bones, now, rather than something she knows with her head. Life—the continuous conscious singular experience of existence—is so impermanent.

"It went great. Do you want to hang out this weekend?"

■ ■ ■

In Eden there were infinite trees, and all of them were permitted to be eaten from, except for two. First, the tree of eternal life. Second, the tree of good and evil. For a long and endless moment (because this was before time had any meaning, because life was eternal, and time therefore did not exist), Adam and Eve lived in paradise. Then the snake who was the devil came to Eve and whispered curiosity into her ear, and so she bit the apple, and learned delineation.

YUJIN

You're awake at obscene hours again. For you, nights are for watching video game streamers and talking with YJ and going for long dark walks because when it's late enough for long enough, you become tired enough not to care about death.

Tonight, you're awake for different reasons. Two hours ago, you finally finished combing through the files on the USB that Megan gave you, and then you had written up all the contents that you understood in your crabbed handwriting.

You had tried to ignore the USB. You have your own problems and life—you have a third date with Youngmi, you have your *own* job, you can't be keeping perfect tabs on YJ's life. It would have been nice if you could have just shipped the USB in the next package that your mother would be sending to him around Christmas, along with a slip of paper containing the password to decrypt it. That would be months, though. And YJ probably needed the information now, whatever it was that his previous boss had thought was so important for him to know.

You had looked Megan up. You hadn't known her last name, but YJ was friends with a "Megan Taylor" on three different social media sites, who mostly posted photos of herself in pretty locations, interspersed with photos of her at conferences. Your instance was in some of those photos, along with a constellation of other Mergebreak employees. The other things you learned about Megan: She seemed successful (but everyone seemed successful on social media), she seemed to be actual friends with YJ (again, not hard to do on social media), and she seemed to really enjoy traveling (the places, at least, were real). You envied that. It was harder to get a tourist visa sometimes, if you had an instance, and you didn't have the money for international travel, so you didn't really get out of Korea.

After that, you had failed to ignore the USB. You knew a little, but you wanted to know a lot. You had plugged the USB into an old computer with the Wi-Fi switched off. You wondered if Megan had known this would happen, if she knew your other self well enough that she thought you would go looking, even if you were told not to.

▪▪▪

The various versions of the Bible offer a woeful amount of detail with regards to Eve's decision to take the apple. The conversation between Eve and the serpent only lasts a few lines. There are no long paragraphs describing Eve's inner thoughts, like why she thinks the serpent might be trustworthy. Why she wants wisdom, or knowledge, or why it takes so little urging for her to question God.

▪▪▪

You had only meant to skim, but the more you looked, the more curious you became. Technical diagrams, white papers, summaries, saved email chains. A good portion of those alluded to existing relationships or ongoing conversations, and some of the business jargon eluded you. You didn't speak business English beyond formalities. But the science you understood, and you knew that YJ wouldn't be able to easily parse it. Or—he could have figured it out, eventually. But only one of you had majored in a technical field, and the other had majored in finance.

You had gotten the science degree, and YJ had gotten the business one. You had agreed on this to maximize your abilities later, after you reintegrated. And you ended up in STEM and he ended up in econ because an American business school would be a better line item on a résumé than a Korean one. You had transferred to KAIST, because you had wanted to get out of Seoul for a bit and it was a good school for STEM. But you had screwed up your interviews, after. Now you work at a small biotech company. You like your job, mostly, although it's not what you thought you would be doing as a kid. YJ did better: first consulting, then Mergebreak. You're on parallel tracks. If you reintegrate, then you'll be able to list all your experience on a single combined résumé.

But for now: You know you understand more than he does, and the more you read, the more you were compelled to distill it down for him, in case he missed the specifics: Mitosis didn't solely contain the ability to disentangle and separate instances, portioning their memories out into the preexisting people. Mitosis was a singular technological breakthrough that effectively controlled the entire instantiation process. The combination of instances. The prevention of their separation. The forced reintegration. Even more technical: the fine-tuned combinations of instances, down to the percentages of the individuals. You could walk through a Mitosis field and become 70 percent your foreign self, 30 percent your domestic self. You could pull the trigger on a Mitosis machine that was placed at a border crossing and stop a person from instancing. You could turn any person into two versions of themselves, as long as they walked through the field that was created by the gate. Any and every Mitosis machine inherently held these capabilities. These were all derivatives of the same principles.

With Mitosis as it had been marketed, it effectively made reintegration obsolete. With Mitosis as it actually existed, it made natural instancing obsolete.

■ ■ ■

Imagine a world without instances. A world where leaving is perfect absence, where there is no ghost left behind. Imagine never knowing the parallel, leaving the past in the past, a world where desire doesn't matter, where there is no blunt knowledge of the implicit truth of the human heart. Imagine a world where leaving is a single choice, where there is the kind blindness of never knowing and the cruel promise that you will stay singular.

■ ■ ■

You're ashamed to admit it: Your first thought was, *I could overwrite YJ.* The same type of thought as when you saw a high building and thought reflexively about throwing someone off, or the part of your brain that imagined slapping ice cream out of a child's hands. You had looked at the technology and thought: *Here's how I could become him.* You had quashed that thought as quickly as possible.

Rubbing your eyes now, your back sore from slouching over your computer, you know that you had to get the information to YJ, if he doesn't have it. You had to make sure he understood what was going on. You finish writing. You save your file. You unplug the USB drive from your computer. You wonder why your instance wasn't told about any of this. Why this information hasn't been released publicly. It's revolutionary stuff. Maybe that's why.

You stretch. You put on your jacket and grab a lighter from the side table. You jam your feet into your slides. You skip the elevator and walk down the clinically lit stairwell, the fluorescent lights and concrete only broken by the occasional cobweb. It feels like you're descending down a great well. Then you push the exterior door open, and you're outside. You think about going to buy yourself a canned coffee or an ice cream bar. You think about stealing a car from the garage and going on a joyride.

You take your phone out. You call YJ. Over data, with video. It takes a few seconds, but the call connects, his face on the screen, identical to your face except for all the things that are different. He's lying on his couch. He must be home early from work. Or working from home. In the scant patch of the floor visible on his screen, you see dirty socks, a candy wrapper. He yawns.

"Yeah?" he says.

"You free now? Anyone over?"

He gestures at the rest of his off-screen apartment.

"What's up? Everything good with Mom and Dad?"

"Yeah, everything's fine," you say. Why's he so nervous? He's chewing on the inside of his lip. What does he have to be nervous about, right now? You have things to be nervous about. You're going to give him something to be very nervous about, you think.

You take your packet of cigarettes from where it lives in your pocket and light one.

"Hey, put that out."

"It's not your body," you say to him. You take a long breath. He almost makes an expression with his face, like he's embarrassed but trying to hide it. You make sort of a gesture with your body like you want him to continue. He looks away.

"How's the job going?" you say.

"It's just a lot of pressure."

"Can't talk about it or won't talk about it?"

He smiles, just a bit.

"Can't."

"I get that. Blink twice if it's your new boss breathing down your neck that's got you down. The guy who's traveling all the time. What's his name?"

"Drew's fine. Just kind of scattered."

"Better or worse than your old boss?" you say. "Megan, right? You end up talking with her about things?"

"No, she's still not answering my calls. Why do you ask?"

"No reason," you say, and leave it at that. You want to tell him about Megan's visit, or that you're going to be sending him a package by proxy, but that seems like too much to tell him over the phone. You wish you were in the same place. This is an impossibility. If you left—you know that you'll instance again. You know that in your bones. You don't need a third version of yourself running around.

But you think this conversation is strange enough that he would use his brain.

"You talk with Soyoung again? She told me everything was set."

For a moment it looks like he's frozen.

"Why're you talking about Soyoung?"

His voice is very even. You frown.

"We're friends," you say. "I think you guys would get along okay. Since me and her, you know, we're friends."

"Just because I said yes to helping her doesn't mean she's going to want to be friends with me," he says.

"Soyoung likes me," you say. "She'd like you. We're the same person. Just to be clear."

"Yeah, I got that. What's with you, today?"

You give an exaggerated shrug. "I'm fine. Just kind of tired. I'm going to head up and go sleep."

"Sure," he says. He looks very calm. "'Night."

You hope he picks up what you're putting down. You hope you're similar enough, still, that your thought processes can be a clean mirror of his, that he'll take your advice and talk to Soyoung, and by then, the USB drive will have gotten to her, and this can all be his problem for a bit.

■ ■ ■

What YJ doesn't understand, and what you have no interest in telling him, is that there's no future here for him to come back to, for the two of you to live here. There's just the military service and Hell Joseon. Maybe the world for him-and-you is better, because then the combined self has an American degree, which helps, but then what? Just a job that takes twenty-three of your twenty-four hours.

Those thoughts make you feel like a bad person. You might be a bad person. You might just be having a quarter-life crisis. But you don't know what else you would be doing with your life. On the bad days, you feel like you are putting your life on hold for YJ to live. And it's stupid. You know it's stupid, that YJ is having a hard time too, but you think he knows the same thing you know, in his heart. After all, you had wanted to leave. Just an accident of consciousness, of remembrance, that left you here and sent him forward.

Your worst fear is that YJ calls you one day and tells you that he got citizenship, but he's not interested in reintegrating, and he is never coming back.

YJ

You're not on a date. Or it is a date, but not in the way you're accustomed to thinking about dates, where this is a step in trying to build something larger. Or it's not a date, because you and Soyoung hadn't defined your relationship other than an impermanent friend-something. Not exactly romantic. Not exactly anything that had long-term viability. You haven't talked about your relationship with her, though you'd texted a little about when to meet up next.

But right now, the sun is shining and you're walking through Central Park with Soyoung.

"Soyoung wanted to do tourist things," she had said when you met her at the Columbus Circle entrance, beneath the big statue. "Stuff she had seen on TV."

"Am I part of tourist things?"

She shrugs. She hands you a coffee. It's your order: sweeter than coffee has any right to be, no milk.

You must look surprised, because the next thing she does is laugh.

"It's just, you and Yujin have the same coffee order. Kind of funny," she says.

"Thanks."

"I didn't want to go alone," Soyoung says. "Seemed a little lonely. And no one else knows about . . ."

"Well, if I'm the only option."

"I just thought it might be fun."

"This is fun," you say. You're surprised to find that you mean it. You're happy to be here.

"Okay," she says, and she smiles, and you feel about seventeen years old.

You weren't lying. It feels really good to be doing something so divorced from the rest of your life and relationships that it can exist in its own little bubble of feeling. And the fact that it's completely temporary is a breath of fresh air. The thing with Petra—the thing with all your relationships—is that you always had to think about whether this was forever. About whether the version of you that had integrated Yujin back into your self could love that person. But here, there's no future. Soyoung, as you know her now, will no longer exist. Whatever she and you do, in the moment, won't last—there's an expiration date built into the whole endeavor. Like having a relationship with a living ghost.

She doesn't look like a ghost, though. She looks very human and alive.

"This part of it is okay," she says. "Soyoung had always wanted to travel more. She would be really delighted to be here. Is really delighted, I guess."

"How do you feel about it?"

She wrinkles her nose.

"Weird," she says. "I'm going to buy one of those bizarre SpongeBob ice creams."

Soyoung grabs your arm—not like a girlfriend would, like a friend would—and pulls you into the park.

You walk down the main artery of Central Park, going past the horses and the carriages and the hopeful drivers, the vendors selling nuts, the tourists walking slowly in a horizontal wedge that spans the entire street. You always feel like you should be doing more *New York* stuff than you're doing (go see a Broadway show, go to the Met), but at the same time, that all feels like tourism for people outside the city. You have work.

"I didn't see anything strange yet in the laboratory room," Soyoung says. "Or—I guess I don't know what I'm looking for yet. But I'll let you know if I get a chance to look at some files or something."

"Thanks," you say. "But really, just describing it would be enough. Don't, like, touch the equipment."

"Okay. First, the technician did intake with me, and then booted the Mitosis machine up, which was in the center of the room. Everything looked pretty *in place*, like, there wasn't anything odd, it looked like a research laboratory. And then, when he gave me the signal, I walked through the Mitosis gate. Other than that, nothing weird."

"This might have been a dead end," you say. "Asking you to look, I mean."

"I mean, I'll tell you if there's anything strange," Soyoung says. "But I don't know what's considered strange."

"I tracked down my old boss," you say. "I'm going to ask her about what's going on. She's working for the IIS now."

You had finally broken down and snooped on Megan's socials, since she still hasn't responded to your texts. You don't know why Megan would be keeping such a distance, though. All you had gotten was the same generic goodbye message everyone had gotten: *Although I'm going to miss everyone I've worked with, I'm excited for this new chapter.* No email address. No phone number. You opened up your web browser search engine and typed in her name. Maybe if you messaged her over Instagram, she'd answer.

This is how you found the page nestled deep in the dot-gov websites that listed her as an employee of the IIS. No headshot, no biography—this page probably wasn't supposed to be public yet. The new chapter. She's working for the IIS. There's no number listed, but there was an email address for the office. So you emailed her from your work email, because there was no reason for Yujin Lee, private non-citizen, to get an appointment with a government official, but Yujin Lee, important corporate talking head, could. But you were in limbo until they emailed you back.

"The instancing immigration division? You think she'll help?"

"I honestly have no idea."

Soyoung lets go of your arm and walks over to one of the ice cream carts. You watch her point at the ice cream on the board. Everything about this afternoon feels fake. A fake date, a fake girl. You're fake too. You'll reintegrate with Yujin. You'll no longer exist.

Now that you've admitted your ambivalence to Soyoung, you can't keep yourself from ruminating about your antipathy. You just—you want his life and his memories. You don't know about being him. You don't know how to talk with him about this.

Soyoung walks back with her ice cream.

"Can you take a photo of me, with the ice cream? For Insta?"

"Should you be doing that?"

"Rose takes selfies. It's for social media camouflage."

You acquiesce. You take your phone out and position it to take a photo for her. You never really take photos of yourself. You don't know whether you should be getting Soyoung's whole body in the shot. Or just her face. You split the difference and take a flurry of photos. She can decide which ones she wants.

She finally takes a bite. The chemical yellow against her mouth.

"Is it living up to your expectations?"

"No," she says, and holds up the ice cream for you to try. You acquiesce.

It tastes like sugar and artificial chemicals. It reminds you of your childhood. Five-hundred-won ice cream bars outside of the FamilyMart. The one that looked like a shark and had a pink bloody strawberry inside. The one that was just a milkshake in a squeeze bottle, where you and Soyoung had competitions to see how far you could squirt it out of the container if you stepped on it. You don't miss your childhood, you don't think, except when you do. *Do you remember when we were kids? Does this ice cream remind you of our childhood?*, you want to ask her.

You lick sugar from your lips.

"This is pretty terrible," you say.

"Isn't it?" she agrees, and laughs. You don't understand how Yujin was never in love with her.

SOYOUNG-ROSE

Soyoung walks into the Mergebreak building and tells the receptionist her name. The receptionist checks a list, and then waves her through to the elevator bank. A couple of people take the elevator with her. She tries to be unobtrusive while she inspects if any of them are wearing MERGEBREAKs. One person. That's more than in most office buildings. Must be a business traveler. Soyoung walks into the Mergebreak reception area, where Gerry looks up from doing something on his phone and smiles politely.

"Hi. Ready to go?"

"Let's go," she says. "How've you been?"

"Not too bad."

He leads her down to floor twenty-six. She's hoping that she can stall him for a little, take a surreptitious walk around the lab. Look for whatever could be useful to YJ. But as soon as Gerry gets there, he turns the Mitosis machine on, and the world goes strange. The space between the gate turns qualitatively familiar and foreign.

She wants to walk through the gate. She cannot bear to walk through the gate. The metaphorical taste of the gate screams against the interior of her brain.

"Please, whenever you're ready," Gerry says.

She closes her eyes. She's thinking about all the things she used to want. She's thinking about what information is shelved in this lab, where she can't read it. Soyoung walks through, and—

I am seventeen and I am studying. It feels like I am always studying. My life feels like it is an endless wheel of routine. I wake up and go to school. I go to cram school afterward. I go do my homework. I fall asleep. I don't dream. I wake up

I am seventeen and I am studying. I feel like I am always studying. Studying for school or studying for the SATs or going to extracurriculars or working on my college application essays and I am always trying to find some way of being extraordinary.

again. I am counting down the days until I take the CSAT.

I punch numbers on my calculator and I write paragraphs and I memorize science facts and I think about my instance and how she must not have to do all of this studying. I looked up how the American school system works and my first emotion was anger, that she could have access to the whole apparatus of higher education without the same ladder that I had to climb. If I did badly on the exam, I would have to take it again the next year.

I complained to my grandfather about this. He is the only person who regularly talks to my instance. He laughed when I complained.

I asked him, do you think my life is easy?

He changed the channel on the television. He didn't look at me.

I do, he said.

Harabeoji, I said. He laughed at me. Next time I am going to complain to Minsoo-oppa instead.

I have been told that I am not competing with the other students at my school, or the national pool of talented teenagers. I am competing with every other Asian girl my age who has the same set of skills that I do. I am competing with every other Asian girl who's good at math and sometimes I wish that I was white (to be the default) or brown or black (for the diversity scholarship).

I have not been told, but I know implicitly that to be competitive against the other Asian girls, I need to get perfect grades and perfect SAT scores and a double handful of SAT 2s and even then this is the floor, not the ceiling. I have been told that there is an unspoken quota of how many Asian girls will be admitted into any good college.

I do more math problems. I feel very much like nobody in the world has ever had the same problems I have had, and I have suffered more than any person on earth.

I know this is temporary. I dream of being a grown-up. I think it will feel different from being seventeen in a qualitative way, and one day I won't have to think about this stuff anymore.

—she falls out the other side of the gate reeling, her knees hitting the ground, the echo of two lives reverberating in her singular head.

YJ

You're in FiDi. You never come down here anymore—you had a job here once, and you remember walking back to the subway late at night, trying not to slip on the cobblestones. You had thought more than once that New York was a small city compared to where you grew up, but the block-by-block changes were more expansive. And it was only small if you didn't count all the boroughs, but it wasn't like you were going out to Ridgewood or Flushing every weekend.

Megan's new office is here, in the old brick building across the street. In the IIS office. You stare at the front. It's a completely different genre of building from the Mergebreak offices, which are wholly encased in glass. The occasional person walks in—government workers in business-casual, and people who clearly need to talk about some sort of instancing or immigration issue. Tired-looking parents towing a couple of kids. Men with brown, deeply lined faces. Then again—you don't know that the people in business-casual aren't also there for some sort of immigration issue. You've been here before. When you were a student, and again, when you were dealing with an issue with the H-1B1 you had at your previous employer. You had worn a button-down. You had also looked like you worked here.

Why would Megan quit to work at IIS? Megan had been on the up-and-up. You knew things about Megan: how she had a genuine belief in Mergebreak's stated mission, how she believed in technology for social change. And it was a good job. She was *high up.* Did Megan want to run for office someday? You would vote for her. Not just because you had thought she and you were friends. She had been the best manager you'd had.

■ ■ ■

The knowledge that was hidden from Adam and Eve was also that of delineation. "Delineation" is an imperfect translation of the original Hebrew, from a word that is hard to define other than to say that it is "the difference between the self and the other self." Which is to say, instantiation.

God, as supreme creator, as all-powerful, as perfect and infallible, as capable of feats beyond human ability of comprehension, created the world in his own image. Adam and Eve, the light, the darkness, the oceans, the animals, heaven and the angels, all of these are imperfect instances of God, different facets of His face.

■ ■ ■

You walk into the IIS building and get milled through the waiting room, telling the bored secretary that you have an appointment, clarifying that it's not an appointment for your visa, and yes, you have to talk with one of the non-public-facing government employees, before being led up the stairs to the second floor where there's a long, yellow-lit hallway with doors and placards. It reminds you of going to office hours in an unfamiliar university building. You get to the door that says MEGAN TAYLOR. You knock on it. This really does feel like office hours.

"It's open," Megan calls.

You push the door open and go inside.

"Hey, wow, it's been a bit," she says, getting up from her desk.

Your eyes dart around the office as the rest of your body moves in for a shallow hug. She brought the same calendar that she had hanging on her wall at Mergebreak. There's a photo of her and her partner on her desk, and one of her and her college friends, and a landscape that you know is of her hometown only because she's told you. There's a bookcase of leatherbound books that you instinctively know she only uses for her videocall backgrounds. Other than the trinkets, it looks nothing like her old office. Where her office in Mergebreak had glass, her office here is plaster and wood.

You don't think that she had any hand in choosing the underlying aesthetics of her office, but you remember how one of your early real conversations with her had been about how appearances mattered. You had both been working late on a report, and the conversation had turned vaguely personal; you've forgotten what you had said, but she hadn't gotten *mad,* though she had gotten serious, and told you about how she felt she had to dress in a specific way, talk in a specific way, for people to take her seriously. That you had it easier than she did. And you had said, *probably, you did.* But in your heart you had felt like: She's your boss, why is she bringing this up to you? You also had to follow a dress code for people to think that you belonged. And at least everyone assumed that English was her first language. You didn't say any of that, because she was your boss.

"Just a bit, yeah," you say. "Hey—my defense, you didn't return any of my texts."

"I know. I was out of the country. Traveling, while I was between jobs."

"Go anywhere fun?"

The small talk feels like a current you are getting pulled along, a dance that you're stepping through by rote.

"Asia," she says. "Japan, Korea—not China, though, getting the visa was too much of a pain."

"How was Korea?"

"It was good! It was—the thing I hated about Japan, was that it feels like you have to be quiet all the time. But in Korea, it felt more vibrant. I was only there for a bit, though."

A part of you wants to ask her to describe Seoul to you. This is the same part of you that wants Yujin's memories.

"Do you ever worry about instancing, when you travel?"

"Not in Asia."

"I messaged you the other day," you say. "You were back, by then."

She smiles sympathetically.

"It's different, if one of the VPs at Mergebreak comes in officially, versus Yujin Lee, someone I worked with, messaging me off the record," she says. "I'm treating all my electronic communications as hackable now. Since it happens to basically every politician doing anything interesting."

"This isn't an elected position, though, right?"

"No, but, well," she says. "It's going to get a lot of visibility soon. Sit down, though, here," she says, gesturing to the little sitting area that's set up near the door. She sits.

"Do you want some coffee? Tea? We only have instant and Lipton, but you know."

"I'm fine," you say, sitting near her. "So, no seltzer tap?"

"No, no more office perks. But, okay. What can I help you with?"

You hesitate. You have a thousand questions, and you don't know what order to ask them in. What you had learned through the last eight years of your career was that people would almost always give you more than they meant to give, as long as you asked the right questions in the right order. But you want to skip to the end, here, to the hard questions, the "why are you working for the government now?" questions, the "what is Drew not telling me?" questions, the "is there something sinister happening here, am I being set up?" questions.

"Drew called me the other day. Told me that I couldn't look at the super-classified research on twenty-six until my clearances went through."

"Yes, that's correct," Megan says. "It's why I *also* told him to promote you after your clearances went through, or at least wait to make you do all the press until you actually knew what the shit was going on. If he didn't want to do the press, he could have pulled someone else in. Let me guess—he's treating you unfairly?"

"He's been fine."

"Don't give me that. He's an asshole, isn't he?"

"He's—like a TV show techbro asshole," you admit. "He's fine. I can deal with him."

She laughs. "Yes! Exactly! You see what I had to put up with? I'm so sorry you have to inherit him from me."

"Why'd you recommend me for your job?"

The smile fades from Megan's face. You wonder if you asked that question too early in the conversation.

"I recommended you because I knew that it would be a sensitive position with a lot of visibility, which Drew would try to influence. So, I wanted someone I could trust, taking over for me. Someone who I could feel alright about working with, in the future, rather than going through one of Thorsson's cronies. And that was either you, Katarina Callow, or Jose whats-his-last-name, you know—"

"Tall Jose, not short Jose."

"Yes, that one. But I recommended you because—you're still here on a visa."

"Did you *want* to give him blackmail material?"

You stand.

"I don't know if you realize this, but you've made it so I can't say no to

Drew. I can't disagree with him. I can't argue with him. I'm doing all this press for something I'm not allowed to look at, and I can't push back on it, because"—you gesture vaguely, weakly—"citizenship."

Megan doesn't know what you and your instance have been working for. And you don't want to tell her about them now, not here. Not while you're arguing. But she knows that you're here on a visa. She's frowning a little now.

"YJ, if he tries anything, I'll just hire you. I'm sorry. I didn't know it would weigh on your mind so much. I did want him to think he could control you, a bit. But if he tries anything, I want you to know that I've got your back. Okay?"

The wind leaves your sails. You sit back down.

"Okay," you echo.

She clasps her hands together.

"So. What else? Wait—maybe we start from something else. What do you know," she says.

You look down at your feet. You need to buy new shoes. It feels like there's always something wearing out. You look up, you take a sip of water, and then you tell Megan the rest. You tell her about how Drew didn't warn you away from twenty-six until you actually went to look for the underlying documentation. You tell her how you know that the Mitosis project encompasses more than the separation technology. And you tell her that you're pretty sure that the funding is coming from the federal government, through some program or other, and that you'd like her to confirm if that's the case.

She nods. She looks out her window, and then back at you.

"Yes. Here's the parts that I can tell you," she says.

Condensco had been a medium-sized late-stage start-up that had been looking for a way to prevent instancing from occurring. Instancing tech had historically been expensive and hard to iterate on. Condensco had received a sponsorship by the U.S. federal government for researching ways to disentangle instances. The catch was that Condensco, and any successor organization, was required to comply with the guidelines established by the IIS, was subject to their limited-but-sacrosanct oversight, and was required to turn over any particularly novel invention for prior approval before public sale. But this was a self-reported standard. When Drew and Megan had acquired Condensco, the requirements shifted to Mergebreak. Any of the Condensco-related projects that were funded by the IIS were technically IIS projects, so only employees with clearance could access them. And so, yes, Mitosis was government-backed, and YJ wouldn't get access to the full suite of information until he was cleared.

"And everything else—I can't tell you, yet," Megan says. "Especially not while we're—at my job. But since you already know about it."

"Why'd you take this job, anyway?"

"It seemed like a good career opportunity," Megan says. She's back to giving you non-answers. You asked too quickly. She glances at her phone.

"I've got a meeting soon. But this was good. It's nice to get it all out into the open."

"Sure, yeah," you say. You stand.

She smiles at you. You think it's supposed to be sympathetic.

"Do you talk to your instance, much?"

Why is everyone so obsessed with your instance, recently?

"Sometimes," you say. "I talked with him the other day."

"I can't imagine what it's like."

"It's a pretty common experience," you say. "A lot of people have instances. They say that projected outward, the number of instances will overtake the number of non-instanced people by 2130, barring mass changes to human psychology or public perception of instantiation."

"Yes, but still—it's hard to imagine, from the inside."

You shrug. You adjust your pants before taking out your phone and pretending to check the train times. You glance back at her.

"Thanks, Megan," you say. She smiles at you again.

"YJ," she says, "I've never lied to you. I want you to have the information to make informed decisions. That's the difference between me and Drew. And I'll tell you one more thing I probably shouldn't be telling you: I recommended you because I thought you'd make the best replacement for Drew, if he was removed."

■ ■ ■

Atheist theological studies majors like to point out that Lucifer, the serpent, the one angel who rebelled, is also an instance of God.

SOYOUNG-ROSE

Soyoung's up too late. She had a 2 AM meeting for her Korean self's job and then had meetings in a block all morning for her American self's job. She had swapped languages, given presentations, smiled in the video window, made small talk with Korean coworkers about "dealing with some family issues, but they're almost resolved," and "how Korea was, other than the family things," with the American coworkers. It was logistically challenging, making sure that no one suspected that there's anything wrong.

She rubs her eyes. She gets out of bed. She might as well go get her mail. A walk will clear her head.

▮▮▮

On top of her mail, there's a package. She hadn't ordered anything, but the address is located in Korea, specifically Yujin's apartment. Soyoung takes it upstairs and rips it open. The top of the box has a note that says *Care package!* along with some snacks, the xylitol gum she likes, and some stationery supplies (fancy mechanical pencils, colored lead). She pulls all of them out. Underneath there's a USB drive, with a sticky note folded on top: *FOR YJ (SY PLEASE DON'T LOOK☹)* and a second slip of paper, which has a string of numbers, and the word "PASS."

It's clearly all window dressing for the USB drive. But why send this to her, rather than to his instance directly? Soyoung has the vaguest memory of YJ having asked about Yujin mentioning her when they talked. She examines the snacks. They're all Korean brands, all things you could buy in the States except without the English-language packaging. The honey twist things, the banana puffs. Kid snacks.

Dr. Crouton meows and comes running up to her. Soyoung bends down to scritch him.

"You think these are treats, don't you? It's not treats. It's problems."

He winds around her ankles. She stands up. Picks up the USB drive and uncaps it. Recaps it. She puts it down and opens the door to the closet where she keeps her out-of-season coats and shoes and other miscellany. A handheld vacuum cleaner. A shoebox full of old cards, from Rose's birthdays. An old diary. One of those preserved roses that an old boyfriend had gotten her, as a gift and a joke—*a rose for Rose!*

Underneath everything, there's Rose's old laptop. It's a college artifact. She uses it for anything that she doesn't want on her work computer. If there's anything suspect on the USB drive, it won't get mixed in with her work files. The ancient machine begins booting up. Soyoung goes over to the kitchen and takes out a bag of the American honey things. She opens it. Dr. Crouton comes running over.

"Again, not for you," she says, and shakes a couple out onto her hand. She walks back over to the snacks and opens the Korean honey things. She closes her eyes. She eats one, and then the other. Crisp, oil, salt, sweet. She can't tell if the difference in flavor is psychosomatic or not. She opens her eyes again and eats a few more before brushing her hands off and sitting down at the computer. She plugs the USB drive in, and gets a notice that it's password protected. She punches the password in and then opens the file folder. The first document she opens is a letter addressed from Yujin to YJ. She thinks about closing it. She doesn't. She reads.

▪▪▪

Adam receives the apple from Eve, who exhorts him to eat it. She can't explain anything more to him. What she learns from the apple is untransferable. There is no way to explain in language the intrinsic understanding she gains from its consumption. All she can say is that it's good to eat, and what they had thought before was wrong.

YJ

Grand Central's crowded; the weekend out-of-towners, a few commuters, a group of Chinese tourists all gawking at the hall. You check the train tables and go to the track for the Metro-North, up to Poughkeepsie. Soyoung's standing there, typing rapidly on her phone. She doesn't look up until you arrive. You smile at her, but you don't reach out to hug her. She smiles back. You haven't kissed her again, since the first time. You haven't touched her since the time in the park. She hasn't moved to touch you again, either.

"How's it going?"

"Not bad. Just sending *sorry, I'm busy!* texts to friends, you know."

"Sure," you lie. "Do you have a lot of friends?"

You have to stop yourself from wincing. It's such a high school question.

"Rose has like . . . a large social network," Soyoung says. "I don't know if I'd call them all her friends. It's been awkward. I've been making a lot of excuses."

"You don't want to see them?"

"Not really," she says. "If they realize—"

"How likely is that?"

"I have no idea," she says. "Would you have realized?"

"I didn't know you, I don't know."

"Sorry, I didn't mean to forget—"

"It's fine," you say, though you don't know how to feel about the way she sometimes conflates you and your instance. She doesn't do it often. But you've noticed in the past weeks, every so often she'll forget. She'll look at you with too much familiarity. Sometimes you like it. Sometimes you don't. You keep saying yes to her, though. "I just—"

The train arrives in a screech, cutting off anything that you were going to say. You wince at the sound. You both turn to the opening doors.

"I miss Seoul the most when I'm taking public transit," she says. She sounds so wistful. You've forgotten how the public transit was, in Seoul.

■ ■ ■

There are sects of Christianity that argue for Adam's innocence. Adam, seduced by his wife. Adam, trusting his only human companion. Adam, being given a little treat by his own flesh. How can you not trust someone like that? Something like that? How can you not be curious, of what they have, and you don't?

But that severs Adam's agency. That makes him a dumb animal, unthinking, accepting anything handed to him. And Adam is made in God's image, just like Eve, just like the serpent.

SOYOUNG-ROSE

"Why upstate?" YJ asks, inspecting the sign for the trailhead.

"I wanted to get out of the city," Soyoung says. "Rose's and Soyoung's memories mesh worst in places that either of them remembers well. But we haven't been here before."

"So that's why the hike."

"Yeah," she says, and starts down the trail. Google maps had said that this was a short, very scenic hike with a beautiful view of a river, that it was out of the way and fairly secluded, and only for moderate to experienced hikers. The mountains make her think of Korea, when she was a kid, and she and her cousins were dragged on hiking trips. The memories are monophonic, singular. She remembers getting sunblock smeared on her face and being forced to wear a hat. She remembers playing on the public playgrounds at the foot of the mountain, stepping from one swinging log to the next, reaching for Minsoo. She remembers floating a paper boat down a stream overflowing with rainwater. The water—she blinks. She turns.

"You pushed me into the water!"

They had been in elementary school, on a field trip. They had been going to some important mountain temple that Soyoung remembered the name of and Rose didn't. They had stopped for lunch on the banks of a river, and the kids had played in the shallows. Yujin had pushed her into the shallows, and she remembered yelling about getting her clothes wet.

"What are you talking—"

"Second grade! You pushed me!"

"What in second gra—oh. Wow. I had totally forgotten about that. I didn't know you would actually fall," he says. "I haven't thought about that in years."

"Neither have I," she says. She had tried to push Yujin back in retaliation, but had only managed to splash water at him. But Yujin had been such a baby at seven, he had started crying. Later the teachers had forced them to apologize to each other: hug and make up. They had, but she remembers not forgiving him in her head, yet later forgetting, the way that children forget.

"I won't push you into any streams," YJ says.

"I asked you to come out here because Yujin sent me some weird stuff related to the Mitosis project. It's for you. It seemed pretty sensitive. I think it might be the things that you wanted me to look for, in the lab."

"What?"

"I don't want to talk about it where people might overhear."

Soyoung starts walking down the path. YJ follows her.

▪ ▪ ▪

Seoul and New York are on roughly the same latitude. The climate is nearly identical, in many respects. Four seasons. Greenery. Seoul is wetter, with great damp rainy seasons when the rain pours. The pine trees are gnarled and twisted and eccentric. But if you go a few hours outside New York at the right time of year, the mountains look almost the same, until you look closely at the trees.

▪ ▪ ▪

They're a little farther up the path now, the trail having narrowed to a single person's width. It's lovely in here. The light filters through the leaves, dappling the floor with flecks of green light. It reminds her of the forest around her grandfather's gravesite. How there was the well-kept clearing and the soft mounds demarking each grave, but if you walked a few meters into the woods, the paths would narrow, the light would dim, and the undergrowth would brush against your ankles.

"I had a weird conversation with Yujin the other day," YJ says.

"Weird how? Weirder than the conversation that you had with your old boss?"

"No. Less weird. But he mentioned that I should hang out with you."

"How long ago?"

"Not long. Earlier this week, maybe? It takes a couple of weeks for mail, so—"

"—he probably sent this before that. What else did he say to you?"

"It was more like what he didn't say. He didn't want to talk about it over the phone, mostly. He was really paranoid about it."

"You're kind of a paranoid person, though."

"I am not!"

"YJ, you are," Soyoung says.

"It really does kind of upset me when you make statements like that about me and him," YJ says.

You glance back. He looks like he's trying to keep his face neutral. You shrug. "Sorry."

"The things you know about him aren't the same as things you know about me."

Soyoung looks forward. She climbs over a few roots. What had been the same about Rose and Soyoung? Enough that she was able to move through the world as she is now, not enough that it felt comfortable. They thought in different languages. They had studied different things in school. They ordered different things at restaurants. They had the foundation of the shared childhood. They had both been the sort of person who had felt things deeply and buried those feelings in the dark sand of her soul. With the clarity of the bright shock of reintegration, she had understood that. She was melodramatic. She had a hard time talking about anything meaningful.

"I took a look at the files he sent, already," Soyoung admits.

"Were they private?"

"Well, in my defense, he sent them through me."

They're reaching a harder part of the trail now, a great mass of hardscrabble stone, the reason that a lot of people turn back before getting to the summit. It's a morass of jutting edges, squeezed out by tectonic activity.

"Do you want me to go first?"

"No. But take my bag. It's got my laptop in there."

"Why'd you bring your—oh, to show me."

Soyoung steps onto the first piece of shale. Going up almost feels like climbing a jungle gym, or doing an easy bouldering course.

She wishes that all her problems were like this pile of rocks. There is nothing to feel about this pile of rocks. There is nothing to imagine about this pile of rocks. There are no decisions to make about this pile of rocks, no complicated emotions, no ownership and what to do with it, no stepping through and experiencing the physical-mental tangle. Just one step, then another. Sweat drips down her neck. She can hear birds calling, responding. The sun is in her eyes, she squints. Her palms scrape against the rock, again and again. She wipes her forehead with the bandana wrapped around her wrist. And then they're at the top.

■ ■ ■

How does Eve feel about eating the apple? Here was the boundary between Eve's mind and her heart. Here was the boundary between her body and the rest of the world. And here was the boundary between good and evil. Here was everything she should do. Here was everything forbidden. She chews, she swallows, and her first thought is to hand the fruit to Adam.

■ ■ ■

"It's going to be hell getting down," YJ says, breathlessly.

Soyoung sits gratefully on a rock. "The loop back is easier, according to the reviews."

"Hikes have reviews online now? Damn."

"Everything has reviews," Soyoung says. "The Mitosis machine? People are going to leave reviews."

"'Two stars. My instancing led to my husband having to choose between my selves, and he said that he didn't want either of them.'"

"Don't joke about that. Taehyung might—"

"Sorry. Do you love him?"

Soyoung frowns at him. YJ looks almost startled to have asked that question. His surprise always makes him look younger.

"Not like we are now," Soyoung says. "I don't think I can, like this. Even if I instanced a second time. It would still be . . ."

How to say that she doesn't understand where love, liking, attraction, where all of that lives in the body. How she's stripped the familiarity from Taehyung and Soyoung's relationship, and now her conglomerate self wonders whether the past was the only thing keeping the relationship solvent. How it makes her wonder, sometimes, if shared history is the single thing that keeps her relationships threaded. She's here, after all, because Yujin and Soyoung grew up together.

She looks back at the landscape in front of her. The first tint of yellow is curling across the farthest mountain. The river is a fat silver snake. On the other bank, there's all the little houses and the black curve of the freeway.

"Most relationships survive post-reintegration," YJ says. "That's statistically proven."

"I think we're far enough away," Soyoung says. She doesn't want to talk about her relationship with Taehyung. YJ hands her the backpack, and she unzips it and pulls out the laptop. She initiates the boot sequence, plugs the USB drive in. Shows YJ the contents of the file.

"The password for the USB is 876212."

"Megan made the password the floor keycode, cute."

Soyoung clicks open the text file. Up pops a no-frills textbox and Yujin's blunt Korean. She hands the screen to YJ. She watches his face as he reads. It's a long letter.

"This is the text file that Yujin included, addressed to you. I read the message, sorry. And I looked through everything."

She wasn't sorry. It had been a long, late night, that had culminated in bad sleep. There was a part of her that hoped YJ would glance over everything and say it was all information he already knew. In some ways, she would have preferred a problem that was dead and buried.

"You said that earlier."

"I just still feel a little bad about it."

"Mm," YJ says. Soyoung stands and walks around so that she can see the screen. He's closed Yujin's message and opened up the first actual file. A report to Megan Taylor and Drew Thorsson—she's pretty sure that's YJ's boss—detailing the status of the technology that would underpin the Mitosis machine, about how it could be installed in a freestanding device with a greater working field radius as opposed to needing the near-skin contact.

"Give me a minute," he says.

"You don't have to look at this now. I'm giving you the USB drive."

"Just give me a minute, please."

He's biting his lip. He looks very out of place, sitting on the jagged rocks in hiking boots and a T-shirt that says MERGEBREAK-CITIBANK 5K across his chest, swiping furiously across the touchpad. She glances down the mountain. This far up, it feels like the rest of the world is very far away.

■ ■ ■

If Eve has the apple, and tells Adam that this will ruin his life but he will learn everything God knows, does he still take it? Or is it kinder to never tell and hand it to him, so he bites guilelessly? Or is it kindest to never hand him the apple at all.

YJ

There's sweat cooling down your back, and you feel the slightest red sting of a sunburn on the bridge of your nose. You've never used a laptop on the top of a mountain before, and it's a hot weight in your lap that you're trying your best not to get sweat or sunscreen on. But mostly you're preoccupied by reading, and your body feels like a piece of meat that you're trapped within, while your mind feels like it's submerged in a vat of electrified water.

■ ■ ■

The knowledge of instancing wasn't the only thing packaged in the forbidden fruit. There was the capability of understanding distance, of understanding that there was a difference between God and people, people and animals, that it was terrible to be naked, that there were things to be done to mitigate their nakedness, that it was possible to lie to each other and to God, that there were things in this world that were simple and that there were things in the world that were complicated.

■ ■ ■

The first file is a long letter from your instance. Not a letter. A set of bullet points and paragraphs and references to various files, beginning with him telling you, *So your old boss visited me . . .* and you have the sense that the document would seem scattered and disjointed to anyone in the universe except for you. For you, the stream of consciousness reads like a clear and flowing river. Item the first, the fact that behind Mitosis, there is a singular, underpinning principle which completely controls instancing. Item the second, this "control" rested not just in being able to disentangle reintegrated instances, but in being able to prevent instances from separating in the first place. A Mitosis gate could be placed at a border and the person crossing could be sure they wouldn't instance. Conversely, two instances, brought within the field of a Mitosis gate, would find themselves inexorably drawn to one another and coalesced, agonizingly, back into a single person. An instance brought into the proximity of a properly calibrated Mitosis gate would find themselves lying on the ground, in pain. It was a weapon. It was a tool. It was the death of instancing as a phenomenon, if it was deployed globally.

Item the third: The gate could be further fine-tuned. It could knit instances together, without the previous necessary skin contact—as long as they were within the radius of the gate. And further, it could provide specific blends of the instances: 20 percent foreign, 80 percent domestic. Or a complete replacement. Overwriting one instance entirely with the other.

Your thoughts turn directly to Yujin. You think about completely overwriting him. You think about keeping a few of his memories—the good things, the things you miss about Korea, the skills he's acquired over the last ten years, but leaving the bulk mostly yourself. You shiver.

"Are you cold?"

Soyoung's sitting near you. She's not looking at your computer. You wonder how she felt, reading this section. If she had the same thoughts you had, whether she looked back at the moment that she reintegrated and thought about how her previous selves would have chosen to lever the proportions in their favor. You think about Yujin, typing this document. You know he must have thought about it.

"Just felt weird, for a moment."

You keep reading. The Mitosis gates could be linked together. You could create a fence with them. You could bisect a room with them. You could create an artificial border in any space. With the Mitosis gate, you could remotely control the process of instancing and reintegration without any physical touch, any underlying personal intention.

This was revolutionary. It was the biggest leap forward in instancing technology since the MERGEBREAK had been developed. It was the biggest leap forward in human technological development since fire, since the printing press, since the jet plane. It could eradicate instancing. It could force every single person crossing a border to instance. It could completely delete an instance's memories upon reintegration—would that be murder? You couldn't think of a business reason that this information hadn't been released at the same time that the original reintegration plans had been announced to the public, unless they were trying to sell the product in stages with higher price points.

Or if the IIS was involved, because the technology was too dangerous. During your meeting with Megan, she had asked you about your instance. She had mentioned that the IIS had oversight. That strange conversation you had with Yujin means he must have seen the documentation that Megan had sent to him, by then. Megan must have expected you to have seen the contents of the USB file before talking with her, or she had been probing to see if you knew what she was talking about.

What could you do with this information? Were you supposed to use it, somehow, to undermine Drew? You could see a path clearly for that: You would bring this information to the public and let everyone know that it had been Drew that had suppressed it. Was that what Megan wanted you to do? No, that couldn't be it. If the IIS was suppressing this information because of how deeply world-shaking it was, then Megan wouldn't take kindly to you blowing the lid. But how were they expecting to keep this a secret, for long? Eventually someone would do the equivalent of jailbreaking a machine. Or a technician would blow the whistle.

Either way, whatever happened, whatever you were supposed to do, you knew this information would make Mitosis an obscene quantity of money if it was publicized and deployed. This would be like being the only company to sell telephones, or the only company to sell the concept of fire.

"How much do you know about the instancing industry?" you ask Soyoung.

"Only what we learned in school."

"This is like looking at the schematics for the atom bomb, but for instancing tech."

"Open the file labeled 'test-dash-schedule-dash-final,'" she says. "I think it's pretty close to the bottom."

You do. It's an Excel spreadsheet that mirrors the one you had looked through to find Soyoung's research study. This one has an extra column, rows you don't remember, unredacted names and numbers.

Soyoung leans over your shoulder.

"Look at the bottom rows."

She points at two rows that are right next to each other. The study that

Soyoung's in, and then right underneath: another study scheduled for the same dates that would test the effects of the reintegration and separation functions at the same time. Recombination at different frequencies, after different amounts of time—microseconds, seconds, full minutes.

"What are the chances that I got accidentally shunted into the wrong study?"

The two studies started on the same date. They had similar barcodes. It was entirely possible this could have happened.

SOYOUNG-ROSE

"Why do you think you're in the wrong study?"

How to explain? Soyoung only has a suspicion. It struck her when looking at the trial datasheet, the dates, the fact that Gerry hadn't told her what trial she was in, because of course you wouldn't tell the test subject what you were being tested for. Instancing studies could be altered based on participant knowledge, since instancing was such a deeply psychological phenomenon. But it hadn't felt like the first time she instanced, going through the gate. She had assumed that was the case because it was an artificial border being created. But now she wondered.

"The dates match up. And the test doesn't feel only like separation."

YJ looks at her. He doesn't understand, she can tell. She wonders what he's thinking.

"If you think that's what's happening, then you should drop out," YJ says, closing the laptop.

"I'm not doing that," Soyoung says.

"Seriously, Soyoung."

"I can't wait for the official rollout, YJ. Both of the trials end with full separation, so."

He's quiet.

"Right?" she says again.

"Sure," YJ says, reluctantly, like he knows the shape of her next sentence. He looks away from her as he slides the laptop back into the backpack.

It's hope, more than truth. It's the fact that she's halfway through the trials and though each encounter has left her feeling unraveled, there have been no permanent effects. It's that she is so close, and she's never going to have another opportunity. Another few weeks and she'll walk out two people. If she pulls out now, there's no future for Soyoung and Rose. She has one goal. The rest is all chaff in the wind.

"I don't want you to get hurt."

"I'm not getting hurt," Soyoung lies. "It doesn't hurt."

YJ's eyes flick from the screen, to her, back to the screen.

"Alright. Fine," YJ says. He stands. "Let's go. Thank you for giving this to me. I'm sorry for getting you involved in this."

"You're welcome," Soyoung says. "Do you still want me to snoop around for you?"

He's quiet for a moment.

"I don't know. I don't—I wish Megan had just *talked* to me," YJ says. "Had told me all of this. Or that Drew hadn't decided he wanted a media puppet."

YJ had told her about how he felt that Drew had hired him partially because he was pliable, because he needed citizenship. He had told her about meeting Megan, and how she had talked in circles. Soyoung frowns.

"Does Megan know about your breakup?"

"No, why?"

"Does she know what Petra looks like?"

"No—Soyoung," he starts.

"So I'll pretend to be your partner and talk to Megan, off the record."

"Please don't talk to her," YJ says.

"I'll just tell her that you know, and see if there's anything else she wants to tell you."

"I can handle myself. I don't need you to fix my problems for me."

"Okay," Soyoung lies. "Let's go home."

▮▮▮

Soyoung isn't investigating YJ's problems solely out of altruism. There's a shred of altruism there, along with a shred of guilt in that she feels a little that she's contributed to his problems. But a larger part of it is: If there is a door, and you have the ability to go to the other side, then would you not go through that door? There is a part of her that is Rose, jumping at the chance to return to Korea. There is a part of her that is Soyoung, desperate to pull Rose into herself. When given a target, she can't not pursue it. This is an intrinsic part of her character.

▮▮▮

They walk down the mountain. It's much easier than the walk up. Near the last fork in the road, YJ stops. He looks at her. His face is serious, intense.

"This changes—I can't help thinking. What if this had existed when we had been younger?"

"Mitosis, you mean."

"The full abilities of it, yeah. Imagine if you could have chosen to instance, when leaving Korea."

He's saying *you,* but Soyoung doesn't think he's talking about her. He's talking about himself and Yujin.

"Let's say they installed a Mitosis machine at Incheon Airport. Would you have chosen to instance?"

"I—I don't know," YJ says.

Soyoung wonders what he's thinking about. How his thoughts must have shifted to interiority. When she had read the papers, she had immediately thought about how her life could have been different if her younger self hadn't instanced, or if there had been some sort of device pressing her back together before she ever even knew she had been separated. She had sat at her kitchen table eating the entire two bags of honey things and thought about a singular future.

Assume she didn't instance. That she could have decided not to instance—would she have done it? She was a kid. Would her mom have told her to do something, either instance or not? Probably. Would she have followed her mom's directions? Yes, because she loved her mother. So then, would her mom have chosen not to instance, when she had left Korea? Would she still have argued with her grandfather? If her grandfather could have chosen whether to instance or not, in what capacity does he cross the semi-stabilized Korean border? How does anyone cross a border? Who gets to choose whether to instance, then? Do parents get to decide for children? Do these get default-placed at every train and airport terminal? Does everyone choose a door to go through: instance, or not? How do you know what you want, if the decision can be made for you?

"Do you think instancing is a good thing?" she says. That's not a question that made sense, before now. Instancing is a fact. It's how the world is. Like gravity and stars and needing to sleep. Except that it's not. The universe is filled with dark matter, embryos can be frozen for decades, planes can fly through the air unassisted. Two steel bars can shape your future.

"If this stuff—if there's a choice. Like, okay. Let's say you get to choose. Do you *want* you and Yujin to exist?"

▪▪▪

This is a thought that was only possible to conceptualize after eating the fruit of the tree of knowledge. Is it good to exist? Is it better to have been created, in any form? Is it right for a third party to create a person out of your rib?

▪▪▪

He looks away.

"The first thing I thought of, when I read what Mitosis could do, was that I would want Yujin's memories, but only the good ones. The useful ones. Overwrite the rest of him with me. I bet he thought the same thing. No—I know he did. And he knows that when I read it, I'll know he did. So, I don't know. Would you have instanced?"

Soyoung shrugs.

"Me now? I want to say no. But I don't know. I liked the idea of leaving. But I wanted to stay, a little. Not enough to stay for real. I knew I was going. I was a kid. I don't know if a kid should be deciding all that. Like, instancing is about—"

"—desire," YJ says.

"I was going to say knowing," Soyoung says. "Like, knowing that you're not going back. That this is permanent. Do you get to know that, as a kid? I guess I wonder, is it good if you don't ever have to ask yourself that question?"

YJ's quiet.

"Yeah, I don't know, either," Soyoung says. "Sorry. I guess I've just been thinking about this a lot. And you're the—well. The recipient of this message."

Soyoung doesn't tell him that she's copied the USB drive onto her personal computer. She doesn't have any plans to do anything with it.

"You didn't talk about it with Yujin?"

"Are you going to? It doesn't seem like something for over the phone."

"No," YJ says. "And I haven't told him about. Um. Us, either."

There is no us, Soyoung almost says. But that would be mean. And there is sort of an *us,* in a way.

■ ■ ■

The acquisition of shared knowledge creates delineation. Adam and Eve against God. Adam and Eve as hiding their sin. Adam and Eve discussing how to proceed, now that they know things, now that they are aware that there are things that they don't know.

■ ■ ■

It's late afternoon by the time they reach the bottom of the trail. The shadows have grown long. They spent the rest of the walk talking about inconsequential things: their plans for next weekend, the scenery around them, and how beautiful it is, about the latest television show that's plastered all over the billboards in Times Square, and how neither of them think it's going to be any good.

The sweat is cooling on Soyoung's skin. She looks around. It's golden hour. The light streams through the branches. They're back where they started. She turns to YJ.

"Do you mind taking a photo of me?"

He looks surprised, but takes out his phone.

"Just here? At the beginning of the trail?"

"Yeah, this is fine. Can you get some of the, like . . . landscape behind me in the frame? So I'm sort of silhouetted there."

"Sure," YJ says, and takes a few steps back. "My shadow's going to be in the frame. Is that okay?"

"It's fine," she says. She doesn't tell him that his shadow in the frame is actually preferable. That for Rose's friends, this implies a date, a good excuse for being busy. It's a paper trail. YJ takes the photo. She has to keep from laughing: He takes photos like a Korean ahjusshi, knees bent.

"Okay," he says, handing her the phone. She scrolls through. She looks happy in the photos. Uncomplicated. She looks like Rose, she guesses, from the color palette of her clothing, from the wide smile. She sends the good ones to her phone, posts them.

"Thank you," she says to YJ. She hands him his phone back. She smiles.

"If it makes you feel better, I'm pretty sure Soyoung would have overwritten Rose in a heartbeat. So."

■ ■ ■

This is a state of affairs that can only exist until God arrives in the garden.

YUJIN

Your phone vibrates while you're at work, and you scramble to grab it. One of your coworkers glances at you. The other is asleep. You pick up your phone and make a sort of apologetic face at them. It's two in the afternoon, and you're just back from lunch at the office cafeteria.

"Hey, it's late," you say to Soyoung. It's still novel to be getting phone calls from Soyoung. You mostly just texted her, or got food together.

"Sorry, were you busy?"

"I'm at work," you say. "I can talk."

"I just wanted to let you know that I got the care package, thanks. And I shared it with your instance."

"Nice. Thanks."

"Cool," she says. You can hear her breath. She hesitates like she wants to say something else.

"Oh, that's it?" you say, tilting your tone teasing. You wonder for a second, if she looked through the files, but you've known her for most of your life. She's never deliberately unkind, and you're doing her a favor, with the Mitosis thing. She probably hasn't opened the USB drive. She wouldn't mention it over the phone.

"Yeah, that's it," she says, not meanly. "I just wanted you to know."

"Things are okay, then?"

"Things are okay," she says. "It's going to be fine, I think. Thanks for passing on—yeah."

"Sure," you say.

She takes another breath.

"Would you have chosen to instance, if you could have? Like if you could press a button and decide to never have instanced. Would you have instanced?"

"No," you say, easily.

"Oh," she says.

"Why?"

"Just thinking," she says. "That wasn't the answer I was expecting. I don't know why."

YJ

You take a shower when you get home. Then you go for a long walk, even though your legs are still sore. You want to think and pacing around your apartment doesn't particularly appeal. You want to call Yujin about this. You don't like that he's a crutch for your thinking. You rely on him too much sometimes, outsourcing your decision-making to him. But there's no decisions here, just—you keep thinking about it. How the ability to completely prevent instancings, cause instancings, rewind people, force them back together—how all of this would combine.

Let's say Mitosis, in its full capacity, gets widespread adoption. Let's say it starts being offered at the airport. You could see this being a service that people buy as they travel: a conscious instancing, or a conscious lack of instantiation. You could see this changing the face of travel, at first at the upper echelons of society, then eventually trickling downward, until the only people who ever have to worry about organic, uncertain instancing are migrants, refugees, and illegal immigrants. You see the shape of the future changing, the same way it changed when the first commercial steamship set sail. You see Mergebreak having a stranglehold monopoly on the market. You see your stock options skyrocketing.

And knock-on effects. Let's say *everyone* knows about it now. Instancing is psychological. Instancing relies on the knowledge that you're never going to return, that you don't want to return. Can you truly know that, in a world with Mitosis? This decouples the action from the emotion. You don't know how this would change things, in the long term. Only that things would change.

SOYOUNG-ROSE

It's raining heavily when she gets to the building, one of those summer storms that like to sweep in and sweep out. New York doesn't get them as bad as Korea does, usually—she remembers through Soyoung's memories, through Rose's filmy childhood remembrances, how the monsoons would pour and then suddenly stop.

Soyoung tracks water into the Mergebreak building. She takes the elevator up and goes through reception. Gerry nods at her. He's standing with a clipboard, talking to a man wearing a blue beanie.

"Almost done," Gerry says.

"Sure," Soyoung replies, and smiles when the man glances at her. He doesn't smile back.

The man looks tired. This is the only word to describe him. There is a slouch to his appearance. His eyes aren't focused, or rather, when he glances in Soyoung's direction, they aren't focused on her, as if he is seeing something beyond her presence, as if he is looking toward some sort of nonexistent horizon. He looks like he's seeing something that does not exist. Beyond that, he's some sort of brown, though Soyoung can't tell where he's from, exactly. His clothes aren't particularly interesting. He's short.

Soyoung hasn't met anyone else who is in the trial, yet, and hadn't expected to. But of course, regardless of which trial she was doing, there were going to be other people enrolled, who didn't know what they were signing up for. She wonders what she looks like, when she comes out of the other side of the machine. Whether she has the same hazy focus, the wandering gaze. Who is she, when she walks out?

"Gross outside, huh? Thanks for not rescheduling."

Gerry's mundane observation shakes her out of her thoughts. She smiles at him.

"Oh, you know. Happy to help advance the cause of science. Was that another person doing the test?"

"Yes," Gerry says. "I can't tell you more. On account of, well, privacy."

"Totally," Soyoung says. *I know something you don't know,* she thinks to herself. She wants to ask him what trial she's in. But she isn't supposed to know about any of that. She only has two options: go forward, or leave.

Gerry punches them in to the testing room. He sets up things at the terminal. Soyoung asks about his weekend. He tells her about going upstate with his girlfriend and their dog. They talk about the dog, whose name is Calpico, and who is a Labrador mix with too much energy. Gerry clearly loves his girlfriend. She bets the girlfriend is Asian—no way is a white guy naming his dog Calpico without her. They met in college. Gerry seems like a genuinely nice guy. Soyoung can't help but wonder: How much does he know about the technology? He knows enough that he's lying to her about the test she's in—unless he's truly just a technician, and has only been instructed about the sequence for programming the Mitosis machine.

"How does this work, practically?"

"I can't tell you that," Gerry says. "Not until we start selling commercially."

He presses the button. The gate becomes a void, and there is no world on the other side. Soyoung does not want to walk through. Artificial emotion induced by the machine. She wants to know. She closes her eyes. She steps forward, and—

I am twenty-five years old and I am hungry. I skipped lunch, a work meeting ran late, and I'm trying to lose a few kilograms so I don't mind, really. But I'm still hungry. My body hasn't gotten the signal that my brain has given it, which is that we are trying to lose weight.

I'm daydreaming about food. I want pizza. I want crisp French fries. I want tteokbokki and twigim. I tell myself I can have this in the future, when I'm skinny. I've lost weight before—everyone loses weight before they start college, it's important to look good for college, even if you looked terrible in high school—but I gained it

I am twenty-five years old and I am making kimchi with my mother. She's telling me I need to learn how to cook. We've never done this before. We buy kimchi from the store and she tells me to wrap it in two layers of plastic wrap and don't eat it forty-eight hours before a date or important interview because it will make my breath smell weird to Americans. I have a vague memory of doing this as a child, with my grandmother, before she died.

People in my family were always dying or leaving. I don't think about these things anymore.

It's less that I like Korean food and more that it's the default food I eat back by drinking and eating out. So I have to go on a diet. Because I want a new job, and if I'm not pretty then it will be harder for me to get a new job, and even more than that I like people not judging me and sometimes I think I should have gotten a nose job and eyelid surgery. Sometimes I think society should be different.

But I live in the world as it is. And I can bear any suffering for my own bright future.

when I cook. But I don't cook for myself. I never really think about where my food comes from. I eat a lot of Trader Joe's prepackaged meals and dinners with my friends in cheap restaurants and I also eat a lot of sandwiches. I don't mind this.

I wonder if my mother is trying to connect with me. I think that this is a really stereotypical attempt to connect with me, if it is. I have read a lot of diaspora novels.

I want to ask her about Korea but it feels like the wrong moment. I don't know what the right moment would be. My childhood feels like a different country. I don't think of it often. It feels like it exists behind a door that often stays shut.

The fresh kimchi smells really good. It smells like spice and garlic and green growing things. I eat a piece.

My mother asks how I like it.

I tell her it's good. She smiles. I smile back. It's a good moment. I don't want to complicate it. So I don't ask any more questions.

—she kaleidoscopes through, falling to the floor.

■ ■ ■

When she gets home, she examines every inch of her skin in the mirror. She wants to see if there are any scars, any acne pockmarks, any moles that can confirm whether she's proportionally more Soyoung, or more Rose. But it's impossible to tell. She hadn't memorized her skin—neither version of her skin. She thinks that she's the same as when she went in. But it would feel that way, wouldn't it? What if they put her back together wrong? But it had felt so different, to become Soyoung-Rose, not just Soyoung, not just Rose.

She gives up. She gets in the shower. Steam clouds her vision.

As she scrubs, Soyoung thinks about the house again. What her mother had said about the house. How she and her mom had such a hard time talking about anything. It would have been easier if her mom gave her clear-cut instructions. If her mom—either of her moms—had opinions. If her mom in Korea had sat Soyoung down and told her that she wanted the house. If her mom here had said *sell the house!*

And she realizes she's thinking about Rose's mom as *her* mom. She doesn't know if it's just that it's a slip of the mind, or if something's changed by going through the gate.

YUJIN

You open the door to your apartment, juggling two heavy bags from Emart. You could have used more bags and more trips to carry the groceries but that would have felt like losing. You're met with your mom and Soyoung's mom drinking tea.

"Ah, Yujin-ah," your mom says. "Say hi to Soyoung's mom."

"Hello," you say politely. You've never really gotten used to talking with Soyoung's mom, as an adult. When you see her—or any of your friends' moms, really—you feel about ten years old.

"Wow, Yujin-ah, how have you been? How's your job? How's your instance?"

"It's good," you say. "He's good."

Soyoung's mom always asks about your instance. You always say that he's good. Soyoung's mom is the only person, other than your parents, who really asks about YJ, and you never know what to tell her. You don't know what your mom tells Soyoung's mom about him.

"Have you heard from Rose? I heard you kids met, when she was here."

You try not to freeze—try to keep your hand moving as you put the green onion into the fridge. You don't know what Soyoung's mom knows about what Soyoung is doing. You know your mom doesn't know anything—unless Soyoung's mom told her. But why would Soyoung's mom ask about Rose, unless she knew?

"I talked a little with her," you say, trying to keep your tone casual. "Not a lot."

None of this is a lie.

"Good, that's good," Soyoung's mom says.

"I don't know how you do it, not checking in on her," your mom says.

"She's got her mom," Soyoung's mom says. "It's not my place."

"But she's your *daughter*," your mom says, and it sounds like an old argument, there's no heat behind your mother's tone.

"Well, we have to keep it separate somehow. She doesn't need two mothers,"

Soyoung's mom says, and sometimes you really do see how Soyoung and Soyoung's mom are related.

"Do you talk about us a lot?"

They turn to you from where they're sitting at the dining table with their coffee and cookies. They look surprised, like they forgot you were here. You keep putting the groceries away.

"Sure, you're our kids," your mom says. And you just kind of nod to that, because you've never felt comfortable talking about this with your mom.

■ ■ ■

There's no one way to globally, singularly characterize the relationships between families and their instances. There were cultures in which the instance was shunned. There were cultures in which the instance was an honored guest, but meant never to reintegrate. There were cultures where upon sight, the instances were forced to reintegrate. There were cultures who sold their instance into bondage—there were cultures who spread rumors about the slavery of the instanced self in order to accuse other cultures of barbarism. There were cultures that killed instances upon their creation. In the global, homogenized west, the instance is an awkward, vestigial thing. Impossible to ignore in the age of global telecommunications and cheap long-distance flights. Some scholars have called the instance a problem of modernity, arguing that in the past, the difficulty of transit created natural divides.

But at the familial level, well—it depends on the family. In most of them, an instance of your son still stays your son.

■ ■ ■

You go back outside after putting the groceries away. You look at the time. You want to tell Soyoung about what just happened, but it's not a reasonable hour. You text YJ instead: *Mom's talking with Soyoung's mom. Kind of funny SY's mom asked if I had talked with R recently.*

YJ types back: *Why?*

You call him. He picks up.

"Why're you awake?"

"Work," YJ says.

"It's three in the morning."

"I'm almost done," he says. You can hear him typing.

"What are you working on?" you ask. You wonder if all these late nights are partially your fault—the data on the USB drive. He's seemed distant, since then. You haven't mentioned it. Megan's sharply bounded concern keeps you from wanting to talk about it over the phone.

"Do you think instancing is a good thing?" YJ says.

"Instancing? Like, the concept?"

"Like the fact that it exists at all," he says.

"It's just a fact," you say. "Like, is gravity good or bad? Is death good or bad?"

"Well, is death good or bad?"

"Soyoung asked me if reintegration was like dying, before Rose visited."

"God, she's strange," YJ says. He sounds really fond all of a sudden. They must have been *actually* hanging out, outside of the favor he's doing for her, outside of the USB drive. You thought you would like the fact that they're friends, but the slight sliver of jealously like a sour candy bursting on your tongue surprises you.

"Death is probably bad," you say.

"Would you want my life, if you had to choose?" he says. "Just, binarily. Between mine and yours."

"I don't know," you say, and you know that he's read the files, that he's read your thoughts on the files, that both of you have had that thought: what if it were only you.

SOYOUNG-ROSE

Soyoung leans against the wall of the testing chamber. At this angle, she can see Gerry's hands as he calibrates the Mitosis gate. She wishes she could ask him what he's doing, or pull out the USB and review the calibration sequence for the various Mitosis capabilities, comparing what she's been given to Gerry's actions.

"What interested you in all of this?" she says.

Gerry looks up. "My parents are both instances. My mom's from Russia. My dad's from, I forget where, a lot of places."

"Oh. Should I be apologizing or congratulating them?" Soyoung tries to tilt the question kind, not cruel. She had assumed that he had sprung fully formed out of an American suburb.

Gerry shakes his head, glances at her.

"Probably both, maybe my mom more than my dad. It wasn't so easy for her. Russia, you know?"

"Not really."

"Like I don't think she's allowed back in the country," he says. "Or she'll get like, the gulag or something."

He gives kind of a self-conscious laugh. He punches a green button, and then turns a dial. "I don't actually know a lot about what happened with them."

"My mom's side of the family is technically from North Korea," Soyoung says. "I get it."

"Yeah, you know."

"Do most of the people who work here have a connection to instancing?"

"I think a lot of the people on the Condensco side have instances, but people don't talk about it much. It's kind of personal. I don't know for sure."

"Sure," Soyoung says.

"Anyway. Ready?"

Soyoung wonders if the study, whichever study it is, is being compromised by the fact that she knows too much about Mitosis now. If instancing is about desire, which is related to knowledge—then to know too much about what's happening might change the results. But that might not matter. The Mitosis machine supposedly bypasses intent. The only intent that matters here is her decision to walk through.

"Yes."

He turns the machine on. She closes her eyes. She walks forward, and—

I am twenty-one years old and I've just gotten a phone call from my childhood friend. I haven't talked to him in years. We drifted apart. It's my fault, except for the fact that it's his fault. I was angry that he asked me out. I shouldn't have laughed. But he shouldn't have asked me out. It ruined things.

But I pick up. Because he is my friend and underneath everything I will always pick up, because of all those summer afternoons at the playground. I care about him.

He sounds bad on the phone. He tells me he instanced.

I ask where he is. He says he's on the air train. I ask if he's with anyone. He says his parents.

I remember what it was like when I was eleven, almost against my will. I hate thinking about this. I am always thinking about this.

I hear him quietly sniff. This surprises me. I don't know why it surprises me. I just sometimes have a hard time thinking that other people have feelings.

A bad and secret part of me feels good that Yujin feels that way. I spend

I am twenty-one years old and I am playing a video game with my high school friends. We are all a little too old for this, but it's school break and it's very cozy, to be sitting in Clarissa's basement squished between Esther and Sujit, while we yell at Yuna, who has the controller.

We're playing *Myst. Myst* is a really old single-player puzzle game about exploring an island that the player has been transported to through a book. We are trying to explore the island and also to find a way off the island, I suppose, although I've lost the plot. There are a series of puzzles that need to be solved to advance the plot.

We used to play games like this in high school and middle school. Single-player games controlled by a single person, with the rest of us yelling instructions. Creating something collaborative out of something meant to be singular. I don't remember why we started. We haven't done it in years. Playing this with them feels nostalgic. It is an uncomplicated joy to yell at my friends, all of us pretending that we are younger than we are.

a lot of time pretending not to have my experiences. I like that there are people in the world who understand how I feel, or have the same experience I do. I think he might be able to. I try not to think this thought; I fail.

I ask him if he wants to meet me at my university, and if he wants to ditch his parents and talk about what happened. I say I will buy him coffee or alcohol or whatever he wants. It's a stupid token gesture. I am trying to tell him that I understand.

It makes him laugh. He says yes.

—she collapses through on the other side.

■ ■ ■

When Soyoung gets home, she opens the files she's copied from Yujin's USB. She reads the instructions for utilizing the machine. For catalyzing the separation process. For activating the reintegration process. For stopping instancing. For starting instancing. What the waveforms on the screen need to look like, for various configurations of instances. What does it mean, that Soyoung's memory reverberated longer than Rose's? She doesn't precisely remember what the screen looked like, beforehand, when Gerry was using it.

In her head, she recites the rest of Rose's memory: They played the video game together, and then they went and got pizza at the place that did the fried chicken pizza, and they talked about who everyone from high school was dating or had broken up with. She's heard that every time you remember a memory, that memory is then rewritten. She wonders what is getting rewritten, in the Mitosis machine. If the reintegration afterward is subtly different. But there's no way for her to know. It doesn't feel like that day in the forest.

YUJIN

The only reason you notice is because you're on Soyoung's Instagram, updating her profile with a Seoul-based location tag. Just a photo of a very pretty cup of a chocolate-coffee concoction, with a high tower of whipped cream and little candy pearls. Aesthetic girl–type post. Aesthetic girl–type drink. You ordered it because it was something Soyoung would buy for a post. Not what she would actually drink. Not what you would order for her, as a joke.

Soyoung's Instagram is all photographs like this—pretty candy-color concoctions, with the occasional photo of her in profile, the occasional photograph of her and Tae, photographs of her and her family sometimes. You scrolled through idly. Then you saw Rose Kang on the list of recommended profiles. You clicked on it.

Rose's Instagram is a lot like Soyoung's. Less cute little cafes, more bars. More photographs with her friends—there's a blond girl that shows up a lot. More photographs of her alone in front of a pretty landscape or a landmark. You scroll back up. Then you stop. The second-to-last photo—a pretty landscape with rolling hills. She's standing, looking tired but happy. There's a shadow of a man in front of her.

You recognize that shadow. It's an absurd thing to say—but you do. That's your shadow. That's your silhouette. That's *YJ's* silhouette, and attached to it is YJ's body, taking Soyoung's photo. You hadn't thought they were still hanging out. You've seen videos of Manhattan. There's no way they're in the city. They're on a trip together somewhere. YJ's the photographer.

You think for a moment. Then you open your shared photo drive to see what YJ's phone has been uploading.

Photographs of Soyoung. Photographs and photographs of Soyoung. Soyoung in front of mountains. Soyoung at a restaurant. Soyoung at the park, holding a SpongeBob ice cream bar. You catch glimpses of YJ in reflections on glass, in his shadow on the floor. Things you wouldn't notice unless you were looking, unless you were the man in the photograph looking for your other self. And maybe this is friendship. But you know yourself. You know who you are, and you know what it looks like when you *like* someone, when you *care* about them, when they're the sort of girl that makes you imagine a whole future with them. You have never seen this expression outside of an accidental glimpse of your reflection in a restaurant mirror.

You've never looked at Soyoung that way—not without the soft cushion of your previous friendship, without the glass wall of knowing she's taken.

"That motherfucker," you say. You almost admire your other self's nerve.

■ ■ ■

In the first world, they split apart and never meet again. In the second world, they grow up together and she falls in love with someone else—more than that, she falls in *commitment,* builds a future and a life with him, and you never want anything at all. In the third world, you aren't yourself, and you haven't known her in the contexts you know her, and she knows you in more contexts than you know yourself, and—

What are you talking about? Attraction isn't love. A crush doesn't mean anything. Have they slept together? You didn't think that Soyoung was that sort of girl. No, that's shitty. What you really don't like is that it's him and not you.

■ ■ ■

You drink the too-sweet coffee. You kind of wish Soyoung was here, Soyoung before everything, who would be the one drinking the coffee and she would have bought you a drink that was truly the worst concoction of all time. Soyoung who you could just ask questions of and have answered. You wish you were YJ, so you would know what he's thinking without needing to ask him. You spend too long looking through the photos. You try and find any other evidence of . . . anything. How Soyoung feels about this. Whether there's a relationship here, or just one-sided attraction. Or if you're just imagining things. But you don't think you are. You know yourself.

You don't know what to do about this information. You wonder whether you should tell someone. But who to tell? You're Soyoung's friend, not Tae's friend, and anyway, you don't have any proof. You can't go to him with a bunch of photographs and say, *Hey man, I think your fiancé's reintegration is cheating on you with my instance.* And you can't talk to YJ about this. You play the conversation out in your head. You imagine being him. You don't know if you would tell the truth, if you were asked. You would dodge the question. You would change the subject. You would say something like, *What are you talking about* and *I thought you told me we should be friends—I was just taking a photograph for her.* And you can't talk to Soyoung about this. It would spiral, messily. And half of Soyoung doesn't have the context in which to know you.

You wonder what they talk about. Whether she's telling him all about you-and-her. Whether he's telling her things about you. You feel like you're in a bad K-drama. Maybe you *should* tell Tae. Why didn't your other self tell you about this, when you called last week?

You finish the too-sweet drink. You decide that, much like the USB drive, there's nothing you can do about this. You feel like there's never anything you can do about anything.

SOYOUNG-ROSE

"You don't have an instance, do you?" Soyoung asks Gerry, while he sits at the terminal and pokes at the keys. She's leaning against the wall in a way where she can surreptitiously watch the screen. She's mentally reciting the steps from the files on the USB. First, Gerry drags a digital slider on the left, which looks like an approximation of the diagrams that she's seen. Second, he's going to—yes, there he goes, setting a dial between ranges epsilon and zeta, next he'll put the calibration numbers into—yes. He's doing everything she expects. This is the calibration for the study she found on the USB drive. The one that's testing simultaneous separation and reintegration. That knowledge doesn't change anything, though.

"No," Gerry says. "I get asked about it a lot, when I tell people where I work."

"I bet," Soyoung says.

"It's interesting. I don't mind it. Alright, I think we're ready. Are you ready?"

"Yes," Soyoung says, and Gerry hits the digital switch and the space between the Mitosis gate goes strange and Soyoung's used to it now, so she closes her eyes and walks forward.

I am twenty-seven and I am going on a hike with my boyfriend, up the old city walls. It's late at night. The spray of lights in the city below is like stars or a movie set. It is beautiful, from above. The path is illuminated by low, golden lights. Sometimes I feel lucky to be living my life. It is sometimes very good and easy.

We're holding hands. It makes us go slower than we would, individually, but his hand is warm and pleasantly envelopes mine and it feels safe and good. I look at him out of the corners of my eyes. He's handsome. I like the thoughts that exist in his head. I think I love him.

We walk and pass other people. It's mostly couples. This is a date spot, I realize. It's romantic. It's velvet sky and soft lighting and sweet isolation and the warm summer night breeze. It's meant to foster good feelings.

We reach the top of the path. This is the highest point of the old city walls. I look over. From here, the entire north side of Seoul is visible. In my mind, Seoul is the only city in Korea worth anything. But I was born here and I've lived my entire life here. I'm biased. I wonder if I would feel differently if I were someone else.

Kang Soyoung, he says. I turn.

My boyfriend sinks down to one knee. He pulls out a ring.

He tells me he loves me. He asks me to marry him.

For a moment, the sky above me feels like a great black bowl and I feel like I am a rat in a trap. But the feeling passes as quickly as it came, replaced with an ecstatic happiness bubbling up in my chest. I am thinking about the future as a good place to go to. I am thinking about doorways being opened. I am thinking, underneath all of this, that I am going to have a good life.

I say yes.

I am twenty-seven and I am sitting alone at a bar, reading a really good book. I am very content. This is not always true. But right now, I cannot imagine anywhere or time in the world where I would rather exist.

—she falls through the gate.

▪ ▪ ▪

After Soyoung goes down to the lobby, she calls Tae. She does it before she can think about it too hard, with the memory of his proposal sitting sweetly in the meat of her temporal lobe.

Tae picks up on the second ring.

"Ah, Soyoung," he says, and then there's a cut-off portion of breath. She knows that he wants to say something but is stopping himself.

"How have you been?" she says. She doesn't feel the bright bloom of affection she had thought she might. This is a strange relief. She does feel the guilt, the vague and shapeless desire to be better to him in a thousand ways. To stop forgetting about him. To be faithful. To consider him *hers* and not an artifact of her prior self's life.

"I'm doing okay," he says. "Are you out?"

"I'm walking home."

"Are you—" he says, and then cuts himself off again. And she knows that he wants to talk to her, but he doesn't want to talk to her like she is, and that he misses her, but she, as he knows her, doesn't exist. But she could just be extrapolating incorrectly. Soyoung's memories filtered through Rose's logic aren't necessarily truth. She shouldn't have called him. She had wanted to test who she was but—this is cruel.

"I miss you," she lies. She doesn't miss Tae. She misses being the person who would have missed him. She misses being the person who didn't know he existed.

▪ ▪ ▪

It occurs to her later, when she's about to fall asleep. She could use the Mitosis machine without a technician, as long as she had access to it.

YJ

You're standing between the chips and the beef jerky, contemplating the merits of sour cream and onion versus salt and vinegar, contemplating whether you should be eating chips after going to the gym. You answer the phone after glancing at the caller ID.

"Hey, did you want to do s—"

"I'm at the natural history museum," Soyoung says. "Megan just walked in, and I'm watching her from across the gallery. I'm going to go talk to her. I assume you want to listen in? I can put you on speakerphone with the volume down."

"What?"

You drop the bag of chips you're holding. The guy at the register gives you a sidelong glance. You mouth an apology while jamming the phone between your shoulder and your ear, bending down to pick up the bag.

"I see Megan."

"How do you know it's her?"

"YJ, I have the internet," Soyoung says.

"Did you *stalk* her?"

"No, I just saw that she had liked a few posts about an after-dark event at the museum."

You're stumped. You put the bag back on the shelf numbly. You think that still counts as stalking.

"It was a little bit of a long shot," Soyoung says. "But I had nothing going on tonight."

"Soyoung, let it lie, seriously. I'll talk to her myself."

"YJ, do you think if you approach her in her office again, she'll tell you the truth?"

You stare at the chips in front of you. There are Original Tasty, Salt & Vinegar, Sweet & Spicy, Dill-icious Pickle, Sour Cream & Onion. You wonder why there are so many flavors that are combinations of two different flavors, how many decisions people made that enshrined Dill-icious Pickle as part of the flavor canon, because you're pretty sure that five years ago you weren't seeing nearly as many pickle flavors as you do now. There is someone deciding what chip flavors go to market. The Drew of pickle chips.

You want to know what Megan meant by *if Drew were removed.* You want her to know that you received the USB drive, and ask if there was anything she wanted to tell you, away from your official titles. You think about where you are in relation to the American Museum of Natural History. A twenty-minute drive, if the traffic's bad. Ten minutes if it's good. You could take the subway, but then you'd have to get off the phone.

"Go ahead and talk to her. Keep me on the line, please. I'm on my way."

You walk out of the bodega, and you hail a cab.

■ ■ ■

In Eden, which was the entirety of the world, there was no hiding from God. God had created everything in Eden. God walked with Adam and Eve as their companion. God had made them in his reflection. God was the one who understood the division between the self and the other. And yet, Adam and Eve attempted to hide their transgressions. Adam and Eve bite the fruit of knowledge. Adam and Eve, so enamored with their new understanding, forget that lying is an old skill, for God.

SOYOUNG-ROSE

Megan is standing underneath a whale. The whale is a full-size replica of a grown blue whale, hanging weightlessly above a dark, two-story hall, illuminated only by spotlights and the luminescent glow of the backlit dioramas. Dead fish and dead birds and dead amphibians, everywhere, arranged as if they're still alive. Soyoung is leaning against a railing, watching Megan order something from the temporary bar cart set up under the whale. The whale is magnificent—she remembers Rose's memories of being thirteen and going on a field trip here and walking under the whale, being unnerved by the weight of it, how it loomed over everything, how it was being held by such thin, invisible wires.

"I'll let you ask the hard things, I guess?" she says to YJ, over the phone.

"Yes, please," he says.

"I'm going to tell her that you know about stuff. And I'm going to tell her I'm your girlfriend. As an alibi."

"I—sure."

Soyoung walks around the balcony, keeping her eye on Megan. Around her, there's a few strangers holding canned spiked seltzers or teeny little plastic cups of white wine or water. She locates the stairs. She likes that the museums in New York do nights like this to get people in their doors. Rose hadn't been back since she was a kid. Soyoung's never been here before.

"I really don't know why I'm surprised you did this," YJ says. "You flew to the States just to ask me to help you get separated. Stalking someone is nothing, compared to that."

"It wasn't stalking. Her socials are public."

"Were you afraid of instancing, then?"

"No," Soyoung says. She thinks back to how it felt leaving, this time. She hadn't thought about it until she was about to land. "I knew what I wanted."

"The thing that gets me," YJ says, "is that with Mitosis, no one would have to be scared."

Soyoung sweeps around the curve of the balcony. She passes the arced windows that show: herons mid-spear of a bluegill; starfish and sea urchins beneath kelp; seahorses clinging to rock formations.

"You know what's a little funny? This is like when Yujin came with me before I met my instance for the first time. For moral support. We got coffee. I asked him whether he thought reintegration was like dying—"

"Why would you *ask* someone that?"

"It made sense in context," Soyoung says.

"I don't think it's like dying," YJ says.

"It's not like dying, for the record. Yujin never really gave me an answer on what he thought," she says. "Okay, I'm putting you on speaker and I'm going to go talk to her. We're in the room with the big whale. Come find us there."

Soyoung takes out her earbud as she approaches the sweeping staircase down to the first floor. She wonders how best to intersect Megan, unobtrusively. It's not like intercepting YJ—that was a planned meeting, and he was a stranger with the face and temperament of a friend. Megan is a true stranger, and all she knows about her is that YJ had been friends with her, as much as you could be friends with your boss.

YJ

You walk into the natural history museum after paying the entrance fee for the after-dark event. They ask if you want to check a coat. You're still in your gym clothes; you check your gym bag. You go through the entrance into the main hall with the huge dinosaur skeletons, currently lit with neon spotlights for the night event.

You're only half paying attention. You've been listening to Soyoung and Megan talk. You think they're probably still in the whale room. Soyoung had introduced herself and had told Megan that YJ received the USB drive. Megan had sounded—not suspicious, but a little guarded. You think that the only reason she hasn't walked off yet is that Soyoung told her that you were coming soon. You're positive that Soyoung's original suggestion—to pretend to be Petra in order to get the information from Megan, wouldn't have worked. But now they've steered the conversation back to calmer waters, talking about the museum.

"Have you guys ever been to the instancing section?" Megan says.

"There's an instancing section?"

"Next to the planetarium," Megan says. "Mergebreak contributed some of the funds, if I'm remembering correctly."

You remember that. You had gone, when it had opened a few years ago.

"Cool."

"We can go check it out, after YJ gets here."

You walk through halls that have half a forest lovingly recreated behind plexiglass, little dioramas of the savannah, tropical rainforests, the tundra. And then you're in the whale hall, looking for Megan, for Soyoung. You spot them near the center of the room.

▮▮▮

There is a school of thought, that God must have placed the forbidden fruit in the middle of Eden for a reason. What use is it, to place something easily accessible and forbid it? It must have been a test. Humanity's actions were in line with God's plans.

■ ■ ■

They turn to you as you approach.

"Hey," you say. "Thanks for waiting."

You don't know that anyone was in a hurry but it just seemed like the thing to say. Soyoung smiles at you. You smile back at her, pull her in for a kiss like you would have done for Petra and hope that Soyoung goes along with it. She does. Soyoung kisses you back, a soft brief brush of her lips against yours before you break away and turn to your former boss.

"Hi," you say. "Fun seeing you here."

"Hey, so good to see you," Megan says. "Was this on purpose?"

"This was mostly date night," YJ says. "But I wanted to catch you outside of the office. You should make your likes private."

"If it wasn't you, this would be creepy," Megan says.

"But it is me," YJ says. "The only me possible. You know, since my instance is in Korea."

Megan cracks a smile.

"It's a bit—YJ, how much have you told—"

"I'll go check out that exhibit," Soyoung says brightly. "And you can talk. I'll meet you later?"

"Sure," you say, and she punctuates her leave-taking with a second kiss. For a moment, you wish it meant something real.

You and Megan walk away from the center of the hall and the looming bulk of the whale over to a corner, where there's a coral reef exhibit with tiny little clownfish and other tropical fish whose names you don't know, pinned into place as they would have swum in life against a backdrop of preserved coral.

"I got your message," you say. "The one you sent to Yujin. I guess you were obliquely asking if I had gotten it, the last time we talked. Why did you give this to me? I appreciate the heads-up, but it seems . . ."

You watch Megan, who is watching the fish, who aren't moving.

"I am going to tell you something too sensitive for the USB drive," Megan says. "I can provide proof once your clearance goes through, if you agree with me on how to handle the situation."

▪▪▪

To deliberately set a trap with the forbidden fruit would be a cruel trick for God to play. To know your creation would act in a certain way and still set them up to fail, that could only be the action of a cruel and unjust god.

▪▪▪

"Okay," you say.

▪▪▪

Or maybe it had all been a test. Maybe if Adam had responded to God without a lie, had he boldly claimed what he had known, then there would have been no punishment.

▪▪▪

"I didn't tell you how the conversation between Drew and I went, when we were trying to figure out what to do with Mitosis. Drew wanted to take the product to market before reporting it. The whole package. Total capabilities. And I wanted to take everything to IIS, so they would bury it," Megan says. "I hadn't thought what we'd develop would be so . . . *deployable.* So unobtrusive. It's the sort of tech that can be hidden in doorways. In lampposts. Hell, you could get two guys to hold them while walking down the street. So, we argued about it. Me, Drew, a couple of others, but really mostly just me and Drew. Because the concept of taking the whole thing to market was his baby. He wanted to follow the tech playbook: Move fast, break things, change the world, or at least secure your exit before the authorities have a chance to regulate. I thought this would get us all put in jail. And, you know, I didn't want to work in a world where *Drew* was in charge of the entire phenomenon of instancing. Like, would you even trust Drew with a kid at the airport?"

"I might trust him at an airport. He seems to know airports."

"Fine, a kid in like, a mall. Kid walking down Fifth Avenue. Anyway, long story short. I won. We brought everything to IIS. Mitosis in all its glory."

Megan looks away from the fish diorama. She shrugs a little, wry smile on her face as she continues the story.

"And that's when IIS got interested. Not in shutting it down. In getting a first cut."

She describes what happened in clinical detail. There were a series of negotiations which had ended with: IIS would continue funding the project, in return for a temporary moratorium on the public knowledge of Mitosis's full capabilities. Meanwhile, IIS would quietly install Mitosis gates at strategic border control points, checkpoints, airports and ports, simultaneously with the public release of the consumer service, which would be bolstered with all the goodwill and branding that Mergebreak had earned in the last few decades. And at the five-year mark, Mergebreak would be allowed to sell full-capacity Mitosis machines to various foreign governments on an approved list, and then would finally be given the right to sell the full-capacity service to individuals. Mergebreak would get what was effectively a state monopoly, in return for cooperating with the IIS.

▪▪▪

Imagine a world where the choice to instantiate is decided through a checklist. Through an interview. Through clean governmental decisions based on the current geopolitical climate. A world where every checkpoint has a machine that neatly severs the past from the present. Imagine a world where an application must be accepted to divide the self. Imagine how neat the world is, here, how the agony of uncertainty is so sweetly removed.

▪▪▪

"So, I was angry," Megan says. "Like, existentially pissed. We were going to be colluding with the federal government on deceiving people? I was going to write a really scathing op-ed and try and get it in the *New York Times* or the *Atlantic* or something. And then I got a job offer from the IIS. They wanted a liaison. So, you know. Now I'm here."

"You changed your mind that quickly?"

For a moment, she looks ashamed. Then some muscle in her mouth tightens.

"It was going to happen with or without me," Megan says. "It didn't matter what I wanted. What mattered was what was going to happen."

You imagine the world with Mitosis deployed as Megan suggests. First, quietly at the borders. Then, in a series of advertised revelations. Services sold to consumers. Mitosis gates sold to other countries. Until it becomes the unspoken norm of public society, the same way that taking your shoes off at the airport was a norm, or checking a passport at the border. Mergebreak was going to make so much money. Their stock price was going to go through the roof.

Megan starts walking to the next diorama. YJ follows her. This one is a double-wide. A school of small silver fish, being corralled by a few larger, predatory fish.

"So that's it. That's everything," Megan says.

"This shouldn't be legal," YJ says. "No—I know what you're going to say. It's not illegal, so it's legal until proven otherwise."

Megan nods. "Like crypto, or the internet. Or cloning. Or, like the invention of the airplane. They haven't created legislation around Mitosis yet, because they don't know what it can really do. To quote Drew, 'We're getting in on the ground floor.'"

The silver fish must have been individually mounted. That's a tremendous amount of work. A tremendous number of dead fish.

"So, what do you want me to do about it?" YJ asks, turning to Megan.

"This is an option," Megan says. "You don't have to say yes. If you don't say yes, then we never need to talk about this again. And that's okay! Seriously, it's okay. I gave you what I gave you because I thought it was unfair you were being put in your position. I'll still back you, if Drew pulls anything. Okay?"

"Okay," you say.

"But if you're game, I want you to publicly leak this information, in a few years. After the rollout. Everything but the schematics—the extent of the full capabilities, the government backing, the deal that Mitosis has with IIS. And I want you to point at Drew as the one who agreed to make the government agreement happen, behind the public's back. I want the board to have a good reason to force Drew out."

You stare at her. She's asking you to be a whistleblower.

"I want you to take his toy away from him," Megan says. "And in return, I'll put in a heavy recommendation for a second promotion for you. You get his job. Mergebreak is fully in bed with the IIS now, and I'm the IIS liaison."

"Why after the rollout?"

"Because—well, this is my project now."

You want her to emit more than the lightest, mildly sheepish tone of embarrassment. You feel that she should feel a greater hypocrisy. To turn around from decrying Mitosis to quietly administering a program that would deploy it, secretly, without the public knowing. You wanted her to be better than the average person, if she had the ability to change lives. You dislike how even if Mitosis is a technology with global, far-reaching implications, it feels like it's a pissing match between two people.

And more than that, you dislike how you don't disagree with how Megan is handling things. You don't know that you would be handling it differently.

"Why me?"

"Who else?" Megan says. "Take some time. Think about it. Then come back and talk to me, okay?"

You look away from the diorama, the silver fish, the sharklike predators.

"I—thanks. I will. I should go find my girlfriend."

"She seems nice," Megan says.

"She's—I'm very grateful to her," you say. You don't know that you'd call Soyoung nice.

▪▪▪

If Adam and Eve had simply practiced lying to each other, rather than first attempting to lie to their omniscient deity, then they might never have had to leave paradise. Or they should have eaten the fruit from both trees. Or they should have been different people, in a different creation myth.

SOYOUNG-ROSE

Soyoung had followed the signs that took her around the space center and into the hall containing the history of instantiation. It was set up as a timeline, with artifacts, reproductions, screens playing looping videos. *Instancing has been with us since our earliest beginnings,* the sans-serif wall text declares. The exhibit runs through instancing as documented in prehistoric and ancient civilizations, through early history, through the modern era. It touches upon the experiments conducted by the Axis and Allied powers during World War Two, the experiments done during the Cold War in the U.S.S.R. and by the CIA, the university-based studies done during the seventies, ending with the development of the MERGEBREAK and leaving on a note of optimism toward new innovations. The exhibit is only mildly sanitized. It acknowledges that until the current day, most instancing research was produced under wartime conditions, and in many cases on political prisoners.

It's not a bad exhibit. When she comes out the other side there's a staircase that leads back to the Peoples halls, the ones that have little dioramas and exhibits of all the various non-western cultures. She walks through them, passing people holding little drinks and looking at the various dioramas. She's always felt a little weird that those exist. She remembers Rose coming here in high school, with her friends who were a grab bag of different ethnicities, looking at the strange little exhibits where their cultures were pinned on display. Indian subcontinent. Africa. Pacific Islander. East Asia. It had been fun—but in retrospect, it was strange that these existed. Soyoung shivers and takes the stairs down and finds herself in a hall full of birds. In the half-light, it's ominous. Her phone rings. She picks up.

"Where are you?" YJ asks.

"The room filled with birds," she says.

"Is it quiet?"

"No one's really in here. It's a little creepy."

"Okay. Gonna come meet you. Stay there."

Soyoung puts her phone away. She sits down on one of the benches.

▪▪▪

There has never been a documented case of a bird, or any other animal, instancing.

▪▪▪

YJ comes from the opposite direction she had walked in, his quick footsteps echoing on the floor. Soyoung turns toward him. He sits down next to her.

"They have a Korean diorama, in the Asian section. With all the old Korean stuff," he says.

"I saw that back in high school. It's still up?" Soyoung says.

"It's still up."

He's silent for a moment, looking at his hands. Soyoung can see little beads of sweat at the nape of his neck, as if YJ's run a long way. He's nervous. She's surprised. The conversation had seemed congenial when she left.

She's about to ask him what's going on, when he tells her, "Megan told me everything. IIS is going to deploy Mitosis at the border, before it's public."

"Mitosis," Soyoung said. "Like—with all it can do."

"Everything. For border control. To prevent people from instancing, when they cross. Probably situational. And then they're going to start selling to other countries, when they get the OK from the IIS."

Soyoung imagines the gate installed at Incheon, at JFK. She's imagining a world where the application to instance is done ahead of time, where it gets processed through churning bureaucracy, the decision made by some faceless government official. The idea of it is deeply distasteful in her mouth.

YJ continues.

"She wants me to whistle-blow on Drew after the government rollout is complete. Basically told me I could have Drew's job if I did. This is insane, right? This is all nuts."

YJ runs his hand through his hair.

"So. What are you going to do?" Soyoung asks. She's imagining the myriad ways a Mitosis gate could be used in an ICE facility.

"I don't know yet," YJ says, lifting his head back up. "I don't like this. But I don't disagree with Megan's approach."

Soyoung frowns. "You *like* the way the IIS handled this?"

"I mean—no. But between the IIS and Mergebreak . . ." he says, trailing off.

She tries to imagine his perspective.

"Better IIS than Mergebreak," she says, watching YJ's face for any reaction. "Better you and Megan than Drew, making the decisions on like—god, this is international, huh?"

He nods.

"If it's going to happen anyway, it doesn't matter what I want. Just what's going to happen."

"Why does it have to happen?"

"The technology exists now. What's the alternative?"

Soyoung gets up. She walks up to the wall with the birds. She hopes that no one else is hiding behind a pillar or a doorway. She takes a circuit. There's no one around the columns, or leaning against the doorway. Just the birds, pinned as if they're in flight. There are so many goddamn types of bird in the world. YJ's gaze follows her around the room.

"Why are you against it?" he says. "Mitosis prevents my situation, your situation. It standardizes the process. If this had existed, you wouldn't ever have instanced."

She frowns at him.

"It's someone else making a decision about how you feel about yourself and the world around you, about the shape of your future, about what you get to know. It's like the military service thing. Or applying for citizenship. Am I being too specific?"

"I'm only feeling a little bit specifically attacked, so go on," YJ says.

"It's the top-down mandate. It's someone else making the choice for you."

"It's the government, it's not your mom or grandfather, Soyoung."

"Seriously?"

"You started it. It's not personal."

"Yujin. This is your old boss asking you for a favor, tempting you with a job if you accept. It's all personal," Soyoung says.

YJ shakes his head. "That's—it's not relevant. Okay. Let's imagine people leaving, I don't know, some fucked-up refugee state. Do you think they want to leave a version of themself behind? Isn't it better for them, that they stay singular?"

"But they still instance, right? Because whatever third world country probably doesn't have the Mitosis installed at their airports or roads or border checkpoints or whatever. Because Mergebreak is selling it, and Mergebreak isn't going to give it out for free, it's gonna depend on whether the government pays for it. So they leave an instance anyway. It's only people who leave like—America, or Korea, or whatever, who would have access to this—if we even think it's a good thing. You're thinking about this like it gives people a choice. I'm thinking about the abuses of power—situations where, I don't know, a government says sure, you can reintegrate here, but we get to decide which memories you keep."

"Okay, first of all, wouldn't there be bad actors in the private sector? You're arguing for a world where this is never deployed at all. And why shouldn't people who have access to Mitosis get it? It's not—it's random chance, where you're born."

"But people don't *get* access," Soyoung says. "That's what I'm saying. It's being forced on them. It's about who has control. You're ignoring my point entirely."

"It's not being *forced,*" YJ says, gesturing with a hand. "As long as you're doing everything correctly, and you're not a criminal or anything, there's no reason for them to choose for you. This would be a cleaner rollout than Mergebreak having to negotiate with every single individual."

"And it all works out for you okay, because either Drew or Megan jets your dual citizenship application to the top of the pile, and you get whatever you say you want, and then you never actually have to tell Yujin what you want," Soyoung says.

"Ow. Okay. That one was a cheap shot," YJ says. "Fine, what would you do?"

Soyoung doesn't know what she would do. She doesn't think that the weight of her future matches against the future of everyone else in existence. But Soyoung knows herself now. Rose ignored her past but jumped at the first good excuse to go back to Korea. Soyoung didn't reach out to her instance for years, and then suddenly sprang reintegration on her. She doesn't always know what she wants. She just knows that all versions of herself are the same sort of greedy opportunist.

"I'd probably put everything online now," Soyoung says. "I'd put everything that Megan told me online, but I wouldn't wait to do it on her terms. I'd upload them to force the IIS to change tack and deal with the public backlash before installing the gates at the borders. I'd release all the schematics. I'd name her and Drew. I'd implicate the IIS and Mergebreak, both of them. I'd send everything to reporters. I'd make it too big an issue to be buried."

YJ's quiet for a moment.

"That would ruin my life," he finally says.

"Well, I guess some things are worth that," Soyoung says, feeling like she's ripping words out of a TV drama. Three months ago, her biggest problem was what she was going to do for brunch.

"Is that how you felt, after reintegrating?"

"Oh, shut up," she says.

∎∎∎

Studies have shown that people are able to wholly hold two contradictory ideas in their head without any cognitive dissonance. An idea, a desire, none of it needs to be grounded in reality. It just needs to be something the holder believes is true. A buried understanding. An unconscious bias. Soyoung doesn't know how to convince YJ of anything. YJ is the sort of man who can work toward a single goal for years. He's the sort of man who can lie to himself for years about what he wants. He's selfish and self-interested and she's seen that there's no version of him that has had a successful long-term relationship. And he's the sort of man who, when he hears that an old friend who he parted with on bad terms needs help, will eventually say yes.

∎∎∎

Soyoung and YJ leave the hall full of birds, walking through exhibits that display the various historical world cultures, through the hall of Asian mammals and then back through the entrance, which is still lit in neon. They blend in with the other people leaving the museum—couples, groups of friends, all the people who thought that going here on a weekend night would be fun.

"I want to talk to Drew, once more," YJ says. "Before saying yes to Megan."

Soyoung doesn't say anything about Rose and Soyoung meeting for a funeral and the way that their talking didn't actually mean any sort of communication occurred.

"Good luck," she says.

They walk down the street. They're going to the same subway terminal.

"Should I not have pretended to be your girlfriend?" Soyoung says.

YJ rubs the back of his neck with his hand. "I really enjoyed that part," he admits.

YJ

You check Drew's calendar for when he is next going to be in the country. It's within the month. You have your secretary make an appointment with him. You want to talk with him in person, rather than over the phone. It's easier to understand a person when you can see their face. You think that many of the issues between you and Yujin are because you can't see him in person. You don't tell your instance about what you learned.

In the meantime, you do your laundry. You clean your apartment. You try not to daydream about Soyoung being your girlfriend. You try not to run through hypothetical arguments in your mind with Soyoung about Mitosis. You sometimes succeed. Other nights you think about her when you can't sleep. The concept of her takes on various roles: impassioned anti-government activist who has a fundamental issue with the American federal government using Mitosis as an arm of American foreign policy; anti-monopoly economist who thinks that giving a single company the ability to maneuver global migration in such capacity would have incredible negative externalities; emotional bleeding heart who thinks that it's just cruel to dictate the world in such grand strokes for people; compassionate pragmatist who says that even if some governments will act in the best interests of their people, there is no guarantee that all regimes would.

You build arguments against your fiction of her, but all of them come down to the same points. There is no suppressing the knowledge of Mitosis indefinitely. The world will change, regardless of how the information is disseminated, and it is impossible to know the optimal path forward. And to do anything other than following Mergebreak or the IIS's directions would ruin your life. You would be fired. You would lose your visa. You would go back home. Would that be so bad? It would be a life you could fit into. But you don't want to go back home.

SOYOUNG-ROSE

Soyoung wakes up to her phone ringing. She blearily punches the button to answer the call.

"Hi, can you talk?" Rose's mom says.

"Yeah," Soyoung says. Sleep gives way to simmering guilt in her stomach: She had meant to call, before. She's been busy, since the night at the museum. Soyoung hasn't seen YJ since. She's been going to the research studies. She's been doing Soyoung's job, Rose's job. She called Soyoung's mother in Korea, who asked when she's coming home. She didn't have a good answer for her.

"Were you asleep?"

"I'm awake."

Her mom sighs like she doesn't believe her, like how she sighed when Rose lied about whether she had done her homework.

"Really," Soyoung says.

"Sure. Okay," Rose's mom says. There's a pause in her speech. Soyoung can hear her breathing. Then Rose's mom takes a long breath. "Okay, so when you were a kid, your grandfather had an opportunity to go back to North Korea. Not a DMZ tour. *Korea*-Korea. To go back to his hometown. You know—he grew up outside of Pyongyang. He left behind his parents—your great-grandparents—and his brothers. I don't really know more than that. He didn't talk about it much. But when he was older, he had the opportunity to go back for business reasons. A business trip that would include going back to his hometown."

"Mm?" Soyoung says. She rubs her eyes. "What?"

▮▮▮

Between 1910 and 1945, Korea was annexed by Japan and formally colonized under the Japan-Korea treaty of 1910, though the process of colonization and the reach of the Japanese influence across the Korean peninsula had begun decades before, since the 1800s. The cultural assimilation of Korea into Japan was carried out in a series of sweeping reforms.

In 1937, as part of the Naisen-Ittai program, the Korean language was banned in schools, and Japanese history was taught in place of Korean history. In 1939 and 1940, two ordinances were passed—Sōshi-kaimei, creating a policy that attempted to persuade ethnic Koreans to give up the Korean-style name in favor of Japanese names.

∎∎∎

"I was thinking about the house. I told you I was thinking about it."

"This isn't about the house."

"It is about the house. It's about *about* the house. So your grandfather talked it over with some of his close friends. And he talked it over with me, because this is before we moved to the States, and he still thought I was responsible."

Her mom takes a breath. Soyoung sits up.

"Mom, I thought you meant—"

"Let me finish, Soyoung-ah. So your grandfather decided he wouldn't go back, because he had heard of people being blackmailed before, after they returned to the South, and being asked for money by their families in the North, but the money didn't go to their families, it went to the North Korean state. And it wasn't like, you kids, who don't care. This would have been his siblings, his parents. He has a brother, at least. Your great-uncle. I don't know, I don't know about his family, too much. You probably have cousins there. And your grandfather had also heard of times where it had been a setup, to forcibly reintegrate the person, if they were someone with technical or political knowledge. They did that, because they didn't have any education in the North. And your grandfather was very smart, you remember. They would have wanted him."

∎∎∎

At its closest point, the distance between the Korean peninsula and the Japanese main island is 193 kilometers. The capital cities of the Republic of Korea and Japan are two hours away by plane. It is possible to eat breakfast in Tokyo and be in Seoul for dinner.

▪ ▪ ▪

"So he didn't go back," Soyoung says.

"Mm," her mom says. "And, you know. He had me and your uncle and your aunts. And he had the business, and the house, and he owned some other property back then, that he sold later. He had always said that he had made the right decision about not going back, to me. But I talked with your mom, the other day."

Soyoung doesn't know who she means for a moment. Her mom? She's talking to her mom right now. She realizes, then. Rose's mom means Soyoung's mom.

"You guys *talk*?"

"No. Just about you. This once. I called her."

"Why'd you talk about me?"

"Because there's just one of you, and you're here."

▪ ▪ ▪

The earliest recorded instance was one and a half years old. A toddler, Jillian Last-Name-Redacted, who instanced when her parents moved from England to France. It's theorized that due to the clear boundary and Jillian's early intelligence, she was able to understand what was happening and had conceptualized the idea successfully in her mind.

It's likely that younger children have instanced, but there is no official historical or medical record. Lots of rumors, though. There is great debate in parent forums for international moves, whether it is better to tell your kid that you're moving permanently or temporarily—if your kid instances without you, leaving a copy of them alone in their country of origin, at the airport alone. People try not to fly with young children, as parents are often worried about how much they understand.

This is the sort of thing you worry about in a first world country. A luxury concern. When your country is being cracked in half and controlled by foreign powers, when your country is being mismanaged by a corrupt government, when you are escaping gang violence, when your minority group is part of a targeted genocide, then you worry about other things. You worry about any version of yourself getting out. You hope any versions of your children survive.

▪▪▪

"So you guys talked about me," Soyoung says.

"Just letting her know you're okay. You should call her more."

"I forget to," Soyoung lies. "Why are you being so *sympathetic* to her?"

Rose's mom sighs, again, loud enough that her breath crackles over the phone. Soyoung remembers her mom in Korea sighing like that, when Soyoung would tell her that she broke a glass or got a bad grade.

"Was it different, if you instanced when you're grown up?" Soyoung says, and winces at the juvenile question. "I just mean—you know?"

"It was hard," Rose's mom says, in the same tone of voice that Soyoung uses when she doesn't want to talk anymore.

"Would you go back? If I go back?"

"You didn't instance, Soyoung."

"I could change my mind. I could stay here instead, still. It's intent at the time, Mom. Not—"

"Did you? Change your mind?"

Soyoung doesn't say anything to that. She can't tell her mom that she changed her mind the minute she was combined. She can't tell her mother that she's doing a research study for technology that isn't yet released to the public, which isn't even testing the technology that she thought it was. She can't tell her that the ultimate purveyor of this technology is the federal government of the United States of America, and that the only reason she knows about this is because the instance of her childhood friend has accidentally become involved. How Soyoung now has information, context, access that no one other than YJ has. How she's an accidental mole.

▪▪▪

In between the trials, Soyoung has been thinking about what YJ is doing. She thinks about talking to him again about Mitosis, but her arguments change from week to week. Some weeks she disagrees with him: The government shouldn't be in charge of people's futures and personhood; there have been no cases where this ended well. Some weeks she agrees. The government already decides people's futures, this just adds a practical layer to it. There is no guarantee that private industry would handle Mitosis in its full capabilities better, without the guardrails. And if individuals had the knowledge—people are panicky animals. People are dumb. People instance when they don't consciously realize they're going, and people leave their families, and people live in a thousand strange ways. And beyond that—maybe it's not YJ's responsibility to blow up his life for this. On the other hand, he should believe in something bigger than his own well-being. He should be willing to take risks for things greater than his life. But that's a train of thought that leads to strange places. Intimidating places.

■ ■ ■

Her mother keeps speaking.

"I had decided before we moved that I wouldn't lie to you about our going to America being a visit or a vacation. I decided that you should know what you were getting into. What we were getting into, Umma and Soyoung. That you deserved to make those decisions. I don't know if I did the right thing, but that's what I thought at the time."

"That's not how it felt," Soyoung says. She doesn't remember most of the lead-up to moving. All of it subsumed for Rose underneath the surprise of being somewhere new. She doesn't remember when her mom told her about this. Neither does Soyoung—for her, it was just the airport trip and then going home.

"I asked you, 'Soyoung, do you want to go to America with Umma?' and you said yes," Rose's mom says.

"I don't remember that."

"Well, you were young."

"But the house," Soyoung says. "Let's go back to the house."

■ ■ ■

Soyoung's grandfather's first language was Japanese. He used to go to Japanese bookstores in Seoul. He never visited Japan before his death. Does the world change for him, if Mitosis had existed when he was alive? If it had been part of the fabric of society? If the gate had been installed when Korea was cracked in half—at what point, though? When in the conflict would it have dawned on the powers-that-be that this war was inconclusive? What if Mitosis had been invented before then—when Korea was annexed by Japan? Does the gate get installed immediately between the two states, xenophobia and anti-Korean sentiment determining that no one from Korea can consider Japan their home? Is it a better world for him, if her grandfather can make the decision that he's leaving the North, and not leave a copy, knowing he's singular? Or if he makes the decision to assuredly leave an instance behind? Or—more likely, he doesn't get to make that decision. Someone else, operating the machine, with a mandate from above, chooses for him.

▪ ▪ ▪

"The house. So, she said that she thought it was something about that, his family history. That he was trying to make sure you had a good reason to come back. Or for me to come back, because of you. But I don't know, Soyoung. I really don't know what he wanted."

"Why couldn't he just tell me while he was alive?"

"Soyoung," her mom says, and doesn't say anything else about that. Soyoung thinks that her mom was sad. Is sad. She doesn't know how to respond.

"Sure," Soyoung says. Closes her eyes. "I have a hypothetical question for you, Mom. Do you think it's important that people know what they're getting into? Would you rather know what's going on, even if it makes things more complicated?"

"Soyoung," her mom says. "I went to America with my preteen daughter."

"Okay. Second question. If I think the right thing to do is going to make my life harder, and probably make a lot of people angry at me, and if I'm not even sure if it's the best thing, but I'm pretty sure this is, like, the best option for *everyone*, not just for me, like, personally, then what should I do?"

Her mom is silent for a moment.

"If you want to sell the house, I think you should do it," her mom says. "It doesn't matter what anyone else thinks. Or what he would have thought. I wish I had figured that out when I was younger."

Soyoung bites her lip.

"I wasn't talking about the house, Mom. But thanks."

YJ

"So," you say. "Thanks for taking the meeting with me."

Drew looks up from his tablet. Today he's borrowing Sara's office, which is covered in photographs of her kid. Drew spins in his chair. Behind him, Sara's kid beams at you from a hundred different angles.

"Yeah, of course," Drew says. "Was gonna get something set up with you when I was in town, anyway. So, good timing on your part. What'd you want to discuss?"

He's smiling at you. He doesn't look jet-lagged at all. You wonder how Drew keeps track of all the time zones he's in.

"I talked with Megan," you say, keeping your voice calm and even.

"Ah."

The smile crystalizes. Something in the cast of his face changes. Not toward embarrassment. A sharpening. You try to ignore it.

"And I just wanted to talk to you about everything. You want to grab coffee and go to the roof?"

His face changes again, softens so that he's smiling at you like he thinks that you're not a threat. You're still playing the same game he is. You smile back. You need him to think you're on the same side.

"Exactly what I was thinking," he says.

▮▮▮

You have a plan. It's a simple plan. You're going to tell Drew that you have all the information about Mitosis now, and that you'd like to hear his side of the story. You're not going to give him any sense of what you want to do. That would require knowing what you wanted to do.

▮▮▮

"So, what'd Megan tell you?" Drew says, after you've gotten your break-room coffee and gone up to the roof. It's cold. You brought your coat this time.

"Pretty much everything," you say. "She confirmed the sponsorship. Mitosis's capabilities. What IIS and Mergebreak agreed on."

"And you don't like it," Drew says.

"I don't like the way Megan characterized it," you demur.

"She got to you," Drew says, and his smug tone makes you want to deck him, sending him flying over the railing.

"Megan's the only person in this who's told me anything real. She's not using me as a media shield in case this all goes south. I'd love to get a good explanation here of how you feel. I'm not trying to escalate this. But I do feel like you've treated me very unfairly here, like I'm some sort of proxy for jerking Megan around and I'm—"

"Woah, hey, calm down," Drew says. He looks really surprised. He looks like you've broken the corporate social contract—which, you have. You don't know where that came from. You had wanted to go into this completely copacetic, you had wanted to insinuate, not accuse. At least you didn't say the last thing, which is that you've been given heaven's mandate to whistle-blow on him and Mergebreak. He shouldn't think you're considering that. He shouldn't think you're capable of conceiving of that idea at all.

"Okay, first of all, we thought your clearance was going to come through sooner, and second of all, it's kind of the IIS's fault that this is taking so long, so that's on Megan, and third of all, you're the face 'cause it looks way better to have an immigrant-type guy as the face, instead of me. I shouldn't say that, but hey."

You start laughing. An immigrant-type guy.

You had meant to play it cool. You had meant to let him finish his piece. But this is the moment he loses you.

▮▮▮

Everything could have been avoided if Adam and Eve had said no to the serpent. But the serpent was an instance of God, like every other being in existence. There was no reason to doubt him.

▮▮▮

Drew laughs too. Like this is a joke you're sharing. Sure, this can be a joke you're sharing.

"So, fine," he says. "Let's chat about it. God, I've wanted to talk with someone else about this for-*ever.* Lay it on me, YJ. What are your problems with me?"

You sit on one of the low outdoor couches. Drew sits across from you, hands clasped. Perfect listening position. He must actually be a pretty effective salesman, if you're not one of his employees.

"I don't have any problems with you personally."

"Oh, come on. You just told me you had beef."

"No—I don't care about that. Do you really think this is the best way forward?"

He makes a sharp gesture with his hand.

"Of course not. I wanted to keep it all private industry. None of this government, private-public partnership junk."

"I mean, not from the good-for-the-company level. I mean the good-for-the-world level."

He leans back against the low chair.

"Alright. I'll give you the pitch. I want you to imagine the invention of the passport, YJ," Drew says. "This is just like that. We're standardizing the international experience. People will be able to choose what they want. Really make the decision, not just have to guess how they feel before they board the plane."

"And—Megan wasn't clear on this. Are they going to be the ones choosing?"

"Ah-ah, don't get sneaky on me. You're trying to bring up the free will, desire thing. You're trying to bring up the government thing. Well, I didn't like that, but it's fine. It'll get sorted out in the wash. It's not going to be Megan clamping down the iron vise on us forever. Next few years will have some really interesting policy decisions—I think it's worth it. We'll sell *everywhere,* 'cause we can fix a problem that a lot of people want to solve. Do you think that the guy running across the border in Tijuana wants to leave a version of himself behind? Do you think *I* like getting on all of these planes all the time so I don't instance? Bet you would have made different choices if you knew for sure what would happen?"

"Sure," you say.

You would be different. You would have made different choices. You had never known you would want to change until you did.

■ ■ ■

You had imagined what would have happened if you hadn't instanced, when you were in college. If you had finished your semester abroad and gone home. You wouldn't be living Yujin's life, you don't think. You had been more ambitious than he was. You wouldn't have met and had your heart broken by Petra. You wouldn't have reconnected with Soyoung. You would have probably gotten a different job. You'd probably still be living at home. You wouldn't have been consciously thinking about immigrating anywhere. You might have traveled more—you might have had more money for travel, and you wouldn't have the niggling fear in the back of your mind every time you got on a plane. You would have seen your parents more. You wouldn't have lost touch with your high school friends. You might be less lonely. Or not: Maybe everything about you was agnostic to where you lived.

■ ■ ■

"What do you think?" he says. "You disagree?"

This is a question that functions as a trap.

You imagine pushing back. You imagine telling Drew that you do disagree. Not that you do. You do and you don't. You think the future he's describing is an inevitability. What does it matter that it comes in one year or five? But you're tired of being jerked around.

"Why are you so scared of instancing? The planes, the travel, the—all of it. Why that?"

He frowns.

"I'll answer your question in a second. I've just always been curious," you say.

Drew looks away from you. At the horizon. The direction he's looking in is a straight shot down a Manhattan street. On the solstice, the sun lines up perfectly down the cavern. You've never seen it, even though you've lived in New York for a long time. You always seem to miss the exact date.

"I've always thought of having instances as—that's your life they're stealing, you know? You hear a lot of horror stories in the instancing industry—*you* know. I know you've got one you like, but not everyone has a good time. I've been traveling a long time. Never really felt attached anywhere—like, a hotel in Amsterdam's the same thing as a hotel in San Antonio, right? I'm concerned that if I get attached, I'll end up instancing when I leave. But hey—I'm lucky enough that the flying makes sense for my job. Back on topic though. What are your thoughts on all of this?"

"I think that you're very lucky to be able to travel like that," you say.

"C'mon, man," he says. "Look, aren't you trying to get dual citizenship out of this? That's the same thing. You just aren't thinking big enough."

"Drew. It's obvious that you promoted me because I need this job for my visa, so you could control me by leveraging the speed at which my application for citizenship is processed."

He's silent for a moment.

"Well, you don't have to say it like that."

▪▪▪

In many ways, the serpent is the model for rebellion. His fall from grace is the precursor to the actions that Adam and Eve take.

▪▪▪

"You know that if you fire me, I'm just going to get another job here, or I'm going to go back to Korea. It'll be fine. I'm not the sort of noncitizen that you can intimidate with deportation. I have options. Sure, they're not my first-choice options. But the trajectory of my life is going to be fine, so you can—"

"You added another person to the recombination trial," Drew says. "Who is she?"

"Soyoung?"

Her name slips off your tongue before you can stop it. You weren't expecting to have to hide Soyoung's existence during this conversation.

"Yeah, Soyoung Kang. Rose." Drew pronounces her name all American, all the syllables slightly wrong. "Who's she?"

"Why were you looking at the trial data?"

"Is she your friend?"

"That's not your business," you say, because you don't know what to say.

"Okay, sure," he says. "But Soyoung, Rose, she's supposed to be two people. She's not registered as reintegrated. So. I'm not going to ask what's going on with her. But."

"Are you *threatening*—"

"I'm not trying to threaten anyone," Drew says. "But I'm saying that even if you don't care about yourself or your instance, that—citizenship, you might care about other people."

▪▪▪

Soyoung sitting in the bar, leaning forward and speaking so intently about her other self. Soyoung sitting on the roof, speaking softly about what had happened to her. The way she smiles at you. The way she handed you the USB drive so easily. The way her mouth felt on yours.

▪▪▪

If Adam was offered the apple before Eve, would he give it to her?

▪▪▪

"So, you know. Let me know what you want."

▪▪▪

You are tired of acceptance. You are tired of just saying *okay*. You are thinking about standing in your living room after Petra left and not chasing after her. You are thinking about every time you've laughed with other people about the pronunciation of your name. You are thinking about when you said yes to the promotion. You are thinking about how many things you have just accepted without asking. You want to tell Drew to shove it. You want to push him off the rooftop.

Fuck your own self's happiness. He's never been in this chair, sitting on the cold rooftop of this building, staring down a man who doesn't care about anyone else. But. Do you care about Kang Soyoung? Do you care about her enough to keep her out of the telescopic lens of your conglomerate? Maybe you're not a good person. Maybe you're just selfish. Do you care about that?

■ ■ ■

"YJ?"

■ ■ ■

What does Soyoung care most about? Would she put her personal desires above her political beliefs? She's the sort of woman who forced her instance to reintegrate with herself.

You know what she wants. She wants freedom, same as you. She wants to be separate. She wants her world to feel familiar again. This is what she wants, as she is now. But what will she want, when she's separate? You imagine being Rose. You imagine having never gone back to Korea in two decades—it's easy, just double the length you've been gone. You imagine being Soyoung—you imagine being Yujin. And his wants are easy to imagine. He's you.

You want to give her everything she could want.

■ ■ ■

Drew is still smiling. Like he knows your thoughts. Like he knows you're going to fold. Asshole. He doesn't know what you're thinking. You're going to ruin him. He'd lost you with his first few sentences. You're going to say yes to Megan. You're going to take his job. But first, he's going to do something for you.

■ ■ ■

You take a breath. You smile at Drew.

"I want you—Mergebreak, Condensco, IIS, whatever—to sponsor Soyoung-Rose's dual citizenship. Both halves of her—the same type of citizenship that I'm going to get. I want you to prevent anyone from figuring out what she did, that she's here illegally, after she's separate, and for her instance to get a first-class plane ticket back to Korea. And I want access to all of the information I was being kept from. All the documents. Everything. I need that for my job. And then I don't go and talk to the news. I don't quit. I keep everything running to the party line. Your line."

"Done," Drew says.

■ ■ ■

After catching Adam and Eve, God delineates the world between the garden and the wasteland and casts them out. There had never been any boundaries before. Adam and Eve did not know what would happen when they left. But they step over the border of Eden and walk forward into the wasteland. When Eve turns back, she sees their instances. This is God's final punishment: to know that a version of them will be in paradise forever.

PART V

Han (n.)

1. Resentment.
2. A culture-bound emotion embodying specific grief, sadness, resentment, a dense knotted string of feeling of all the bitter sorry sadness, processed into a singular compact word.

Jeong (n.)

1. Attachment.
2. The opposite of han—no, not the opposite, the opposite the same way that chocolate is the opposite of vanilla, the way the sun is the opposite of the moon, i.e., two unrelated concepts that are nevertheless spoken of together—is jeong. Jeong is connection. It's that you and I are tied by some strange little string of fate. It's that I love you. It's that you and me, we grew up together. I know you down to your bones. We are going to find each other again.

SOYOUNG-ROSE

Her doorbell rings and Dr. Crouton starts meowing. Soyoung looks out the peephole. It's YJ. She opens the door.

"Hi. I brought dinner. I'm sorry to just show up. Can I come in?" YJ says, holding a bag of takeout as if an apology. It smells like—Korean food. Chinese-Korean food. Like a strange mirror of the last time Soyoung had Korean-Chinese, which was when she was cleaning up her grandfather's house with her cousin. There's no good place for this outside of Flushing.

"Where did you get this?"

"New restaurant opened near the Jay Street–MetroTech stop," he says. "Is that your cat?"

"Don't let him get at the food," Soyoung says, and opens her door a little wider. Soyoung wrinkles her nose. "Why are you here?"

"I talked to Drew," YJ says. "Can I come in?"

Dr. Crouton meows again. Winds around her ankles.

"Yeah," Soyoung says, and lets him in.

■ ■ ■

Odysseus is given hospitality throughout the duration of *The Odyssey*, by strangers and by friends. The ancient laws of hospitality dictated kindness when you met a stranger who was a long way from home. It was likely they were an instance, and one who had no one else to turn to other than the kindness of strangers. They needed to be welcomed. Their home belonged to their other self.

■ ■ ■

YJ puts the food on the counter. He looks around the room as if the concept of a living room is foreign to him. Rose doesn't live anywhere exciting—it's blue walls and an Ikea couch and posters that have been upgraded from bare thumbtacks to frames.

"You have a nice apartment," he says.

Soyoung is thrust into a memory—Yujin in Soyoung's college dorm room, telling her that her room, with the single bed and messy desk, looked nice.

She does the same thing she did back then: She says, "Thanks."

Soyoung doesn't ask YJ any more questions, because she suspects that silence is going to be more effective. Instead, she goes to her fridge and gets them both cans of seltzer. The whole situation feels a little like when Rose ran into one of her hookups in the broad light of day. Just, awkward.

YJ takes the food out of the bag. Plastic containers of noodles, deep-fried pork, sauces. He glances at her.

"I'm going to sauce—"

"Sure."

He pours the sweet-and-sour sauce on the pork. The black bean on the noodles.

"I talked to Drew," he says again. "I wanted to get his measure about—you know. Before I really committed to Megan's plans."

He pauses. Hands her a bowl of noodles.

"I meant to keep everything calm, but it got a little heated."

"Heated how?"

YJ sits down with his own bowl of noodles. He puts the bowl of tangsooyook and little yellow pickles and raw onions between them.

"You know when I say that he's *really* American?"

"Sure," Soyoung says.

"Like the sort of American who calls himself an expatriate," YJ says. "He just pissed me off. I lost my cool. He was being an asshole and I basically told him to fuck off and I didn't need him, and that I wasn't interested in what he could offer me. Then he tried to blackmail me, using you."

"What?"

"I want you to know that I didn't agree because of my—Yujin's—citizenship stuff. Job stuff, whatever, okay?" he says. "To be clear. That wasn't a factor. But then he mentioned you."

"He knew about me? YJ—"

"Let me finish. He knew about you, and he knew that I knew you, and I argued with him, and I got him to agree that he wouldn't bring your situation to anyone's attention, and that furthermore we would sponsor your and Rose's dual citizenship, after you separate, so that both versions of you get to go—wherever you want. So, I got him to give us that, and after everything's done, I'm still going to follow Megan's plan. I've decided. That's what's happening."

YJ is looking at her like it's a relief to tell her, like she should be happy with the decision he's made for her. That he's given Soyoung the answer he thinks she should want. Soyoung is thinking about her grandfather's house, how it was a gift with strings, a physical object that was supposed to shape her feelings and actions. How her other self stood in front of Rose and offered her entire life as a gift that she should have wanted.

"I never asked you to do that," she says. "This doesn't solve any of my problems. I wanted to be separated—"

"That too," YJ says. "You get that too. You finish the trial as planned, and then—"

"You told your company about me?"

Soyoung is thinking of YJ's mindset. What YJ believed was true about her.

"Did you do this because you think you can get with Rose, afterward? That it'll help your chances in the long term?"

Hesitation in his expression. If he says no, Soyoung is going to slap him. If he says yes, she's going to rip into him for being a coward. She cares about him. He's the echo of her friend, but she cares about him separately from Yujin now. And he is being a condescending, patriarchal asshole, making decisions for her, setting wheels into motion that she never asked him to, just because he thinks he knows what she wants. Because he's extrapolated from what little he knows about her, and he's decided that what she wants is what *he* would want.

"It wasn't my first intention," YJ says. "I promise. I just thought—"

"You just thought that you could make a decision for me and I'd go along with it. And I guess that makes you feel like some sort of white knight. This lets you save face, it lets you respect yourself. You're not going along with Drew for *yourself.* You're going along with it to help a girl. And I bet that feels better, right? It gives you an excuse to collaborate with Megan, right? An excuse to get your super promotion? It lets you believe you're not just going along with shit, and saves you from making your own decisions, ri—"

"Soyoung," YJ says. Like the word is a stone dropping from his mouth.

"Do you know how much easier it would be, if I didn't want to help you? If you weren't asking me for things? If you weren't messing up my life, getting between me and Yujin? I'm sorry I wanted to give you all the things I was trying to get for myself. The things I've been ruining my life for. You think I'm some sort of coward? Fine. I don't care. But you're only still here because I didn't report you to the IIS."

The silence in the room is as loud as the scream of the brakes of a jet plane, touching down on the tarmac.

"That was too much," he says. "I'm . . . I'm going to go."

"You're missing the point again," Soyoung says. "But yes. You should go."

"I would never have reported you," he says, and she points at the door.

YJ

You get your coat and you walk out the door without saying anything else to Soyoung. She doesn't say anything to you. You were too scared to look at her face on your way out. You were too afraid of what you might see. You feel like you did after Petra broke up with you, except that had been all tepid, polite conversation, and this was the chill aftermath of a hot argument. But it's the same feelings in your heart: that you're being misunderstood, that you're being punished because you can't read the inside of someone else's mind. You feel like you are always making the wrong decisions. You shouldn't have said what you did. You didn't mean it. You were just angry.

You're a half hour away from home. You don't really want to go back to your apartment. You walk slowly down the dark, tree-lined street. You don't know where else to go, except home.

■ ■ ■

It's a disproportionate consequence, really, for God to divide the world and send his creations out into the wilderness just because they made one mistake. They had no idea what the punishment would be. It was the first time this had ever happened. The punishment doesn't fit the crime.

■ ■ ■

You end up defaulting to taking the subway back to your apartment. It's less crowded than the way over, the commuter crush having dissipated. You snag a seat and try and distract yourself with a game on your phone, but the little animations of bubbles exploding don't cut the gnawing bad feeling out of your brain.

Too many people want things from you, that's the problem. Megan wants you to follow her plans. Drew wants you to follow his. Yujin has wanted your life for your entire existence. Soyoung-Rose wanted your help before you even met, and what does she want now? She wants you to somehow come up with some . . . solution to the Mitosis problem? She wants you to thread the political needle that fits whatever sense of ethics she has, while not screwing yourself over? She wants you to blow up your life? No one is asking you for things that are reasonable to give.

You don't know what point that Soyoung said you were missing. Unless she meant that she cared about the Mitosis rollout, how IIS and Mergebreak would handle it. Which was ridiculous. Of course you knew she cared. You had argued about it. You didn't like what was going to happen, either. But you had to live in the world as it existed. You couldn't create Soyoung a different one.

I'm sorry, you type and erase.

I was trying to stand up for you, you type and erase.

You think about it for a moment. You imagine being Soyoung.

I really wouldn't have said anything, you type. You stare at the words for another moment. You erase them. You set your phone on do not disturb, and put the phone back in your pocket and close your eyes. You know this is a dumb thing to do on the subway, but you do it anyway.

▪▪▪

There is no way for the man on the other side of the Auraji to know if the woman wants him back.

▪▪▪

You manage to keep yourself from checking your phone again until right before you go to sleep. Then you finally take a look at your glowing screen, squinting in the darkness of your lofted bedroom. There's nothing from Soyoung. You want to send Soyoung paragraphs. You want to explain everything you're thinking. You want to believe that by explaining every line and facet of your thought process, you could convince her. You know this is a bad idea.

There was a thing you used to do, back when you were in school. When you wanted to procrastinate on a subject, you worked on a different class's assignment instead. Lateral moves. Math problems exchanged for history essays. History essays exchanged for English workbooks. It made it easier.

You exit out of your messages and you go to your contacts. You go to *favorites* before remembering she isn't there anymore. You find Petra's number. You hesitate, and then call it.

You hope she picks up. You hope she doesn't pick up.

She picks up.

"Hi, Jay?"

Her voice is bright, and it sounds like she's cooking something while she's talking to you, there are vague kitchen sounds coming from her end. You're thrown into a vivid sense memory of all the times you cooked with her. You haven't been cooking much since she left.

"Why did you break up with me?"

The words fit in your mouth like they belong there. You've wanted to say them for so long.

Petra's quiet on the other end. Just the sound of a tap running, the click of a burner being lit. She has you on speaker. You close your eyes. You imagine her in the kitchen. Drinking a glass of wine and stirring something. You imagine yourself in the room with her. Bringing her tongs or a cutting board or a second glass of wine.

"What could I have done, to fix things?" you say. "What did you want from me?"

She's still quiet. You close your eyes. You feel very alone in your bedroom. Then she finally speaks.

"Jay, I think the things you could have done about our relationship, or the things I could have done, were all things that we would have had to have done a long time ago. At the beginning of everything, when we started dating. There wasn't anything left to do, at the end. I didn't want anything specific from you. I just—it wasn't that serious. You hadn't given me the opportunity to make it serious. I guess, in my heart, I just wanted to leave."

"Okay," you say. You don't feel any better about Soyoung, but at least it's a different sort of hurt in your chest now. You feel as hollow and as light as a shell. "Sorry to bother you. Thanks."

SOYOUNG-ROSE

Soyoung puts the food away. She gives Dr. Crouton his dinner. She sits at her kitchen table under her single overhead light with her phone in front of her. She's thinking about how everyone is so bad at knowing what anyone else wants. About how people can be so bad at knowing what they want for themselves. About where the line is, between wanting and knowing. How you can go and be sure. How you can stay and never be sure. How a foregone conclusion is only a foregone conclusion after the fact of its happening.

She knows now that YJ isn't going to do anything with the Mitosis information. He's going to go along with the desires of everyone around him and he's going to think that this was the right decision. No. That's cruel. You can't ask someone to destroy their life because you think it's ideologically correct. Soyoung does lots of things that she doesn't believe are ideologically correct: eats factory-farmed meat, throws her recycling in the trash, lies all the time to her friends and family.

YJ shouldn't have brought up her citizenship status, the fact that she was in the country illegally. That was low.

Soyoung had told YJ that if she was in his position, if she was the one person in the world with the ability to enact change, she would release every single bit of information she had, not on the terms that were dictated to her, but on the terms she chose. She had said it flippantly, but it had been the truth. She realizes now that she had expected YJ to take action. But she's capable of taking action, too.

▮▮▮

It would have been easier for Eve, had she never eaten the apple.

▮▮▮

So how would she release the data? Soyoung gets up, goes back to the fridge to pull the noodles out. She shouldn't have put them into the fridge; she's now in the realm of technical problems, not the sort of fuzzy relationship issues that make her nauseous. She dumps half the noodles into a frying pan.

She would want to disseminate the information as widely and legitimately as possible, in a single burst. She would want backups sent to various individuals and organizations to keep the information from being scrubbed or suppressed. She would send everything to the press—a couple of Rose's college friends had become journalists. She would upload everything to social media sites and instancing forums. She would send everything to Mitosis's competitors. She would hire someone to buy a billboard right behind the Mergebreak billboard that hung over the I-95 highway—no, that was silly. But was it? She had never done anything like this before.

The obvious persona for Soyoung to adopt would be that of a Mitosis trial participant, who had infiltrated the system while going through a research study. This had the added benefit of being true. It could be useful to co-opt the name of an existing organization as well—associate herself with Anonymous or something. Borrow some legitimacy. That might be overcomplicating things.

She stirs the noodles.

And what to send? She has verbal confirmation of the IIS's plans from YJ. She has the USB drive containing all the documentation on how Mitosis works, the research trials, Yujin's notes. She doesn't have any written confirmation of the IIS's plans—a write-up will have to do, and hopefully people don't think she's tinfoil-hatting. Getting to the Mitosis terminal could cushion her from being called a conspiracy theorist, but she doesn't have access to the lab.

Although—getting to the lab wouldn't be impossible. All she needs to do is to get through the front gate, up the elevator, and into the lab on floor twenty-six. The front gate needs a standard employee keycard. The second, specialized keycard would get her into the elevator that goes to floor twenty-six—the one that she's seen Gerry use, the one she knows that YJ also has. And on floor twenty-six, there would be a door to the lab, protected by a keypad passcode. But she knows the passcode: It's the same as the USB, as confirmed by YJ's offhand comment, weeks ago.

So the only thing she needs are the keycards. But those wouldn't be hard to get. She just has to get YJ's wallet. How to get his wallet?

Soyoung pours the noodles into a bowl and picks up her chopsticks.

The easiest way would be to pretend to reconcile, and under the guise of reconciliation, palm the wallet. Pretend to make up, steal the cards while he's in the bathroom or something.

She sits back down at the kitchen table with her food.

Using YJ's cards would implicate him. She might cost him his job, and with it his life in America. She wants to keep YJ's hands clean, but it feels like this is the only path forward. She doesn't know how to steal Gerry's card without him noticing, he pays too much attention to her in the lab. And she doesn't know any other employees. So, YJ's cards are the only option. Hopefully YJ has the good sense to claim that they had been stolen. It might be enough to give him plausible deniability.

This could all work.

Soyoung eats her noodles. She contemplates the future. She vaguely remembers in Japan or China, that you're supposed to eat noodles on the New Year because it symbolizes long life.

Soyoung has one crucial psychological advantage over YJ: She has nothing to lose. Soyoung, as she is now, is a temporary amalgamation, prepared for her own unraveling. She has no future, and her component parts hold futures so divorced from her current reality that their fate is an abstract question.

She could do the heist after finishing the research study, after being disentangled. But would her two selves still want to upload everything? She's thinking about how Soyoung was selfish, how Rose was selfish. She's thinking about how their combination, her conglomerate self, is selfish. Selfish enough to leave her family without warning, to put off the question of her childhood home's ownership for months, to lie to her mother, to use her childhood friend for a favor even when it might get him fired.

She can't wait for the study to finish. But if she got into the lab, she could use the Mitosis gate on herself, after downloading the data from the servers. If she were to separate in that moment, she thinks her future selves would continue the course of action she's set for them.

Soyoung rubs her eyes. Walks over to the bathroom and opens the medicine cabinet. Pulls out a bottle of ibuprofen and shakes two out onto her palm. Pops them in her mouth and drinks some water from the tap. Closes the cabinet. Her reflection looks back at her. Memories fade. Months ago, everything about her face had felt subtly wrong. Now she just looks like herself. She looks like her moms.

She's thinking about how it felt, for Rose to go back to Korea for the funeral, how it felt for her to return to the States, to walk through the airport. She imagines the future, if she doesn't go through with this plan. Pretend that YJ keeps his job. Pretend that Soyoung finishes the trial and is separated. Pretend that Rose goes back to her life in New York and Soyoung gets on the plane and goes back home. Soyoung probably gets married. YJ probably asks Rose out. She probably says yes. And around them, the world changes silently, invisibly, unless everything is dragged kicking and screaming into the light.

Because in the light, everything changes. The knowledge itself would be transformative. Instancing is a psychological phenomenon. It has always been about intent. Just releasing the information about Mitosis could change migration, even beyond access to the machine itself. To know that complete control over the process was possible by machine would change the way people think about the permanence of leaving. The world that Soyoung lived in—the one where leave-taking could be permanent, might never exist again.

Like leaving home, like going back for the funeral, like Soyoung pressing her hand into Rose's: It's a foregone conclusion. She's going to do what YJ won't.

So: She needs YJ's keycards. Once she has them, she also needs a distraction. She needs something that will so occupy YJ's mind that he won't be thinking about his wallet, or won't look at whatever security breach information that she accidentally flags. So, what would distract him?

Ah. She bites her lip. She knows what she's going to do. It's going to be a little bit cruel. But. He was cruel to her, first.

YUJIN

You're going on a very long walk in the middle of the day. It's hot. It's humid. You think it's going to rain soon. You're probably going to get caught in the downpour. You should get on the bus. You should take the subway. You should tell—who do you tell? You don't talk about this sort of thing with your friends.

The breakup had come out of nowhere. Youngmi had met you for a date on the stupid bank of the stupid Han River, and while you had been eating the stupid little lunch that she had made for the two of you and the stupid little cup noodles that you had bought from the nearby convenience store, she had told you that she didn't see a future with you. She had been really nice about it, which was the worst part. She had given you the old line: It's not you, it's me. You had pressed her, though. You had asked, *no, what's the real problem?* And then she had told you that she just wasn't feeling it. That you had seemed distracted. Uninvested in the relationship. That she wanted to get married in the next couple of years, and it didn't seem like you had similar goals. That you weren't wholly committed.

The worst is that you can't disagree with her: You've been too distracted—busy taking over parts of Soyoung's life, worrying about whatever YJ's gotten himself into. But you had liked her. You had really liked her. You had thought there might be a future with her.

Your phone begins to ring. You're not in the right headspace to talk to anyone. You fish it out of your pocket anyway. Soyoung's calling. You don't want to pick up. No, you do want to pick up and start unloading on her. That's too much. You want to pick a fight. You're going to tell her that she's going to just deal with the rest of her unraveling on her own and if Soyoung gets found out, Soyoung gets found out. Ah, you want to make her mad.

You pick up the phone.

"I talked with your instance. YJ doesn't want to reintegrate," Soyoung says.

"Ah," you say. You feel lightheaded. The back of your shirt damp with sweat. The sun beating on your neck. You feel sick to your stomach. You feel a great and terrible lightness. You want to sit down. You want to never get back up.

■ ■ ■

The version of Odysseus that stays home, how does he live? There are no grand epics about him. There are no poetic verses that describe his condition.

■ ■ ■

"When did he tell you?" you say, your voice sounding like it's coming from very far away. You start walking again. You don't know what else to do.

"Recently," she says, which is nothing. "He told me not to tell you. But I'm telling you. He doesn't know how to tell you. He knows that you want—"

"—to reintegrate," you say, numbly. A horrible thought rises through the soft matter of your brain. "Did meeting you convince him? Did he change his mind because he met you, and he saw how much you hated it? Did I do this, by agreeing to help you? By making that connection for you? Soyoung. You've ruined my life."

She doesn't say anything to that. In a sick way, that feels good. She's a proxy for who you want to hurt. You're mad at her. You're mad at yourself. Both yourself here, and yourself, the other yourself, the one you want to be. You keep walking. You need to get out of the heat. You can't have this conversation on the bus or in the subway.

"I'm really sorry," Soyoung says. "But wouldn't you rather know the truth?"

White-hot anger. Like her question is an attack. Like you deserve things happening to you because of how you feel.

"That's not the point—the point is that I am trying to help you, and helping you is ruining my life—and, are you fucking him?"

"What?"

"I saw the pictures on his phone," you say. "Is that how you found out? Are you fucking him? Does he tell you things because you guys are—"

"He took *pictures* of us?"

"Of you," you say. So there is an "us."

"That's not—Yujin," she says.

"What does he have that I didn't?"

You don't even really care about this. You don't love her. Maybe this would make sense, in a world where you loved her. Where you had been waiting in the wings to swoop in at the moment of romantic distress, but you didn't, because you *aren't a creep*. And it makes you mad that YJ would try for that thing.

"Yujin—" she says, and she sounds so sad. You don't care.

"Soyou—"

"I kissed him once," she says, all a rush. "I like him. I like him differently than I like you. Sorry. I didn't tell you. Nothing's going to happen, because all of this is temporary, okay? So I didn't tell you. I don't tell you everything."

"You mean he kissed you," you say, wiping the sweat from your forehead. She doesn't say anything to that. You stand up.

"I know him," you say. "He's probably in love with you. We fall in love stupid."

"Yujin—"

"I don't want to be in love with you," you say. "I liked what we had."

You walk into the convenience store. The door does its little chime. The air-conditioning hits you like a delicious truck. You still mostly feel numb. Fine. Whatever. In some ways, this is the relief of forgone conclusions. Of course he doesn't want to reintegrate. Of course this has come to pass. Of course you get broken up with. Hell Joseon.

"I guess I won't be," you say. "He won't reintegrate with me, so this isn't my problem."

You walk over to the water. You pick up the closest bottle. Soyoung is very quiet. You guess this is all over. You guess you aren't going to reintegrate now.

"This isn't how I wanted to ask. And I'm sorry. I'm really sorry. I'm not always a good friend. I take you for granted. I don't tell you enough. I ask you for too much. I could have told you about YJ not wanting to reintegrate weeks ago. But I didn't, because it felt like it wasn't my secret to tell. It was yours. His. I felt like whatever problems existed between the two of you were your problem. Either he'd tell you or he wouldn't. And I guess, I'm only telling you now, because I want something from you. I shouldn't tell you this. This is terrible of me. But if you help me with this, I'll never ask you for anything again."

"Why should I help you?"

She's quiet for a long moment.

"Do you want the house?"

"What?"

"My grandfather's house. If you help me with this one thing, I'll give you the house. You can pay me like, a thousand won or something."

You almost put the phone down. You sit heavily on the steps leading to the river and stare at the horizon, the other side of the riverbank, the apartment complexes, the rolling hills, the stores and offices and houses and all the people working, living, eating, breathing in them.

"Are you crazy?"

"I'm serious!"

"What is this actually about?"

Soyoung loved that house. That's the thing. You don't know how Rose felt about it, but Soyoung had loved that house. She wouldn't have sold it to a friend. To family, maybe. But not to you. It's serious, then. It's not kiddie romance bullshit. There's actually a problem.

"I can't talk about this over the phone," Soyoung says.

You could do a lot of things with a house. You could sell it. You could live in it. You could give it to your parents. You could raze it and put a little apartment complex there. You could run a restaurant. You could use the house as fuel for a future that doesn't include YJ.

"I don't need your house. What's the favor?"

She takes a deep breath.

"I need you to call YJ and distract him, at a predetermined time. I need you to distract him so badly that he doesn't respond to anything from work, any notifications, nothing. You could accuse him of not wanting to reintegrate with you. You don't have to say that, but I think it'd get his attention—"

It would get his attention. If he knew that you knew, if you raised a fuss. If you argued with him. He'd argue back. This is what you are for each other, sometimes. A safe punching bag, except this one would be a real fight. Knuckle to knuckle. Skin to skin—you could touch him. Your flesh on his. You could reintegrate, if you were physically pressed against each other. Skin.

Physical touch. You realize—what's stopping you from going to New York? Just your life here. Just the fear of instancing. But you wouldn't instance now, no, you know that in the deep black pit of your soul. This wouldn't be permanent. You know how the Mitosis machine works now. You know that every leave-taking can be temporary.

And you want to drag him back. You want him to feel what you feel. You don't want him to get to leave you behind forever. You want to suck his memories into your self. Better for you and YJ to be stuck in Korea, better for you to be conglomerate and miserable. He doesn't want to reintegrate? You don't care.

"Soyoung. I'll do you one better. I'll show up in person."

"In person?"

"In New York. I won't instance if I leave," you say. "I know it. I want to confront him. I can convince him in person."

"You're really enthusiastic, all of a sudden."

"I know what I want to do now," you say. "Call me with the details, when you have them."

You hang up.

YJ

Can we talk?

Soyoung's text surprises you in the middle of a meeting. You have to fight to keep your face neutral while one of your coworkers talks about the fourth quarter projections.

Sure, you text back, underneath the table.

Your place? Friday?

The fourth quarter projections are looking pretty good. You wonder how much better they'd look, if Drew had been allowed to go through with his full-scale Mitosis rollout.

Sure, you text back again. You want to say something like, *sorry about everything.* You want to say, *you misunderstood me.* You want to ask, *are we good?* But you don't say anything. After your call with Petra, you feel a little burnt out on questions like that. You've gotten your vulnerability out of your system.

YUJIN

The airport hasn't changed since you were there last, characterized mostly by the high, airy ceilings with the rows and rows of check-in desks. Incheon Airport was the first airport you ever went to. You remember thinking that it was so large, when you first saw it. Like it was a spaceship. The last time you were here, you were nineteen.

You've only got your backpack and your passport and your boarding ticket on your phone. Around you, there are families with their suitcases piled high on carts and their children bobbing and weaving; couples in matching outfits; white foreigner tourists. This feels illegal. You dodge around all of them and get to the Asiana desk. Checking in all goes smoothly. The desk lady looks confused that you don't have any luggage, not even a carry-on. But she checks you in and then you're through and to the security check, where you churn mechanically through the line. You take your laptop out, your shoes off.

You go through the scanner. You pick up your laptop and put on your shoes.

Then you get in line for the customs and immigration booth. They have electronic terminals now—the last time you were here, they still had people stamping the passports. You get in line. You're thinking about the last time you were here. When you were still singular. Back then, you had been thinking about: your dorm room, what homework you hadn't finished for your classes. You hadn't been thinking about anything at all.

▮▮▮

There are offshoots of Christianity that claim that upon death, the soul is instanced. The good and noble part gets to go to heaven. The bad, nasty, sinful part goes to hell.

▮▮▮

You get in the line for citizens. You are thinking about homecoming. You are going to grab your other self and you are going to pull him into you. You are going to make him understand. You are going to stay yourself. How dare he treat you this way. How dare he not tell you, like a coward. You are going to inflict your life on him like a curse. You step through the immigration booth. You keep walking. You don't think you've left anything behind. You are going to come back. You are going to get everything back.

SOYOUNG-ROSE

"I'm sorry," YJ says, before saying hello, before any other greeting. "It was below the belt, what I said. I was angry. I'm sorry. Genuinely."

Soyoung blinks at the open doorway, at YJ standing in it. He doesn't move. "Can I come in?"

"Sorry, yes."

YJ opens the door wider, and Soyoung steps through. It's a blunt reversal of the other week, when he had come to tell her about the meeting with his boss. She hasn't brought food, but in every other aspect these meetings are the same except that she's the one with an agenda.

Yujin just texted her that he's boarded the plane. Tonight, Soyoung's going to break into the Mitosis lab.

The living room is cleaner than when she last caught a glimpse. It looks less like a bachelor pad. It's a little obvious that someone moved out. There are blank spaces in the apartment—an empty space in the bookshelf, an empty picture frame on the TV console.

"Can I get you—water? tea? A drink?"

"I'm okay," Soyoung says. "I just thought—we could clear the air."

"Sure, yes. Um."

He makes a gesture with his hand, as if to ask her to begin. She walks over to his living room. YJ sits down on the couch. She doesn't know if she should sit down. This is all tremendously awkward. This is more awkward than asking him for access to experimental technology.

"What do you want, from Soyoung and Rose, after?" Soyoung says.

YJ shakes his head.

"I don't want—"

"Maybe 'want' is the wrong word," she says. "I'm asking nonjudgmentally. Just, why?"

"Why do I like you?"

"I wouldn't put it so high school. But—I guess, what were you hoping for?"

He leans back on the couch. Stares at the ceiling. Soyoung looks around the room. Where's his wallet? She doesn't suppose he has it on him when he's at home. It's probably where he keeps his keys. Her eyes dart around the short hallway. There—on the side table. Next to the key ring. His wallet.

"I've been thinking a lot about the future," YJ says. "If I don't reintegrate. If I don't go back to Korea. If I do go back to Korea. All the combinations. And I was thinking about what you might want, after. I know Soyoung's in love with someone else. But I guess I kind of hoped that there was a chance that Rose and I might be—compatible. After."

"Compatible."

"It sounds bad when I say it like that, I guess. I just meant—I like you. I like you a lot. And I know you like me—some amount. Some amount of liking. As friends, as—me and you, it felt like we had some sort of connection, right? Like if we met at the right place, the right time, I could—"

He sits up. Rubs his face. His cheeks are red.

"I'm really pouring my heart out here, Soyoung."

"I thought this was a rebound, for you. Something casual."

"If it was anyone but you, it would be," he says, and each word is enunciated perfectly, like he's pulling teeth.

▪▪▪

When the man on the other side of the Auraji wades to the side where his lover stands, he must expect some kind of homecoming. Something commensurate with his efforts. He must think that his desire is matched, that there is a reason for him to leave. But it's just a story. Maybe instancing for unrequited love is more romantic.

▪▪▪

"So, um. I guess this isn't reciprocated."

It is. That's the thing. It could be. She likes him, bad decisions and all. He's indecisive, he's too much of a people pleaser, he doesn't always know what he wants. He waits too long and lets the world happen to him in the meantime. But every version of him is kind. He is the sort of person who helps his friends, when asked. Underneath everything, he's someone she would be happy to come home to. She's not yet in love with him. She could see a world where a version of her loved him.

"I'm not saying it's not," Soyoung says. "I'm just saying—I don't know how Rose will feel, after."

"Okay," he says. He's smiling a little.

"But you shouldn't have let that dictate what you were going to do, with Mitosis."

"Soyoung, like you said, it's all personal."

They could fall into an argument again. They could end up circling the drain, arguing in circles. But she thinks this is enough to lure him into a false sense of security.

"Can I actually get that cup of tea?"

"Sure," he says.

He gets up for the kitchen. Soyoung walks over to the bathroom and while her body is covering the motion of her hand, she swipes his wallet from the side table.

She closes the bathroom door behind her and locks it. She sits on the toilet. Stealing his wallet was easier than she thought it would be. She pulls out the cards. Credit cards, ID, small change. Sandwiched between the credit cards there's a blank white piece of plastic, and a second card that has YJ's name and photograph. He looks a little sad in the photograph. Soyoung feels bad for a moment. But not that bad. She takes both cards and slides them into her back pocket.

Soyoung closes the wallet. She flushes the toilet, runs the sink. She opens the door with the wallet palmed loosely in her hand behind her as she smoothly walks past the side table and redeposits the wallet on the table before walking back.

She leans against the counter. Studies YJ. The line of his body. The way he moves his arm while grabbing a cup. This is the last time she'll see him. She won't exist, soon. This is the last time they'll interact. She should go. It would be less suspicious, to leave. To go home, and spend a couple of hours pacing before she goes into the Mergebreak offices.

He glances at her.

"What?" he says. "Why are you looking at me like that?"

She's going to miss him, that's all. She's going to miss being the her that can miss him, the way she feels about him now. She's never going to see him again. She just doesn't want any more regret.

"Come over here," she says, and he walks around the counter, and she pulls him close, and kisses him on the mouth, and his hands land softly on her hips, and then grip harder, as she uses her fingers to unbutton his shirt, one button at a time.

■ ■ ■

There must have been a length of time, if only the length of the walk between the center of Eden and the gate, where Eve had thought about all she was going to lose. Everything she would never see again. The trees and the animals and how she would never be able to look at Adam naked without knowing that he was naked.

■ ■ ■

She leaves, after. He wants her to stay. He's falling asleep, he grabs softly at her wrist when she lifts from his body. But she goes. She has things to do. She kisses him, open-mouthed, while he's still lying naked in bed, and she pulls on her pants, her bra, her shirt, her socks, her shoes, and then she leaves.

In the elevator, she presses her hand against her pocket, to make sure the keycards are still there. They are.

YUJIN

Soyoung gave you the address, the time, the place. You had googled *how to get to Manhattan from John F. Kennedy Airport* and given up and decided that you would call a rideshare. Or maybe you'd take a cab. You liked the idea of taking a yellow cab in New York—it was silly. A hint of novelty on your mission. *Mission*. That sounded so serious. You didn't know what else to call it. Your little errand.

Going through the airport had been garbage—you hadn't expected the airport to be such garbage. You had expected New York airports to be better. You had read all the signs okay, at least. You hadn't expected some of the signs to have Korean subtitles—along with Chinese, Spanish, a bunch of other languages. And there were *so many white people*. And black people. And brown people. It was the people more than the buildings that got to you. You haven't seen this many non-Asian people in one place since your semester at NYU. But everything in the city was slightly askew. A little off, from what you knew. You didn't dislike it. In another life, you would have enjoyed the opportunity to explore.

Now you're standing in YJ's apartment lobby, waiting for the elevator. He lives in an okay building, you guess. You didn't get any looks coming in from the doorman. Why would you? He probably just thinks you're YJ, coming home from something.

The elevator comes. You get in. Elevators in the United States are subtly different than most of the elevators in Korea—you can't quite articulate what the difference is, but there's a palpable strangeness, the same way that everything here has felt like the world tilted to the left.

You want YJ's familiarity with the country. You want his easy understanding of how to call a cab, how the streets are set up. Your anger had cooled to a low simmer on the plane ride. But you still want your revenge. You want to fold him into yourself and have him understand how he has wronged you. You want his life. You'll settle for taking him back into yours.

You get out of the elevator. You know he keeps his spare key underneath a doormat. You're going to let yourself in. You had told Soyoung that you're going to distract him—you were lying. No, not lying—what you're going to do is going to be very distracting. You don't plan on giving him time to talk. You're going to walk up to his sleeping self and push your body onto his. And then you'll be him. You'll know everything, if you reintegrate. And if you change your mind—if your future, reintegrated self changes his mind—then he knows how to separate himself. But you—you know how you feel. You didn't instance when you crossed the border, anyway.

▮ ▮ ▮

Imagine that Adam gets to walk back into paradise. Imagine him looking at his nude self. That motherfucker who has never known anything but paradise. Of course, that naked asshole got his own punishment: He can never leave.

SOYOUNG-ROSE

Soyoung walks out of the subway. It feels like she's awake after a long time being asleep. Adrenaline. She's shrugged off the last of the warmth from YJ's apartment, and the temperature has dropped since night fell. When she went in, it was still light out. Now, the streetlamps are on, the world's all fluorescent and shadow, LED billboards. A sinister sort of half-light. No, don't pathologize anything. Her ruse hinges on her seeming as unsuspicious as possible for as long as possible. Part of that requires pretending everything is normal, down in her subconscious.

This is the last easy moment for her to back out. She could go home. She could go back to Korea. But it feels like it had felt for Soyoung, when she had decided to reintegrate with Rose. The certainty. How she reached for her other self's hand and it was like her body was moving before her mind could tell her what to do. She was wrong, then. She doesn't think she's wrong now.

■ ■ ■

It's easier, if Odysseus gives up on going home. If he accepts the gods' punishment. But there's no world in which Odysseus doesn't try and go home, now that he's failed to die in a war.

YJ

You wake up from a dead sleep. For a single second, you're confused. Some animal sense in your body jolts you to awareness, and in a series of staccato realizations, you see that there's someone in the room with you, standing over your bed.

"Soyoung?" you say, blearily.

"Shh," the shadow says.

He has your voice. Adrenaline shoots through your system. You throw the blankets up, scramble across the sheets.

"Shit!" the shadow says again louder, stumbling back, blanket in his face.

You scramble to your feet, tumble off the other side of the bed, try to get a good look at him as he pulls the blanket off. In the slim line of light from between your curtains you see him, in features more than in his totality. Here is his nose, the shape of his skull, here is the gleam of his eye, his jawline, here is your face in kaleidoscopic totality and you have the completely inane thought: *Yujin can't be in the States, Yujin is in Korea.*

Yujin lunges toward you.

■■■

The fisherman in his house, with his knife outstretched.

■■■

You throw a pillow at him. You throw your watch at him. You throw Petra's alarm clock at him. You run around the bed. Yujin stumbles into your closet. You don't want to hurt him. You run jaggedly around the bed, swerving past his outstretched hand. Your heart beats with the compulsion that you can't let him touch you. You're naked. You're not wearing a MERGEBREAK. He's not wearing one, either, you bet.

"Ow—Don't—" he starts to say in Korean, but you're throwing your dirty laundry at him and you're not thinking clearly. Your whole being is suffused with fear, the cortisol and the adrenaline, your nerves jangling all disjointedly, why's he here, why's he coming for you, what happened between you and him that he's here, what does he know, don't let him, don't let him touch you—

He lunges at you. You jump back, nearly trip down the steps from your loft, manage to slide your way down without falling. He comes after you.

"Why are you—" you shout, clambering over the sofa.

"—you didn't want to—" he shouts back before slamming his ankle into the glass coffee table and swearing.

There's a part of you fascinated by everything about him. You've never seen him in the flesh. Here is the way he moves, the same as you move. You've slammed your legs into that coffee table a million times. The way he grimaces when he's hurt. That's all you.

"—who told you?" you say, running to the kitchen. You look at your knife block. Your half-formed thoughts kaleidoscope on one another. No. This is insane. You look back up. He's looking at you. You're looking at him. He's thinking what you're thinking, you know. You won't do it. You're a coward. You don't want to kill yourself. You're a normal person. You're not a murderer. And he knows that you know that he's thinking this.

So you grab the knife.

Yujin stops. He knows that you don't mean it. But the knife is a physical object. The knife gives you distance. He has to pause. It doesn't matter what he thinks about you. It matters that there is a physical object between yourself and him, that you could use, that maybe ten years has given you enough distance that you *could* use it.

"Let's just talk," you say. "How are you here?"

He gives you a look like you're stupid.

"Plane."

"Did you instance again?"

"Of course not," he says. "We're going back, Yujin. I'm going back."

He speaks in complete banmal, almost derogatory.

■ ■ ■

Does Odysseus, seeing his other self slaughtering the room full of suitors, think to himself: I wish I were him? Does he feel relief that he is finally taking action?

■ ■ ■

"Who told you?" you say. You know the answer in your heart. There's only one person who knows where you would be, tonight, that you were asleep, because mere hours ago she was lying next to you. Did Soyoung sleep with you because she knew what was going to happen? Was she colluding with him? *Why?*

"Soyoung," he says. He takes a step forward. You don't step back. He knows you're bluffing. You know you're bluffing. You can't be bluffing.

"You're here to reintegrate," you say.

"What I don't understand is why you wouldn't just tell me," Yujin says.

How to explain. You know your faults. You are always spending too much time deliberating. You think that you can get all your dominos in order and knock them down. You have plans. You don't execute. You withhold information. You didn't want to tell him because you knew in your heart what you wanted but you thought you could put him off as a problem until the clock ran out.

You contemplate dropping the knife. You contemplate letting Yujin walk into you and becoming one person again. Give him what he wants. You know you could reverse it—you could be separate again, within the hour. But—the way that Soyoung talks about her past selves. How the person that she is now doesn't want what her previous selves wanted, how the conglomerate self has different goals, beliefs. What if the person you become, what if they don't want to separate? What if Yujin overpowers their desires? What if you change your mind?

So, not that. You've got the home field advantage. You're going to run.

You put the knife down and pick up a pan and throw it at him. You jump up and slide across the counter, but it doesn't work the way you expect and you end up skidding pathetically, halfway across, and you can see Yujin reaching for you and you feel cool acceptance, ah, this is all it is. This is what everything is. All you're thinking is *sorry I've been such a shithead. Sorry I promised you things that I didn't deliver. Sorry that I left you in the chrysalis of our previous life.*

YJ-YUJIN

So, in this story, the fisherman lives.

▪ ▪ ▪

Yujin's head hurts. His other self—his prior self—had good aim. He lies on the counter, staring at the ceiling. He knows everything now. Full download, cascade—it's like what Soyoung said. Reintegration doesn't feel like the movies make it feel. It's not a slideshow of memories, not like watching a clip show of moments. It's like being stranded in deep water. It's like feeling seaweed wrap around your legs and pull you under, every thought dragging up a new set of associations, memories. YJ's apartment is suddenly familiar, foreign. It's home, it's alien, it's home again. Whatever he's thinking about is being magnified through two perspectives.

He closes his eyes. He's thinking about the last few seconds before recombination. Yujin hadn't expected him to freak out. He had hoped that he would be able to touch his other self before he woke up. Yujin's head now is filled with the memory of him with the knife, standing before his self. Like he meant to use it. Like he knew that they weren't the sort of person to hold a knife like that, that they folded at every opportunity.

He was strangely relieved that he wasn't that sort of person. That there was, underneath everything, no raw red throbbing hatred of his other self, the recombination of their selves wasn't an act of continuing violence, it was just the single stab and the coalescing. He remembers thinking about Mitosis—overwriting himself. Both versions of him. Ah—there's the shame at his own greed. There's the relief that Yujin hadn't tried the other version of this reintegration—somehow luring YJ to the Mitosis machine and overwriting him, and that YJ hadn't gotten away, hadn't lured Yujin into that same trap in fear of what Yujin might do.

He felt like himself, whoever himself was. Yujin, probably. He would think of himself as Yujin, because in his head, YJ had also been Yujin, more often than not, and Yujin had never thought of himself as YJ.

"I was so mad," he says to himself. "I wouldn't have been so mad if you had just talked to me, once or twice."

"I didn't know how to bring the subject up. On either end," he says, after a long pause. "I was tired of stasis. I was tired of the perpetual motion machine."

"I guess I felt like I had been suffering for no reason," he says.

Yujin scrubs his face with his hand. He casts his mind back—the last few weeks, the series of events and decisions that led here. The feelings, winding back from the facts. Soyoung had asked Yujin to distract YJ. Soyoung had come over to YJ's apartment earlier. Soyoung and YJ had slept together and Soyoung had been the one who initiated. Soyoung and YJ had argued, multiple times, about Mitosis, about the IIS, about how she thought he had some intrinsic, intangible duty to act.

She wanted him to make decisions different from the ones that he'd made. She wanted to be separate. Yujin was supposed to be a distraction—a distraction from what? Yujin frowns. He gets up. Soyoung had come here to get something. Get something, or plant something. But they hadn't talked about anything suspicious. They had mostly talked about relationship things. Would she have been blackmailing him with their relationship? With the possibility of a relationship? That made no sense.

"She didn't have to do that," he says to himself.

He goes to his wallet. He flips through his cards—his general passcard and the passcard for floor twenty-six are both gone. He knows where Soyoung is going. She's going to the Mitosis lab.

▪▪▪

Every future person in the universe will learn sin, after Eve bites the apple. It is an inevitability.

▪▪▪

Yujin dresses. Button-down, pants, a jacket. Formal. Like he's going to work. He should look like he's a professional, not like he just got off the plane.

Yujin doesn't know what Soyoung is going to do. Whether she's going to take everything and dump it onto the internet, whether she's going to record the inside of the Mitosis lab and dump that online, too. Would she send the Mitosis specs to reporters? Will she write a manifesto and post it? He has no idea.

Yujin tries calling her, while putting his shoes on. The call goes straight to voicemail. Of course she's not picking up. He tries from Yujin's phone, racking up a huge data charge with the international roaming. She still doesn't pick up. Is she in the lab, already? Or just in an elevator or a subway?

Yujin doesn't know. He doesn't know what he's going to do when he meets her. He knows he has to hurry. Soyoung has an enormous head start—but she had timed her plans with Yujin's arrival in the apartment, he thinks. He might be able to intercept her.

It's the strangest thing, but: Yujin feels good. He feels alive. In the middle of this motion, there's no past, no future. Just the present, the single ongoing action. Maybe both of his selves had been living in stasis for too long. Maybe both of his selves should have been trying to change, all this time. What's been stopping him? Only his own self.

▪ ▪ ▪

He calls a cab, stumbles into the first one that pulls over. It'll be faster than the subway, this time of night, and if he pays in cash then there's no record, not like with a rideshare. He doesn't know whether this is going to matter, but—he's trying to be careful.

"Hey, you can't get blood on the upholstery," the taxi driver says in a thick accent that Yujin can't place. He touches his ear. It feels wet.

"I won't," Yujin says. YJ hadn't thrown the pan with any precision, it must have scraped against the side of his head.

"Rough night? Girl kick you out?"

"Kind of, yeah."

Girl did kick him out, in the sense that this is Soyoung's fault. Yujin dabs at the blood on his ear. It smells like iron. They say that head wounds bleed a lot. He wonders if ears count. He calls Soyoung again. The phone immediately goes to voicemail. No connection. He tries again. Still no connection.

Yujin dabs his head with his sleeve. He's going to go to the Mitosis offices. He's going to swipe into the building, break into the lab, and he's going to confront Soyoung and he's going to figure out what she's thinking, even if he has to unravel her to do it.

"Can you take me to Fortieth and Seventh?"

SOYOUNG-ROSE

This late at night, the Mergebreak building is a cold black monolith studded with the occasional pane of light. Soyoung walks in through the front door like she belongs here, because as long as she looks like she belongs she won't be stopped. The lighting in the lobby is still blunt daylight-strength fluorescent, and she nods to the single doorman sitting at the desk. He nods back. Soyoung knows she looks respectable. She had fixed her hair on the subway.

She palms YJ's keycard so that the face and name are against her hand, pressing it against the card reader. She holds her breath.

The gate opens, and she steps through. The night doorman doesn't give her a second look. It's so easy, when you have the right keys. When you look like you belong.

She pushes the button for the elevator, shifts from side to side while the numbers tick down on the little screen. She's trying to act normal—there's probably some security guard in a room somewhere, reviewing all the camera footage. The elevator arrives and she gets in.

Soyoung chews the inside of her lip. She's thinking about her plan of attack. She's thinking about all the other times she walked through the Mitosis gate. She's thinking about what it might feel like, to go through clean. The elevator stops. The door opens. She walks quickly over to tap the second keycard at the second elevator. Punches in 26. Gets in the elevator and rides down.

She walks through the empty reception area. Her reflection against the glass windows is her only companion.

At the door to the lab, she types in the keycode on the number pad, which turns a cheerful green. She opens the door. She turns on the lights and walks into the familiar laboratory. She's spent so much time in here. The sound of her footsteps echoes off all the metal. She goes to the terminal and turns it on, before pulling a hard drive out of her jacket pocket, which she plugs into the machine. She starts the download, and then goes over to the physical files. She's going to take as many photos as she can.

YJ-YUJIN

Yujin throws cash at the cab driver before running out of the car and into the lobby. There's a night receptionist sitting at the desk, looking half asleep.

"Hi," Yujin says. "I work for Mergebreak, and I left my phone in there earlier today, but I forgot my keycard. Can you verify me and give me a temporary passcard?"

It's late. Far past working hours. But this is a building that houses law firms and tech offices and two different investment banks. This is a Manhattan skyscraper. There's always someone working.

"Sure," the night receptionist says. He runs Yujin through the verification procedure that Yujin remembers doing every single time YJ had forgotten his keycard. The night receptionist nods.

"We're good."

He manually opens the gates, and then Yujin's walking through. The crossing is momentarily mind-bending—he's walked through this gate a thousand times, he's here for the first time—but he manages to keep his expression and his gait steady until he gets to the elevator. When it arrives, he leans heavily against the wall. Scrubs his face in his hand. What was that? What the hell was that? It felt like his brain was melting out of his ears, though the feeling's gone as quickly as it arrived.

He gets to the Mergebreak reception area and faces the second hurdle. He doesn't have a card that'll let him summon an elevator to floor twenty-six. But there's a stairwell that goes down the heart of the building, accessible from every Mergebreak floor without a keycard. If he takes that down, there'll be a keycard reader at the door that separates the stairwell from the actual floor. Those doors are made of frosted glass. Mergebreak has a whole team dedicated to network security, but Yujin bets that nobody is watching for physical intruders this deep into the building, someone who had already gotten past the prior levels of security, who would know where to go, like YJ does, like Soyoung does. The glass door would break, given sufficient force. And every floor has a civilian firefighting kit, which Yujin remembers from YJ's memories of having to do fire drills every six months. There's a fire axe in the kit.

This is a terrible idea. But he's so close. And he only has so much time.

Yujin grabs the firefighter's kit from behind the receptionist's desk, opens it, and pulls out the fire axe. It's a cool, heavy weight in his hand. Then he makes a beeline for the stairwell, going three floors down the brightly lit oubliette. He feels like a horror movie protagonist, carrying the axe, going down the stairs before reaching the glass door.

It is a clear and fragile thing. It delineates space with its presence. He could turn back now. Until he acts, this can all be undone. This could all just be a bad dream.

He takes a deep breath.

Yujin swings the axe, crashing through the glass, before stepping through, running down the hall to the laboratory. As he runs, he's thinking about how good it felt to break through the glass. How good it felt to ignore all the barriers that are stopping you from getting what you want.

SOYOUNG-ROSE

The files finish copying over from the terminal. Soyoung carefully disconnects the external hard drive and opens the program that controls the Mitosis gate. The gate begins to do something adjacent to humming. She ignores the not-humming and plugs in the USB drive containing the calibration instructions that Megan shared into the computer next to the terminal. She begins to calibrate the Mitosis gate, comparing the terminal display to the USB's instructions at every step. She needs to get this right. Even though she's watched Gerry do this and she's mapped his movements to the descriptions and technical diagrams that Megan provided, it's different doing this live.

She plugs another spatial coordinate in. The hum changes pitch. She feels repulsion. She frowns. Maybe she set the gate's field too wide. She hadn't seen Gerry show any expression when he was the one sitting here. She plugs a different set of coordinates in. The feeling of repulsion fades. Good. She doesn't want to accidentally step in before everything's calibrated.

There's a crash from somewhere outside. She freezes. Breathes in sharply. Nothing. That was nothing. Just the building settling. Or a night janitor. No one else would be here, this late. She bites her lip. Keeps calibrating the machine. Pulls a slider slightly closer. Changes the frequency a few levels down. About three-quarters done, she thinks. She had assumed this would take less time, but she supposes Gerry was a professional who built parts of the interface, and this is Soyoung's first time using it.

The sound of the number pad clicking. Fuck. Yujin didn't do his job. He didn't intercept YJ fast enough. YJ must have noticed his cards were gone, and extrapolated who had stolen them and for what purpose.

Nearly there. Two more dials to turn, a few more keystrokes. She goes quickly, one hand on the dial while the other bangs at the keyboard. She needs time. She needs to stall him. She needs to *stop* him. She has one tool. The machine in front of her.

She bites her lip. She makes three decisive keystrokes.

The door opens.

YJ-YUJIN

Yujin walks into the room and is thrown into the diffuse emotion of nostalgia, punching him in the chest. *Remember being a kid, playing in the sandbox with Soyoung. Remember walking to school and sitting in class. Remember leaving Korea, getting on the plane and thinking that it's an adventure.* The feeling suffuses the air. It makes him stop; it makes his knees weak.

"Mitosis does that to everyone, the first time," Soyoung says.

Yujin pushes past the feeling in his chest. He takes a step forward.

"Soyoung—"

"Don't step closer. If you take three more steps you're going to be in for a really weird, bad time."

He stops.

"I've set the radius of the field to its maximum," Soyoung says. "I don't want to hurt you. But I will, if I have to."

"Soyoung," Yujin says. "What are you doing?"

She doesn't answer his question. She keeps typing at the keyboard while watching him.

"The more you know about what I'm doing, the more implicated you become. You said you didn't want this to be your problem, so just turn around. Walk away."

"You used my ID, I'm already implicated. You told Yujin how YJ felt to make him come here; you slept with YJ to get my keycard; you lied to Yujin for months, and—"

She looks at him, no longer typing. Wide eyes. She's staring as if she can read his mind, understand what's happened to him. As if to see something is to understand it.

"You reintegrated with yourself," Soyoung says. "That was what Yujin meant by 'a distraction,' wasn't it? Am I right? Who am I talking to right now?"

"Yujin," he says, because that's his name, that's YJ's name, that's every version of his name, and he starts laughing, because the absurdity of the last few weeks is finally getting to his head. Oh, how knowing changes things. Oh, how lying when you have a secret is different than lying by accident, how having two histories in your head is different than being singular.

"Please leave," Soyoung says. "I know you don't want to be involved."

Yujin shakes his head.

"I said it before, I'm already implicated. You stole my cards. I'm the first suspect."

"Tell them I seduced you," she says.

"Did you?"

"No," she says. "But I don't know if I could make you believe that."

How have he and Soyoung come to this? They used to play together. Their biggest problems used to be begging money off their mothers for chips after school. He can't know her heart now. He can't know why she does anything at all.

YJ could stand here all night. Soyoung could stand here all night. He thinks about what he knows about Soyoung. Soyoung, once she has direction, chases that desire to the end of the earth. She has no compunctions about asking the world to bend toward her favor. Soyoung was trying to live in a way that was temporary, and it made her careless. There is no way he's going to convince her to stand down. He knows her, he thinks. He hopes. He and she, they could stand at an impasse forever. But that leads to both of them being caught in the morning. If he just got to her, physically, he could overpower her. And he wants to do that: He wants to catch her wrists in a hold and pull her out of this room. He wants to take her back home with him.

"Soyoung, I think the only person you're ever interested in is yourself, and all the rest of us are collateral," YJ says. "But I really don't think you'd hurt me on purpose."

▮▮▮

Odysseus blithely leaving Ithaca, assuming his wife, his son, his other self, will welcome his return.

▮▮▮

YJ steps forward.

▪▪▪

Adam taking the apple, assuming that Eve will never hurt him.

▪▪▪

Nostalgia crashes over him like a wave, sweeps him apart into his component parts, the punch of powerful feeling hitting somewhere behind his heart and lungs, and it makes him choke, it's such a surprise, it makes him want to vomit, and he's still moving toward the gate, body in motion as if propelled by the yearning, the desire to rewind time, it's been so few hours since he's been reintegrated, and he tries to stop but he falls over his own feet, and he's crashing forward, and then he's gone, and then he feels something around him, and god, he feels so—

SOYOUNG-ROSE

Soyoung sees Yujin step into the radius of the Mitosis gate and collapse.

Later, she's going to think about how she should have turned off the gate, she should have let whatever was going to happen to Yujin happen, she should have bluffed with a smaller radius. But in the moment, before she can think, he's falling, and his form is going strange and fluid, like taffy being pulled, amorphous untangling, and she's terrified for him and she's running forward to catch him, action before conscious thought, and then she's in the radius, and—

SOYOUNGROSEYJYUJIN

I am seven years old and I am standing on the bank of a stream. Sunlight glints off the water. There's a sudden sharp push at my back and then I'm falling forward and I'm yelping and–

I am thirteen years old and I am SOMETHING IS WRONG eating dinner with my family. It's not that exciting. It's just soup and rice and some banchan. I want to be eating–

I am seventeen years old and I am standing in SOMETHING IS WRONG the middle of a quiet side street in the middle of Seoul and my friends are walking ahead and Yujin is talking to me and I am being SOMETHING IS WRONG given something I don't want and I don't know what to do but–

I am twenty-four years old and I am falling in love with Petra. I am sitting on the couch next to her and we are SOMETHING IS WRONG watching a movie. It's a romcom. I don't really like romcoms, SOMETHING IS WRONG and I don't think that she does either, but she had promised her SOMETHING IS WRONG friend that she would watch, and I've been roped into it. I

I am seven years old and I am standing on the bank of a shallow stream. In front of me, my friend is leaning over the water. I want to put my hand on her back. I want to scare her a little and hear her laugh. I want her to look at–

I am thirteen years old and I am excited about graduating middle school. I think SOMETHING IS WRONG I can be someone new in high school, who isn't tied to my previous self. Who isn't the new kid from Ko–

I am seventeen years old and I feel like my heart has been ripped out. This is the first time I've felt like SOMETHING IS WRONG this. I will never feel like this again, every future heartbreak will be a lesser echo of this SOMETHING IS WRONG moment. The worst thing is how Soyoung is laughing, but–

I am twenty-four years old and I am watching English language SOMETHING IS WRONG programming on the foreign language channel. SOMETHING IS WRONG I think it's a television show, but I'm not sure. I'm eating breakfast while I watch. My parents aren't awake yet. Sometimes SOMETHING IS WRONG I think about moving out of my parents' place, but I haven't pulled the trigger don't mind. I guess I like doing things with Petra even SOMETHING IS WRONG if they're boring, or hard. I would rather be sitting here than anywhere else. On the screen someone tells a joke. She laughs. I look at her. This is when I realize I'm in love. I could not mistake this feeling for anything—

I am twenty-eight years SOMETHING IS WRONG old and I am staring at my other self. SOMETHING IS WRONG She's saying SOMETHING IS WRONG something, and I understand the words she is saying but I SOMETHING IS WRONG don't understand the intent behind it. Regret isn't so bad. Regret SOMETHING IS WRONG is nothing compared to desire. You have to move SOMETHING IS WRONG forward. SOMETHING IS WRONG You have to know how it feels. You have to burn your hand SOMETHING IS WRONG on the SOMETHING IS WRONG stove SOMETHING IS WRONG and—

SOMETHING IS WRONG SOMETHING IS WRONG SOMETHING IS WRONG SOMETHING IS WRONG SOMETHING IS WRONG SOMETHING IS WRONG SOMETHING IS WRONG SOMETHING IS WRONG SOMETHING IS WRONG SOMETHING IS WRONG SOMETHING IS WRONG SOMETHING IS WRONG SOMETHING IS WRONG SOMETHING IS WRONG SOMETHING IS WRONG SOMETHING IS WRONG SOMETHING IS WRO—

yet. My mother always makes a face when I start talking about it. SOMETHING IS WRONG She tells me that one of me is in America, she wants to keep the other. SOMETHING IS WRONG I know that she doesn't mean it in a bad way, but it leaves a bad feeling in my—

I am twenty-eight SOMETHING IS WRONG years old and I am staring at my other self. I'm done saying SOMETHING IS WRONG everything SOMETHING IS WRONG I need to say. I feel satisfied. I feel like she understands—she must, right? I SOMETHING IS WRONG have explained SOMETHING IS WRONG myself. She is SOMETHING IS WRONG enough SOMETHING IS WRONG me that I can speak freely and be understood SOMETHING IS WRONG. This SOMETHING IS WRONG must be SOMETHING IS WRONG r—

SOMETHING IS WRONG SOMETHING IS WRONG SOMETHING IS WRONG SOMETHING IS WRONG SOMETHING IS WRONG SOMETHING IS WRONG SOMETHING IS WRONG SOMETHING IS WRONG SOMETHING IS WRONG SOMETHING IS WRONG SOMETHING IS WRONG SOMETHING IS WRONG SOMETHING IS WRONG SOMETHING IS WRONG SOMETHING IS WRONG SOMETHING IS WRONG SOMETHING IS WRONG SOMETHING IS WRO—

SOYOUNG

In the memory, you're standing in your grandfather's house. This isn't real. The world around you has the soft filmic quality that dreams have, the clear and soundless clarity that can only exist in the mind. It feels like the interior of the memories, when the Mitosis machine would rip you apart and stick you back together. The moment before you're spit out. You would be more worried, but none of this is real and you don't have the capacity to be worried.

You're standing in your grandfather's living room. There are pictures of your cousins and you on the walls. There is a jug of barley tea on the table in front of you. This is how it looked when you were a child. In reality, you and Minsoo stripped your grandfather's house bare months ago.

"So," a voice behind you says. Your voice. "I didn't have that one on the bingo board."

You turn around. Rose is sitting at the kitchen table. You remember sitting at the table, how Rose is sitting the same way you sat there as a teenager. You did a lot of homework at that table.

"YJ stepping in."

"Yeah."

You probe your memory. You remember Gerry telling you, at the beginning of the trials, that after being unspooled the memories of the last few months would become washed out, apportioned between you and your instance based on some sort of weighted internal valence. The last few months feel clear in your head. You remember being Soyoung-Rose. You remember the series of decisions that led to this outcome. Beyond that, in the current moment, you have only your own memories of the past, not Rose's. It's a strange segmentation.

Rose gets up. She inspects the kitchen. You follow her.

"How do you think we come out?"

"I think it just ends. Same as every other time."

"No, I mean—how do we come out? How do—separate, or together?"

"I don't know," you say, and you realize that you're not speaking any particular language with Rose. You think a thought. It verbalizes. She understands. You're inhabiting the space between thinking and speaking. There are no languages here.

"Fair," Rose says.

You step out of the kitchen. You inspect the living room. You're sure if you went upstairs, you would find your old bedroom.

"Hey, I want to check out the upstairs," Rose says, and then she starts walking that way, so you follow her.

ROSE

You head for the stairs. You thought that being separate would make you feel clearer in the head. You had thought it would be more of a relief. But it just feels like—there's no difference. It just feels like you. You're worried about the same things you were worried about before the laboratory: what to do with YJ, what you are going to tell your mothers, how you are going to get Soyoung to the airport.

And you're worried about the files, the copies of the archive, the fact that when you leave the dream, you're going to be a trespasser in an office building, and there's going to be two of you, and YJ will be there, and you don't know what condition he's going to be in. You remember thinking that you'd figure all of this out after. That you'd buy a plane ticket, and upload the files from Korea. She had left the details for you and your other self.

You're surprised that, even with the manifold problems she's left behind, you like the memories of your conglomerate self. She didn't ruminate. She acted, rather than thought. She saw a problem and followed the clean bright line to its conclusion. She wasn't kind, but in the end, she had prioritized what she felt was good for society over her own personal gain. She might have been selfish, but at least she had been selfish in motion. She was better than you had been.

▮▮▮

The world where the fisherman sits at his own bedside and asks his instance how his life had gone is a quieter one. There's no bloodshed, in that world. Maybe there's some conversation. Maybe he runs back for the undersea court. But there's no bone-deep knowing. No two worlds in his chest. No knife, either.

▮▮▮

You walk across the living room. Everything in the room seems so much smaller than it did when you were younger.

"I'm sorry," your other self says. "For reintegrating us."

You stop halfway up the staircase. You look down. Soyoung's looking back at you, clear-eyed, the set of her mouth serious. You remember reintegration: the immediate feeling of regret, of remorse, of sadness, of furious anger. She had never apologized—she had never been able to. An apology to the self would have meant nothing.

"I didn't expect you to feel that way."

"Well. I just want you to know. I'm sorry," Soyoung says. "You don't have to forgive me or anything, but I just wanted to say it."

You look away from her. You keep walking up. You are thinking about the last few months. You are thinking about all the hurt, the confusion, how the mélange of her life and your life felt, and how it felt to be someone who was able to ask your questions and finally get your questions answered. Someone capable of going into this house without fear.

"It's okay," you say.

SOYOUNG

You walk behind Rose as she opens the door to your old room. This is probably pulled from your memories, not hers. You remember it better than she does, you had lived here until you went to college. But it looks like your room from when you were eleven. Cartoon posters on the walls. The pink bedspread you got rid of when you were fifteen.

Rose falls onto the bed. It's the sort of comfortable, pleased motion you remember being able to make with your body that you've never seen from the outside. You lie down next to her, slowly, giving her time to get up if she wants to. She doesn't. You look up at the ceiling. The fluorescent lights, the water stains. It's an old house. You don't miss being a kid.

"Why the house, do you think?" she says.

"I mean—I guess we've been thinking about it a lot. Or trying not to think about it."

"I don't like what it says about us, that stealing Mitosis was easier than deciding what to do with the house," When you don't respond, she says, "I remember there being glow-in-the-dark stars."

You finally respond.

"We took them down when we were ten, remember? I wanted to have a grown-up room, going into middle school."

Silence again. It's nice, in a way. The quiet clicking of the alarm clock that you kept on your nightstand. The sound of wind in the trees outside.

"What do you think happened to Yujin?"

"I don't know," you say again. "I didn't think he'd walk in."

You're worried about him. You're really worried.

The clock ticks. You close your eyes and open them. Still no stars. Just your memory of them.

"What do we do with the house?" she says.

▪▪▪

Why the house? Why situate this trip through the unconscious here? What does it represent? The house is your childhood. The house is your grandfather's postwar consolation prize. The house is a gift. The house is a trap. The house is the world as it used to be, as it could be, as it could have been.

■ ■ ■

It's your turn to be silent. You want to give her the answer she wants, this time. You feel like you've made enough misery for her. But you don't know what she wants.

"I want to hear what you want to do with the house."

"I want to sell it," she says, and it sounds like a confession. "Or, no. I want to want to sell it. Or I want to want to give it to Minsoo, or something. Or to you. But, no. I don't really want—"

"You actually want to keep it."

"I want to be the sort of person who wants everything that comes with keeping his house," Rose says. "Or the sort of person who truly doesn't care. Like, how I wish I missed him. I want to miss him, more than I miss him. I miss—"

She rubs her eyes.

"I don't think you get to choose who you miss," you say. "I thought you could, but—"

"—yeah," Rose says. "But if I don't miss him, why the *fuck* am I so attached to the house?"

You don't have an answer for her, there. She doesn't seem to mind, she just dries her eyes on her sleeve and then you're both getting up, because there's the sound of someone calling from downstairs.

YJ-YUJIN

The first thing Yujin thinks when he opens his eyes is: This is it. I died. The Mitosis gate tore me apart and I died and this is heaven. He's staring at a patch of pale blue sky ringed with a halo of treetops. He turns his head. Trees, a brick wall behind them, little pieces of shrubbery in front. He gets up, the world tilting around him, and he realizes he's in the backyard of a house. Yujin remembers this house. It's where Soyoung used to live, as a kid, where they kicked around a kiddie soccer ball together. Where they played with toy lightsabers.

Yujin walks forward through the scrubby grass. It's quiet here. There's none of the ambient Seoul city noise that he remembers. He wants to talk his problems over with someone. The person he would talk his problems over with was himself.

"This is probably a dream," he says to himself. "Or some sort of psychological phenomenon. Representative. I hope my brain isn't getting fried."

There's nothing that he can do if his brain is getting fried.

"I'm in the Mitosis field, most likely. This is all happening in my mind."

Yujin gets to the back door of the house. He opens it.

It's an old house. Old leather sofa, *really* old television. Smells a little like incense. It hadn't seemed so old when he had last been here, but the last time he was here, he was a child, a single memory that both Yujin and YJ had shared.

"Hello?"

He calls out into the room. He's not expecting any answer, but he hears someone upstairs.

SOYOUNG

You look down at Yujin. You think this is the combined version. Not just his Korean self, or the American YJ. When you saw him earlier, running into the room, it was something in the set of his shoulders that made you think it was both of him, together, and he looks the same as then. He looks up at you.

"Why are there two of you here?"

"Why aren't there two of *you*?" Rose says, leaning on the railing. She's watching him with bright eyes. She came to the same conclusion you did.

"You programmed the machine," Yujin says. "You tell me why this is happening."

"I didn't think you'd step in," you say.

"Well, I did," he says.

"You shouldn't have—"

"*You* shouldn't have," he says. "What the hell were you thinking? Let me guess. You're here to rip the files off the server. You're here because you want to separate before uploading everything."

"So what if I am? What are you here for, then? Are you here to stop me?"

"Yes," Yujin says. "This is crazy. You can't just do this kind of thing—steal my IDs, break into my office, spread corporate secrets across the internet. You can't just *do that*."

"What's crazy is that you'll just go along with what Megan and Drew want," Rose says.

"Why's that so crazy? Is the world where everyone has access to every single schematic to build their own Mitosis machines, with no oversight, to use them on people like you used it on me, is that not crazy? Is that *better*?"

"Is it better if you don't know what you're walking into when you get on that plane, is that what you're saying?" Rose says. "It's better not knowing who you're going to walk out as on the other side of the immigration checkpoint? Not knowing who you're going to be when you cross the border? Do you prefer it that way, Yujin? Just knowing that it's going to be whatever the IIS wants. Is that better? Not asking for the details because what you really want is to have someone else make that decision for you? Because it's easier to accept things happening to you than it is to make a *choice*? Things happen because you *do* things, Yujin! You can't just let them happen. People deserve to know."

"That's not how it'll happen," YJ says. "There are guardrails—"

"How can you be sure," Rose says. "That's been my entire point. How can you be sure of what's going to happen? How can you trust the individuals in charge to make the right decisions for every single person on earth? How can you trust yourself to do that? YJ couldn't even trust Yujin. *I* couldn't trust myself."

"Rose—" you say.

She turns to you. "No. I'm mad at you, too. It's okay, though. I understand how you felt, now. I don't regret what happened, I only regret how it happened."

"I'm sorry," you say again. "If I could have understood what you meant—"

"—if you had understood what I meant by regret, then you would have been *me,*" Rose says.

Rose turns to Yujin. She puts her hand on his shoulder. You watch the way he leans toward her, unconsciously. You suddenly miss Tae. It has been so long since you missed Tae. But the missing has the tint of nostalgia, as if your relationship with Taehyung is something that is already lost. Ah, he's going to be so sad. There is no world where you don't hurt people.

"Yujin. I don't want to argue with you. Can you just answer one thing?"

"Fine," Yujin says.

"If there were no consequences to your life. If you could get away with everything. If you weren't scared of retribution. How would you really handle Mitosis?"

YJ-YUJIN

Yujin frowns. That's not a question that makes sense. There's no world without consequences. To ask Yujin how he would act in a world without consequence is like asking him how he would act while living on the moon. It's hard for him to imagine. So often, the parts of him that are cautious subsumed the parts of him that are brave.

But. He remembers the way that it felt, to chase after himself. How it had felt like freedom, to face himself in his bedroom and damn every version of his future self. He imagines being that person.

Soyoung and Rose are both silent, watching him through identical eyes. They're fishing for something. He sighs again. In a world without consequences, it feels wrong to tell them anything other than the truth.

"If there were no consequences, I'd pause the border rollout," he says, finally. "Everything else about Mitosis, I'd let the IIS handle, because I think that's better than letting any single person at a private company control this—whether it's me, or Drew, or whoever. But what I'd do doesn't matter. We don't live in a perfect world. There's no way to thread that needle."

"Fine. But which is a better world: one where everyone has the schematics, or one where just Mergebreak does?" Soyoung says.

"Soyoung," Yujin says.

"Tell me right now that you're happy with Drew and Megan deciding how instancing works for the rest of the world. To set the standards we're all going to have to live with. Tell me that, and we'll stop."

Rose is silently nodding next to her. As if they're in total agreement, one speaking for the other.

He's thinking about the first night at the bar. He's thinking about seeing Rose in the shopping street, Soyoung in the basement of the Shinsegae Department Store, Soyoung-Rose in his living room. He's thinking about convictions so strong they exist in a plurality of selves. He wishes he had that sort of conviction.

Yujin had it, in the end. Yujin had flown to the States the minute he had learned how YJ felt. He remembers being Yujin, all those years in Korea, alone. And it had *felt* alone, in a way that YJ hadn't thought it did. YJ had assumed that Yujin had felt like he was part of a community, that he had family and friends. And he did. But it was a lonely feeling, waiting for the rest of your life to start. A frustrating feeling, knowing that your life depended on the actions of someone an ocean away. It hadn't been good, to depend on someone else. It hadn't been good, to be so blind. He knew that in his heart now.

▮▮▮

The English word "nostalgia" is derived from the Greek word "algea," the plural personification of pain.

▮▮▮

"No. I'm not happy," Yujin says. "No, I don't think that this is a *good* status quo. But like I said—we don't live in a perfect world."

"You don't have to perfectly agree with everything that might happen. You just have to agree that it's better if there's more time, before the rollout. That it's better if people have a little more information," Soyoung says.

Yujin sighs.

He wants to be the sort of person who could have flatly told Soyoung no, the first time, the sort of person who could have not pulled the thread of the whole conspiracy, who could have accepted the first bribe and asked no more questions. But he's not that person. If he was, he wouldn't be standing here. Always a part of him, doubting. Doubting whether he's doing the right thing with his instance. Doubting whether he should help Soyoung. Doubting whether he should play Drew's games. Doubting whether he should take Megan's deal. Doubting whether he's ever made the right decisions. Doubting whether Mergebreak and IIS should hold the keys to the technology.

"Fine. Okay. I get your point. But, Soyoung, it's not better for my life, if Mitosis leaks."

"But you don't have to be the whistleblower," Rose says. "All I'm asking is that you let me go through with this."

"My ID shows that I entered the building," YJ says. "And Drew gets a log of every time someone accesses twenty-six. And I broke a glass door, earlier."

"No, your ID got stolen by a corporate spy, who stole your wallet at a bar. When you realized the cards were missing, you ran to the office and broke in to catch her, but she used the Mitosis gate to psychologically overwhelm you. It's dangerous technology. You did all you could. You risked your life! But she knocked you out. She got away," Rose says. "Give me a fifteen-minute head start, stumble out of here, and hit the fire alarm. Call Drew, pretending to be YJ. And I bet you'll instance again, when you fly back to Korea. One of you goes, the other stays. Nothing that happens here has to be permanent, except for your memories."

He thinks about it for a second. It would work. Mergebreak wouldn't want to involve the police in the theft of company secrets. Megan might be mad, but first she would be worried about him. Drew would use it as another string on him, until Megan snipped those threads. And personally, Yujin would have to decide how to handle his reintegration. That's a separate issue. In the short term, Soyoung's plan would work.

"How do you know you're doing the right thing," he says. "You're creating a more complicated world this way."

"If we're wrong, I can live with regret," Rose says.

■ ■ ■

The man on the bank of the river. The man standing on the bank of the bay, knowing he might drown.

ROSE

Yujin nods. One sharp dip of his chin.

"Okay," he says.

"Okay," you say. "Just like that?"

"Just like that," Yujin replies. "Take Mitosis. I'll let you go."

He says it with such finality.

"Thank you," you say. You don't have anything else to say. You just stand there staring at each other stupidly.

Yujin looks away first, and back around at the walls surrounding you.

"So how do we get out, then?"

Your instance speaks.

"Yujin, do you remember—the week before I left for America. You came over with your mom, because our moms wanted to talk. And we watched cartoons until we got sent outside to play, but we were kind of old for that, so we asked if we could go to the store instead."

"Yes," Yujin says, a puzzled expression on his face.

You remember that day. It had been an unremarkable afternoon, other than going to the store. You remember how it felt like freedom, being allowed out on your own, together. You went to the store, you and him. You bought cheap candy. He bought a soda. You had used the rest of your money to buy one of those ice creams that you can split in half, and you had eaten it together. You remember it being a good day.

"Every time, before, during the testing, the experience ended with the end of the memory. I think that's the end of this one. I think we just walk out the front door to get out."

You and Yujin both look over. The front door looks—it looks like the front door to your grandfather's house. You remember walking through it so many times. You remember being too scared to go in, six months ago. You hope you see it again someday.

Your instance walks forward. You begin to follow her. She seems to know where she's going.

"Soyoung, Rose—are we good?"

You stop. You both look back at him. Yujin has an expression on his face that you can't read. Are you good? You and him. You have more to talk about, topside, you think. If you're lucky, you'll have time, someday.

"I think so," Soyoung says.

"I mean, like, in the grand scheme of things. Because I care—"

"Yujin, we're good," you say, and you reach for his hand, and you pull him through the door, and—

SOYOUNG

—You fall out of the gate, reeling. You stumble to your feet. You don't feel any pain, or nausea, you don't feel *bad,* the way that you felt bad in all the test runs. You hear the sound of something else falling to the floor. You shake your head. You feel like yourself, like *Kang Soyoung.* You think it's just you in here, now—you don't remember growing up in the States, but you have the remembrance of the recollection, like a faded memory, imprinted in the folds of your brain. You look down at the mess. Rose is getting up from her hands and knees. Yujin is collapsed next to her, singular. The Mitosis machine is inert. The only feelings you can identify in your brain are the ones coming from your heart.

You crouch over Rose.

"Are you okay?"

Rose looks up at you.

"Let's keep the house," she says. "I want us to keep the house."

"Sure," you say. "Okay. Yes."

ROSE

You click at the terminal. Soyoung is sitting next to Yujin, who still hasn't woken up. You hope he's okay. You'll let Soyoung worry about him right now. You're scrubbing your fingerprints from the server—this is a you job, not a Soyoung job. You're the one who knows how to use the command line interface.

"I have a theory," Soyoung says.

"Okay," you say, glancing up from the terminal. She's got Yujin's head in her lap.

"I think in his own terrible way, he was trying to give us choices," Soyoung says. "Our grandfather, I mean. Not YJ. If you wanted to come back. If you wanted the house. I don't think he thought that we'd actually listen to him, if we didn't want to reintegrate. I think he just . . . wanted to put it on the table."

"He should have used his words," you say. You try for spite and it comes out stale.

"Well, he's dead," Soyoung says, and it makes you laugh. She's funny. You're funny.

"Yeah, he's dead."

"I'm sorry we didn't get what you wanted—the perfect separation," she says. "Unless you don't remember, and only I remember."

You remember the last few months in clear detail. Beyond that, Soyoung's life is like the memory of a memory. Like a reflection in a window.

"That's okay," you say.

"We can try again, while we're here?"

▮▮▮

The night on the mountain, your grandfather's dead body in his tomb. The way you felt, looking at her. The way she pulled toward you with such guileless motion. The night when you picked up your phone. The way it wasn't a question, of course you were going to go back. How all your actions were foregone conclusions.

▪▪▪

You look at Soyoung. Soyoung looks at you.

▪▪▪

The way there was no choice but to release the files. How there was no self capable of any other decision. How you are trying to learn from your own selfishness. How you had liked the person you had been, with her. How the ability to take action had felt better than watching, ruminating, stasis. How you want to be someone who is able to move through the world and admit to themself what they want, and how you want to be a person who is able to understand when there are more important things than what you want. How you think that the two of you, together, would be a more effective instrument.

▪▪▪

"Do you want—?"

"Only if you want," she says.

You've been her before. She's been you. She doesn't move forward. She holds out her hand, palm up, like a question.

You take her hand. For a moment, it's warm. And then—

YJ-YUJIN

Yujin wakes up. This time, the first thing he notices is that he's warm. He's lying on something soft with a shiny shock blanket pulled over him. He opens his eyes. He turns his head. Soyoung-or-Rose is poking at a laptop.

She looks over at him. "I was a little worried you wouldn't wake up."

Yujin slides up. They're still in the Mitosis laboratory. Soyoung sits next to him.

"Do you remember what happened?"

The dream—the feeling of separation, of reintegration—is dissipating like so much smoke in his brain. He remembers getting thrown through memories, scraping the inside of Soyoung and Rose's brain. He has the passing thought—*ah, if we could give this experience to everyone, there would be world peace*—and it's brought crashing down through the remembrance of what his selves did to get here. He gets it. He understands how they felt. He just—he would have done things differently, had he known.

"Yes," Yujin says. "Soyoung, is Rose here? Did you stay reintegrated?"

Soyoung shrugs.

"I put myself back together," she says.

The rest of his memories trickle in. What he had agreed to. What they had talked about, inside. How he had agreed to help her, to let her run and take the blame for releasing all the Mitosis data.

"Where will you go?"

"I'm not telling you," Soyoung says. "You shouldn't know anything about that. For plausible deniability."

Yujin imagines her boarding a plane. He imagines her going to Korea or to a country without an extradition treaty with the United States. He imagines her on a sunny beach, wearing a tiny bikini like a Bond girl. He imagines her in a small interrogation cell, strapped to a polygraph machine, as if she's James Bond.

"Do you think you're going to be okay?"

Soyoung smiles at him. All bravado, teeth shiny and white, the same smile that she had as a kid when she was about to skewer him with the lightsaber.

"I'll be fine."

She gets up and goes back to the terminal where she begins packing up her hard drives. She's not looking at him when she speaks.

"But I don't think we're going to see each other again, after this."

Yujin wants to say, "Of course we will."

He wants to say, "Despite how you nearly destroyed my entire life, I am so glad to have known you."

He wants to say, "I love you."

"Okay," Yujin says. "Okay. Good luck."

"Thank you," Soyoung says. She looks around the room. She adjusts her jacket a little. She walks over to Yujin and cups his face in her hands and gives him a long, lingering kiss. Then she draws back.

"I'm going now," Soyoung says. "Despite everything, I really loved getting the chance to know you. All versions of you. Fifteen minutes. Remember."

And then she's gone.

SOYOUNG-ROSE

She takes the elevator down. She's got a flight to schedule. She's got to grab her luggage from her apartment. She should be thinking about the logistics of the data leak. She should be thinking about getting through customs. She should be thinking about how Dr. Crouton is going to cope with a fourteen-hour flight, and how maybe she should just let Clarissa take him. She should be thinking about how this is going to be her last time back in the United States for a long time, and she should call Rose's mother and tell her that she loves her. She should be thinking about how to break the news to Tae, about breaking their engagement. She should be thinking about hiring a lawyer.

But she's thinking about gardens. She's walking into the cool Manhattan night, and she's thinking about how nice it will be, to walk through the gate to her grandfather's house, when she gets back to Seoul.

YJ-YUJIN

Yujin sits in the middle of the lab. He's set a timer on his phone: fifteen minutes. He feels the adrenaline leeching out of his pores. He's thinking about futures. He's thinking about the feeling of Soyoung's lips against his. He's thinking about the fact that Yujin is supposed to go back to Korea, and came over yesterday on a tourist visa. He's thinking about how he's going to have to go to the airport and separate again, sending a version of himself back so that he doesn't have to explain what happened with Yujin.

He stares at the Mitosis machine. It would be nice if he could use it instead of instancing again. But he can't use the machine here. It would be obvious if anyone ever looks at the security camera footage of the lobby—one man enters, two identical men leave. And they *will* be looking at the security camera footage. After Soyoung releases everything, Yujin knows that there will be a granular postmortem of every angle of footage the security cameras were able to capture.

The artificial calm on the quiet laboratory will be shattered. Soon, he'll have to walk back into the real world, and there'll be a lot of chaos, despite what Soyoung said, what he had agreed to. There's going to be a whole circus of internal and external investigations, and while Yujin can see the path through, where he ends up okay, his innocence is only earned by pinning everything on the nameless spy. Despite what Soyoung suggested, despite how Yujin's going to try and give her a head start, he doesn't see how she stays nameless for long.

He wonders how the future will treat her. How it would be hard for her in the coming months. She would be facing all of this alone. All she has is information, and the hope that someone will listen. There is a part of him that wishes he could have gone with her. A part of him that wishes that when she said *let me go* he could have said *let me come with you*.

Now, he wishes that he had said that to her.

He blinks. He rubs his eyes. The cold white steel of the Mitosis machine leaves a luminous afterimage on the back of his eyelids. It would have made certain things easier, if he had gone with her. His defection would add institutional weight to her cause, if she wanted to take that route. But it would have made certain other things harder, as well. Without him working from within, there will be no visibility into how Mergebreak and the IIS will spin this. He could soften the search for her, from inside the machine. Misdirect them. Lie about her.

He wishes he had an instance he could send with her. It's not what she would want, though.

Yujin checks his phone. He's been sitting there for ten minutes. He stands up. He folds the shock blanket up and puts it in his pocket. He grabs a microfiber cloth from a workbench and starts wiping down the terminal. He bets that Soyoung didn't think about fingerprints, unless she wiped them away while he was knocked out. If so, he's just being condescending. He thinks for a moment, and then brings the cloth over to the gate and begins to wipe down its thin frame. Just in case.

The gate is made of two stainless steel poles that have a join in the middle. They're built slimly enough to be concealed in a larger structure, and he has to be careful while polishing the seams. He pauses at the join. The gate is easily disassembled. It could be hidden up a pair of pants, or against a person's back, with enough tape. He puts the microfiber cloth down. He goes back to the terminal and studies it. The control panel is attached to a pedestal. Unscrewed, it would be smaller than his torso.

He could take the Mitosis gate. He could bring it to Soyoung. If she had the prototype, no one could deny her claim. And he could separate himself. He could let her separate him. She wouldn't want him to come with her, like this, but maybe there is a part of him that she would want to keep. Give each self the parts of him that she needs. Maybe she'd like to have the part of him that knows about the inner workings of Mergebreak. Maybe she'd like to have the part of him that loves her. Or maybe he should stop assuming what she's going to want. Assuming what people want is what caused him to end up here in the first place.

So maybe he'll just ask.

He picks up a screwdriver from the cabinet next to the terminal. He goes back to the gate. He inspects the joint. The screw. The half-inch of metal keeping the Mitosis gate threaded.

He thinks for a moment. Maybe YJ would have been paralyzed by this choice. But Yujin? He would have taken the chance and run with it. That's what he had done, anyway. He came to the States. He reintegrated.

This could go wrong in so many ways. But he wants to be the sort of person—the sort of people—who are brave.

■ ■ ■

The knife, the apple, the river, the wine-dark sea. The distance between knowing and not knowing. The distance between action and inaction.

■ ■ ■

"Okay, let's do this," Yujin says to himself, and begins to dismantle the gate.

SOYOUNG-ROSE

The sound of rapid-fire knocking on Soyoung's door echoes through the living room. Soyoung freezes, throws a blanket over the new laptop and the other computer junk that she's been setting up, the hard drives that she's already begun copying all the data from.

It's Yujin. He's peering against the peephole as if he'll be able to look inside. It's been two hours since they last saw each other, for what Soyoung assumed would be the last time. Soyoung yanks the door open.

"Why are you here?"

"Let me in," Yujin says. "I'll leave in a second, if you want me to. But I have to show you something."

Soyoung lets him in. He's standing awkwardly, but other than that, he looks pretty much the same as two hours ago. She's oddly happy to see him, like her hindbrain hasn't caught up to the current circumstances.

"Did something go wrong? Did I trip an alarm on my way out or something?"

"Nothing's wrong," he says. "No alarms or anything. I just—okay, it's easier to show you."

Yujin takes off his jacket. Then he starts unbuttoning his shirt. Soyoung's too surprised to tell him to stop stripping. She wants to know where this is going. With every button, it becomes obvious that there's something taped to his chest. The shirt falls to the ground. There's something strapped to his arms, too. Polished steel. Soyoung squints.

"Is that the Mitosis terminal? And—oh my god, it's the gate. You disassembled the gate and—you duct taped everything to yourself and stole the prototype?"

"Yes," he says. "Can you help me get this off?"

Soyoung goes to grab the kitchen shears.

∎∎∎

The fisherman, walking back to the edge of the sea. Eve, walking into the wasteland. Odysseus, wiping the blood of suitors off his limbs, marveling at his instance's memories of his homeland. The woman on the bay, catching her lover's instance in her arms. Whatever happens next is whatever happens next.

▪▪▪

Soyoung snips across the tape, gingerly pulling the cut edge away. It must hurt, but Yujin doesn't complain. He's holding his arm above the table, where they've put a blanket to catch the piece of the Mitosis gate when it falls. The peeling duct tape reveals inch after inch of skin as it's removed.

"Why'd you do this?"

"Well, at first, I thought it might be useful for you. Physical proof goes further than files. You can put it in checked baggage, give reporters a demonstration or something."

"You're assuming I'm taking a plane."

"It's what I would do, if I were you," he says, and winces as the tape rips hair off his skin. The first piece of the Mitosis gate falls on the blanket with a soft thump. It's a one-of-a-kind prototype, and it's sitting on Rose's old Hello Kitty blanket.

Yujin removes his arm and holds the other one over the blanket, and Soyoung repeats the process. First the cut, then the pull.

"If you don't want it, if you don't think it's useful, I'll take it back. I'll come up with something. But I wanted to ask you one more thing."

"Sure," Soyoung says. "And I do want it."

She hadn't thought about stealing the gate. That had seemed too audacious to even suggest. But having the Mitosis gate would be useful. As a prop, a tool, or just to be dismantled and reverse-engineered.

Soyoung pulls more tape back. Yujin holds his arm very still. He's not looking at her when he begins to speak again, slowly, and then all at once.

"You asked me to let you go, in the lab," he says. "Not to help you. You couldn't even imagine a reality where I'd help you. And I guess you were right. Who I am now isn't someone useful to you, wherever you're going. And maybe I'm more useful to you like this, here. I'll cover for you as much as I can. As much as my stupid self-preservation allows. But there is a very large part of me that wants to go with you. And if you want me, I'm yours. Whatever parts of me that you want to take with you."

She stops removing the tape. She stares at him. Yujin doesn't change through the viewing. He continues to look like himself. Like Yujin, like YJ. She wonders what parts of him prompted him to say this. To ask her to use the Mitosis gate to carve him into whatever she might want of him.

"You changed your mind so quickly. Why?"

"Why does anyone do anything?" Yujin says, shrugging with his good arm. "Because I want to. Because, Soyoung, I want to go with you, and I will miss you very badly when you're gone."

"You're asking me to decide who you are," she says. "Who you become."

"Yes," he says. "Make me someone who can go with you."

Soyoung looks back down at his arm and continues to tug at the tape. The skin underneath is red and irritated. The second piece of the machine falls onto the blanket. He's asking her to make him into someone she wants. It's not her grandfather offering her his home that he had lived in for half a century. It's not her mother offering her America. It's not Soyoung standing across from Rose on the mountain, offering her entire life in the single clammy palm of her hand. It's something different entirely.

Does Soyoung want him? Their decades of friendship. Meeting again for the second first time. The way it feels easy to talk with him. His slightly chapped lips. The way his skin feels now, warm against the tape, warm against her hand. The difference between what she wants, and what she wants to want. The difference between what she takes and what she is given. How this would be hard, when it had been so easy to reach for herself.

She doesn't know if she trusts herself for this. This is harder than deciding to steal Mitosis. But Yujin is looking at her, and she doesn't want to look away.

■ ■ ■

The fisherman's heart, beating between his lungs.

EPILOGUE

A man and a woman board a plane. They're carrying two backpacks, one carry-on, and one cat carrier. Neither of them look like they've gotten much sleep. There are dark circles under the man's eyes, and the woman is clutching a to-go cup of coffee like a lifeline. They had argued about the cat carrier, and the cat inside. The woman had won—the cat is a powerful argument against them being fugitives. The man had acquiesced. They're holding hands.

The plane is about to take off. In the plane's baggage hold, there is a piece of checked luggage that contains a set of steel bars and a control board. After the plane takes off, an avalanche of emails, uploads, and messages is going to be sent from a secure server, hitting every relevant newsroom, forum, and social media site.

In an office building approximately six miles away, a man sits at his desk. He's on the phone, and he's arguing. He doesn't look worried. He doesn't want anything that the man on the other end can offer him. On his chest and legs, there are still patches of hairless skin from where someone ripped duct tape off too quickly. He's thinking about the man and the woman on the plane. He's refreshing his newsfeeds every thirty seconds. He doesn't want to miss it.

The headlines drop. The plane takes off.

Outside, the world changes.

ACKNOWLEDGMENTS

Nothing is created in a vacuum, and *Sublimation* would not exist without the support of an entire auditorium's worth of people. The book you're currently holding in your hands would be much poorer without their input and support.

Immense thanks for my editor at Tor, Carl Engle-Laird, and to my editor at Picador, Ebruba Abel-Unokan, for your help in improving the many versions of the draft by leaps and bounds, and to Tor assistant editor Matt Rusin, for your help making that possible as well. Thank you to everyone at Tor—specifically thank you to Isa Caban, Anthony Parisi, and Eileen Lawrence on the marketing team, Tiana Tolbert for the social marketing, publicists Cassidy Sattler and Sarah Reidy, managing editor Rafal Gibek, production editor Jeff LaSala, production manager Jim Kapp, Jamie Stafford-Hill for the incredible jacket design, Greg Collins for the fantastic interior design, copy editor NaNá Stoelzle, proofreader Jessica Warren, cold reader Tania Bissell, and the entire team at Picador. Thank you all for your incredible work in turning my draft into a physical object, and getting the word out about this book's existence.

And, thank you to my agent, Steven Salpeter, for your work in championing *Sublimation* from its earliest form. Speaking of which, thank you to Neil Clarke, for publishing my short story "Homecoming is Just Another Word for the Sublimation of the Self" back in 2021, which was the seed from which this novel unfolded. Thank you to Ashley Chang for reading the first draft of the short story, and thank you to Sydney Jeon for reading some of the earliest versions of this novel's beginnings and encouraging the creation of the full story.

Thank you to Allison Mills and Roshan Pulapura for reading truly ridiculously countless versions of this novel—and Allison, a second thank-you for all the cat name brainstorming. And thank you to Emily Temple-Wood, Jocelyn James, Carolyn Zhao, Alex Kang, Jamie Ahn, Ashley Chang, Ethan

Reed, Cayla Fay, Amanda Silberling, and the lovely people in the OGOF discord server for the support and beta-reading and cheering my writing on. And thank you to everyone else who edited, read, supported, and otherwise created the conditions for *Sublimation*'s existence.

Thank you to my partner, Joe Kachmar, for your support and affection while I brought this novel into the light of day. And finally, thank you to my mom and dad for always supporting my writing and creative work, for encouraging me to pursue my dreams, and for buying me every book I ever asked for. I love you all.

ABOUT THE AUTHOR

Amanda Silberling

ISABEL J. KIM lives near New York City in an apartment filled with books and swords. She is the author of numerous short stories and has won the Nebula, Locus, and the Shirley Jackson Awards. Her work has been translated into multiple languages and reprinted in multiple best of the year anthologies. When she's not writing, she's practicing law or podcasting. *Sublimation* is her first novel.